Frank W. Calkins

Indian Tales

Frank W. Calkins

Indian Tales

ISBN/EAN: 9783337089191

Printed in Europe, USA, Canada, Australia, Japan

Cover: Foto ©Andreas Hilbeck / pixelio.de

More available books at **www.hansebooks.com**

FRONTIER SKETCHES

BY

FRANK W. CALKINS

———

CHICAGO:

DONOHUE, HENNEBERRY & CO.

Frontier Sketches.

DONOHUE & HENNEBERRY, PRINTERS AND BINDERS, CHICAGO.

CONTENTS.

INDIAN TALES.

I.

OLD STUMPY.

In the spring of the year 1866, the writer's family moved westward from West Bend, Iowa (a small settlement on the Des Moines river, where we had spent the winter), a distance of forty miles across a wide, bare stretch of prairie, into the valley of the Little Sioux. Here we settled upon a homestead, having to go eighty miles to the nearest land office, at Sioux City, to take out the necessary papers.

Our nearest neighbors, with the exception of five families who had accompanied us, were fifteen miles away.

In order to give the reader some idea of the raw newness of the country, I will add that our nearest marketing points—Fort Dodge and Sioux City—were each eighty miles away. All that distance we had to go in order to dispose of a few pounds of butter, or to buy a pound of sugar.

To build a house of lumber was not to be thought of, though my father did manage to get a quantity of floorings, sheetings and shingles made from native ash at a sawmill twenty miles down the river. From these he finished a comfortable log cabin, into which we moved upon one of the first days of May.

As I have said, our nearest neighbors lived fifteen

miles away, but we soon discovered several of a nomadic sort, who made their appearance periodically, and lived in "dug-outs" along the river. These were old fellows who hunted for a living, and, in their own dialect, had "trapped the kentry off'n on fer years."

One evening, just after we were fairly settled in our new cabin, and while we were seated at supper, there appeared in the open doorway one of the oddest-looking creatures imaginable. It was a little old man, with a reddish-gray beard and long, thin hair of the same color; and though I was then but a boy ten years old, I can at this moment shut my eyes and recall the image distinctly. The dumpy figure standing for a moment, one foot upon the door-sill, one dirty hand resting on the casing, the greasy, patched, old "wammus," deer-skin pants and big beaver cap are still vivid in my recollection.

"Come in," said my father, as the queer old fellow stood hesitating with a grin upon his face. "Come in and have some supper."

"I'm obleeged to ye, mister; don't keer'f I dew," and he stumped into the room, half falling over the sill and stumbled across the floor in a clumsy, awkward fashion. "Got no feet," he exclaimed, " 'cep'n only a wooden un an' a stub.

"Ben a-trapin' round here some this spring," he continued, hitching up to the table. "These is my grounds, from the forks down here to the head of the Stony. Got a dug-out up'n the High bank nigh Round Grove. Got 'nother up on the Sioux nigh the 'Lakes,'" —a local name, still used, for the group of lakes mentioned above,—"an' I've got a nuther out on Rock River, an' another up'n Minnesoter on the Lacky

Parle." (*Lac Qui Parle*, lake which speaks.) "Change off, ye know; fer when t'aint good trappin' on one ground, most gen'ly 'tis on 'nuther."

Having thus oddly introduced himself, he began using his knife and fingers upon the food passed to him, eating rapidly while he answerd the various questions my father put to him. He sat next to me at the table, and I noted that his clothes were woefully greasy, and had a smell about them which I came to recognize later on, when I trapped my first muskrat. I left the table before I had finished supper, but sat in the doorway, where I could watch our queer guest and listen to what he said.

During the course of the meal, we learned that his name was Charles Weeks, and that he was born near the shore of Lake Champlain in New York. He had come West in '35, and had trapped in northern Iowa and in Minnesota ever since. For thirty years, in fact, since he was a boy of nineteen, this man had wandered over and lived on these uncivilized prairies, and the greater part of the time he had lived alone.

After supper it began to rain gently, and my father and I hastened to finish the remaining "chores."

When we came in, dripping from the rain which meantime had begun to fall more rapidly, the old trapper was still sitting by the fire, for even though an evening in May, the storm was a cold and thoroughly disagreeable one.

"Knowed this was a-comin'," said the trapper. "Reckon ye'll hev to let me roll in on yer floor here fer the night. I could 'a' huffed it home to my dug-out ten years ago, when I stud on two feet, 'stid of two stumps, an' I'd 'a' thought nothin of sech a sprinkle es this; but them days is gone by."

My father assured him that he was welcome to stay, and then asked if he would tell how he came to meet with such a misfortune as the losing of his feet; and I will give his story mainly in my own words, rather than in his backwoods dialect.

"Oh yes," he answered. "It's a pityful yarn, though, and I don't generally like to say much about it. It happened about ten years ago over on the Des Moines. I was staying that fall with a gritty chap that moved up from Fort Dodge, and squatted on a piece of Des Moines bottom-land. He had his wife with him, and a baby about a year old, I reckon, as pretty and as slick, too, as a muskrat kit.

"Symmons—that was the man's name—had built him a log shanty, and he had a yoke of oxen and a cow, and had broken a five-acre lot that spring, and tried to raise some potatoes and sod-corn; but he planted too late, and the frost killed every hill of them early in September.

"Well, at that time I had a dugout not far from where he'd settled, and I had some flour and coffee, and a lot of traps cached near by, and so when I came down from a summer's hunt up in Minnesota, to begin my fall trapping, Symmons wanted me to go as a partner with him for a season. Seeing he was so hard up, and that he could furnish me with a decent place to live in and a cook, I concluded I'd go in with him.

"You see, in those days, and now too, the buyers came around late every fall and spring, and bought all the fur the trappers had taken during the fur seasons. So we decided that when we had sold our furs that fall, I was to take Symmons' oxen and wagon and make a trip down to the Fort for a winter's supply of groceries and such things.

"Well, we did do famously for a couple of months. All the slews were unusually full of rat houses built that summer, and there were plenty of beaver and mink on the river and creeks.

"Everything went off well enough with us until one day about the last of November. Then we had trouble enough, and it came quick and unexpected.

"A lot of Sioux had sneaked into our parts unknown to us, and one night they lay in ambush in a grove near the cabin, and as it happened as we went to the cabin Symmons was ahead of me, he got all their bullets, and I got none.

"Poor fellow! They killed him the first fire, for he wasn't expecting anything of the kind, as there hadn't been any Indian trouble in our parts for over two years, and so he was carrying his pelts along without even a gun with him.

"I had mine, though, and as I was on the other side of the river from them all, I made a break to get away. Then the Indians rode to the shanty and burned it, and drove off the cattle.

"They didn't find Symmons' wife at home, though, for she had heard the firing, and had run off with her baby and hid in some thick willows down the river. It was nearly dark when they got to the house, or I reckon they would have found her easily enough, for I had no trouble finding her, shivering and crying in the brush the next morning.

"You may be sure she was glad to see me, poor thing, for she thought we'd both been shot; but she and the baby were nearly frozen, for it was very cold in the night.

"But she wouldn't be satisfied to go away without looking after Symmons, until I told her I had found him and buried him in a sand-bar. We were poorly equipped for cold weather, and 'specially for the tramp between us and where her folks lived at Fort Dodge.

"When she knew what we must do, she got right up with her little one and said she was ready to start. Well, we set off at once, down the river. I carried the baby and she carried the gun, except when we saw any game, and then I'd try to get a shot, and I did kill a duck and a rabbit before noon, and made a fire by firing my gun into a mess of dry leaves. By this fire we cooked and ate them both for dinner.

"When we'd got through our meal, and had got upon high land, I found that we had reached a point where we must make a tremendous circuit round the west bend. But it had grown warmer, and I concluded to risk it, knowing that we could make it before night if it didn't storm; for the woman was clean grit and a good traveler, and the baby seemed to feel contented as a kitten after its dinner of broiled rabbit.

"Mis' Symmons, though, couldn't keep from crying all the time, and every little while she'd burst out afresh, and I'd say something to try and keep up her sperits, but you can believe that I didn't feel more than ordinary cheerful myself about that time.

"Wal, we hadn't made more than half that stretch of prairie before I saw there was a big snow-storm brewing, such a storm as I reckon they never get anywhere except here on these prairies." (These storms have since become well-known under the name of blizzards.)

"That made me uneasy enough; for I knew if one struck us away from shelter, we shouldn't stand one chance in a hundred of getting through alive. But the storm did strike us, and we did pull through. The snow came, with a tremendous northwest wind, when we were about three miles out from the river, and in five minutes you couldn't see six rods from the end of your nose, and it turned cold so suddenly it seemed like slapping you in the face with an icy blanket, after coming out of a warm room.

"Mis' Symmons happened to be dressed purty warm with a flannel dress and a cloak that she could pull over her head; she hadn't time when she fled from the Indians into the woods to get her bonnet, and the baby hadn't scarcely any clothes on, but she had wrapped it in her cloak all night.

"Well, when that storm came, I made up my mind there wasn't any show for us, but I thought I'd try and save the baby. So I jerked off the fur socks that I wore inside my rawhide 'packs,' and pulled one of them on over each of the baby's legs, and tucked its arms inside of them, too, and then I pulled on my packs and put the little cretur inside my coat, next my bosom, and we hurried on. The wind was in our backs, and that was one grand thing, and I knew if we could keep on for the next half-hour we could make the timber on the river; for all we had to do to get our direction was to point straight with the wind.

"I made Mis' Symmons hang to my coat-tail, and then I took her off at a good dog-trot, with the wind helping us on.

" But it was a terrible jaunt ! The wind blowed harder and the snow grew thicker every minute; and the
cold seemed to cut clean to the bone. It wasn't five
minutes before I knew my feet were both freezing. No
great wonder, you see, after pulling off warm fur socks
and then putting my cold feet back into them frozen
rawhides.

" But I hugged that baby and went ahead harder and
harder; and that plucky Mis' Symmons she hung to me
and kept up, and finally we made the river, and got
into a sheltered place behind a hill.

" It wasn't dark, and so while she held the baby and
walked down a path in the snow, I got together a pile
of dry wood and made a fire. Then I took my knife
and cut a big heap of brush and made a kind of shelter
over the fire so the snow wouldn't sift down on us, and
then I took my gun and went along the bottom of the
hill and shot a grouse and a couple of rabbits, and
brought them in.

" By that time we had a first-rate fire, and Mis' Symmons had got down by it and examined her baby, and
had found it wasn't frozen anywhere ; but, poor woman,
she'd begun to thaw out herself, in spots, and she was
suffering terribly.

" As for me, I had worked all the time like a beaver,
and I'd kept every part of me warm but my feet. They
were frozen solid, from the ankle down, and felt like a
couple of sticks.

" I thawed 'em out in snow by the fire ; but I couldn't
tell you what I suffered that night. Mis' Symmons
wasn't frozen badly anywhere, just her toes and some
frost-bit spots on her shoulders and hands. Her cloak

had saved her head and ears, and my big beaver cap, like the one I wear now, had saved mine.

" We managed to cook the rabbits and eat them, and to feed the baby, which didn't make any fuss at all, but went to sleep in its mother's arms.

" It was a frightful night; but somehow we lived, all of us, she a-dozing by the fire and holding the sleeping baby, and I cutting and piling sticks upon the fire.

" Well, the next forenoon, about the middle, it cleared off. We had cooked and eaten the grouse for breakfast, and I'd got a big heap of dry wood round the fire, and so I told Mis' Symmons that I knew where there was a ' dug-out,' four or five miles below, and if she thought she could keep herself and the baby warm, I'd go down there and prospect.

" She said she could, and wanted me to go; so I walked off, and got down there after a couple of hours' hard wading, expecting to find the dug-out empty, and not fit to stay in; and wasn't I the happiest man to find two trappers that I knew occupying it, and fixed up as snug as you please!

" They were Bill Goss and Jim Freeman, God bless 'em! And the way they took me inside and put me in warm blankets, and then took more and went after that woman and her baby, was a blessed thing to see, I tell ye."

The old trapper drew his dirty sleeve across his eyes, and every other eye in the cabin was wet with sympathy.

" Well, they took us in and nursed us," continued the old man, "and when the weather became clear, Bill put on his snow-shoes and went down to the fort and

got her folks who lived there to come up after her with
a team and sled.   And they got a doctor, too, to come
up to see me; for my feet had been getting awful
bad.

"When her folks came they took her home, and the
next spring they all moved back to Mississippi, and I
never saw her or the baby again. I didn't get round
again for a good while, and when I did, I'd lost one
foot and ten toes, and I've been stumping it over the
prairies ever since; that's why they call me 'Old
Stumpy.'   Still, I don't know but I'd do the same
thing agin—pore creturs!"

II.

McLEOD'S ADVENTURE.

Among the earliest settlers of the Wisconsin valley were "Bob" and "Bill" McCleod, known to later settlers as "The Mc*Cloud* Brothers." Long before—the date is not exactly known—the tide of emigration began to turn northward from the exhausted mines of the "Lead Region," Bob and Bill had built their log cabin on the north side of the river, and settled themselves—at least for a time—under a picturesque bluff, in what is now known as Richland county.

They were hunters and trappers of true backwoods origin, and belonged to that rough and hardy class of men who have for more than a century led the vanguard of our civilization into the wilderness. They were large, fierce-looking men, who usually shunned neighbors, and had little to say to those whom they met.

They kept up an inveterate feud with the Winnebagoes and Pottawatomies, whose hunting-grounds encroached upon what they were pleased to call their own. This feud was continued long after the treaties of peace which settled the difficulties that were the causes for the Black Hawk and the Winnebago "Wars."

The McCleods hated the Indians with a fierce and unrelenting hatred, and were cordially hated in their turn, and also greatly feared by the roving bands of savages who knew them.

Bob, at least so it is said, had sad cause for his hatred of the Winnebagoes, for during the Indian troubles of 1827, a party of three young bucks had made a raid upon a small settlement in Missouri and had taken several persons, among them young McCleod's betrothed, a girl of sixteen years.

For six years Bob mourned her sincerely, and then during one of his trading trips to Prairie Du Chien he met his long-lost sweetheart and knew her instantly. But she was the wife of a Winnebago, and had almost forgotten her own people, so thoroughly had she become Indianized.

From that day Bob grew morose and vindictive, and his brother shared in this feeling. Neither of them ever married. In their difficulties with the Indians—and they were known to have had many—they were not, it is perhaps just to say, always the aggressors.

It is known that on more than one occasion the brothers were in danger from parties of Winnebagoes and Pottawatomies, who had come upon their "hunting-circuit" with the evident intention of either killing the white men or driving them across the river, but such was the address, the watchfulness and boldness of Bob and Bill that in every instance they were enabled to escape, and sometimes to inflict serious punishment upon their enemies.

Once a single Winnebago in the night boldly perched himself among the branches of a scrub oak that grew at the foot of the bluff, and with gun cocked and ready, waited patiently for daylight, when he expected to kill one or both of the brothers as they came out of their cabin-door.

As it happened, Bill had gone out early in the evening to watch deer at a "lick" in one of the hollows above. He did not return until daylight, and as he came around the point of the bluff with a saddle of venison upon his shoulders, he caught a glimpse of a moccasined foot dangling below the limb of an oak between himself and the cabin. With great caution he crept nearer to the object, and saw that an Indian was crouching among the leaves. As soon as he had obtained a clear view of the intended assassin, he drew his rifle and shot him. Bob, who had been out all night the day before and was sleeping late—late for *him*—was aroused by the shot, and came out rubbing his eyes with one hand, and with a cocked rifle in the other.

The Winnebago had a bright, new army musket, and if the brothers had been at home and—as frequently happened after getting their breakfast—had come out of their cabin-door together, he might have killed them both, and this was no doubt his design.

At another time, while Bill and Jules Piquith—a "Canadian Frenchman" who was trapping in company with them—were away on a trading trip, Bob had a "bout" with a Pottawatomie, which came near costing him his life, and in which the Indian certainly was the victor.

It was in June. Bill and Piquith had gone down the river with a boat-load of furs—their "spring catch"—to market them at Prairie Du Chien, which was the nearest trading-post. One evening, several days after their departure, as Bob was returning down the river, in his dug-out, from a visit to some "set-lines," at a famous catfish-hole which he had discovered at the lower end of an island, he saw a canoe shoot out from the mouth of a creek, some hundred yards ahead, and glide off down the current.

It was dusk, but Bob thought he knew the canoe. It

was Bill's dug-out, and somebody was taking a most unwarrantable liberty in paddling it about.

He and Bill, with a considerable amount of labor, had each fashioned a light "dug-out," or canoe, from a pine log, for his own particular use in paddling about to their traps and on fishing excursions. Each used a broad paddle of cedar, and could propel his light craft through the current at a surprising rate of speed.

These canoes were among their most valuable possessions, therefore Bob was highly incensed upon seeing a stranger making off in one of them.

" *Hi thar !* " he yelled. " You feller ! "

But the stranger paddled swiftly on without seeming to have heard.

Again Bob called or rather roared at the retreating canoeman, " Hi, you ! Land that dug-out ! " And then, seized with a sudden conviction that the trespasser was "one o' them Pottawats from Muscada," the irate hunter caught up his rifle and leveled it. He found it too dark to sight with any accuracy and, hastily laying down his gun, resumed the paddle.

And then began an exciting race.

The Indian, of course, knew that he was pursued, but evidently relied upon the growing darkness to protect him from the white man's rifle, and upon his own dextrous use of the paddle to make his final escape.

In the latter point, however, he was much mistaken. Bob was a man of great strength, and an expert in the use of his broad paddle ; an implement so large as to be clumsy in the hands of an Indian used to the light blade with which his birch-bark craft was propelled.

In less than a mile's run McCleod came up with the Pottawatomie.

The Indian was on the look-out, and when Bob's canoe had come up within a few yards of him, quickly dropped his paddle and caught up his gun.

Bob was just on the point of reaching for his own gun, but so quick were the Indian's movements that the hunter had only time to throw himself backwards as the Pottawatomie's gun cracked. The bullet whis-

tled over his head harmlessly enough, and Bob straightened up, with a hoot of derision.

The Indian, to expedite his movements, had dropped his paddle upon the current and Bob saw that he was now vainly reaching for it, while his canoe was drifting.

And now, instead of "wastin' an' wishin'," McCleod determined to run the Indian down, that is, to upset his canoe and strike him on the head as he struggled in the water; but as he was about to drive at it, over it went, and the Pottawatomie disappeared in a sudden plunge into the water on the other side. Bob thought he understood that movement. Shooting his canoe forward until it had passed the drifting one, and then catching up his gun, he watched sharply for the Indian's head to appear below. It was not so dark but that he could see the surface quite plainly for a number of yards on either side, and he knew that the Indian could neither swim very fast, nor remain very long, under water.

He watched several seconds, but in vain, **for** no head appeared, and then suddenly began to suspect the trick that had been played him. He was just about to turn and take a look at the overturned canoe, when he felt it grate against the stern of his own. He threw his rifle around, with a quick intuition of what was about to happen, but he was too late. McCleod never knew exactly how it was done, but as he turned, his canoe was given a violent wrench at the stern, and he was pitched, gun in hand, neatly out into the water.

The Indian had either come up *under* the over-turned canoe, or just behind it, and as it drifted down against Bob's craft, the wily fellow had seized and upset it, well knowing that with his rifle wet and himself in the water, the white man would not be a formidable foe.

Bob came to the surface spluttering, but clinging instinctively to his rifle.

"Hoo! hoo!" shouted the Indian. "How you like?" McCleod turned his head, and saw the Pottawatomie making off, swimming toward the point of an island— the channel was studded with them—some fifty yards below; and, angrily determined to punish the Indian at all hazzards, he immediately struck out and gave chase.

Both swimmers were encumbered with their rifles, but the Indian had several yards the start, and proved himself as good a swimmer as the white man. He reached a ridge of sand, against which the deep current was wearing, as much in advance as he had started, and quickly drawing himself up, faced about and clubbed his gun. By the time the Indian had executed this maneuver, Bob had come within striking distance, and suddenly realized that he had made another mistake.

Just as his feet struck bottom, the Pottawatomie leaned forward—the Indian was standing up to his knees in sand—and struck viciously at him with the barrel of his gun. Bob had barely time to throw his head to one side, and the blow fell with benumbing force upon his right shoulder, and glancing, knocked the rifle out of his hand.

Bob had the presence of mind to throw himself quickly backward, to kick vigorously with both feet, while he "pawed the water" with his left hand; his right he could not use.

This energetic plunge undoubtedly saved his life, for before the Indian could recover, to deal another blow, he was out of reach. He now swam on his side out a few yards into the current and treading water with his feet awaited the canoes, which were drifting down toward him. The Indian plunged into the water, secured Bob's rifle, then he stood on the bank and shook both guns at the discomfited hunter.

"Hi, you!" he yelled. "You want gun you come git." Then he dropped the guns, laughed, slapped his legs, and hooted at the enraged Bob all the derisive English of his vocabulary.

As for McCleod, he had nothing to say, but bore his misfortune with outward stoicism, like a savage in this respect at least, and when the canoes drifted alongside, he managed to get himself astride the bottom of one, and by the use of his uninjured arm and his legs to paddle it ashore at the main bank. Leaving the Indian to capture the other and make off at his leisure, Bob went home to his cabin to nurse his wound and his wrath.

It was some days before he could use his right hand, even to feed himself. He had a musket and plenty of ammunition at the cabin, and with this weapon he was obliged to content himself, until it came his turn to make the fall trading trip.

He never saw his rifle again, although the canoe was accidentally discovered the following spring. It was hid near the mouth of a creek, not far from the then deserted Pottawatomie village.

III.

AN EXCITING BOAT RIDE.

"Isn't that the mouth of White River?" I said to Capt. Isaac Brodhead, of the river steamer *Treadwell,* with whom I had taken passage for a trip up the Missouri not many months ago. The evening was advancing. We were standing on deck, enjoying the moonlit scenery, and had just come up opposite a gap in the low hills, showing a valley, up the bottom of which I could see a long arm of shining water.

"Yes," answered the captain, who stood leaning upon the taffrail. Presently he came to where I stood, and seated himself on the rail, with his back to the water.

"I made the money to buy this boat, or ruther the one that I owned before this, off that river," he remarked, and the remark was in a tone that plainly invited a question.

"And how was that?" I asked.

"Trapping," he answered. "Twenty years ago there was more fur to the mile along the banks of White Earth—that's what we called the river then—than on any other stream of its size that runs into the Missouri.

"Fur brought a good price then, too," he continued. "A trapper could make money in those days, if he cared to save. Most trappers are too free with their cash. It wasn't so with me, though."

He sat thoughtful after this, and at length I ventured a question.

23

"Did you go out alone when you trapped on the White Earth!"

"No, of course not. The business was too dangerous; and then two or three men could trap to better advantage than one. I used to trap with two fellows named Thad Peters and Gil Villemont. We started out in September, and did not get back on to the Missouri till the middle of the next May, or later. '

"For two seasons we went up White Earth in a big skiff, and when we come back, it was loaded so full of pelts that two of us had to walk along shore, while the other steered the skiff.

"The last time we had to make a big dug-out canoe, pack part of them in that, and take it in tow. We could have made another for two of us to ride down in, but it was such a desperate lot of work to dig one out with the tools we had, that we'd ruther walk. We always kept another boat cached near the mouth of White Earth, an' when we struck the river, we pulled this out of its hiding, calked it, and sailed down to Omaha, where we spent our summers and sold our fur.

"In the fall we loaded our boats on some up-river steamer, which took them and us back again to the mouth of White Earth, and landed us there.

"But the third season we took with us a bigger boat, a flat scow skiff large enough to bring us back and all the pelts we might take in the season. She was twenty-one feet long, eight and a half wide in the center, with planked sides twenty-two inches high. She had two sweep-oars on the sides, and a steering oar that would work on either end.

"She was a queer kind of craft, made so as not to draw much water going up the river, for at that season the water was always low. In the spring, during the freshets, the stream was generally deep enough in mid-channel for the heaviest river craft, and that was the time when we came down with our load.

"Well, we set off in the big boat at the mouth of White Earth about the first of September, and by the middle of the month we had worked our way a hundred and twenty-five miles up the stream to the mouth of Porcupine. Here we had a dug-out hut, stoned up in front, which was Injun-proof (at least while we were inside of it), and which we used for our winter quarters.

"We had been lucky in having never seen an Injun in that vicinity, or when we were passing up or down the river. There was not, however, very much risk of meeting them, unless it was at a camp or a crossing, and in those days the savages never seemed to hunt along White Earth, except in early summer, when the deer and elk came down to the bottoms to raise their fawns and calves, where there was tall grass and good hiding-places.

"In fact, the only two tribes that we were afraid of were the Brutês up on the Missouri and the Oglallas down on the Niobrara, and we ran the risk of encountering them, as fellows of our craft always took their chances of meeting the redskins twenty years ago.

"But we got through the winter very satisfactorily, and did not meet with any misadventure until we were coming down the river in the spring, with our furs, and were within a day's run of the Missouri. The boat was loaded with pelts. We had on board sufficient provision for the run down to Omaha, so that it was not necessary to land. We had made a week's bread ahead, and had placed flat stones in the scow on which to build a fire. Dry willow tops and limbs of trees could be gathered as we went along, to cook meat and coffee.

"Our furs were baled, and wrapped tightly in buffalo skins, and these were packed around the sides of the boat, so that the oars would just work over the top of them.

"There was but little need, however of using the oars for the river was high—all back over the bottoms—and the current in the middle channel was swift and strong. It took us along about five miles an hour, and we should have probably reached the Missouri by noon of the second day without seeing an Indian if we hadn't camped over the first night.

"Just after we had shoved out from shore on the morning of the day before we reached the Missouri Gil Villemont sang out:

"Look over there, boys! We've got company!"

"He was in the bow, or the end that happened to be the bow at the time, and pointed to the prairie to the right. Thad and I looked. What should we see but what seemed to us a hundred Indians, more or less, on ponies, galloping down a long slope towards the river!

"For a moment we were so surprised that we just sat and stared at them, when all at once the gang discovered us, and brought their ponies to a standstill instantly.

" Mates,' said Gil, I'm sure they are Oglallers, for they always go in droves. - We had better get out of gun-shot They can't come after us on horseback.'

" Gil and I seized the oars, while Thad steered, and turned the boat out of the channel over on to the 'swash-water' of the bottom land.

⋯ The Indian no sooner saw us move than they set up a yell that could have been heard a mile away, and came dashing down to the water's edge. It didn't take many sweeps of our long oars to run across near the other shore, and then there was nearly a half-mile of deep water between us and the savages.

"'They can't bother us much now,' said Thad, 'for neither their guns nor their arrows will reach us here, and we shall get to the old 'Misery' by night. So let them pow-wow if they want to, or they can foller us down the river, as they choose.''

"'Yes,' said Gil, who was a queer-talking fellow, and drawled out his words when he wished to make a point; 'yes, but remember, lad, this is May and the ice is out. We've hed warm spring rains a-plenty, and thar's nothing under the sun to keep part of those rascals from swimming over behind us, ef they should take it into their heads to tackle us from both sides at once.'

"That wasn't a pleasant view to take of our situation, and we hadn't gone two hundred rods before we saw that that was exactly what the savages intended to do for in a few moments a part of them rode into the water and started for the opposite bank. Then they slipped off behind, and each savage caught his horse by the tail and steered him across.

"We at once steered our boat back again into the middle of the channel, and as the stream broadened out below us for a mile or so, we had a chance to prepare for defense before we should reach narrow places where the Indians would have a chance to shoot us.

"We had each a rifle, muzzle-loader, of course; for that was before the day of Winchesters. Among us

we numbered **five** big six-shot revolvers. We were
well-armed for the times ; but what were three men in
the face of a hundred Indians? Even if we had a
thousand guns, we couldn't use but one apiece, at a
time, and one of us must attend to the steering of the
boat.

"We judged, too,that the Indians were Oglallas, from
the fact that they evidently came from the south, and
had a large number of ponies with them besides what
they rode ; and we concluded that they felt sure our
boat was loaded with valuable furs, that could be
traded for guns and ammunition at the agencies. It
would be a great prize for them, and we felt sure that
they would do their best to capture our cargo.

"Gil, who'd had more than one skirmish with Indians, planned our defense for us. He had us stack the
fur-bales in three different places, one at the stern, one
at the bow and one midway—a row on each side, so as
to shelter each of us completely, while settin' between
them. Then he took his place in the stern to steer.
It was a cramped position and the most dangerous
one; for when he came to a strong side current, he'd
be sure to have to raise up, in order to git the right
sweep for his oar-handle. But he was a brave fellow.

"'Now, boys,' said he, when Thad an' I'd got fixed
in between our stacks, each with rifle, revolvers and
ammunition in front of him, 'I want you to keep cool,
boys. Don't show yourselves to get a shot. In fact,
don't shoot at all unless they get on a point in front of
us, at some of the narrows. Then we shall have to
drive them back; for then I must stand up and steer
hard to keep the boat from the shore. Gil drawled

this out in his slow, queer way, and Thad and I promised to heed his suggestions.

"In the meantime part of the Indians had crossed, and now both squads of them were galloping down, one on each side of the river, to reach some of the narrows in front of us. A mile or so ahead there was a place, such as you'll find every once in a while on all small streams, a place where the high-lands came crowding the valley in on both sides, and of course the flood of water is pinched up into a narrower channel. Luckily for us, though, in this place which would give good arrow-range from both sides, the water was swift, much stronger and swifter than anywhere else.

"Well, both gangs came crowding down into the very edges of the water and ranged themselves out in lines. Then they got off their ponies and stood in the water behind them, so as to protect their bodies; for the rascals were'nt any more ready to take chances in those days than they are now. Thad was in the bow. He was a hare-brained fellow, but a good shot. As soon as we had drifted near enough, so that we were within rifle-shot, he rose up, rested his rifle over the top of his barricade, took a long, close aim, and fired.

"Gil and I both craned our heads to see if the shot did execution, and I saw the nearest pony on the right bank rear up and fall over into the water. The Indian behind him scampered to another pony; whereupon the whole gang set up a yell and began firing their guns and shooting arrows from both sides of the river.

"Of course, we were obliged to stick close to cover. The arrows skipped and whizzed over our heads, and the bullets struck the planks like the clatter of hailstones. 'Twas fortunate that we had the furs packed in several folds of hard, dry buffalo skins; and it was still more fortunate for us that we had them at all, for we never could have passed those two lines of fire without being hit, for some of the savages fired their arrows into the air at such an angle that when they came down they fell into our boat. More than one feathered shaft buried its head in the planks on the outer edge of the boat, but not one happened to hit us.

"We made the run of the narrows in about a minute, and neither of us was wounded. As we passed below we held a bale of skins at the back end of the boat, so as to stop shots from the rear. In a minute more we were out of reach. Gil laid the steering-oar out straight behind, and we swept along, swiftly, down the center channel.

"As soon as we were fairly out of range on another broad stretch of water, we looked up to see what the Indians were doing. We rather hoped they would now leave us alone after wasting so much ammunition; but we were disappointed, for they rode along the highlands, on each side, and swarmed beside us like two flocks of black buzzards hovering over a wounded buffalo. They knew there were more narrows ahead, and they evidently hoped that in some of them the current would not favor us as it had in the one we had just passed.

"Well, after floating something more than five miles, we had another gauntlet to run, and here Gil had to raise his head and arms above his barricade, to give an extra sweep, so as to steer us out clear of a strong side-current, splitting off at a little island and runnin' in sharp against the other bank. He could see ahead enough to tell what turn of the oar was needed ; but as he was giving the sweep, an arrow struck the brim of his wool hat and the shaft ran clean through to the feathers. There it stuck.

" 'I've got a new ornament to my head-dress,' said he, cool as you please, as he leaned back again between his bales.

" In a minute or two we were out of the reach of their arrows again, and runnin' down-stream, between two lines of thick trees, that the water roared and swashed amongst with a noise that half-drowned the yells of the savages. And they did yell, fearfully, every time we passed them. -

" This was but a specimen of our experience for eight or ten hours that day. The rascals were loath to give us up; and hour after hour they followed on, swimmin' the mouths of creeks, keeping well to the front, and shootin' at us whenever there was the slightest chance of hitting the boat.

" But they either got discouraged, or else short of ammunition at last; for a little before sundown they pulled up, looked after us awhile, then set off on their return up stream.

" We got up then and stretched our legs and examined the boat and the furs.

" More than fifty arrows were sticking in the planks and into the buffalo-skins of the bales, and there were plenty of bullet-marks, too. It fairly looked as if the old scow had feathered out, the arrows were so thick. But I assure you we were glad to get off without any of them in our skins. Gil was nearly beat out; and I

took his place until about dark, when we shot out into
the Missouri, then pulled across and camped on the
other side for supper.   We went on, however, as soon
as we had rested our cramped legs a little by walking
about ; and a week later we got down to Omaha, safe
and sound, with over three thousand dollars' worth of
furs."

IV.

A RACE FOR LIFE.

Several years before the first real settlers came to build their log houses on the banks of Spirit and Okoboji Lakes, the wandering trapper and fur-hunter had discovered both their beauties and their uses.

These fine lakes now furnish a summer resort for hundreds of families in Iowa, and for tourists from nearly all the Northern and Eastern States. Yet when James Freeman and David Utter built their trapper's hut, a little more than thirty years ago, at the north point of West Okoboji, there was not a settler's cabin within fifty miles of them. Fifteen years ago, the three sheets of water, Spirit, West and East Okoboji Lakes, that every pleasant day in summer are now flecked with yacht sails, had then known no boat larger than a canoe.

James Freeman's first advent into this region was some time about 1852, he believes, though for a long period of his trapping life the years went on with him so much the same that he says he "gits 'em kind o' mixed."

He first saw the region when out one summer elk-hunting with a party of "Johnny Green's Tribe" of Chippewas. He was so delighted with the lakes that he came back with his traps and spent the fall and winter there, living literally in a hole like a badger's dug back in one of the banks. He had such success that season that, upon returning to Prairie du Chien in the spring, his lean ponies loaded down with rat, mink and fox skins, he easily found a partner to go back with him the next fall.

It was a young man named David Utter who went out with him upon the second trip.

On account of the large number of rat sloughs which lay to westward and northward of the lakes, they made their winter quarters on the beach at the upper end of West Okoboji, which was quite bare of timber, and even bushes. But the bank was high, and sheltered their cabin from the northwest winds, which, in this part of the country, nearly always bring the fiercest storms.

They cut hay for their ponies and built a comfortable shed, and passed a very prosperous, though, as it happened, on account of steady hard cold, a rather monotonous winter.

Spring came again at last, and the early summer brought the trappers back loaded with furs to James's usual market at Prairie du Chien.

The two men kept quiet about the rich trapping grounds they had discovered in the far northwest of Iowa, but nevertheless when they returned to the lakes the next fall, they found a large log cabin built in the woods at the lower end of West Okoboji, and four young men, brothers, from the vicinity of Prairie du Chien, inhabiting it. These newcomers had been exploring the region, and had discovered, by the stakes left sticking in various places to mark it out, the grounds already claimed by Freeman and Utter, and had staked out grounds for themselves, taking in "Gar" Lake, the "outlet," and several miles on both banks of the Little Sioux river below.

As the four young fellows—their patronymic was Gilman—had shown such thorough regard for James's and David's rights as trappers, the latter could find no fault with them, and the six trappers came to an amicable agreement to hold the lakes in common against all future pioneers.

James and David took up their old quarters, seven miles from the Gilmans; seven miles of beautiful, clear water, plentifully stocked with fish, which formed a constant source of supply for the trappers' rude table. Fur and game were as abundant as ever, and the outlook for the season was bright.

Yet misfortune came to them.

In the first place, David was taken down in October with malarial fever, caught, no doubt, by exposure in the rat-sloughs. James was compelled to stay constantly by him for several weeks, though the Gilman boys took turns, coming across in their canoe, to sit up nights with him.

One night, when David had taken a turn for the better and James was sleeping by his side, their four ponies were stolen from the shed, and the settlers never saw them afterwards. The animals were probably taken by some solitary Indian, or else by a party of them.

This was not only a serious loss, but a deep cause for alarm to all the trappers. James and David had never seen any sign of Indians in all their trapping there, except old *tepeé* stakes and a few decayed fish-drying racks along the beaches.

As David grew better, however—such is the hardihood of the trapper—James left him bolstered up on the bunk, and began to put out the traps again.

It was now late in the fall, and though there was no snow as yet, there had come a cold "snap" that froze two or three inches of rough ice over the surface of the lakes.

James had been out twice with the sled, putting traps along the beach, baiting them with fish, and the third day as he was returning just before sundown from his beat, he happened to look off over the high prairie to the northwest, when a sight met his eyes that gave him a sudden and great alarm.

It was a party of horsemen coming down towards the lake. He watched them a few seconds, and though they were fully three miles distant, he was certain they were Sioux.

"Some of 'em," he said, "have ben sneakin' round 'n' stole our hosses, 'n' now they've gone back fer others tu drive us out o' here."

As near as he could count, there were more than thirty of them, and he concluded at once that their bold manner of approach was to be accounted for by their numbers.

James knew them of old for a daring and relentless horde. But he did not wait to study the situation long; he plied his skates in a straight shoot for the cabin, which was a half-mile to the north, almost directly in the face of the coming horsemen.

He kept his eyes upon the latter, however, and soon saw that they had discovered him and noted his movement, for they whipped up their ponies. and headed them directly toward the cabin.

But he could reach the cabin first, and he thought if David were only well they might have time to barricade and fight off the savages; but Utter was not yet able to stand on his feet, and he must be saved at all hazards.

James' plan was quickly made, as he dashed forward. He reached the cabin by the time the Indians had made a mile run, as he conjectured, after he came where the bank hid them from view. Bursting open the "shake" door, he rushed inside, without untying the sled-rope from his belt.

David was sitting up in the bunk, his back to the wall, busily trying to mend an old pair of moccasins with his "buckskin needle" and a "waxed end." Without giving him time to say a word, James caught down his partner's rifle and pistol which hung on the wall, thrust them and the ammunition-bag into David's hands, and catching the blankets around the astounded invalid, gathered him forcibly into his arms, and carried him out and deposited him upon the sled, just outside the door.

"Injuns," he said, when Dave had caught his breath enough to ask what was "all this racket about?"

"Better leave me 'n' scoot, if there's many of 'em comin'," suggested David, coolly.

"Not a thought on't, ol' boy; you jest grit yer teeth 'n' hang on, 'n' I'll pull ye through tu Gilmans'."

"Gimme your gun, too, then," said Dave. "I can hang to both of 'em 'n' the sled too."

His growing excitement gave him strength.

"All right, Dave, ye kin try it," said James, who was now busily strapping a small box of powder and lead upon the rounds of the sled, between Dave's legs; when he had secured the latter he strapped Dave's legs down, too.

"Can't roll off if ye try, now," he exclaimed; and he

delayed yet a moment longer to fasten the blankets around the poor weak boy's body. "Now we'll streak it, Davy, straight shoot for Gilmans'!"

Away the brave fellow darted, dragging the sled with its precious freight at his heels.

As soon as he had got out on the lake from under the bluff where he could glance back over the high bank, the intrepid skater saw that he had not a half-mile the start of the Indians. They were coming as fast as their ponies could carry them; and they set up the usual hideous yelling when they sighted the whites.

"Lot of 'em, ain't they?" said David, in his squeaky, weak voice, after twisting his neck for a look at the Indians. "They'll try to ketch us on them p'ints down yender, Jim."

"Yes!" shouted Freeman. "Don't bother me with talk; I've got ter *work* now!"

James had understood the danger from his very first thought of this plan of escape. The two points of land that project into the water, the one on the left, about three miles down the lake, and the other on the right, nearly opposite the Gilman cabin, would either of them give the Indians a chance to cut him off, if they could get out on them before he passed.

If the ice had only been smooth, he would have laughed at his pursuers, well knowing that he could reach Gilmans' before they got half-way down the lake; and once with those four sturdy, well-armed fellows, there in the woods, he would not fear fifty Indians. But the ice was rough, and do his best, he knew he could not drag that loaded sled and make more than twelve miles an hour; and the chances were that the ponies on the smooth prairie would considerably exceed that rate. Still he hoped for the best, and skated at his handsomest pace.

As he and Dave had expected, the Sioux saw their advantage; and without losing a moment, they divided into two parties at the head of the lake, and came yelling down both shores at the top of their horses' speed.

It was a hard race for James. On the left-hand side, an inward curve of the lake gave that party of the savages an advantage; but on the other hand, an outward sweep of the shore would compel the others to go round. In ten minutes the Sioux on the left bank were neck and neck with the skater; and their shouts came across the quarter-mile of ice with startling distinctness.

"Better cut me loose," squeaked David; "you can't save us both, old fellow."

"No, never!" growled Jim, and then bending forward and hugging the shore a little closer, where the ice was more smooth he lent his energy to a splendid trial of speed, that carried him ahead of the foremost Indian, and passed the point in advance of him—the whole gang of them whooping and screeching frightfully to flurry the fugitives. Several shots were fired; the bullets pattered on the ice behind the sled, but did not strike it.

David could hardly contain himself at this successful run. He cheered and crowed, in his weak way, but so earnestly, nevertheless, that it warmed the heart of the brave, cool skater. It added a mile an hour to his speed, he said, "ter hear Dave squawk."

Fast as he was skating, however, he kept a cautious

eye on the Indians who were now flying along the
right-hand bank, to cut him off at the lower point.
They were gaining ground and rounding the broad
curve of the shore. ˌFive or six of them seemed to be
mounted on swifter ponies than the rest, and were considerably ahead, riding scattered out in line, their
bodies lying nearly flat along their animals' backs, so
as to catch as little wind as possible, and each Indian
plying his *quirt* with downward strokes and desperate
energy.

"*S-c-r-r-t-t!* *S-c-r-r-t-t!* Jim's skates scratched
over the ice-ridges, while Dave sat "stiffening" his
back, hugging the rifles and watching the Sioux.

It had already begun to get dusk a little as James
and his sled came within shooting range of the point.
The foremost Indians had already reached the extreme
end of the little cape, and were jumping from their
ponies for a run across the ice. James veered off
somewhat; but he dared not go much out of a direct
line for Gilmans'; for if the Indians should once succeed in getting between them and the cabin of their
friends, there would be no hope of escape.

The trapper was now terribly fatigued; half an hour
of such tremendous exertion was beginning to ˍweary
his muscles. Nevertheless, he nerved himself for one
more desperate rush, and then, as Dave afterwards
said, he "went like lightning."

The growing darkness saved them; for six or seven
of the savages had left their horses and got out within
easy range as they passed the point, and spreading out
in line on the ice, began firing guns and shooting
arrows at them.

Bullets, buckshot and feathered shafts whistled past

and over them; but they were going swiftly; the twilight favored them, and strange as it may seem, they got past without a wound. .

The Indians did not follow them, probably from knowing that the other trappers were in the woods just ahead. After a few minutes more, Jim slowed up

Bullets, buckshot and feathered shafts whistled past them.

to get breath; for he had nearly lost it entirely in his last hard effort.

David was too tired and "done out in his back" to crow much this time. The jolting and jerking of the sled in the roughest spots had been a hard strain upon his feeble strength.

As they neared the woods, they saw three figures

hurrying out on the ice to meet them. The Gilman boys had heard the last firing, and had rushed out to see what it meant. James panted forth his story in a few words. The ride did not injure David. He rapidly recovered.

V.

A BAD "MEDICINE MAN."

About ten years ago—it was the autumn of 1877—
the writer, being at that time one of a firm of contractors engaged in furnishing hay and wood to the
Government posts on the upper Missouri, met with an
adventure which may prove interesting to such as like
accounts of personal encounter and peril.

Upon referring to my diary for that year, I find
that on the fourteenth day of September, being then
at Fort Randall, I had set off to return to Yankton.
I had reached Fort Randall, some time previously, on
one of the freight-steamers which brave the currents
and sand-bars of this most fickle of all navigable
rivers, but had failed to finish my business there in
time to catch the return steamer of the Benton Line;
and when, at length, I was ready for the journey, I
found that I should not be able to get a boat down the
river again for at least three weeks.

As I could not possibly wait so long, I went to our
"wood camp," some fifteen miles above Fort Randall,
and procured a horse and saddle from one of my
partners who had charge of our working force
stationed at that point.

As my home was on the river, some miles below
Yankton, I had fully two days' ride before me, and
there was no agency nor post near the end of my first
day's ride; consequently I should be obliged either to
camp by myself, or spend the night in the hut, or
tepeé, of a Yankton Sioux.

43

I concluded to adopt the alternative of lying out by myself; for I had been inside a great many Indian habitations, and had learned to prefer the pure air of the open prairie to the odors of a *tepeé*, and my own cookery to that of any squaw. Indeed, I would not have hesitated for a moment about the matter, but for the fact that, at the time of which I write, it was not a safe plan for a lone traveler to make a night camp, even among the most reputable of the reservation Sioux.

He might sleep in their *tepeés*, among their families, with comparative safety. He could not be made way with there, without incurring a risk which the cunning rascals well understood. But a lone camper, sleeping in the woods, or on the prairie, was still a strong temptation to the enmity of the "white man's hater," as most of the Sioux loved to call themselves.

It was, at this time, a frequent occurrence that some lone trapper, or traveler, between the posts on the upper Missouri was missing, and such an one usually was never seen or heard from again

From our wood camp, within three years, two men had disappeared mysteriously—one a trapper, named Bret, the other a Norwegian wood-chopper.

But such is the hardihood of pioneers, living amid constant dangers, that I gave but slight heed to these things; and having procured a loaf of bread, some bacon, coffee, a small skillet and a tin cup, at the wood camp, I packed them with my blankets, tied the bundle on behind my saddle, and thus equipped, set out, with the determination to camp where night should overtake me, and to be in Yankton within thirty-six hours.

The day was exceedingly warm for that time of the

year, and I was obliged to travel slowly, the more so since my horse was rough-gaited and a poor traveler.

At noon I pulled up near the log cabin of a Yankton Sioux with whom I happened to have an acquaintance. His name was *Kotonka Washta* (Good Buffalo), and, for an Indian, he was possessed of remarkable intelligence and industry. He owned seventy ponies, six cows, fourteen dogs and three squaws; and the latter had cultivated, during the summer, a considerable field of corn, pumpkins and melons.

Kotonka himself was not at home, but from his women I bought a few roasting ears, picked from a patch of late sweet corn, and a couple of melons, which were "prime ripe" and luscious.

The afternoon was hotter even than the morning; the air was "muggy" and at times almost stifling. I could hardly spur my horse along at any reasonable pace; and, at last, after I had made about fifteen miles from Kotonka's place, he became exhausted and refused to go further.

It was now about five o'clock, and I picked a camping spot near at hand and made preparations to spend the night there. The place which I chose was a little knoll on the high land, overlooking the valley of a small creek which here runs into the Missouri.

It was not in a region that I liked; but I was compelled to accept the situation, so I unsaddled my wretched horse, turned him loose for the present, and began to make arrangements for my supper. I went to rest early, thinking that if my horse should prove able to travel, I would get up and be off by two or three o'clock in the morning.

There were several sets of old *tepeé* stakes standing

along the bank just at the foot of the knoll; and as I knew from past experience that these were excellent material for camp-fires, I went immediately down to pull some of them up for the purpose.

While doing so, my attention was attracted to a dense thicket of plum-trees, which grew along the creek below me, and looking closely, I saw that the tops of many of them were red with fruit. This was an attraction not to be resisted; and dropping the stakes which I had pulled, I made my way through the copse of hazel brush and small scrub-oak bushes which grew on the side hill, and soon found myself in the midst of the very finest plum-grove which I had ever seen.

There were growing here several varieties of the wild plum, with red, yellow, and variegated skins. Nearly all these were now "dead ripe"; and under many of the trees the ground was thickly strewn with those that had fallen from over-ripeness, or been shaken off by the wind.

The trees were tall for the kind, and stood thickly together, completely shading the ground, which was almost bare of vegetation beneath their boughs.

I selected a tree where the fruit upon the ground best suited my taste, and after giving it a thorough shaking, which brought down a small shower of large, bluish-red plums, I squatted upon the ground, and began eating and filling my hat. This enjoyable business had proceeded for some minutes, and both the hat and my internal capacity had nearly all the fruit they could hold, when I suddenly felt a sensation of the near presence of some living thing!

I can not describe the feeling, but there came over

me a warning sense of being watched by human eyes, and of being in personal danger. This feeling was so keen and alarming, that for a moment it held me spell-bound, and I dared not look to the right or the left. Almost unconsciously, though, my right hand stole back to my hip and grasped the handle of a Colt revolver (the only weapon which I carried) that hung in a sheath at my belt.

Then I glanced quickly up—to the left—and found myself, as I had expected I should, looking squarely into the malicious eyes of the ugliest being it was ever my lot to face. The visage was bedaubed with a hideous coat of paint, green on the cheeks and lower jaws, with circles of black under the eyes, and with vermilion stripes across the forehead.

The savage wore a green blanket around his shoulders, over which peeped the horn of a bow and top of a quiver of arrows. He had a black, slouched, felt hat on his head, and a pair of blue soldier's trousers belted at the waist.

He was standing not thirty feet distant from me, partly concealed by the slim trunks of the plum-trees, and stood stock-still when I first caught sight of him; but I could distinguish his position plainly enough, to see that he had been stealing toward me on tip-toe, and that his right hand rested on the hilt of a knife in his belt! His eyes were like those of snakes.

I confess that I was startled. He was a Sioux medicine man—one of a class of as venomous wretches as ever moved in human form.

But without moving from my squatting position, I whipped out my Colt's revolver, and "pulled down" on him.

" *Huh!* " he grunted, in evident alarm, and then stepping out into an open space, he threw up both hands, and exclaimed, " No shoot! me heap friend! "

The scoundrel! I knew better. As he stood there, I eyed him for a moment, trying to make up my mind whether I ought to shoot him down, and avoid farther risk, or order him off, and trust to my wits to escape the arrow which I felt sure he would now send through my skin if he was given a chance.

But bad as he looked, and treacherous as I knew he was, I could not bring myself to shoot him.

" Go on! " said I, at length, in as savage a voice as I could command. " Go! "

He walked past me, and disappeared among the plum-trees—never looking once to the right or left.

When he was out of sight I got up, and backed quickly and softly away, in the opposite direction, until I had got out of the plum thicket, when I turned and hurried up the hill through the hazel brush and oak shrubs. You may be sure that I kept my eyes on all sides of me as I went—and I had need to; for before I reached the edge of the copse, that painted rascal rose up from the brush not fifty feet away, and let fly an arrow. I saw him rise up just in time to make a spring to one side, but his feathered shaft hurtled by terribly close to my body.

I had my revolver cocked in my hand, and instantly returned a bullet for his arrow, as he dodged down into cover again.

I was a tolerably quick shot in those days, and I think I hurt him, for he jumped up with a yell, dropped his bow, bounded zigzag away through the bushes, and got out of sight and range in a remarkably short space of time. Yet, as he ran, I sent two more shots at him, but, of course, without any certainty of aim. He was out of sight and reach in a few seconds.

I then went back to my packs and the horse on the knoll, and thought over the situation.

After reflection, I concluded that my falling in with him was probably a chance meeting. These medicine men are very solitary in their habits, and this one had probably been prowling about by himself after their fashion. No doubt he had been in the plum grove there, and watched my coming at his leisure. Seeing me busily occupied in filling my hat and my mouth with plums, he had determined to steal up behind me, and kill me. Now that I had so signally thwarted him, he would have, I felt sure, a double incentive to murder me, that I might not report him at the forts, yet so confident did I feel of having hit him pretty hard, that I did not much fear his coming back. Nevertheless, as soon as I had cooked and eaten some supper, I packed up and started on again, by the hazy moonlight, determined to move as far, at least, as I could get my horse to go.

I crossed the creek at a point considerably above the plum thicket, where there was no brush, and thence pushed my horse along at a good walking pace over the rolling prairie. The old beast did better in the cool of night, and stood up to his work so well that by nine o'clock, next morning, we got into Yankton. I still have the medicine man's bow—an ash one tipped with buffalo horns—as a souvenir of our little fracas in the plum thicket.

VI.

One hot evening in the summer of 187–, the writer, with three other young men, was camped on the banks of the South Platte river, some seventy miles above the little station of Julesburg. We had unharnessed the horses of our big wagon, and picketed them out to feed near the high stockade of a solitary ranch station. Over the top of the stockade posts the grass-grown roofs of several adobe cabins were visible. On the roof of one of these a half-grown antelope kid was industriously cropping the herbage, and by its side lay another, serenely asleep, its head thrown back over its shoulder.

Beyond the stockade, and adjoining it, was another inclosure of several acres, surrounded by a high board fence; a large stock corral, in fact, in which several ponies were standing, lazily whisking away the flies, evidently too much overcome by the heat to make any further exertion. These and the antelopes were the only signs of life about the place.

"Guess this ranch takes care of itself," remarked one of our party, who, at that moment, was attending to a skillet of venison steak over a fire of dry drift-sticks, which we had picked up on the bank of the river. "Guess old Cliff would stir up these fellows, if he knew they all went off 'n' left the houses with a couple of tame antelopes for guards."

On first halting for the night, we had rattled at the

gate of the stockade, in the hope that we might be let in and given a chance for fresh water at the well ; but the gate was barred inside, and the premises were apparently deserted. We rather wondered at that, for we had heard of this ranch, and knew it to be one of the "Cattle King" Cliff's out-posts—a "round-up" point for the east half of the great range over which his thousands of cattle fed, winter and summer.

But as we sat down to our supper of biscuits, steak, canned tomatoes, and coffee, we heard the big gate of the stockade squeak on its hinges, and a moment later there sauntered out to us a tall, strapping young fellow, in a woollen shirt and buckskin leggins. He had on his head a wide-brimmed, white wool hat, with red leather band, and on his feet high-topped, high-heeled boots, at the counters of which jingled a pair of Spanish spurs.

There was also a pair of big "Colt's" in his belt His woollen shirt was open in front, the sleeves were rolled up to the elbows, and the deep tan-color of his arms matched well the bronze of breast, neck and face. He had the biggest and fiercest of black moustaches, and a pair of sharp black eyes to match it.

A remarkable figure, perhaps the reader may think, but one that, with some modification of form or feature, will soon grow familiar to the camper in the "cattle country."

"Hullo, fellows!" said this specimen cow-boy as he came up and leaned his elbow upon the hind wheel of our wagon.

"Hullo!" said we; and then, in the short, suggestive parlance of the country, we asked, "Eat?"

"_You_ bet!" was the cheerful rejoinder, and the

stockman flung himself down into the circle about our oil-cloth, was helped to a pint cup of coffee and some tomatoes, and helped himself liberally to biscuit and fried antelope.

"Got nothin' but cold grub in the ranch," he explained between mouthfuls, "an' it's too mighty hot to make fires now. Nobody here but me ; boys gone up on Lodge Pole to run in strays. Be'n asleep all the afternoon. Rattled the *gate*, did ye? Wal, now, I must be a snoozer! Curis what risks a man'll take in this country. Now, here's you fellows trailin' about all alone, the four of ye, an' me here a-sleepin' alone in a 'dobe, an' six hundred Cheyennes turned loose on the country above!

"Fact," he said, coolly, noticing our looks of surprise, not unmixed with alarm. "Yes, sir; runner come down from the ranch above 'n' warned me yisterday, They've gutted one ranch up there, killed a cow-man, 'n' run off a lot o' stock; expect 'em down here any time. A lot of 'em come down here last year, and caught us snoozin', right in broad day noon, too."

The reader may be sure we were not a little alarmed at such news, though we hardly knew whether to credit the fellow's words or not.

He might be trying on the cow-boy's and miner's favorite pastime—that of "stuffing," or frightening, "tenderfeet;" but he gave us further particulars in an honest, matter-of-fact way, and after supper invited us to haul our wagon inside the stock corral, and to spend the night with him in one of the adobes. So we concluded at length that he was acting—as, indeed, afterward proved to be the fact—in good faith.

Having accepted his invitation to a shelter for the

night, we were soon established in one of the long, cool adobes.

Our horses had been picketed as close to the stockade as the grazing limit would allow.

"You'll have to take the resk on the stock, in course," said Briggs—he had given us his name in the course of our conversation. "We all have to take them resks, but I reckon there's no danger to yerselves in here. The Cheyennes caught us napping here once, as I was a-tellin' ye, an' they won't calc'late on doin' it again.

"Tell ye about that, if ye like. 'Twas kind o' scaly times for Gowan an' me, but there was a heap o' fun in it too."

Of course, we were only too glad to listen to his account.

"It was jest about a year ago now," he said, "when Ed Gowan and me was keepin' the ranch alone, while the other three boys—there's gener'ly five of us stays here—was up river a-helpin' brand a new lot o' steers jest druv in frum Texas.

"There wasn't nobody along the river a-thinkin' of Injun trouble then, an' as for Ed an' me, we hadn't seen one for nigh a year. We stayed close round the ranch here, though, for a week after the boys went off. Then we begun to feel mighty restless.

"Then, too, we was expectin' the boys back ev'ry hour. We calc'lated 'twouldn't be no harm to leave the ranch for a half day's hunt. We was tired o' beef an' bacon, an' we knew where to go to find plenty of antelope."

"We saddled our ponies, an' struck out that afternoon. We rode up into the 'rock country,' 'bout twelve miles north o' here, among the big cañons an' cuts, an' we found plenty of antelope. We'd killed five by dark, but by the time we could gather their saddles an' pack our extra horses, which we'd took two, an' get back to the ranch, it was nigh daylight next morning.

"The boys hadn't come, so, as we was mighty tired an' hungry an' sleepy, we turned our ponies in with the other stock in the big corral, and got us some breakfast; then we piled onto a couple of bunks, and was soon sleepin'.

"I was woke up by a punch in the ribs, an' when I'd come to myself 'nough to get my eyes rubbed open, I saw that there was a half-a-dozen naked, greasy Cheyennes in the room, standing around a-grinnin' at us. I saw, too, that Ed was awake, an' that they'd gathered up all our shootin' irons, an' that we was both pris'ners, in our own shanty.

"I needn't tell ye that we both felt mighty foolish and badly scared, though we put on as bold a face as we could. Ed was the bravest though, and the coolest. He'd ben a trapeze performer along with Montgomery Queen's big show. He was all muscles an' siners, up to all sorts of tricks, and as spry as a cat.

"Wal, sir, soon as Ed saw how 'twas, he reached out his hand to the nearest buck, an' says, says 'e, 'How do brudder?'

"'How?' says the Injun, an' all of 'em grunted an' grinned.

"But jest then there was a terrible commotion and a-yellin' ' outside, an' two or three of the Injuns rushed out. The others wanted to see the rumpus, too, I 'xpect, for they turned to us, and motioned us out of the door. We got up, and walked out, with an Injun

in front an' two behind us. As we got out the door,
we heard a frightful yellin' outside the stockade.
There was six or seven Cheyennes dancin' and screechin'
like they'd gone plum crazy. But the biggest fun was
what was goin' on inside the stock corral, and we soon
saw that the dancin' bucks was a-laughin', though *you'd*
never guess at that by jest listenin' to 'em.

"You see one of their fellows, thinkin', of course,
he'd have an easy job, had rode into the corral to drive
out the stock—there was thirteen ridin' ponies and

three or four colts. But there was a customer in there
that the Cheyenne hadn't reckoned on. It was a big
jack, jest the ugliest, orneriest critter ever you set eyes
on. He never 'lowed any strangers inside that corral
if he could help it, an' he gen'ly could, an' that was
one reason we kep' him.

"Wal, he'd got after Mr. Cheyenne, an' he was goin'
for him most savagely

"When we first saw the race, the Injun was clear up

on his pony's neck, a-clingin' for dear life, and the jack
was right up alongside, with his jaws wide open.   The
Cheyenne had lost holt o' his reins, an' was jest hangin'
over on the opposite side of his horse's neck, and there
they was, goin' round and round, the jack a-grabbin'
an' bitin' at the Injun, an' a-brayin' an' squealin' till you
could a-heerd him a mile.   An' the best of it all was,
that them Cheyennes outside all seemed to think it was
the biggest kind of fun.

"Talk about an Injun's not laughin', why, fellows,
they nigh busted their throats.   They clapped their
hands onto their stomachs, an' doubled up like jack-
knives.   Ed and me laughed, too.   I don't believe we
could 'a' helped it if we'd known they'd kill us the next
minute.

" But matters soon begun to get pretty ser'ous inside
the corral; the Injun darsn't git off his pony, for he
could see mighty plain that the jack was after *him*.

" He'd 'a' got the fellow, too, if his pony hadn't a-ben
such a smart little critter; the mustang seemed to
know that his master was in danger, for he kept flying
right round in a short circle, keepin' away from the
fence, and keepin' the jack on the outside o' his circle.

"But the Injun' was awful scared, he couldn't use his
weapons if he had any, an' he just hung on an' yelled
to the others, for help I 'xpect, though, of course, we
couldn't understand.   But it must a-ben, for pretty
soon they stopped their laughin', an' all but two that
was left to guard us jumped on their ponies, rode into
the corral, an' with a big whoop made a dash for the
jack.

" I didn't have time to watch the outcome of it, for
all at once I see Ed jump at one of the guards, an'

—

strike out. The Cheyenne went down like a stone, an' before I could gather my wits enough to make a move, he turned, sprung onto the other one, wrenched a Winchester rifle out of his hands, an' knocked him down with it.

"I thought it was time then for me to take a hand in the fight, an' seein' the first Injun that Ed had hit tryin' to git up again, I made a jump for him, an' snatched his gun out of his hands; it wasn't much of a job, for he was half stunned yet from the rap Ed had give him.

"'Come on, Jim!' I heard Ed say then. '*Don't shoot!* Get inside the gate!'

"I was glad enough to obey orders, I tell ye, an' leavin' the two Cheyennes to come to their senses, I followed Ed at a run. We got inside the stockade, an' barred the gate, then we run into this 'dobe here, an' fastened the door.

"'You bet they won't come for us now,' said Ed, 'I'm fixed for 'em, an' so are you pretty well,' an' lookin' at him I saw he'd not only got the last Injun's Winchester, but he took off his belt of cartridges, an' brought that, too. I had a Springfield carbine in my hands, so we didn't much fear 'em.

"They made an awful racket outside, but they didn't fire a shot, an' pretty soon things quieted down, an' we heard 'em drivin' off the stock.

"After a while we unfastened the door, an' got up on top of the 'dobe, an' then we could see the whole gang drivin' our ponies across the hills to the north.

"'Guess I didn't hurt those fellows much,' said Ed, 'but look, they've made an end of old Jack;' an' sure enough we could see him in the corral chucked full of arrows. They had to kill him I 'xpect, or he'd ↳ run 'em all out. The next day the boys come down, an' one of the range bosses, an' I 'expected we'd get the bounce; but when he heard how 'twas, he jest laughed, and sent for more ponies."

We stayed that night with the young ranchman, and pushed on again the next morning, but learned, on reaching the ranches above, the day after, that we had narrowly escaped a brush with a large party of Cheyennes. They had passed over the trail not more than two hours ahead of us, on their way south again, evidently fearing pursuit from the troops at Fort Collins and Cheyenne. Such was life on the plains but ten years ago, where now are large and thriving settlements, as safe from Indian raids as the good old city of Boston.

VII.

A WOMAN'S BRAVE EXPLOIT.

As early as 1834 a few hardy pioneers ventured to build cabins upon the western banks of the Upper Mississippi, and to move their families into them. One of these bold men was William Gleason, who, with a yoke of oxen, a cart containing household effects and a cow, moved with his young wife from the lead mines at Mineral Point in the spring of the year mentioned, and settled at the mouth of the Little Pinnicon (little turkey).

He was attracted thither by the tales of two young trappers whom he had met at the old French town of Prairie du Chien, the winter before. They told him of the black, rich land in the valley of the Little Pinnicon, with scarce a stick of timber in the way, though the bluffs on either hand were lined and covered with oak, butternut, hickory and poplar. Their stories of bear, deer, beaver and mink stirred his hunter's heart.

These young men—Simpson Briggs and John Ellery —had marked out each a squatter's claim, and, not intending to spend their lives as mere trappers and hunters, wished to have neighbors. In the end, Gleason agreed to come, and accordingly set a time when, with his wife and his goods, he would be at Prairie du Chien, where the young men agreed to meet him.

True to their word, Briggs and Ellery were awaiting

them in camp at the "Prairie" when Gleason and his wife arrived. The two trappers guided the settlers on a three days' journey over prairies and among wooded hills, and finally brought them, with their effects, to the bank of the great river at a point opposite the mouth of Little Pinnicon.

Here a strong *bateau*, with mast and sail in the bottom, lay hidden among rocks. The enterprising trappers had provided themselves with this boat as a means of freighting their packs of deerskins, buffalo hides and furs to markets down the river. Its size and strength enabled them in two trips to set the Gleasons, with their household goods and stock, upon ground which was henceforth to be their own.

There a surprise awaited the newcomers. As they mounted the bank of the little creek at the mouth of which they had landed, John Ellery pointed to a little tree-grown knoll some two hundred yards distant.

" Yonder's your cabin ready fer to move in," said he, " an' thar's good water in a spring down thar not fifty steps frum it."

"Thar's room enough fer four," said Gleason, as, a few minutes later, the party surveyed a comfortable log structure with strong "shake" roof and stone fireplace and chimney.

" Yes," said the young wife, gratefully ; " and it shall be both yer homes till ye bring wives of yer own up the river."

Thus did the generous and brave backwoodsmen aid each other in the pioneer work which has laid the foundation of populous states.

That evening the party of four sat round a rudely constructed table upon the puncheon floor of their new

home, and ate with great contentment a supper of warm
biscuit, broiled duck and coffee. The next day, by
the aid of the oxen and a stub of a plow, a "single
breaker," a "truck patch" was ploughed, and before
the sun set was planted with seeds which had been
carefully hoarded. A week later more than three acres
had been thoroughly "stirred" and planted to corn,
squashes and pumpkins.

A fine crop was raised that year, bringing in autumn
such abundant variety to their table that this little
band of pioneers felt themselves to be living in the
very "lap of luxury." Of game—the house when the
men were at home was an arsenal of guns—they had
such abundance as three good hunters, with ample
opportunities, could secure. Even Mrs. Gleason was
provided with a gun, a short, flint-lock fowling-piece,
which she knew how to use, and upon which she put
much reliance for protection when the men were all
away from the cabin.

Briggs and Ellery were often away upon trapping
and hunting excursions. In September they rode away
upon their ponies to the west to shoot buffalo, and
walked back at the end of the hunt leading their ponies
heavily laden with hides. They had to go only a three
days' journey from the river to strike the Buffalo
"range," now dwindled from its former vast proportions to the limits of the National Park in Wyoming,
where a straggling band of buffaloes still exists, protected by United States soldiers.

These isolated settlers lived in constant danger, for
the country all about them was the common hunting-
ground of bands of Winnebagoes, Pottawatomies and
Musquakies, and occasionally Sioux. These last were

far more to be dreaded than the others, as Black Hawk's war had given the lesser and nearer tribes a wholesome fear of the soldiers, stationed at various posts throughout the region.

No Indian was trusted, unless thoroughly known to be the white man's friend, and of the three men living at the Little Pinnicon, one always remained near the cabin. When the trappers were away, Gleason stayed close at home, busying himself with the building of stables, yard and fence, or with improvements upon the cabin. To the latter he added in time a bedroom for himself and wife, and a general storage-room for provender of all sorts.

Flour, coffee, sugar and other necessities were got at Prairie du Chien by Briggs and Ellery, who made the trip in their *bateau*.

Early in autumn straggling bands of Indian hunters sometimes stopped at the Pinnicon cabin to beg for "tobae" and "sug," which, as the supplies were limited, had to be denied them.

Winter came and passed without incident to the settlers, save such as their hunts afforded. These were often stirring or amusing, and their recital served to make the evening pass pleasantly before the crackling back-logs of the fire-place.

Thus time passed until "planting-time" came and went, and still the little band remained unmolested. About the first of June, Briggs and Ellery, with the *bateau* well loaded with the "spring catch," set out for Prairie du Chien.

They had been gone twelve days, and their return was momentarily and somewhat anxiously looked for by the Gleasons, who were out of flour and some other necessities. It was on the morning of this twelfth day that Bill, as his wife and the others called Gleason, came hurrying to the cabin.

"Sallie," said he, with much excitement, "there's a big band of elk 'bout a mile up creek, an' I'm goin' after 'em! Won't be gone long."

"Go ahead, Bill," said his wife. "I can take care o' myself a few hours." He snatched down his rifle from its pegs, and hurried out.

He had been gone not much more than an hour, when a young dog chained near the door began to bark. Mrs. Gleason looked out, and saw coming down the river, half a mile away, a string of horsemen whom she knew at once to be Indians.

She watched them a moment. Whether it was the manner in which they rode, or the fact that she was alone that alarmed her, she did not know, but accustomed though she was to the lonely life of the frontier, she was frightened. She immediately shut and bolted the door, and with table and stools hastily barricaded the two small openings which served as windows, leaving a corner of the one at the front open to serve as a port-hole. Then she looked to her gun, and freshened the priming.

By this time the sound of horses' hoofs had drawn near the cabin and halted. Sallie Gleason's face was very pale at this moment, and her hands trembled, yet she did not hesitate, gun in hand, to take her place at the opening in the window.

She saw enough at her first glance to warrant all the precaution she had taken. Naked, hideously bedaubed in paint and evil-eyed, such a villainous-looking lot of savages she had never before seen.

There were seventeen of them drawn up in a squad a few yards distant, and they were surveying alternately the cabin and the growling dog.

The Indians were armed with bows and arrows and lances, with but two guns in the crowd. Mrs. Gleason saw at once that they were Sioux. Standing far enough back in the darkened cabin to prevent them from seeing her, she looked through her port-hole directly into the eyes of these dangerous visitors.

For a few moments they sat their ponies silently, giving no hostile sign. Presently one of them, with a guttural word of command, turned his animal's head and with a vicious cut of his quirt set off at a gallop, and the whole troop followed him.

Sallie Gleason breathed more freely as she watched the galloping squad cross the creek and ride out of sight beyond a point of bluff some half-mile below. She thought of her husband, and felt certain he was not in the direction they had taken. She opened the door and windows and resumed her household occupations, but kept a sharp watch in all directions.

Several hours passed with no incident to arouse her fears afresh. At noon she made preparations for dinner, expecting Bill soon to return. Then she took a pail and started for the spring for water.

She reached the top of the gully through which the little creek ran, and was about to descend to the spring when she saw something near the mouth of the gulch that gave her instant alarm. It was a single feather dyed red, projecting above the ridge of a clay bank that marked a turn of the creek's channel.

She had seen that feather three hours before and remembered it. It slowly disappeared. She turned about and hurried back to the cabin, expecting every moment to hear the Indian yell and feel an arrow pierce her body. But nothing further occurred to alarm her then and she reached the cabin in safety.

Once more she barred all entrances and prepared to defend herself to the last. She understood now, she thought, why the treacherous fellows had ridden away so unconcernedly. They had intended the action for a blind. After riding out of sight they had dismounted and having slunk back under shelter of the river-bank had entered the bed of the creek where they were now lying in wait for a chance to shoot down the inmates of the cabin.

That the Indians had not killed her when they had the opportunity was a source of thankful wonder. It could not be, she believed, that they had not seen her, but they must have thought themselves undiscovered. Thus she speculated in fear and excitement.

Through an opening in the front window her eye took in the broad expanse of the Mississippi beyond the ambush of the savages. Suddenly there came into view, not a mile distant, the well-known sail of the *bateau.*

Her first feeling was one of delight; but almost instantly the true situation flashed upon her and she realized the purpose of the ambush. A deadly fear for her trapper friends seized upon the brave woman's mind.

She saw it all now. The Indians had discovered that sail away down the river, and knowing where the boat would land they had, after their cunning and treacherous fashion, stolen back to lie in ambush for the unsuspecting boatmen. She had not been seen on

her excursion to the spring because the Indians were
intent upon other victims.

She kept her eyes on the boat; it was coming
slowly on with a light breeze in its favor; the boys
seemed to be plying the oars lazily.

What could be done to warn them? It would be
certain death to her to go outside and make any movement likely to attract their attention. Even if they
saw or heard her, they might well fancy her to be
merely greeting their return.

Then she thought of the "Wild Goose Bar," and a
plan of action came like an inspiration. The Wild
Goose Bar was a drift of sand which extended into
the river from a point several hundred yards above the
mouth of the creek. It connected with a small island,
or rather peninsula, about a hundred yards from shore.
The geese in their autumn flight often alighted upon it
at night in great numbers, and this had given this
sand-bar its name.

From the lay of the ground back of the cabin-knoll,
Sallie knew that she could reach a point very near to
the bar without being seen. If she might but safely
run the gauntlet of the sand stretch to the covert of
the willows upon the island, she would be able to warn
the coming boatmen.

There was no time to lose. By the time she could
reach the island the *bateau* would be close at hand.
She opened the back window and, gun in hand,
crawled through and ran down the side of the knoll
into a little "swale" which extended for some distance
parallel with the river's bank. Once on this low
ground she bent forward so as to keep her head out of
sight and hurried up to a point which she knew must

be about opposite the sand-bar. Then boldly rising upright she ran swiftly across the intervening ground to the river-bank and slid down its steep side to the foot of the bar.

The keen eyes of the Indians had seen her at last. They guessed her purpose and set up a howl like the cry of a pack of wolves. Looking aside in her flight along the bar she saw them emerge, a yelling swarm, from the creek-bed, and give swift chase up the bank of the river.

They shot arrows at her as she ran, but the range at first was too great, and the shafts fell in the water or stuck lightly in the sand behind her. Oddly enough she thought of the scores of wild geese that had been fired upon from the bank and killed upon the sands over which she was fleeing.

That hundred yards seemed a long distance. The Indians gained swiftly upon her and before she could reach the island their arrows began to whiz spitefully past. She would certainly have lost her life had not the boatmen, who were rapidly drawing near, opened fire at this critical moment. Their long-range rifles scattered the Indians and sent them instantly flying.

Sallie had just breath left to note that there were more than two men in the *bateau*, and then she fell exhausted and fainting upon the wet sand at the edge of the island.

When she became conscious, Briggs and Ellery were kneeling by her, one on either side, fanning her with their hats. Her clothing and hair were drenched with the water they had thrown in her face to revive her.

Looking up, Sallie saw two tall strangers leaning on their guns and looking upon her with sympathy and interest. They now came forward and each in his rough way—for they, too, were frontiersmen—uttered expressions of grateful admiration, mingled with not a little wonder, at the feat she had performed.

When Gleason returned and the story was repeated to him, he said, simply, but with wet eyes: "Ye're a brave woman, Sallie, but I'll never leave ye alone agin, so long's thar's danger from Injuns."

That night John Ellery set out for Prairie du Chien in a canoe, and a few days later a squad of cavalry scoured the region in search of the Sioux. They did not find the Indians, who no doubt knew of their presence and mission, for the settlers at Little Pinnicon saw no more hostile bands.

The strangers who had come with Briggs and Ellery were men with families, true pioneers in search of fresh lands. They were so well pleased with the Pinnicon Valley that they marked claims adjoining the others, and each brought a wife and children into the "Little Pinnicon settlement."

VIII.

(From an Old Diary.)

On the night of the 13th of July, 1875, the writer left the neighborhood of Ft. Laramie, W. T., in company with thirty-four others, enroute for the Black Hills of Dakota.

We left the region of the Fort " between two days, "as they say out West of those who, for any cause, get out of a neighborhood by stealth. For nearly two weeks we had been in camp on the bank of the Laramie river, under strict surveillance of a sergeant's guard, when, for some reason, the patrol failed to put in an appearance on the night mentioned, and at midnight we struck camp, hitched to our wagons, and "rolled " up the Platte.

We traveled hard until nine o'clock the next morning, when we drew into a sheltered cotton-wood grove and hid for the day. Just before noon a sergeant's squad of fifteen cavalry-men rode by at a gallop on the look-out for us, at least ostensibly so, for there was little doubt in our minds that they saw our wagon-tracks leading away from the freight trail, and purposely shut their eyes to them

Instructions from Washington made it necessary for the commandant at the post to halt all northern bound out-fits at the Platte, allowing none to cross over until the Government's commissioners should gain possession of the Black-Hills portion of the Sioux Reserve by treaty with all the tribes concerned ; but when soldiers were sent out after trespassers who had escaped across the frontier of the reservation, they were usually not very anxious to bring them in.

The next day we swam our stock across the Platte, which was too deep at that season to ford—and rafted our wagons and effects, which consisted of mining-tools and "grub," mostly—on a raft made of five dry cotton-wood logs. It took the whole of day-light to get the eight wagons and their loads across, and we camped that night upon the extreme edge of the Indian lands.

In the morning our motley crowd gathered in front of one of the wagons, and we organized to pass through the country in military fashion. A French Canadian, an old plainsman, named Michaud, who talked plain English, was chosen captain, and an uncle of the writer, who was a veteran of the Rebellion, selected as second in command. There were several old miners from Colorado and California, some citizens of Cheyenne, three buffalo hunters, a Spaniard from the City of Mexico, a New Mexican "Greaser," and "pilgrims" from the States, among whom the writer was youngest.

That day we moved over the rough, barren hills which lay between the Platte and Raw-hide Butte, past "Bridger's Hole," a famous rendezvous of the old-time trappers, which Michaud pointed out to us. As we moved forward we presented quite a military appearance; marching on either side of the wagons, with shouldered guns, were the members of our party not employed in driving or as scouts. Two horsemen rode several yards in advance upon the only saddle-animals we had ; two on foot also kept pace with the wagons at some distance on either hand.

At night a guard was stationed on four sides of the camp, outside the circle in which our animals were picketed, for we were upon exceedingly dangerous ground. Both Sitting Bull's and Spotted Tail's young men had cut loose from the agencies, as we had learned at the fort, and we were likely at any moment to be "jumped" by a strong party of them.

On the third day out from the river, just as our small train had entered a valley between two stretches of high, rough hills near the head of White River, the scout upon our left, some two or three hundred yards away, came running down the hill-side at the top of his speed, shouting, "Injuns! Injuns! Corral the wagons! Corral the wagons!"

There was a general hustling toward the wagons of the other out-riders and scouts at the same moment, and in almost less time than it takes to tell it our wagons were drawn up into a circle—each team sheltered by the wagon ahead of it—and our little force, bristling with arms, gathered in an excited crowd within the corral thus made.

No Indians were in sight as yet—and the scout who had given the alarm was telling that he had caught sight of "a hull raft uv' em dodgin' 'mong the rocks up yander," when suddenly, above the tops of some of those same rocks were seen a number of signal flags and hats in motion. This was plainly an indication of a desire to hold communication with us.

Our "Greaser" now came forward, and made it known to Captain Michaud that he could speak the Sioux tongue, as he had lived for several years among

the Cheyenne Sioux, and offered to go up to the buttes
and talk with the Indians.   He was, of course, told to
go, and a few minutes later, as he mounted the steep
bluffs, we saw a number of nimble fellows scramble
down from a ledge of rock and seat themselves in a
circle about " John, " as we called the New Mexican.

They talked busily for some time, the Indians gestur-
ing in an animated fashion, then all arose and passed
out of sight behind the point of rocks which the
Indians had descended.

We waited impatiently for some time, when about
twenty horsemen came in sight and rode down toward
us, the "Greaser" with them.   They came within a
hundred yards or so, then halted, and John rode down
to us on one of their ponies.

In answer to anxious inquiries, he said that there
were at least one hundred and fifty of Sitting Bull's
and Spotted Tail's young bucks over on the other side
of the buttes, and that they wanted (and I fancy now
there was " an uncommon want in their tone ") to know
what we were doing upon Indian lands.   The head
chief, John said, would like to come down and hold a
talk with the " head man " of our party.

Captain Michaud sent John back to tell them that
the party who had come with him could advance and
he would talk with them, but that no others must come
any nearer, or we should fire upon them.

It was a wild-looking and gaudily bedecked lot of
fellows who rode down and dismounted in front of us.
They were togged out in bright-colored calicoes and
beaded buck-skin ; their faces were hideously daubed
in paints—yellow, green, black and vermilion.

They wore belts of cartridges around their waists

and over their shoulders, and were armed with Winchesters and needle guns; altogether I think they were the fanciest lot of redskins, and the most formidable in appearance, that I have ever seen. They flung themselves off their ponies, dropping the reins in front of each animal, and then seated themselves in a semicircle a few yards in front of our corral. We noted, uneasily enough, that there were a swarm of others up among the hills looking on with interest.

Those immediately before us, however, indicated their peaceful intentions by producing and filling a long peace-pipe, and after each buck had taken a whiff and blown it out through his nose, this pipe was proffered to our captain by the chief. But Michaud, who had advanced with the interpreter and stood confronting them, stepped back, dignifiedly folded his arms, and told John to say to the chief of the Sioux that he considered himself a much greater man than any before him and the pipe should have been presented to him before any of them had touched lip to it.

I have never seen so hideous an expression as came over the face of the chief as the interpreter repeated Michaud's words in Sioux. He threw the pipe upon the ground and, amid the grunts and black looks of his warriors, began a haranguing, in which, according to John's interpretation, he charged us with coming upon the Indian lands to steal them away from their rightful owners; they (the Indians) knew where we were going, he said, but we could never get there, as the country in front of us was so rough and broken that no wagons could pass through it, and he illustrated this by waving his hands up and down to show the hilly nature of the region, and swayed his body side-

wise to indicate the tipping over of our wagons. He
then further declared that the Indians would not let
us go among the mountains to seek the yellow dirt,
but would attack us and no doubt kill us all if we
attempted it.

  -This was the substance of John's interpretation,
though the harangue was drawn out at much greater
length, and if we could judge by the grunts of
approval with which the surrounding braves greeted
almost every sentence, the speech must have been a
very good specimen of Indian oratory.

  Michaud's reply was brief and characteristic of all
we had known or afterward learned of the man.

  "Tell them," said he to John, "to jump their hosses
an' git, an' to go mighty quick, too!"

  There was a chorus of angry "Huh's" as the
Indians scrambled to their feet and sprang upon their
ponies again. They scurried away, though, evidently
thinking that after such threats as their chief had
made had failed to intimidate us, we must be determined customers. In three minutes there was not a
Sioux in sight.

  They all disappeared behind the buttes in a twinkling, and then we held a council of war in which it
was admitted by the older frontiersmen that our expedition was one of extreme danger, and that our
chances of getting through with whole skins were, to
say the least, not more than even. Some of the party
were badly frightened and wanted the whole outfit to
set out at once upon the return. Michaud, however,
quickly put an end to that project by declaring that a
retreat would bring the whole swarm upon our heels at
once. We had faced just this danger, he said, from

the moment we had crossed the Platte river and ought
to have expected to meet Indians, and it would look
extremely silly in us to run at first sight of them.
The only thing to do was to move right on, using the
same precautions as before.

The timid ones were silenced and we moved on.
That night we camped upon a high bench of land, and
when it came on dark we discovered signal fires burning upon three buttes in as many directions. Appear-
ances were so alarming that we dug rifle-pits around
inside our wagon-corral. I remember that my turn to
go on guard, with three others, came that night from
nine o'clock till twelve. I probably experienced as
many sensations of awful lonesomeness and fear as
any young fellow of nineteen, new to the situation,
would be capable of. The memory of those three
hours is yet vivid.

Morning came, however, with no further sign of Indians, though the signal fires were visible during most
of the night. We traveled again until noon over a rough
country, meeting with no incident of note. But during
the noon camp, John, our Greaser, left us and went
out among some hills a half-mile distant, and did not
return until we were hitching up for a start. When
asked if had seen anything of the Indians he shook his
head, and when pressed as to whether he thought they
were following us, he said, "Mebbe so, mebbe not." It
was noticed by those nearest him that he was particularly silent and taciturn all that afternoon, though
they paid no great heed to his mood. But at night
when he drove his team out fully three hundred yards
from the usual corral, and camped by himself, our suspicions were fully aroused.

He had taken no part in our organization at Ft. Laramie, and his name was not on the role for guard relief, and as he had never been taken into our councils, Michaud did not interfere with his movements. During the evening, however, a number of the men went out to see him and find out, if possible, his motive in camping off by himself. They found one of his horses tied to the wagon; John had taken the other and gone. They waited an hour or more; he did not return and they came back to camp and reported, and for the next hour our party gave themselves to surmisings and speculations. Some declared the Greaser was "in cahoots" with the Sioux, while others only feared that might be the case, and were willing to admit that John might possibly be on the lookout for our interests, as it was plainly clear that he had nothing to fear on his own account.

Captain Michaud was ready to give the New Mexican the benefit of a doubt, as was also our lieutenant, and it was agreed that an extra guard should be stationed near enough John's wagon to report the hour of his coming in and any developments which might follow.

Morning came, and still the Greaser's horse and wagon stood out there on the prairie with no sign of their owner. The guard picketed out the animal where it could graze, and we moved on after breakfast, leaving both wagon and horse.

Night, or rather evening, found us upon the edge of a high plateau overlooking the Cheyenne valley, with our goal, the Black Hills of Dakota, plainly in view, and a stretch of rough "breaks" dropping away in front of us. We were just about entering at the head of a tortuous cañon which had been explored and found passable by an advance scout. We had to get down into it and camp, or go without water for our stock for that night, but as the foremost teams were driving down a steep pitch which lead into the gulch, a shout was raised behind which brought the whole outfit to a halt. "Hold up! Hold up in front! Th' Greaser's a-comin' on hossback, comin' like th' wind! Wait'n see what's up!"

Those of us on the rise looked behind, and sure enough there came John, whom we knew by his white horse, riding at the top of his animal's speed, and swinging his old sombrero violently back and forth. He pulled up, however, when he saw that we had halted and were waiting, and came in among us at a trot. Shouts greeted him from all sides.

"What's th' matter, John? Where's yer other hoss 'n' wagon?"

"Eenjun gitta ma hoss an' wagn," he replied, as he dismounted and rubbed his animal's steaming neck and shoulders. "Eenjun gitta me too, boota he no keep; plenty Eenjun een el aroyo, de canyon!" and he swept one hand toward the yawning gulch in front of us.

Incredulous and suspicious looks were exchanged upon this announcement which did not, to most of us at least, seem at all likely, as our scout had just returned from the canyon and had reported the coast clear. We looked down over the barren breaks and there was no sign of life of any kind save a scanty growth of buffalo grass and scattering pine shrub. But Michaud came forward and asked John how he knew the Indians were in the canyon.

His reply in broken English was very brief. He had gone out among the Sioux last night he said, and they had proposed to him to join them in an attack upon the whites when their wagons should attempt to pass through the broken hills of the Cheyenne. They had detailed their plan, and when they found he would not join them, had made him a temporary prisoner, and had placed an Indian as guard over him who was to release him at sundown; he escaped during the afternoon, he would not say how, and had ridden hard to overtake us. He had made enemies of his friends, he said, and the Indians would capture his wagon and other horse and kill himself if they ever got a chance.

All the time he was talking, our captain looked him steadily and sharply in the eyes, but John bore the scrutiny with composure, adding to his information that in order for our party to get safely through the breaks it would be necessary to drive further down the "Ilano," where he knew of a long ridge which we could descend with the wagons without danger of surprises, as there were no "aroyos" near enough for the Indians to fire from.

Satisfied of the truth of John's account, Michaud ordered back the wagons which stood with locked wheels upon the side-hill below. As the teamsters circled about and drove up again toward the top, there broke out away down among the gulches a long-drawn chorus of shrill yells which set everybody in the outfit agape and staring!

The sounds died away in a wail while we were gaping for a sight of the screeching red-skins, for such we could not doubt they were who made them. But that was all; not an Indian could we see nor did we hear any sound more than this one outbreak of rage and disappointment, attributable, undoubtedly, to their dis-

covery of John's appearance among us, and the knowledge that we were now fully on our guard against any
attack they could make upon us.

"Queer varmints them Injuns!" said Michaud, at
length. "Boys, this Greaser's saved our bacon sure;
we'll follow where he leads now."

I remember that a grim smile, or rather grin, came
over the dark, wrinkled features of the New Mexican
at this and his small shrewd eyes twinkled with satisfaction. We did follow him after that until three days
later we arrived safely at Camp Custer on French
creek, whither a few venturesome miners had preceded
us. Here we managed to raise a sum of money for
John, which paid him in part, at least, for the loss of
his wagon and horse so freely sacrificed to save our
lives.

Eleven days later, Colonel Benteen, with a detachment of United States cavalry, captured the whole lot
of us and escorted us across the Missouri, where we
were very rightly told to remain until the Government
should acquire a clear title to the lands we had
trespassed upon.

IX.

SEQUAPAH.

The following story of early adventure in one part of the Northwest is told by old Mr. Morgan Apleigh, an old farmer, who was one of the first settlers of the lower Des Moines Valley. He was a boy when he moved to Iowa, in 1836. During the next twenty years he made many hunting and trapping excursions to the North and West, in search of fur and peltry, and sometimes went either alone or with companions four or five hundred miles into the great wilderness which stretched away on every side but one, and which was tenanted only by Indians and animals.

Many were the adventures of this hardy pioneer. Generally he had for companions several of the young men belonging to the frontier settlement in which he lived, and also an Indian of the Iowa tribe, who not only served as guide, but also as protector against danger of attack from many of the Western tribes, whose language he understood, and with whom he was acquainted.

It was with a party of nine, including Sequapah, the Indian, that Apleigh met with a perilous adventure early in the 40's, and which he relates in language much as follows:

"It was 'bout forty-five years ago, I believe. We'd had a dry season; didn't raise any crops to 'mount to anything, an' 'bout the first of September I told the ·'d folks I couldn't stay at home any longer; I'd got to get out o' that clearin', 'n' be doing something agin.

"So I went across the river 'bout two mile, where the Clancy boys lived, Art and Logan, too see 'em 'bout goin' out west of the Missouri after beaver an' buffalo hides. 'Twas after dark when I got to their cabin, 'n' I found 'em both down on their knees mouldin' bullets; they had the floor covered with 'em, 'n' I remember I like to have broke my neck treadin' on 'em.

"Well, after the boys had had a good laugh at me, Art up an' tol' me that they had 'lowed to come over an' see me in the mornin' 'bout goin' with 'em on a hunt they'd been a-plannin' at a rasin' they'd been invited to over on Plum creek. They'd got five of the men over there to agree to go, perviden' Sequapah, an Iowa Injun that lived 'bout twenty miles 'bove us, would go along.

"Sequapah had ben off with me, an' with Art an' Logan Clancy, on many a huntin' an trappin' trip. He'd ben 'mong the Sioux a good deal, an' was 'quainted with a good many of their head chiefs, 'n' could palaver as well in Sioux or Omaha as he could in his own Iowa tribe.

"Of course I fell in with 'em, as that was jest what I wanted to see 'em about. So the next day Logan went after Sequapah, an' brought him down, comin' past Plum Creek, so as to let the men there know the Injun was ready to start.

"Well, the long an' short of it was that in three days we started, nine of us, with three teams an' wagons, an' five ridin' horses besides. We had cloth covers for our wagons. The canvas Art an' Logan Clancy had got at St. Louis, together with some

buffalo guns for me an' themselves. Besides our ordinary huntin' rifles, we had five buffalo guns in the
crowd. These guns were short, heavy rifles, for close
shootin'; barrels 'bout eighteen inches long, an' shot
a slug—twelve to the pound—'most as big as a man's
thumb.

"We steered for the Platte River, an' rafted the
Missouri not far 'bove where the city o' Council Bluffs
now stands. The Platte Valley was the best huntin'
and trappin' ground in the hull Northwest in them
days. Buffalo, elk, deer, antelope, beaver, every
kind o' game except grizzlies, was thick as grasshoppers.

"There was one drawback to huntin' then, though,
that usually kept white men out o' the country. It
was the huntin'-ground of both the Lower Sioux an'
the Pawnees, an' 'twas generally bad business when a
white man met up with a band of either of 'em.

"I went out there many a time, though, between
1840 an' 1861, but Sequapah was generally with me,
an' he was so well 'quainted with the Sioux, that I
went boldly 'mong 'em with him, an' they never
offered me harm.

"But with the Pawnees 'twas different. Sequapah
didn't know any of 'em; couldn't understand their
lingo, as it's altogether different from the Sioux an'
Iowas, who have many words alike, an' can generally
manage to understand each other.

"So we usually made out to do our huntin' an'
trappin' in them parts as close to the headquarters of a
Sioux band o' hunters as we could make it pay; an' they
bein' at war always with the Pawnees, an' 'most always
the strongest, we managed to dodge the Loups,

except on three or four trips, when we did run some
pretty narrow chances with these red-hot rascals.

"An' the trip that I'm talkin' 'bout was one of 'em.

" 'Bout fifty miles from the Missouri we struck a
strong band of Yanktonais Sioux, some three hundred
of 'em, camped on the bank of the Platte. Sequapah
knew the head chief an' a lot more of 'em, an' after we'd
spent a day restin', tradin' an' *powwowin'* 'mong 'em,
we moved on up twenty-five or thirty miles, an' pitched
our camp near the mouth of Shell Creek.

" We had to camp in a rather exposed place on
account o' gittin' water, but we picked the best ground
we could find, on a slopin' ridge that ran down to the
creek-bed. It was exposed enough, though, there bein'
a bushy gulley on either side, an' each o' the gulches
within a hundred yards, an' we had plenty of reason to
wish ourselves a thousan' miles away from it inside
o' three days.

" It ain't exaggeratin' but leetle to say that the country
was black with buffalo, an' the creek a-swarmin' with
beaver, an' we 'lowed to have the biggest kind of a
harvest in robes an' pelts.

" The second day out we brought in twenty-eight of
as fine buffalo pelts as ever I laid eyes on; but that very
night two o' the Plum Creek boys, Hank Bean an' Dave
Torsey, come in with their ponies a lather of sweat, an'
their hats gone, fresh from a hard run, to get out o'
the way of a swarm o' Injuns that had chased 'em
almost into camp, they havin' dodged 'em in one of the
gulches above. They said they believed there was
more than a hundred of 'em, an' it was proved pretty
soon that they hadn't put the figger too high.

" Well, we set to work at once to make ourselves

safe from their arrers, if they should pitch into us, as
Hank an' Dave 'lowed they would, as soon as they
could get us located, an' find out our numbers.

"We took the three wagons an' formed a squar' of 'em
with an open side to'rds the creek, as there wa'n't
much danger o' them comin' up the slope from that
direction. Then we took our fresh buffalo hides, an'
nailed em' four or five deep to the tops of the wagon
boxes, so that their lower edges laid on the ground, an'
that *wall o' hides* is just exactly what saved us from a
general massacre.

"We didn't look for an attack, though, before mornin',
if it came at all. Sequapah gave it as his opinion the
boys had been run in by a fresh band of Sioux, an' that
he could pacify 'em once he got amongst 'em. He said
he didn't b'lieve Pawnees, unless the whole tribe was
together, 'd dare to come in so close to the big Sioux
village below. We picketed our horses on the slope,
an' leavin' Art Clancy an' a Plum Creek fellow named
Rowley on guard, the rest of us rolled in, an' went to
sleep.

"I don't know how long we'd slept, but not long,
when we was brought standin' by sech a storm of hid-
jus yells as never had come to my ears before. It come
from both sides, '*Yi! yi-hi! Yeouoogh!*'

"We all began to grab for our guns the instant our
wits come to us; an' just about then Art Clancy an'
Rowley shot inside our wagon fort.

"'Ravines are full of Injuns on both sides, boys,'
said Art, 'but they haint shot an arrer yet! They've
come up the bottom o' the gulches turrible sly, fer that
yell's the first I've heard of 'em.'

"Sequapah had been asleep with the rest of us inside,

and now we called on him to explain the queer performance, for we'd expected to have arrers an' bullets come
thick as hail after sech a yell, an' not a bullet nor a
arrer was shot at us, nor had the Injuns made another
sound, 'ceptin' that one gen'ral shriek.

"'Huh! um Sioux, Oglallas, me guess,' said Sequapah. 'Um no hollar like um Yanktonais, no like um
Wapekuta, no like um Cheyenne, me heap guess um
Oglalla. Um a heap fool, holla *yi hi;* fink when he no
shoot evly body he lun look then he heap shoot um,
Huh!' an' he spit hard on the ground to express his
disgust. 'Huh! me make a heap talk now; then he
light off go away me guess.'

"On sayin' that, he climbed up on one of the wagons,
--we'd taken off the sheets,--laid his gun across the
top of the box, an' stood up bold as a lion.

"He yelled out something in the Sioux language, then
called over two or three names that I knew : '*Hoton
Washtado,*' meanin' 'He with a very good face,' an'
'*Petit Corbeau,*' 'Little Crow'--both Sioux chiefs, an'
then, without waitin' for 'em to reply, began flourishin'
his arms and makin' a speech.

"He was a reg'lar Injun 'bout likin' to make a
spread. I've often thought since that I never saw nor
heard anythin' so perfectly redic'lus as his performance
that night.

"I can see him yet, every time I shut my eyes, as he
stood up there atween the wagon-bows a-speechifyin'
an' layin' it off with both hands, talkin' first at one
ravine an' then turnin' to the other. Talk about an
Injun's bein' dignified, why, Sequapah made more noise
than any Fourth o' July *orater* I ever heard !

"Desprit as the sityeation might turn out for us, we jess had to laugh.

"There was a moon that didn't go down till after midnight an' it was light enough to see off quite a distance. While Sequapah was talkin' we was all peekin' over the tops of the wagons tor'ds the ravines, some on one side an' some on the other, an' putty soon Injun heads began to pop up in both directions, seemin' to shoot up out o' the grass at the edge o' the slopes.

"Pretty soon there was a whole string of 'em standin' up on both sides, lookin' like a picket fence in a mirage, a listenin' with all their ears to Sequapah's oration. The nearest ones must 'a' been 'bout eighty steps away. It wasn't light enough to see 'em distinctly, but there couldn't 'a' been less than half a hundred on each side.

"Sequapah kept on with his speech, jabberin' away in Sioux for nigh ten minutes I should guess. I could understand a few words an' heard him tell 'em : 'Oglalla wash-tah-do pe-o-peh, Ko-sah-wahu,' and Pawnees ha wai-kahu! sich-e wa-nich-ee!' which meant that he was braggin' up the Oglalla Sioux and callin' the Pawnees miserable fellows, no good for any purpose, an' as the two tribes was always at war with each other he expected to make frien's with 'em, takin' it for granted, o' course, that they were Oglallas.

"Well, he wound up finally an' waited for an answer. One of 'em then, on the right-hand side, who seemed a foot taller than any o' the rest, came for'ard a few steps an' begun talkin' back in a deep voice that sounded harsh as a grater.

"Sequapah listened a few seconds an' then, 'Huh !' he grunted ; 'no understan', um Pawnee !'' an', mad as

a hornet to think he'd wasted all his elokence, he
grabbed up his gun an' blazed away at 'em, then, quick
almost as lightning he turned, give a jump, an' shot
down amongst us like a metiur.

"Then there was music! Such screechin' and howlin'
I hope I may never hear agin; an' the bullets an'
arrers came peltin' agin' the wagons an' the buffalo-
hides like a dozen boys was throwin' han'fuls o' gravel-
stones at 'em; they'd *click* on the iron, *chug* into the
wood and *thump* the skins, an' ev'ry time there'd come
a shower of 'em there'd rise up a horrible babel o'
screeches.

"We ducked, o' course, the minute Sequapah shot at
'em, an' then we lay close, reservin' our fire for a charge,
if they should git bold enough to make one. Four
thicknesses o' buffalo-hides hangin' loose was plenty
of protection agin any weapon the Injuns had in them
days, but there'd been several cracks left at the hubs
of the wagon-wheels an' ev'ry few minutes an arrer or
a bullet or a shot would whistle through one of 'em.
They was accidental shots, o' course, fired at the
wagons, but 'fore we got the cracks located so as to
keep out o' range of 'em Jim Rowley 'd got a buckshot in his wrist an' Logan Clancy'd had a piece o'
scalp raised across the back of his head by an arrer.

"We lay huggin' the ground for two hours or more
with a storm of yells an' shots on each side, an' nobody fired at an Injun but Art Clancy an' Sequapah;
they took turns in loadin' their big buffalo guns nigh
to the muzzle an' firin' 'em over the tops of the wagons,
so to let 'em know that we had big guns amongst us
and plenty of ammunition. This prob'ly discouraged

'em from makin' a charge, an' after a while the firin'
slacked up an' everything got quiet.

"But they hadn't give up, we soon found, for some
of us kept watch through cracks after the firin' stopped,
an' 'twasn't long till an Injun was seen sneakin' out
tor'ds the horses. Two or three shots sent him scut-
tlin' back into the gulch agin.

"Then after a bit, we discovered that a number of
'em had climed into the tree-tops across one of the
ravines an' was tryin' to shoot their arrers over onto
us. They couldn't get up high 'nough, though, an'
failed to get their arrers inside our corral. We sent
some bullets over after 'em an' they give that up.

"Everything was quiet until morning after that,
'ceptin' now an' then a few whoops, and when daylight came, and when it got light enough to see, we
made a sudden discovery inside our little garrison.

"Sequapah was gone!

"He wasn't inside the corral, an' no one had seen
him go out. It had been quite dark for two hours
back, an' we knew at once that he'd slipped out an'
crawled off down the slope an' that he'd gone in
hopes of gitten' away an' bringin' the Sioux to our
rescue, but as we'd heard some fierce yells down
tor'ds the mouth o' the ravines not long before we
were afraid he hadn't made it.

"That was a terrible day for us; the Pawnees had
settled down to a reg'lar siege. We could see a few
of their streaks o' smoke comin' out the ravines where
there were fires and where, prob'ly, some of 'em were
cookin' their breakfasts. But there was enough of 'em
on the watch, an' we couldn't expose so much as a

finger without havin' a shower o' bullets, shot an' arrers sent at it.

"Art Clancy an' I managed to build a fire an' roast some steak, which we handed 'round to the boys. Logan had his head bandaged and Rowley had his wrist wrapped in some cloths they tore from the linin' of Jim's coat.

"The horses had been picketed close in, an' all but three of 'em was there by their stakes whinnyin' for water. Three o' the farthest ones had either been cut loose durin' the darkest part o' the night or they'd got scared at the firin' an' broke away.

"Wall, the day wore on, an' that afternoon another o' the Plum Creek boys got hit, a bullet glancin' off one o' the wagon-tires an' buryin' itself in the top o' his left shoulder. It was a severe wound an' used him up. We done the best we could dressin' it and made him a comfortable bed to lay on.

"The afternoon passed an' still no sign of frien's. Night came on, an' wore away. How those poor horses whinnied for water! two more of 'em broke away in the night.

"Daylight came agin an' found us 'bout as despairin' a set of men as ever was besieged. We'd have made a break to get out an' cut our way through in the darkness that night, if 't hadn't been for the wounded ones we couldn't leave 'em nor git away with 'em.

"It was lucky we didn't try, for just about sunrise down came the Sioux, swarmin' over the hill an' down the ravines like a fresh-stirred nest o' hornets. They came streakin' down, lyin' low on their horses an' yellin' like demons, an' they cleared them gulches o' Pawnees 'bout as quick as I can tell it.

" Sequapah was with 'em, an' he came ridin' straight
to us an' seemed as tickled as we ourselves that he'd
brought the Sioux in time.

"The Yanktons followed up the Pawnees an' fit
with 'em nearly all day ; they killed a good many of
'em, too, and got back three o' our horses.

"The next day we hurried back an' camped at their
village. Here the boys nursed their wounds an' the
rest of us hunted an' trapped. There wasn't many of
'em that cared to git far away from the Yankton
village agin, an' as we had to share our ketch with the
Sioux, we didn't go home as well loaded as we had
expected.

" There was enough of peltries, though, so that when
we came to carry 'em down to St. Louis they brought
enough to pay well for our time, if not for the danger
we'd undergone."

OUTJUGGLED.

" Now turn your tongue loose, Mac and tell us a good story; some wild yarn. We don't want any fancy stuff, but a real adventure, something exciting, out of your own knock-about experiences on the frontier."

It was during our hunting trip up Red River into Texas and the "nation's" territory. We had camped that night in the shelter of the bluffs, and had a roaring camp-fire burning ; for a blustering " norther " had come down on us. Mac had figured as a traveling magician.

" Well, gentlemen," Mac responded at length, and in compliance with our urgent, hilarious demand on him, " I *will* tell you a little thing that happened to me once on a time, and not so very long ago, either. It was last fall, in fact, and came off at one of the Comanche villages.

" About the middle of November, I was trailing my cart and show truck over the " Sill Route " once more, and I camped for the night at the Comanche town, as I'd done a dozen times before that. I knew the bucks, every one of them, or thought I did, and I felt no fear at going among 'em alone, though before I'd always carried a driver.

" Well, I hadn't got my supper cooked before a lot of young braves came down to my wagon and engaged me for a show that evening in their new school-house ! Well, they've got one, a big log house, with a board

floor and seats.   It had just been built, and they'd got
an edicated half-breed girl to teach.

"I told the young chaps that if they'd help me rig a
little staging and put up my curtains and raise me five
dollars, I'd give 'em a first-class show, with all the
latest performances in legerdemain.

"Well, these young bucks that I was speaking of
come down in 'bout an hour with half the town, young
and old, big and little, at their heels, and away we
went, cart, horse and all, over to their school-house,
which was built in the woods 'bout forty rods from the
village.   In a very short space of time, we had a narrow staging rigged, and I hung my calico curtains
'cross the front of it, packed in my truck-chests, and
while the house was a-filling up plump full of the black,
greasy-faced beggars, I got ready for business.

"They raised me the five dollars in silver and paid it
cheerfull as you please; the beggars'll give their last
cent either for a drink of whisky or to see any kind
of a queer performance that is new to them.

"Well, I opened up on 'em.   I performed with rings,
with cup and ball, and set 'em all a-gruntin' and *a-
chuggering* with delight.

"Then I loaded a pistol, marked the bullet, and let
'em examine it; and then handing the pistol to a young
buck I told him to shoot me squarely between the eyes.
That was too much for them Comanches; they just
gripped their seats and grunted like a lot of wild hogs
that you've just jumped in a thicket of sweet-briers.

"That young buck's hand trembled like a mule's ear;
but he pulled down on me, gritty like, shut his teeth,
and cut loose.   Then them Comanches just rose to their
feet and yelled!   But I stepped down out of the smoke

"I performed with rings."—Page 93.

and motioned 'em back into their seats, and got 'em quiet agin.

"Then I opened my lips and showed 'em the bullet between my teeth, and when they'd all seen it there, I took it out and passed it round. It had the same marks as the bullet they'd seen me put in the pistol.

"But I hadn't done with 'em yet; fool that I was, I proposed the rope performance, and called on two of their best men to come up and tie me, telling 'em that I could get out of their knots before one of 'em would have time to saddle a pony, if the horse were right there.

"I produced my rope, a good long one, three-eights, and stout enough to hold a two-year-old steer. I lay down on the platform and told 'em to come on and do their tying. At first they all seemed a little scared of trying; that bullet business, you see, had made 'em a little shy 'bout fooling round me.

"Presently a big, tall, ugly-looking old buck, wearing a green blanket round him and a lot of dyed turkey feathers in his hair, came up on the stage and motioned to a stout young one, sitting near, to come and help him. The young chap trotted up, and they went at me.

"I swelled out my muscles with all my might; you know how the trick's done; but, gentlemen, before they got half done, I knew I was cornered.

"I saw it in that old black villain's wrinkled, scowling face and in his murderous, snaky little eyes. He was one of their *medicine men*, probably the greatest of the tribe. The old brute was jealous of me; and knowing there was nothing any more supernatural about my tricks than about his own heedyus juggling, he'd made up his mind to corral me in one of my own performances.

"Well, gentlemen, that rope was passed round my wrists in a twinkling, and drawed so tight that I winked hard with the pain, and I felt the veins swell almost to bursting.

"From my wrists they passed the rope tight around my waist, then took a half hitch around my *neck* and knotted it under my arms. Then they went for my legs with the other end of the rope, and tied my ankles (I'd taken off my boots) so tight that my feet ached before they'd finished knotting.

"I laid there and never opened my mouth; I wouldn't even let myself think till they pulled the curtains on me. When they got through, I told 'em to draw the curtain and shut me in so that I might set my medicine at work on the ropes. I saw the old medicine-man grin as I give the order. He shoved the young fellow off the staging and pulled the curtains to, leaving *himself inside*. Then I heard a surprised grunt all over the house, and I began to *think*.

"I let my muscles relax and shrunk up like a turtle; but them knots shrunk with me, and I found myself helpless as a baby; and there was that old grinning wretch bending over me with his snakish black eyes just glittering in triumph!

"'Guess you've got me, old man,' said I; 'what are you going to do about it?'

"He bent over me, and made a hissing noise with his mouth, a noise that sounded exactly like the buzz of a rattlesnake's tail. Everything and everybody in the room was as still as a tomb-stone. I couldn't hear a breath outside. All at once that wretch stopped his hissing, and with a quick movement jerked my head up between his knees, jammed something between my jaws, whipped a red scarf out from under his blanket, and passed it around my head and mouth—*gagged* me, in fact, tight as a double-sinched bucker.

" 'I've given my last show on this earth,' I thought. Then the old villain backed down off the platform and slipped out from under the curtain.

"There was a general grunt of curiosity and astonishment outside, and a heap of admiration, for their old juggler was mixed up with their racket.

" '*Silence !*' growled the old wretch in Comanche. 'Silence! I have breathed upon the bad medicine-man of the whites. If I had not done so, his vile, poisonous breath would have slain every warrior in the room. At midnight every one of you would have died. Just as the moon rose above the tree-tops, your spirits would have left your bodies. Your squaws and your children would have been given to them crawling snakes, the Creeks and the Choctaws in the East.'

"Of course I'm only trying to give you the substance of what he said. I don't understand their jargon, only well enough to get their general meaning. When the old man ceased speaking, the crowd just got up and shrieked in the awfullest blood-curdling yells you ever dreamed of! for a minute I thought my time had come, and that I should be torn to pieces by the screeching mob, but the old man shook his medicine-rattle at 'em and down they sat again, quiet as you please.

" 'Listen !' he said. 'Go home now, my children, to your *tepeés* and sleep ; come not here till morning, when you'll find the bad medicine of the whites harmless as the water of the Coder. He shall not hurt you. Go,

and leave me with the medicine-dog ; for I must breathe
again upon him, and my breath will take away all his
charms and all his magic. He shall ketch no more
bullets in his teeth. Go, my children, for my breath is
sacred and can be of no good until all the members of
my tribe are in their lodges.'

"And do you believe it, they all got up and skipped
out of there, every mother's son of 'em ! There I was,
left alone with that heed'yus old beast. I had worked
desputly all the time he was talking, trying to draw
my hands from the rope. I loosened one of 'em
just a trifle, enough to know that in half an hour
of hard work I could bring my wrist through, by peel-
ing all the skin off with it. Well, when they'd gone
and the last sound of 'em died away, the old juggler
stuck his face inside.

"'I go now' says he, I go to my *tepeé* to prepare my
medicines against the medicine of the white dog.
When I come again the white man's magic shall all be
mine ; he will tell me all his medicines.' Then he came
inside, felt of all my knots, made himself sure of 'em,
and then went out and left me.

"'So that's your game, is it?' thought I, and I
began to take hope at once. I hadn't time to think
over the situation ; I just worked like a beaver, with
the sweat pouring off me like rain off a slicker.

"It was a struggle for life ; for of course I hadn't a
doubt but the medicine-man meant to kill me, whether
I told him any of my tricks or not. He would smother
me like a cat in a sack, and pretend to his tribe that
his breath had killed the medicine-man of the whites,
when he would possess himself of my trinkets and be
the greatest man that ever trod a Comanche town.

"Well, he was gone longer than I had any reason to hope for; and after a time I wrenched my right hand through the loop that held it. And I peeled it, too, peeled it horribly. But after that the work was easy; I got my arm loose, got my jackknife out of my pocket, managed to open the big blade with the stiff, swelled fingers of my other hand. Then I cut and slashed for a minute, tore the bandage off my mouth, and spit out a deer's-horn charm. I was nearly smothered with my efforts; for of course I couldn't breathe through my mouth till I got the scarf off; but I soon gained my breath and sat up, a free man.

"Then I began to think and to act. My right hand was just streaming with blood, and an idee struck me. I smeared it all over my face, till it was perfectly red with blood. Then I got up and fished a white sheet out of one of my chests, a piece of 'white factory' that I'd used in some of my tricks. I put that around me, turned down the lantern and the other light inside the curtains, got out my six-shooter, then leaned back against the wall and waited.

"It was nearly half an hour yet before I heard the old heathen coming. He stole in, soft as a cat, and slid along up to the curtains. I always carry three lamps with me. Two of them were burning in the room; but he seemed puzzled about the light behind the curtain. Presently he opened a crack and peeked in. What do you think I saw? The horriblest face ever a human being wore! The cheeks painted a blarish green, half-moons of ghastly yellow under the eyes, a jet-black ring about the ugly, grinning mouth, and three blood-red stripes across the forehead; while the

little black eyes shone with a fierce, beastly glitter that
couldn't be described.

"He'd got himself up in a more fearful shape than I
had. He was going to scare me; but he didn't succeed
—not any!

"He gave a surprised 'whooh' as he looked on the
floor; there was nothing there but a bloody spot. I'd
cleared away the ropes and tossed 'em one side. Then
he looked up and I stepped forward, jerked the curtains
one side, and exhibited my git-up to him. With a
sharp yell he threw up both his hands, and there came
over his bedaubed face the ghastliest look of fright it's
ever ben my fortune to behold. I wish I could have
painted it; I should be famous to-day.

"But I didn't give him any time to recover; I jumped
for him, and struck out as I jumped. He went his
length on that platform like a beef-ox. Then I grabbed
the pieces of rope and before he came to himself enough
to realize what the movement meant, I had *him* tied;
yes, and had that old deer's-horn charm between his
jaws, bound there with his own red scarf, tighter than
wax!

"I'd bound him with limp muscles, and he was there
to stay! He came to himself in a minute and glared
at me frightfully.

"'Ha! ha!' says I. 'You'll *breathe* on the white
dog, will you—*you?* Lay there and learn to let the
medicine of the white man alone!

"But I didn't waste time palavering at him. I
hustled my things out of there, hitched onto my cart,
and skipped out and away; and, gentlemen, I never
went fooling round any Comanche village agin."

XI.

THE OLD JUDGE'S STORY.

" I have lived on the frontier all my life, beginning as a boy in Ohio, and regularly moving west with each fresh migration of settlers, to newer territories, where the sod was still unturned, and though I have gone through with some rough experiences, as all pioneers must, yet I have never had any serious trouble with my fellowmen, either white or red, save on one occasion. That was in the summer of '53, the year after I had settled at my present farm on the Iowa River bottom-lands."

It was after this manner that "Old Judge Crego," as he was commonly called, used to preface his account of his pioneer troubles with the Muskquakie Indians, in the early days of Iowa's history. The old gentleman had been a county judge in Illinois or Indiana, the writer has forgotten which.

" Yes, I had trouble then ; serious trouble, too. It happened in haying time, about the last days in July. We were living in a new log-house on the east side of the river, myself, my wife and child, and our hired hand, a young fellow named Aleck Wingate. We had one child, our little Susie, five years old.

" Our cabin was then the highest mark of civilization —in one sense at least—upon the Iowa River, for there were no settlers above us, and the nearest family below was seven miles distant. We were, indeed, well out upon the frontier ; yet we had lived there for more than a year, meeting with no foes more dangerous than the wild beasts.

"We knew there were hunting-parties of Indians frequently roaming about the country, chasing the herds of elk, which were then very numerous along the upper Iowa and its western branches. But these Indians, we were told, belonged to the friendly Iowas, Musquakies, and to Johnny Greene's tribe; and so when a band of some thirty, calling themselves Musquakies, came and camped at the mouth of a creek two miles above us, we felt no uneasiness at their presence, our only annoyance coming from the begging propensities which they speedily developed.

"They would come singly, and in twos and threes, stalking in at the door generally at meal-time, and beg importunately for 'bled' (bread) and 'sug' and 'tobac,' the latter an article of which Aleck always kept a bountiful supply on hand. Aleck and I were then at work harvesting a twelve-acre field of wheat, which we had managed to get in the spring before; and as this field was in an opening in plain sight of the cabin, we were, during the first week of the Indians' stay, always within call of my wife, who often sat in the open door, with Susy playing at her feet, and watched us as we cradled, bound, and 'set up' the grain.

"But when we went at our haying, on the wide marsh which lay upon the west end of my land across the river, we were much farther away.

"One morning, about ten o'clock, I should think, as we were at work, Aleck looked up—he was mowing just ahead of me—and threw down his scythe with a shout of surprise.

" ' Look ! ' he cried. 'Is Mis' Orego crazy ? '

" Some twenty rods distant my wife was running through the grass, with Susy in her arms. I saw in an instant that she was terribly frightened. Susy, too, was screaming.

" ' Why, why, Em ! ' I shouted, when she came within calling distance ; ' what does this mean ? Is it Indians ? '

" She came out onto the mowed ground, and threw herself and child down upon a swath of hay, and there she lay for a minute, gasping for breath, while Aleck and I, who had both run to meet her, stared at her and at each other in indignant amazement, for we had both by this time divined something of what her story would be.

" ' John, ' she gasped, at length, 'there's an—Indian —at—the house ! He—he—shook me—pulled my hair —and—and—*kicked Susy !* '

" I waited not to hear another word.

" ' Stay with them, Aleck ! ' I shouted, and was off at full run.

" My wife screamed to me to come back, but my temper was started, and I was determined to punish the insolent wretch if I had to chase him into the midst of his own camp.

" I splashed through the river, and when I reached the cabin, and dashed in at the door, I found that savage wretch seated cross-legged on the center of our table, stolidly gnawing a lean pork shank which my wife had boiled for dinner. The pulling of a squaw's hair and the kicking of a papoose were affairs of such minor importance in his tribe, that he probably could not conceive that I should be violently angry that he had exercised a man's supreme privilege in my home.

Or more probably, he merely thought my wife had run out of doors and hid herself and child, until he should go away. Be that as it may, I gave him no time to think or act after he saw me. I knocked him over, table and all.

"He threw the table off with an angry grunt, sprang to his feet, and started out. He went away slowly. I knew Indians well enough to know what the fellow meant by that sullen, dignified gait: he would have his revenge.

"I felt that I had been hasty; that, in fact, I had done a most unwise thing, notwithstanding the Indian's brutal treatment of my wife and child. Not that I was sorry to have punished the fellow, and turned him out of my house, but I had placed myself and family in extreme jeopardy by my hasty course of action. If I had taken him and bound his hands, and then driven him back to his camp at the muzzle of my rifle, both he and his fellows would no doubt have looked upon it as a merited punishment for his trespass upon my premises; but to have struck him I knew was an indignity to which no brave would tamely submit.

"Events afterwards proved that I judged the matter rightly.

My wife and Aleck came hurrying to the house after me, both scared half to death, and when I told them what I had done we held a council.

"We concluded without much argument that it would not be safe to leave the house alone, and of course that Em and Susy could not be left alone there for a single hour, so long as that party of Indians remained about. So we finally arranged that old 'Tad'

Newcome, a one-legged trapper, who lived in the woods three miles below us, should be hired to come up and stay at the house during haying, and, if he would, until the trapping season set in.

" One evening, as Aleck and I were driving up from the ford with a load of hay—we had taken my horses and the wagon over after we began haying, so as to haul home and stack a load every night—we met old. Tad, stumping towards us, his hat off, his face white and working strangely, and his actions showing that something terrible had occurred.

" ' Whoa ! ' shouted Aleck, who was driving ; and he looked up at me.

" I slipped off the load and stepped out in front of the old trapper as he came up.

" ' For Heaven's sake ! ' I exclaimed, what *is* the matter ? '

" ' Jedge,' said he, with a kind of gasp, as though the news choked him, ' *they've got the babby !* '

" I staggered back against the hay like a drunken man. For a moment it seemed as though the blood had all left the surface of my body and gone to my heart, and I felt so faint and sick that I could not speak.

" ' Jedge,' said the old man again, and his voice shook as though he had an ague chill, ' Jedge, I—I—I never dreamt'—but he broke down and could not finish.

" ' My wife,' said I, getting my voice, ' is *she* safe ? "

" He nodded his head and pointed to the cabin.

" By that time I had gathered my senses enough to note that Aleck was flying around the horses, unhitching and throwing the harness off them like a wild man.

"I saw what was his purpose, and my wits seemed to come to me with sudden sharpness.

"'That's right, Aleck,' said I; 'off with everything but the bridles.'

"'Now,' said I, turning to the old trapper again, 'tell me how it happened, when they took her and which way, and tell me quick!'

"'It war 'bout a hour ago, nigh, I sh'd reckon,' he answered; 'the leetle thing run round back o' the cabin, whilst I was settin' smokin' in front, 'n 'er ma wus a-workin' at 'er ir'nin' inside. We didn't notice 'bout 'er bein' gone long, 'n' purty soon I heerd, or thought I heerd, a kin' o' smothery screech out back to'rds the age o' the woods. I run roun' an' couldn' see nothin' o the babby ner nothin' else, 'n' es I wus a lettle scart, I called to 'er ma ter come 'n' help me fin' the young un, an' said I guessed she'd strayed off down to'rds the creek. That scart yer wife ter'ble, 'n' though I didn't say nothin' 'bout Injuns, I knowed she was a-thinkin' of 'em, 'n' we scattered out in the woods.

"'Wal, jedge, we hunted 'long 'nough fer me to run acrost a fraish Injun track on the age o' a gopher knoll. I didn't say nothin' 'bout that ter the wife though; but she jes give it up purty quick, 'n' says she ter me, says she, "Go 'n' git John quick, 'n' tell 'im the Injuns 've got our babby," 'n' then she p'inted fer the cabin, a-weepin', oh, ter'ble!

"'An' now, jedge,' he went on, all the time, in a hopeless tone of voice, 'I don' wanter diskerridge ye, but it's my honest opinyen ye'll navver see that babby alive agin. Them Injuns is sech revenging critters; but *he* went down the crick, jedge, 'n' *you* wanter go

up crick; min' now, what I tell ye, *up* crick ter their
camp 'n' thout no guns, nor we'pons o' any kind; 'n' ef
the Injuns is thair, ye want to ride right in, 'n' demand
that babby, 'n' demand 'er *strong*, 'n' if they've got 'er
alive, ye'll git 'er, 'n' if they haint, ye won't,' and with
that the old fellow turned and stumped off towards
the house.

"By this time Aleck had the horses ready for mounting and was waiting. We jumped on to their backs
and rode off up the river. I did not dare wait to go
and see my wife; I felt that I must and would find my
child alive.

"I do not think Aleck and I were more than fifteen
minutes reaching the Indian camp. It was located in
a beautiful fur-oak grove, five lodges, or *tepeés*, being
grouped in a cluster at the mouth of a creek. It was
dark, and the camp-fires were flickering in front of
each lodge as we rode up; and we could see a number
of bucks, squatted smoking, about the two central ones.

"They paid not the slightest attention to us until I
had dismounted, given my rein to Aleck and walked
into their midst. I looked them over quickly and
carefully, as I answered 'How do' to their grunted
salutations, and soon my eye fell upon the identical
Indian whom I was searching for. He was sitting
with his face turned partly away from the fire, and
was looking doggedly down the long pipe-stem at
which he was pulling stolidly. I knew his ugly visage
instantly and stepped in front of him, but still he did
not lift his eyes.

"'*Get up!*' I commanded; and Aleck afterward said
that my words sounded like the click of a gun-lock.

"The Indian sprang to his feet with an angry grunt,

and looked at me with eyes that glowed, in the fire-light, like two coals; while his companions rose to their feet also, with guttural exclamations.

"'Where is my child, my little girl?' I asked, keeping my voice as calm as I could, though I felt it quiver as I spoke.

"The Indian gave an impatient shrug, and made a gesture of not understanding, but he began backing away as though to avoid further questioning.

"I stepped forward, and reached out my hand to seize him by the shoulder, or the throat, I was not particular which, and as I did so I heard Aleck's voice, sharp and keen with warning:

"'*Judge!* look out!' and then I felt a stunning, crashing sensation in my head, and went down under a blow given treacherously by an Indian behind me. . .

"It must have been an hour or more before I came to myself, and when I did so I found myself upon the ground where the Musquakies had left me, whether for dead or not, I never knew. The Indians had pulled up their lodges, mounted their ponies, and fled.

"When I had recovered enough to take in the situation, I got up, and staggered off toward home. I turned so dizzy, sick and faint a dozen times before I reached home, that I felt certain I was about to drop down and die; but at last I got there, and opened the door, half expecting to find everybody gone, or murdered, and what do you think I saw?

"There was my wife, sitting in our old rocking-chair, in the middle of the floor, holding *Susy asleep in her arms!*

"I fainted dead away. I was brought to my senses by old Tad and my wife, who had worked over me for a long time, and when they finally got me so that I could sit up, they told their story.

"About an hour and a half, as they judged, after Aleck and I had started for the Indian camp, as my wife lay sobbing on the bed, and the old trapper sat gloomily in the arm-chair, they heard a child's voice, little Susy's, crying at the door. My wife flew to it, and snatched up her child, and old Tad, without waiting an instant, snatched his cap and rifle, and fearing that Aleck and I had got into trouble, started for the Indian camp. He found the camp deserted, but did not see me, and then came back, to find my wife working over me, and almost in despair of my life!

" Where Aleck was, they did not know; but he soon came in to inform us, and with him came several men on horses, from the settlement below, where he had ridden with all speed to bring them to the rescue.

" He had tried to warn me at the camp as the redskin who struck me lifted his hatchet, but his outcry was raised too late. He had seen me go down, struck by the flat of the Indian's hatchet; and then, as a number of them turned threateningly toward him, he wheeled the horse around, and made swiftly across the 'Big Bend' to the settlement below. He hoped to rouse them, and cut the Indians off, as he correctly guessed that they would beat a quick retreat. He had not doubted that they would kill me out of revenge. They were all surprised, and not a little rejoiced, at the turn of events.

" We did not pursue the Indians, all agreeing that no good could come of it after what had happened. By a good deal of questioning we got out of Susy, that a 'bad black man' had carried her away, and took her

to his queer *house* where the 'naughty folks' frightened her so that she dared not 'talk or cry,' and then
that 'after a while' the 'bad black man *brunged*' her
'home again.'

"I do not know what the Indians had meant to do
with her; but after what had happened at their camp,
they no doubt feared either to keep her, or harm her,
and so had brought our child back to us.

"That was the only trouble I ever had with Indians,
and was the last, in fact, that we ever saw of any of
those Musquakies."

XII.

WAPPER-JAW JOHN.

I remember "Wapper-Jaw John," the gray-haired Winnebago, who, when I was a boy, used occasionally to visit the neighborhood in which I lived. Despite his strikingly deformed and ugly face, people who knew him seemed always to be kindly disposed toward him. They bought his curiously-wrought willow and splint baskets, and often gave him food and a night's lodging.

His face was angular and deeply wrinkled; the under jaw was set with a curious twist on one side, and it twitched and grimaced grotesquely when he talked—and he could talk only brokenly.

He was a harmless old fellow, with a good deal of shrewd sense. He was unlike the other members of his tribe, and kept apart from them. The other Winnebagoes, so far as we knew them, were worthless, begging vagabonds, who to the number of a hundred or more visited us semi-annually.

John did really earn an honest living, and was never known to beg, although, like other wandering Indians, he carried his "papers," a lot of written testimonials certifying him to be "a good Indian." Two or three of these precious documents were of considerable length, and they narrated John's services and friendly exploits in behalf of white people in times of Indian outbreaks. He carried the papers in a beaded buckskin wallet in a pocket that he had made for this purpose in the breast of his coarse shirt.

One of these accounts covered several foolscap pages. It was written in a close, fine hand that was perfectly legible, though the paper was yellow with age and wear.

I remember the evident pride and satisfaction which John displayed, and the great care with which he handled this paper, when, occasionally, he presented it to some member of our family to be read or inspected. He always got it out when he came where there were children or young folks, for they liked to hear the story repeated.

At this date I cannot, of course, remember the exact sentences in which John's narrator had told of his brave and humane exploit, but the incidents are still fresh in my mind.

It was in June, 1832, several weeks after the outbreak of the Sacs and Foxes, remembered as the Black Hawk War, that Wapper-Jaw John rendered heroic service to a venturous little family of settlers in one of the narrow valleys among the bluffs opposite Sauk Prairie. At this time, according to Smith's "History of Wisconsin," the Sacs and Foxes—

"Had scattered their war parties all over the North, from Chicago to Galena, and from the Illinois river into the Territory of Wisconsin. They occupied every grove, waylaid every road, hung around every settlement, and attacked every party of white men that attempted to penetrate the country."

This condition of affairs had lasted nearly a month, compelling settlers on all hands to gather themselves and their effects at fortified points and into hastily constructed block-houses. Yet in this perilous time one family, a young man and his wife and child, whose home was upon the extreme northern frontier, were living in complete ignorance that there was any Indian outbreak.

Early in the previous April James Streeter had moved up from northern Illinois with his small family, and had settled upon a squatter claim in a pocket of the Black Earth Valley. He had the property usually possessed by the "mover" upon the frontiers in those days; it consisting of a yoke of oxen and a wagon, a cow or two, some chickens, and a few simple household utensils.

After their arrival upon the claim, the young settler and his wife were kept so busy in building a small cabin, and in clearing, breaking up and planting a small patch of ground, that they found no time to cultivate acquaintances in a region where their nearest neighbors were nearly twenty miles distant.

As the coming of this family into the region was unknown to the other settlers, its members failed to receive warning from the couriers who spread the news of Black Hawk's uprising among the hills south of the Wisconsin river. Fortunately for the Streeter family, its whereabouts was also unknown to the hostile Indians, the cabin being a little beyond their usual range of attack.

The husband and wife worked on undisturbed until a cabin had been built, and three acres of ground thoroughly broken up and planted to corn, potatoes and garden seeds. The plants had come up, and had been hoed once, when the couple found that their small stock of provisions was nearly exhausted.

The nearest market for the Streeters was Dodgeville, more than twenty miles distant from their claim.

It was necessary that one of the couple should stay at home to watch the cows and the growing crops, and Mr. Streeter set out alone for Dodgeville, with oxen and wagon, to get flour and other needed articles.

He started on his journey just after sunrise one morning. His wife finished her morning's work about the cabin, and went out with a hoe to work in the field, taking with her the child, a little girl four years of age.

Though living miles from any neighbors, the hardy women of those days often stayed alone while their husbands were gone for days, and sometimes for weeks, upon hunting or trapping excursions, or to distant marketing points.

Mrs. Streeter worked for some hours "hilling up" young potato vines, while Elsie, the little girl, played with a small kitten, their one domestic pet. With a sudden scream, the child came running to her mother, and caught her by the dress. Mrs. Streeter looked about in alarm, fearing that a rattlesnake had bitten the child, and discovered the cause of her fright to be an Indian who had come out of the brush a few rods distant, and was approaching them.

Although she was not afraid of Indians, she was annoyed that one of them should come while her husband was away. She knew that often they were lawless and thieving when they discovered women alone.

As the Indian came toward her, his face mowed and grinned so curiously that she felt an impulse to laugh until she saw that its expression came from a deformity.

"*Hoogh-oogh!*" he grunted, as he came up. "You go, you squaw, *puck a chee* heap klick! You go longa me! Heap Injun comin'!" and he pointed up the valley. "We go yonder!" pointing this time toward the Wisconsin.

The woman was frightened at his words and manner, notwithstanding that he tried to laugh and look as pleasant as his queer features would permit, and though he had no weapons in sight.

"Men kill heap. Me no hurt. You go. We heap *puck a chee*," and he reached down to pick up the child.

The little girl screamed with terror, and Mrs. Streeter caught her up and stepped back.

"No, I will not go with you!" said she. "You're a bad Injun, and you're lying to me!" She had quickly concluded that the Indian merely wished to entice her away while his companions pillaged the premises.

Again the Winnebago—for it was John—tried to explain to her that he meant to be friendly, and to aid her to escape from danger.

"Heap *Outagamie!*" (Fox Indians) said he. "Men come, shoot, kill. Kill papoose, kill white squaw. Squaw go me, so," and again he motioned toward the river, and, by imitating the act of paddling and by sweeping his hand forward, signified that he would take her across it in his canoe.

"No, you go and leave me!" said the woman, sternly. "I won't go with you. Go!" she repeated, pointing toward the woods, and then she turned, with the little girl in her arms, and started toward the cabin.

Instantly the Indian sprang foward, then snatched the child from her, and, catching her by the shoulders, forced her down to the ground upon her face, and quickly tied her arms. He had evidently come prepared to carry out his plan by force, if necessary, and the poor woman felt that her instinct had been true. Not daring to struggle, she submitted to be bound a captive.

Elsie, the little girl, had started to run into the woods, but John caught her, and took her, screaming, into his arms. He walked quickly back with her to Mrs. Streeter, who had risen, after a struggle, to her feet.

"Come," said he. "You go longa me now, heap klick! Me take papoose. We *puck a chee*," and he started toward the river, beckoning her to follow. He had Elsie in his arms, and there was nothing for the now thoroughly frightened and trembling woman to do but to go with him.

It was several miles to the river. The Winnebago hurried forward at a half trot, the child crying piteously at every step, while the distressed mother, nearly out of breath, kept close at his heels, trying to cheer her little girl with words of affection. John was probably too stolid to care greatly for the papoose's wailing, or for its mother's distress of mind, but he was intent upon doing them a friendly service, and no doubt was carrying it out with as much kindness as he was capable of exercising.

At a little after noonday they came to the river at the mouth of a creek, and here John put down the child, which he had carried and led alternately, and going into the edge of a willow thicket upon the bank, dragged out a long canoe, which contained a gun and some blankets. The canoe he slid down into the water, and ordered Mrs. Streeter to get down the bank and step into it.

With her hands bound as they were, she found it

difficult to get into and sit down in the "tittlish" narrow trough, but she finally managed, without tipping it over, to take her place in the bow of the slight craft.

The Indian then carefully placed Elsie upon her knees in the centre of the canoe. "No touch um," he commanded, tapping the sides of the canoe. "Keep a heap still." The little girl, tired and subdued, dared not so much as stir. Then John picked up a paddle which he had laid upon the bank, got carefully into the canoe at the stern, shoved out into the river, and paddled the frail craft swiftly down the stream.

The anguish of the poor woman was keen as she thought of the husband who had so recently been with her, and of the uncertain fate of her little child and herself. She could not believe the Indian's story that he was rescuing them from danger. His violence and his rapid retreat, and this journey upon the river, leading to the west and away from the white settlement, could to her mind mean only that he was carrying them away into that wretched captivity which she knew that more than one woman and child had suffered at the hands of savages.

Brave woman though she was, she gave herself up to despair.

All that day the canoe sped rapidly down stream, keeping as close under the bank as possible, and it was not until after sundown that John landed and got his captives out upon the bank where they could rest their cramped limbs. He then undid a roll of blankets and got out some dried meat, which he offered to Mrs. Streeter, motioning that the papoose could feed her. The woman could not eat, but by coaxing induced the

tired and hungry little girl to swallow a few scraps of
the raw, tasteless venison.

After a time the Indian untied Mrs. Streeter's hands,
being careful to keep between her and his gun.   Then
he motioned to the blankets.

"Squaw make um bed," said he ; " heap sleep."

Glad of so much freedom and a chance to rest and
to comfort her child, Mrs. Streeter made a rough
couch, took Elsie iu her arms and lay down upon it.
The little girl was soon asleep, but the mother lay narrowly watching the Indian, waiting for a chance to
escape if he should drop asleep or relax his guard in
any way.

She got no opportunity, however; John sat near at
hand, leaning against a tree, stiff and upright, with his
gun across his legs.   After about two hours of rest, he
ordered her to get up again and get into the boat, telling her to "take papoose."

She carried the sleeping child down the bank, and
while the Indian steadied the canoe at the stern, got in
at the bow.   John threw in the blankets, got in, put
his gun between his knees, and took up the paddles.
All night they floated swiftly down the river, the long,
steady sweep of the Indian's paddle doubling the rate
at which the canoe was borne by the rapid current.

Mrs. Streeter endured her anxiety and fatigue as
bravely as she could, not daring, on account of her
child, to make any demonstrations ; but she was all the
time on the watch for a chance to escape from her
captor.

At a little after sunrise the Winnebago landed upon
a bar at the north bank, and ordered her to get out of
the canoe.   After carrying Elsie asleep in her arms all

night, she found her own limbs to be so cramped and stiff that at first it was impossible to use them. Seeing her condition the Indian swung the stern round, dragged the canoe out upon the bar, and helped her out.

He now, for the first time, aroused in her a little hope by saying: "Heap white mans, heap soje," pointing to the northwest. "Walk, sun so," showing her where the sun would be when their journey should end. He again offered his captives the dried meat, and the pangs of hunger compelled both woman and child to make a hearty meal.

After they had rested awhile and got the cramp out of their legs and arms, the Indian pointed out the direction in which they were to go, and ordered Mrs. Streeter to walk ahead and lead the little girl. He let them walk slowly, keeping a rod or two behind them, with his gun and blankets. After three hours of tramping they came out of the woods upon a hill overlooking a broad valley—the Mississippi Valley—and then the Indian came eagerly forward.

"See," he said, his face grinning and working with evident pleasure as he pointed to a distant cluster of buildings upon the bank of a wide river which lay in front of them. "See, *Plala doo shang!*"

It was the frontier fort and trading post of Prairie du Chien. Mrs. Streeter had heard of this place, but had known only vaguely where it was situated.

She now perceived that her captor had intended all his acts in friendliness. An hour later she and her child were safely housed at the fort, and her delight and thankfulness at this outcome to her adventure may be imagined.

Mrs. Streeter's alarm for her husband's safety was

great until John, whose services were again secured,
made a trip to Dodgeville and brought him across the
country to her. Mr. Streeter had discovered their
danger, from meeting a body of soldiers on the second
morning after his departure from home. They had
accompanied him hastily back to his cabin, only to find
it burned down and the premises deserted. He had
mourned his wife and child as dead until word was
brought by the Winnebago of their rescue and safety.

XIII.

A DESPERATE ESCAPE.

The dreadful Indian massacre of '62 depopulated whole counties of newly settled territory in a single day —the 18th of August—and drove from the Minnesota frontiers thousands of people in a few days' time.

During this eventful period there were many thrilling and desperate adventures and hairbreadth escapes. The local historians who published narratives gathered at haphazard at the time, did all they could to cover the ground of incident. The main facts and causes of the bloody uprising have been compiled and preserved in several volumes published at St. Peter and St. Paul.

In one of these*, several paragraphs are devoted to the murder of the men in charge of the stores at the isolated trading post on the eastern shore of Big Stone Lake. This account briefly relates the desperate escape of a French and Indian boy, Baptiste or "Bat" Gubeau—as this common name among the Canadian French is frequently abbreviated.

In the Minnesota massacre it was Little Crow's ruthless policy to exterminate all the the whites west of the Mississippi. Every one with white blood in his veins who could not or would not take part against the settlers was to be killed. Contrary to the usual rule in Indian wars, the fur-trader, from the very circumstance that he fancied he was safe, fell a swift and easy victim to the rifle and hatchet of the Sioux.

---

* *Indian Massacre in Minnesota*, by C. S. Bryant, pages 150–151.

All the employés of the four stores and warehouses
at Big Stone, Myrick's, Forbe's, Robert's, Pratt & Co.'s,
were either French *habitans* or half and quarter bloods
of that extraction. Among those of mixed blood was
the "warehouse boy," Bat Gubeau.

On the 21st of August four of Robert's men, Bat and
three Canadians, Patnode, Laundre and Pachette, were
cutting hay on a marsh near the lake shore below the
post. They were at work in their loose shirts and
leggins, mowing with scythes, one following the other.
Without a second's warning a party of "Blanket"
Sioux came up out of the tall grass a few rods distant
and began firing upon them. Patnode, Pachette and
Laundre, who were ahead of Bat and most exposed to
the Indian fire, were killed almost at the first shot.

Young Gubeau saved his life from their fire by quick-
wittedly throwing himself on his face as though shot,
lying across the swath and blade of his scythe.

The Indians scalped his comrades and stripped them
of their hats and shoes; then several of them came to
him and turned him over. He knew his captors well,
and could understand their language almost as well as
the *patois* of his Canadian parents.

"Don't kill me," said he. "Why did you shoot those
men? They were always your friends."

"We killed them," one replied, with black looks,
" because all whites and fur men have always cheated
and lied to the Indians, and we'll kill you because you
are a dog of a mixed blood. We shall kill you when
the sun goes down, after a scalp-dance, and after the
squaws have burned the Indian blood out of your body
with brands from their fires."

This is, in effect, what the savages said, as near as Baptiste could interpret it in his broken English.

The speaker was a Wapekuta medicine man, well known at the trading post as a malignant hater of the white men and a constant fomenter of bad-feeling among his own people.

While two of the Indians were tying Bat's hands behind him with strips of buckskin, the medicine man began prancing around and telling, in a boastful chant, the murders which had been committed upon the white settlers at the Lower agency, at Beaver Creek and Birch Coolie. He sang boastfully that but two suns more would pass before every white man west of *Minnehaha* would die. The Sioux nation, possessed of the guns and ammunition taken from the dead settlers and soldiers, could hold its country and beat back the white people always. Then he warmed up and began recounting, after the whooping, sing-song fashion of his kind, the exploits of himself and the others with him.

The possession of a prisoner who could understand their peculiar chants and the braggings in which they so liked to indulge was unusual good fortune. The vauntings of the medicine man seemed to act upon the savages like the baneful charm some reptiles are said to exercise. One by one they threw aside their weapons and joined the medicine man in his weird leaps and chantings about the prisoner.

Bat said not a word, but sat quietly, his shrewd eyes watching for a chance to break through the ring and escape. He was strong, lithe, and a swift runner, and a plan of action soon came to him. He felt that it was desperate enough, but it was his only chance.

A bayou or narrow bay ran up from the lake into

the marsh upon which he and his companions had been cutting hay, and the head of it was distant not more than a ten minute's run. This strip of water was grown thickly about with rushes, and was from four to six feet deep.

If he could break away, escape his pursuers' shots and outrun them, he thought he might find a hiding-place among the rushes until night should come on.

About the time he had canvassed the chances of this plan, the Indians about him had begun to wind up their dancing, with a peculiar gyrating movement known among them as the Moon-Dance. In it the dancers wheel slowly about bow-leggedly, tetering first upon one foot and then upon the other, and swaying the body from the hips in a snake-like movement. The head is rolled in imitation of a lolling bear and the arms are worked writhingly while the wriggling savage sings, in a most lugubrious, grunting tone: *" E-yungh, e-yungh! Hi-yee, hi-yer! E-yongh, e-yongh!"*

The prisoner kept his eye upon one of the Indians, whom he knew—for he knew them all well—to be the best runner among them. As this one swung around between himself and the line of retreat he had marked out, Bat sprang up and with an agile jump planted both heels of the army shoes he wore in the "small" of the dancer's back.

The Indian went down with a screech of pain and surprise, as the keen-witted Canadian passed over him and shot away toward the lake.

Certain that he had disabled their swiftest runner, Bat felt chiefly concerned for the moment in dodging bullets and arrows. He sprang this way and that at as sharp angles as he could, and at the same time make good headway.

The Indians caught up their guns instantly upon seeing what had happened, but luckily only a few of their arms had been reloaded, and the shots aimed by Indians, breathless with the exertion of a shrieking dance, missed their target. Throwing down their guns, the whole party gave chase, yelling frightfully, as is their fashion.

Bat glanced backward, and saw then spreading out in pursuit, the swiftest runners heading straight for the bayou on either side. As there was no longer any danger from bullets, the boy put himself down to his utmost speed, and bent his head toward the nearest point of rushes. He was hampered by having his hands tied behind, and the triumphant yells, which sounded a little louder at each passing minute, caused him to fear greatly that they would overtake him.

Over mowed ground, through tall grass for several minutes he ran like an antelope. He had gained a number of rods the start of the Indians while they were picking up their guns and firing, and this advantage was what saved his life. He reached the low bank of the inlet in advance of the foremost Sioux, but so near were they that, as he plunged among the rushes, a hatchet thrown by one of them switched past his head and dropped into the water in front.

He threw himself headlong into the water, and dived amid the rushes. Then he pushed himself along by kicking in the mud at the bottom. When his breath gave out, he raised his head out long enough to get a fresh breath, then ducked it and shoved ahead.

In this way he was speedily out of sight and reach of

the Sioux, who did not follow him into the rushes. His
pursuers spread out, and hurriedly surrounded the
bayou in the hope, no doubt, to catch him in the grass
as he attempted to crawl out upon the other side.

But Bat had no notion of going out of the bayou at
present. He found bottom shallow enough to stand
upon, and then began working his wrists out of the ·
thongs which bound them. This he was soon able to
do, as the water-soaked buckskin stretched at every
strain.

He then waited and listened. Soon he heard Indians
talking upon the bank of the bayou opposite his entrance.
They were looking for his trail at the edge of the
water, and asking each other if he had crossed, and
which way he would go. Finally one of them said,
"No, he's in there; the dog will not come out." Then
all was quiet.

Bat would not stir again, for fear he should be discovered by the rattling of the rushes. The time wore
on heavily. Toward night mosquitoes rose out of the
water, and pestered him frightfully. He dared not
thresh about, for fear his whereabouts should be discovered and fired upon by lurking Indians. · Bullets
and buckshot were to be dreaded, even though rushes
enough intervened to hide him completely, although
the bank was only a few rods distant on either side.

As the vicious insects alighted upon his face and neck
in swarms, he discovered a method of alleviating his
sufferings. Every few seconds, as his face became black
with them, and their stings began to make him wince,
he would quickly and softly lower his head under
water, and hold it there as long as he could keep his
breath. The cool water soothed the irritation of their

Soon he heard Indians.—Page 126.

bites, and gave him refuge from them a good part of
the time.

Darkness came at last, and with it a breeze which
rustled the rushes, so that he could stir about without
attracting attention by noise. He now speedily made
use of his legs and arms in working his way down
nearer the lake, where, in a thicket of tall cornstalk
grass, he crawled out of the bayou, feeling stiff and
water-logged.

He lay among the stalks resting and listening for an
hour or so, and then, bending low in the grass, made
his way to the high land prairie, a mile or more distant.
Not daring to attempt to reach Fort Ridgely through
the country which he had learned from his captors was
overrun by the Sioux, he set out for St. Cloud, nearly
two hundred miles distant on the Mississippi.

He traveled three days and nights, occasionally
dodging war parties of Sioux. During that time he
lived upon roots and grass; these he chewed and
swallowed the juice. At length he walked into the
streets of St. Cloud. There was a large gathering of
settlers there, and the buildings, mostly of logs, had
been fortified and put in a state of defense.

There was a crowd of men in front of the first store
he reached on entering the village. Faint and
exhausted, Bat pushed through them, and asked
inside for something to eat. A number of settlers
and others immediately came inside, and in rough
tones asked him what he, a half-breed—he was a
quarter-blood—was doing among the whites.

Bat told his story in broken English, but the crowd,
incensed at the hundreds of murders committed, and
the loss of friends and relatives, were in a frenzied

state of fury at the sight of one belonging to the race
which had committed such ravages.

"He's a miserable spy!" shouted one of them. "A
sneakin' Sioux, come among us to see how many they
is uv us! Let's hang him!"

Beardless, more than naturally swarthy from exposure, haggard and ugly in countenance from hunger and
fatigue, Bat's appearance was against him. The
crowd fiercely took up the cry, "Hang him!"

The nearest men sprang forward and secured the
unfortunate fellow. His hands were speedily tied
with cord; from the stock of goods a rope was procured, and he was hustled out of the store by the
incensed settlers, who declared their intention of
stringing him up to the first tree on the river bank.
It was useless to plead or struggle, and despairingly the
poor exhausted youth allowed himself to be dragged
along the street. But a villager, who had the year
before lived at Big Stone, pushed into the crowd to
have a look at the prisoner, and fortunately recognized
Bat at once.

"Hullo!" he shouted. "Stop this, men! I know
that boy. He's one of Roberts men at Big Stone."

This, of course, put an immediate end to the pro-
ceedings. An innocent life had nearly been sacrificed
to the intense feeling wrought up over the treacher
ous and wholesale murders so recently committed by
Indians and half-breeds all about them.

It is hardly necessary to add that the men were
sorry enough of their conduct when they learned of
Bat's innocence, and that they treated him afterward
with all the kindness of which they were capable.

XIV.

Prior to 1857, a large tract of lake territory lying between the Upper Des Moines and the Big Sioux Rivers was infested by one of the most villainous bands of Indian outlaws which the Indian policy of the government has ever called into being. It was the band of eleven, led by Inkpaduta—Scarlet Point—who in the winter of '57, massacred a half-hundred settlers in their scattered cabins about Okoboji, Spirit and Pelican Lakes, and carried a number of women into a captivity far worse than death.

These Indians, disaffected Wapekuta Sioux, had been outlawed from their own tribe for the murder of their chief, Tosagi. They were the pest and terror of settlers in middle and western Iowa from the time that scattering colonies first came in, until their depredations and atrocities culminated in the Spirit Lake massacre. On that occasion whole settlements were annihilated, their inhabitants being generally taken by surprise, and killed inside their snowbound cabins.

Previous to this massacre, which resulted in the capture and punishment of a part of them and the disbanding of the rest, these Indians subsisted by begging and plundering among the frontier settlements, by hunting and fishing about the Northern lakes, and by a sort of blackmail upon the Wapekutas, whose village was in the pipe-stone region.

The village of Inkpaduta was on the Upper Des

Moines, near the Minnesota line. It was more than a hundred miles from any settlement, until the ill-fated squatters of the Spirit Lake tragedy settled about the lakes. There were no troops stationed within a week's march, and the frontier settlements were too weak and scattered to offer organized resistance.

Occasionally bold trappers, in spite of numerous warnings of the dangers, established and maintained their trapping grounds within the hunting circuit of Inkpaduta's band. Among them was Jake Boyer, a fearless frontiersman, who went among Indians regardless of danger—one of the sort of adventurers whom, strangely enough, the savages seldom molested.

Jake knew Inkpaduta and his followers. He visited their village every fall and spring to trade ammunition or trinkets for furs.

On one of these excursions he carried a double-barreled rifle which he had bought in Dubuque. It was a fine weapon of German pattern, silver-mounted, and had cost him a hundred dollars. The Indians were much taken with this gun, and one of them, Feto Atanka—Big Face—wanted to swap a pony for it. Boyer told him that nothing less than twenty-five prime mink skins would get the gun; that when he could produce so many whole skins, smooth and white inside, he would swap. These terms of trade were made known by signs and by the use of such simple English words as the Indians understood.

A few months later, in autumn, Boyer was visited at his cabin on the Ocheyedan by several of Inkpaduta's band, among them Husan—One Leg, Makpi Opetu, —Fire Cloud, a son of the chief, and Big Face. Boyer found them squatted in front of his dug-out upon the side of a bluff, as he came in from a morning round of his traps. They rose as he approached with his rifle across his shoulder. After a friendly round of "How-Hows!" Big Face drew from his blanket a bundle of black-looking skins. "Huh!" said he. "Me bling um mink, you give um up gun."

Jake saw at once that the mink were warm-weather skins and worthless. No doubt they were the pelts of all the minks taken or shot by the members of the band during the summer and early fall months, and had been entrusted to Big Face in order that so fine a rifle might belong to one of the band.

The trapper drew back, and shook his head in refusal to receive the skins. He was about to explain, what they perfectly knew to be true, that the pelts were of no account, when, with a sudden spring, Big Face was upon him. The others instantly sprang forward also, and Boyer's rifle was wrenched from him. When he was forced to let go his gun, he dodged quickly into a thicket of bushes which grew up to the door of his habitation.

The Indians fired several shots after him, but he was not harmed. He reached his canoe, in which he kept a squirrel rifle for shooting muskrat and other small game, secured the weapon, and made his escape through the tall grass of the bottom, whither the Indians did not pursue him.

He made his way to a settlement sixty miles distant, and tried to raise a party to go and hunt Inkpaduta's band, and drive them out of the region; but he could not find half a dozen men within a circuit of thirty miles who had interest enough in his cause to make it their own. But he found one adventurous fellow, who went back with him to his trapping grounds on the Ocheyedan. Upon reaching the dug-out, they found, to their surprise, that its contents had not been disturbed. Lying inside the door was the identical pack of worthless mink skins which Big Face had brought to trade for the rifle. The traps were also all in their places.

Evidently the Indians had been somewhat alarmed after Jake's escape, and wished to leave the impression that they had been dealing in good faith, and had kept to the letter the bargain which had been made for the gun.

This fact gave Boyer confidence, and he boldly set about his trapping again, determined to watch his opportunity, outwit the Indians, and recover his valuable rifle. During the next month he busied his brain every day with schemes, and finally hit upon a plan which he determined to carry out at once.

Leaving his companion in charge of the dug-out and the trapping, he set out for Fort Dodge with two small ponies packed with the fall catch. At the Fort, which was merely a frontier trading station, he sold his furs, procured ammunition, blankets and some trinkets to trade upon, and set out for Inkpaduta's village, as he had been in the habit of doing at that season of the year.

In spite of all that had happened, he expected to make the savages believe that he was still friendly to them, and could not afford to lose their fur trade for such trifles as the loss of his rifle and the attempt on his life. He did not believe they would dare injure him again, for they would surely know that he had spread the story of their attack upon him at the settlements, and his going to them directly from the Fort would naturally make them cautious how they offended him. After getting among them, he hoped to recover his much prized rifle by a stratagem.

He found only a few old squaws and children at the Des Moines village, but was informed that the bucks were camped at Lost Island Lake, where they had gone to hunt for elk.

It was but a half-day's ride to the place, and he discovered the tepeés of the band as he approached the lake shore at sunset. The most of the Indians had got in from the day's hunt, and, as he rode up, were lying about the fires, waiting for the women to boil some meat for their evening meal.

They got up and gave some grunts of surprise as he approached, but immediately broke into most cordial "How-How's!" and grinned in a way that betrayed their pleasure that he should come among them in so friendly a fashion. He had always dealt more fairly with them than traders were in the habit of doing.

Big Face, One Leg and Inkpaduta were among those who greeted him. He shook hands with all, telling them he had come to "swap" again, and acted as though nothing had happened. They were immensely pleased, and one of the young bucks assisted him in unpacking and then picketed his ponies with their own.

That evening and the next morning were spent in trade; and for a half-dozen red blankets, some ammunition and beads, Jake came into possession of all the beaver, mink and muskrat skins the Indians had.

After the swap had been completed to the satisfaction of all parties, Jake proposed to Inkpaduta that he and a picked number of his men should ride over to his tepeé on the Ocheyedan—a little more than a half day's ride—and hunt elk at the head waters of Stony Creek, where he knew that a big herd of them were feeding.

He had no winter's meat laid in, he told the chief, and since he had traded his large gun to Big Face, he had no rifle that carried a ball large enough to kill an elk. If he would go over with his men and kill him— Jake—two big elk, he would give the chief the smallest pony he had brought with him.

Inkpaduta was taken with the offer, and evidently took all the trapper had said in sincerity. He consulted his bucks and found them all eager to go, as the white man had described the herd as a big one.

The camp was hastily struck and the whole party set out for Jake's headquarters, where they arrived that evening and camped for the night. Jake had told Inkpaduta of his partner who, he said, had no gun but an old musket that would only shoot small shot.

That night, when they were alone in the dug-out, Jake instructed Williams, his partner, that as soon as the party should have got out of sight, he was to pack what furs he could on the pony left him, *cache* the rest with the traps, and make haste for the nearest settlement on the Little Sioux.

Next day, at noon, the hunters were camped near the source of the Stony, and scouts were sent out to look for the elk herd, which was sighted before night.

A plan of the hunt was determined on before they slept, and as Jake was consulted, he so managed that he was to be of the party. They were to go in three squads, enclosing the band in a triangle, in which rode Big Face with Inkpaduta and one of the chief's sons, Roaring Cloud, or Makpeahotoman.

Big Face had made no attempt to conceal the rifle, which was still in his possession; in fact he had carried it with a good deal of flourish and display, evidently proud of owning such a piece of property.

Before daylight next morning the hunting parties were mounted, and circling the region where the elk had been seen. There was a keen wind blowing from the northwest, and as the elk were in that direction the herd was surrounded without difficulty. Two parties converged, one from the north, another from the west, and the third, in which was Jake, moved slowly forward from the southeast.

It was the plan that the herd should be driven toward this last party, who were to rush in upon their front and turn them about. This would bring the whole hunting party upon them.

In one respect the plan was perfect. At about sunrise the big drove was seen by Inkpaduta's party, and Boyer observed, with no little satisfaction, that the elk were coming directly toward him.

They came right on without seeming to see the hunters, who had spread a little and lay close along the backs of their ponies.

There were more than two hundred elk, and Boyer said it was a splendid sight to see them come on, the bulls in the lead; "an acre of branchin' horns", as he expressed it, "movin' down swift like the front of the wind in a blizzard."

When the foremost elk were within gunshot, the Indians straightened up and with loud yells dashed their ponies at the face of the herd. But instead of turning, the whole bunch spread out like a fan and went by like a shot, scattering continually as they sped on.

The Indians whirled their ponies and gave chase, having fired several ineffective shots, and as each selected his game the manœuvre drew them rapidly apart. This was precisely what Boyer had hoped for, and he followed Big Face, keeping him all the time in view. The Indian soon overtook a fat cow-elk, whose calf got in her way and impeded her progress. Big Face rode alongside, shoved the muzzle of his gun almost against the cow's side, and killed her instantly.

He had fired one barrel before, and with a whoop he now circled his pony about, sprang to the ground and stood over the dead elk, evidently satisfied with his morning's work.

This was not what Boyer wanted at all, for there were still other Indians in sight. In fact, nearly the whole party was by this time racing along in pursuit of the herd.

But, knowing that he had not a moment to spare if he would allay suspicion and catch Big Face with unloaded gun, he drew up alongside. Quickly dismounting, he stepped in front of the Indian and covered him with the light rifle, which he had not unloaded.

"Give me my gun or I'll shoot," said the trapper, sharply.

Big Face saw that he was tricked, and that Boyer had the best of him. Like all of his kind he was a coward at heart, and with a sickly grin of fear he laid the ill-gotten rifle against the elk's body and stepped back.

" Now, let go that pony and walk off ? " commanded
Jake, with a meaning gesture. The Indian obeyed and
hurried away toward the retreating elk at a pace the
meaning of which Boyer knew well.

Jake's first move was hastily to load his recovered
rifle with heavy charges, having kept balls in his
pockets that would fit the bore. Then fastening his
small rifle to the saddle of the pony he had ridden, and
tying that animal to the lariat dragging at the neck of
Big Face's pony, he mounted the Indian's horse, turned
and rode northeast toward the Minnesota settlements,
which were then the nearest white habitations.

Just as he started, he looked back over his shoulder
and saw Big Face making frantic gestures from the
top of a knoll about a hundred rods away. But the
whole party, elk and all, had passed out of sight into
the valley of the Stony, and the last that Jake ever
saw of the band, as he spurred his pony in the opposite
direction, was the outwitted Big Face waving his
arms.

It was a daring stratagem which had secured him his
rifle and a " pony for damage," and one which a man
less hardy and keen-witted would never have planned,
and certainly could not have succeeded in carrying
out.

Inkpaduta and his men evidently gave the big elk
herd a long chase, without any notion of what had
happened in their rear. If any of them had seen Big
Face and Boyer near the dead elk, they must have
thought the white man had stopped only to take
charge of his game. At any rate they did not overtake
Jake, who pushed rapidly on to Lake Shetek, where at
a settlement he was safe from Indian assault.

- Later, he joined Williams at Fort Dodge, having passed through Inkpaduta's country in the night. After that he trapped west of the Big Sioux, as he considered the lake region " unhealthy " for him.

XV.

HOW HE GOT IT.

"Jorgensen, can you bring me down, on your next trip, a piece of pipe-stone big enough for the top to a center-table?"

This request, which looks and sounds plain and innocent enough, was addressed, some twenty years ago, by a St. Louis merchant to a Danish fur-buyer, with whom he dealt, buying of him, every few months, a boat load of peltries, brought down from the upper Missouri country.

The Dane, Odolph Jorgensen, a short, thick-set, blue-eyed fellow, wearing a fierce, stiff mustache, stood in front of the merchant's counter, stowing in his wallet the drafts just received for his last boat load of furs.

He looked up at the questioner with a shrewd twinkle in his blue eyes.

"Yaas, for two tousant dollars," he answered, laconically.

The merchant stared.

"Why, man, it aint such a fearful undertaking!" he put in, with a good deal of astonishment.

"Yaas," said the Dane; "it's vort that, efry saint."

"All right!" returned the merchant—he was wealthy. "I'll give you two thousand dollars for a piece of pipe-stone, regular in shape, three feet by five, and two inches thick or more."

"I pring ut down een Nofaimber," answered Jorgensen, and that ended the conversation.

140

Odolph knew that he would risk much, his life even, in executing such a commission; but he had grown hardy in five years of fur-buying in the Indian country. Yet if he could have known all the danger involved in entering upon the "Neutral Ground," and carrying off a block of the sacred pipe-stone, he probably would not have taken the risk.

As it was, he determined to go about it at once, and in the only way he approved of doing business—an honorable one. He had no right to take even a pebble from the sacred ground of the Indians without their consent, and that could only be obtained at a heavy cost, and at no small danger of treachery.

Nevertheless, he put his barge in tow of a steamer, —he shipped his peltries down in a flat-boat on his own account,—and with his assistant, Hans Obermann, boarded his boat and went up the river to Yankton, his headquarters; and from there, leaving Hans in charge of his affairs, he took a horse and rode straight for Yankton Agency, some sixty miles farther up the river.

On arriving, he went to the tepeé of a Yanktonais chief, whom he knew, and who could speak English brokenly, and, after much preliminary talk, told the Indian what he wanted, and offered the chief one hundred dollars to go with him to the pipe-stone country and help him get a block of stone.

The chief listened in sullen surprise at first,—they are all extremely jealous of allowing white men access to the pipe-stone quarries, even as visitors,—but at length the promise of so great a sum of money began to have its effect, and he finally agreed that if "Odolph" —as Jorgensen was known to him—would give him one hundred dollars, the pony he had ridden up there, two new blankets and five pounds of tobacco, and would keep the matter perfectly secret, he, the chief, would go and help him get the pipe-stone.

After much higgling, Jorgensen agreed, and the chief, *Niché Kotonka* (Bad Buffalo), mounting one of his ponies, after a consultation with some of his "bucks," set out with the Dane on the return trip to Yankton. From this point Jorgensen, accompanied by Obermann and Bad Buffalo, who joined them two miles out on his pony, drove north in his wagon to the Pipe-Stone Region. They reached Pipe-Stone Creek, at the foot of the quarries, one beautiful evening just before sunset.

After camping and eating supper, the Indian mounted his pony, and told Odolph that he must go up the stream to where the spirits of two women dwelt in the rocks, and "make medicine" to them before they could touch the stone. He cautioned both the Danes not to lay so much as a finger, or look upon a piece of it until he had returned.

Jorgensen knew of this superstition, and, humoring the Yankton's caution, he and Hans lay upon the grass and smoked their pipes until *Niché Kotonka* came back. It was then dark, and all three rolled their blankets about them and slept till morning.

After breakfast the next morning they hitched their horses to the wagon, and the Yankton led the way to a quarry where the stone, in thin strata, cropped out on the side of a shallow ravine.

This famous pipe-stone underlies but a small strip of territory along the creek which goes by this name, and is found cropping out in numerous small ravines and gullies; and in these places, where it is easiest of access, the Indians go to procure it.

As they only get small pieces for pipes, and various little ornaments which they fashion with knives and other instruments, and polish by rubbing, there has, of course, been no very great diminution of quantity at the quarries. It is now well-known that this peculiar soft rock is susceptible of a very high polish, much more mirror-like and beautiful than that which can be put upon the finest of dark marbles.

It was the extreme beauty of this polish upon Indian ornaments, and the knowledge that, owing to the jealous guardianship of the Indians, there would be considerable difficulty in obtaining so large a piece of the rock, that had induced the St. Louis merchant to offer Jorgensen a large sum for a block of table-top size.

But thus far all had gone famously in the enterprise. The stone was found easy of access at the quarry to which Bad Buffalo led them. And, with the help of a sledge-hammer and crow-bar, Odolph and Hans soon succeeded in breaking into proper shape and dimensions a fine block of mottled stone, varying in color from light pink to the deepest ruby red. The most common color is a dark red, or nearly " liver color."

The Indian then demanded and received the one hundred dollars, which Jorgensen had agreed to pay him before starting upon the return. The other property was to be turned over at Yankton. After this had been done, they set out upon their way back. The chief, by agreement, was to accompany them all the way, as a safeguard, should any party of Sioux accidentally discover their trail and the object of their trip, or come upon them with any hostile intent—

something which any white traveler might expect in those regions at that time.

That night they camped on the east bank of the Big Sioux, at the crossing, or ford, of an old military trail, one they had followed for some distance in coming out of Yankton. The next morning, when Odolph and Hans awoke, the chief was gone. Odolph had left him on guard at two o'clock—they had kept guard by relief—and the rascal had stolen out to his pony, mounted and ridden away. He had taken nothing, however, not belonging to him, having refrained, probably, with the hope of leaving behind an impression of honesty and fair dealing.

Jorgensen suspected treachery immediately. He remembered with alarm the consultation with the braves at the Agency, of which he—and the chief knew it—understood not a word; also the strict injunction of secrecy which Bad Buffalo had laid upon him, and the now doubly alarming and significant fact that the chief had not entered the town of Yankton at all, but had stopped all night with a half-breed some miles above, and had contrived to join Hans and himself the next morning upon the prairie where there would be no witnesses.

All that had seemed natural enough at the time, knowing, as the fur-trader did, the peculiar characteristics of the Indian.

Now, however, the thought came to him with startling significance that *no white man had seen the Indian in their company at all.*

Odolph felt sorely chagrined at his short-sighted confidence, and told his fears briefly to Hans.

"We must put that stone in the river," said he, "and

get out of this country by some other way than we came, and we must do it soon."

Hans was badly frightened, but he obeyed commands with his usual sturdy faithfulness, and in a short time the two had crossed the river in their wagon, having dumped out the precious stone into four feet of water, and were driving hurriedly down the valley on the west side. They pushed on this way for several hours along the valley and across the points of numerous bluffs that pushed out into it, and then halted in the mouth of a deep ravine, where they determined to lie in wait until dark, and then drive straight—or as straight as possible—across the prairie for Yankton.

Odolph reasoned that if they could reach that point without being seen by Indians—for he firmly believed that a party of Bad Buffalo's bucks were lying in wait for them along the military road—the chief would conclude that he had dodged them and got safe through with the pipe-stone, and they could very safely go back in time and get it. On the other hand, if, as was more than likely, they *were* caught, the rascals could have no cause for picking a quarrel.

The sequel proved his surmises correct, but, as will be seen, his tactics availed him little as a means of preventing trouble.

After halting in the ravine, the Danes picketed their horses upon the side-hill, ate a cold lunch of raw bacon and crackers, and then threw themselves upon the grass, with their carbines beside them, to wait the coming of night or whatever of adventure the afternoon might bring them.

They had not a great while to wait for an adventure most unwelcome in its nature.

They had lain an hour or two, and Odolph was stretched upon his back with half-closed eyes, when Hans suddenly sprang up and exclaimed in frightened tones: "*Min Gud, Odolph! De komme at dræbe os!*" (They are coming to kill us.)

Odolph sprang to his feet in time to see appear upon the ridge the last one of a squad of Indian horsemen who had come over the northern bluff and were ambling down toward them.

There were eighteen or twenty of them, all bucks, and armed to a man with carbine and musket.

"Those fellows mean mischief, Hans, sure enough," said Jorgensen, speaking in their native tongue. "Stand back here away from the wagon, a little behind me, and do as you see me do," and throwing his carbine carelessly across his left arm, the fur-buyer awaited the Indians' approach with all the careless assurance he could assume.

As the squad drew near, Odolph and his frightened companion saw that the faces of all of them were hideously bedaubed with glaring paints, green, black, yellow and vermilion.

They were scattered out in single file before reaching the bottom of the ravine, and the leader—a chief if Odolph could judge from his toggery—rode directly to the wagon, without so much as deigning to notice the white men, leaned forward upon his pony's neck, and peered scowlingly into the box.

He looked earnestly for a moment, and then, uttering an angry grunt, glowered savagely at Odolph, who looked him shrewdly and keenly in the eyes and said "*How!*" as pleasantly as he could.

But the Indian was in a bad humor, and without

replying to this civil salute, he turned to several of his repulsive-looking bucks who had now ridden up and gave a few guttural words of command.

A half-dozen or more of them instantly sprang from their ponies and giving the lariats in charge of others, speedily pulled the blankets, "grub-box" and other contents out of the wagon, gave the blankets to the chief—there were only two rolled together in a bundle —then, with their hatchets, they fell upon the wagon-box and began hacking it in pieces. While they were doing this two of the mounted Indians rode out, pulled the picket-pins and led Odolph's horses away up the ravine.

Jorgensen and his man stood looking helplessly on, well-knowing, in fact, that they must do nothing else if they would save their lives.

The angry Indians soon demolished the wagon, chopping the "reach" in the centre and piling the wheels and fragments of the box in a heap together. They then scratched matches — of which they seemed to have a good supply — and lighted splinters in several places at the bottom, and in a few moments the whole heap was enveloped in flames. They stood back and laughed as the blaze crackled about the wreck, and maliciously eyed the two Danes as though they wished they might dare to fling *them* also into the burning mass.

However, they made no hostile demonstration *then* —owing, no doubt, to the fact that the two white men stood with the muzzles of their carbines pointed toward them—but after making sure the fire had made too great headway to be put out, the dismounted ones got on their ponies and the whole party rode off up the ravine.

" Now," said Odolph, as the last Sioux disappeared over the summit, " we must run for it, Hans. We must make the river and get across at once, or we'll never get out of this hollow alive."

They did run as swiftly as their short Danish legs would carry them.

The river was not more than two hundred yards distant, but even as they reached the bank they heard the clatter of horse-hoofs upon the bluff above. Looking back, Odolph saw that the whole troop were riding along the ridge at a headlong gallop and evidently making ready to fire upon them.

" Into the river, Hans !"he shouted, and they plunged in. The bank was sloping and there was no shelter unless they could reach the timber which grew upon the other side.

The water came up to their armpits, and, holding their carbines above their heads, they pushed through the current at a rate that made it boil behind them.

They had not more than reached the middle when the Indians drew up on the crest of the bluff above and began firing down upon them. The bullets pattered "chook ! chook !" close about their shoulders.

" Down, Hans ! down to your nose !" shouted the ready-witted fur-buyer, and sinking down until only the tops of their heads and the muzzles of their carbines protruded above the surface, the imperiled Danes *scooted* through the water like hunted deer.

The moving heads presented small marks at that distance, and some of the Indians dismounted and came bounding down the steep side of the bluff to get a close shot as the white men *came up on the opposite bank.*

But Odolph understood this game also, and heading down stream—he was in the lead, for Hans faithfully followed in every move—he made for a big fallen tree that leaned out from the bank and had formed a sort of boom for the lodgment of a mass of drift-stuff. Behind that they would be safe.

The Indians saw this move and with yells of disappointment halted, fired a few ineffective shots and then hustled back to get out of range of the carbines which they well knew were loaded with waterproof cartridges and would be turned upon them in a moment from behind the drift. The whole party then hurriedly withdrew out of sight.

Odolph and Hans, who had both reached the shelter of the drift, now crawled up the bank and walked out among the trees to where they could safely pull off their dripping clothes and wring the water from them. Here they stayed, on the watch, until dark, when, having seen no signs of the Indians prowling about, they set out in the direction of a Norse settlement, which they knew to have been made some twenty-four miles to the southeast, near the head of the Floyd river.

They reached the sod shanty of a Norwegian just after daylight the next morning, and were hospitably received. They related their adventure, and a few days afterward, securing the services of an ox-team and two of the settlers to go with them, they made a second and successful journey after the pipe-stone.

It was brought back to the settlement and subsequently taken to Sioux City and shipped to St. Louis on the first downward-bound steamer.

It is needless to say that *Niché Kotonka* never put in an appearance at Yankton, and in fact, though Odolph had occasion several times afterward to pass through the "Agency," he never could succeed in getting a sight of the treacherous chief.

The pipe-stone was received by the St. Louis merchant and paid for. It made a beautiful table-top, and yet remains in possession of the family. It is greatly admired by guests, not only for the exquisite polish of its mottled surface, but also as a witness of the Danish fur-buyer's determined fulfillment of a perilous contract.

FRONTIER SKETCHES

BY

FRANK W. CALKINS

CONTENTS.

FRONTIER SKETCHES.

I.

A PIECE OF FRONTIER STRATEGY.

In the early days of the settlement of Wisconsin there were neither land surveys nor government laws by which lands could be held with perfect security by the settlers. There was, however, in most counties an unwritten law, much like that which governs claim-taking in mining districts, and which generally protected the claimant who complied with its requirements. These requirements which were adopted in nearly all the new communities as "neighborhood by-laws," and in most of them strictly enforced against all persons who tried to violate them, were usually something like the following:

The claimant, if he were of age or the head of a family, was entitled to one hundred and sixty acres of timber land and the same amount of prairie land, which he must first locate, and then proceed to measure by " stepping it off."

There was usually some one in every organized township who was regarded as an expert in measuring land. Eight hundred and eighty steps of three feet each along the four sides of a square, beginning at a given landmark and returning to it, were allowed as a quarter-section.

The corners were established on the prairie by marked

stakes, and in timber by blazing trees and carving the taker's name or initials upon them. Then within a reasonable time, say three months—the time was not definitely fixed—the squatter must build a cabin and move his family, if he had one, his effects if he had not, into it, and there make his home until the land should be surveyed and "come into market," when, by appearing either himself or in the person of the "township bidder," at the regular "land sale" for his district, bidding the minimum price, one dollar and a quarter an acre, and paying the money to the registrar of the land-office, he received a government patent which made his claim valid and final.

It was not well for an interloper to attempt to jump one of these claims, or to bid more than the minimum price above a claimant who had complied with the by-laws of his district.

Generally, as I have said, the squatter, who complied with these "right of discovery" land laws, was safe enough to hold his claim, and if he had not the ready money saved to pay for it at the land sale, he could easily borrow it of money-lenders in his district. But sometimes there were disputes, in which whole neighborhoods took sides, and occasionally a squatter's claim was the scene of an affray in which blood was shed.

Two young men, Jacob and Jared Stebbins, who lived in the region between Blue Mounds and the Wisconsin, very early in the history of that country, belonged to the pioneer class above mentioned. Their father had moved up there from Galena some time before the Black Hawk troubles, and, though they were but lads of sixteen and seventeen, they had taken part in the defense of Mound Fort, and in the battle of Wisconsin Heights.

As they grew up and Jake came of age, they became ambitious to have land of their own. They had helped clear grub, break up, fence and cultivate one hundred acres of land on their father's "patent" in Mound Creek Valley, and now it was high time to begin for themselves.

Up to this period the broad Wisconsin, unfordable except in the driest seasons, had acted as a check to the tide of Northern and Western settlement in their district. There was much choice land upon the other side, and some two years before Jake was twenty-one the boys had been across the river hunting, and had staked and blazed claims for themselves—two "quarters"—upon one of which they had subsequently erected a snug log cabin, which they had covered with boards of their own make.

They spent the greater part of two winters in this cabin, hunting and splitting rails during the short days, and during the spring, summer and autumn while working on their father's place, they watched jealously for any movement toward a settlement on the "other side."

The winter before Jake came of age several other claims were taken, above their own, on the west side of the river, on Sac Prairie, one of the most fertile prairies of the state. The boys now determined to move over finally so soon as they should gather the spring crops upon their father's place.

In March, upon going home from their claim, they left their cooking utensils and other belongings inside the cabin, and closed the door and window by nailing some heavy strips across them. It was not until May, after corn planting, that they moved across the river. They swam over two yoke of steers, their breaking team, and rafted across their wagon, ploughs and some other effects. It took them nearly all day to cross, and it was late in the evening when they reached their cabin.

The cabin had been built in the edge of the valley timber, and they had cleared a space around it. As they drove out into this open space, they were surprised by the yelping of a dog, which came rushing toward them, and flew at the faces of the steers, so that they halted and lowered their horns to fight off the brute. Jared ran forward and drove the animal away with his whip, giving it a cut which sent it back to the cabin.

"Somebody's here?" said he.

Jared went forward. The dog snarled at him from under the covered wagon as he approached. As he came up to the cabin, he saw that the boards had been ripped from the door, and that a light was shining through a crack.

"Hallo, thar!" he called, standing close to the door.

There was a moment of waiting, a murmur of voices inside; then the door swung inward, and the tall, gaunt figure of a middle-aged woman stood in the open space.

"Who be ye?" she inquired, gruffly.

"I'm one of the owners of this claim," said Jared, "an' wo'd like ter shar' the cabin with ye till we c'n get some supper."

"Wal' ye can't come in hyer!" said the woman, coolly. "This hyer claim an' this hyer cabin b'longs

"Who be ye?" she inquired, gruffly.—Page 8.

ter us?" and she stepped back to shut the door in his face.

Jared was hot-blooded and was naturally angry at this turn of events. He sprang towards the closing door, and threw all his weight against it. The woman was large and strong enough to have offered stout resistance, but she was taken by surprise; the door flew out of her grasp, back upon its hinges, and Jared was propelled against her with a force that made her stagger half-way across the room.

Jared had gained admission, but found himself facing two big, bony men, who had arisen from their stools before the fire-place as he burst the door in.

They sprang at him, knocked him over, sat on him— one on his shoulders and the other on his legs—and then, with buckskin straps, proceeded to bind him hand and foot.

Jared struggled for a moment, and then, finding it useless, gave it up. He was soon relieved of the weight of his captors, but lay helplessly bound upon the floor.

All this had happened so quickly that when Jake, who had heard the scuffle, had tied the steers and come cautiously up to the door, gun in hand, he found himself confronted by the muzzles of two rifles, which protruded through a crack which had been made by removing a board from the nearest window.

"Drop that gun!" came from within the cabin.

But instead of dropping his weapon, the quick-witted young settler sprang to one side, and ran behind the wagon, under which the belligerent dog was still barking. Then he called to his brother:

"Say, Jerd, have they hurt ye?"

Jared shouted back that they hadn't, but that two men had tied him hand and foot.

Jake picked up a club and threw it at the dog to drive it away; then he called to the men to know what they meant by such outrageous acts. One of them—the old man—answered back that they had taken up a man for assault and battery, and meant only to protect themselves and their rights.

Jake told them they had no business inside the cabin, which belonged to himself and his brother; that this claim had been made and held for two years, and that they were liable to prosecution for assault on his brother.

The elder man answered back that he and his son had found an old trapper living in the cabin; that they had bought his right to it, and laid claim to the land, and, what was more, they should hold it against all comers. It was also stated that a colony of settlers from Illinois had come in some three weeks before, having crossed the river at "The Portage," and squatted along on that side; that a general meeting had already been held, and the usual regulations adopted, and that the speaker inside the cabin had been chosen constable until a regular election was held.

The young fellow was astounded and chagrined at this intelligence. The situation was puzzling enough, for he saw that these claim-jumpers had greatly the advantage over him. He and Jared could really prove nothing; not a settler on the other side whom they knew had ever visited them here or knew of the location of their claim except by heresay. Their only callers had been two or three stray trappers and an occasional Winne-

bago Indian who had at various times spent a night
with them.

It was one of those trappers, a rascally-looking fellow whom he remembered he had disliked, who had
pretended to sell this claim to the present occupants—
and there was a whole neighborhood to stand by them
in possession.

The situation was discouraging even if Jared had
not—according to the code of the region—been lawfully
arrested for an assault.   Jake went out near his own
wagon and sat down on a stump to think.

The night was not dark; the moon was shining
faintly and a light wind was moving the tree tops, and
as Jake sat with his face between his hands in a brown
study, the figure of a person came across his range of
vision. A boy emerged from the woods a short distance
west of the cabin and came toward him.   As he
approached the dog ran out and began leaping upon
him.

"Hullo, mister! w'at ye doin' out hyer?" The
voice was that of a lad of fourteen or fifteen.

Jake answered, warily, that "he'd jes' druv up a bit
ago, an' was wonderin' where thar might be some
water fer the oxen."   He added that he thought it
rather late to wake people up to find out—there was
no light that could be seen from the cabin.

"Oh, I'll show ye," said the boy.   "It's 'bout forty
rod, though, the way ye'll hev ter drive t' git down ter
the crick."

"That don't make any differ'nce—the distance,"
said Jake. "I want to camp by water,"—which was
true enough, as matters had turned out.

Thereupon he untied his oxen, turned his wagon

about and drove after the boy, who led him back very nearly over the way he had come. Jake, looking back as they entered the timber-line, saw the cabin door swing open, and some one come out and look after them. But fortunately the boy was straight ahead and could not be seen, and the man, who had probably come out to see what was going on upon hearing the wagon rattle, turned again and entered the cabin.

It was fifteen minutes' drive down to the creek, by the nearest approach for a wagon, but, as Jake well knew, the stream could be approached on the opposite side of the cabin, which was situated in a bend of it, by a very short cut through thick brush. It was from that quarter, in fact, that he and Jared had brought their water for cooking purposes.

However, it just suited a plan which had flashed upon him that the boy should be at the pains of selecting for him the best camping-place—it got them out of sight and hearing of the cabin.

Jake walked well up by the steers and talked to the boy as they went forward and learned, as he had expected, that the lad was the son of the man who had jumped his claim. The boy said he had gone over to a neighbor's who had just moved into a new log-house one mile west and was to have stayed all night, but finding that a number of land-seekers had claimed the neighbor's hospitality, he had spent the evening at play with their boys and returned. He said his father's name was Burrel.

They reached the creek, and Jake, having quickly matured a plan of action, stopped his oxen and while untying a long, slender lead-rope from the horns of the "near" steer at the head of the team, kept the boy near his side by talking to him.

When he had secured the rope, however, he turned, flung an arm around his listener, and with a quick trip threw him to the ground. The boy struggled and screamed with fear and anger, but Jake quieted him with a stern command and then, holding him fast, told him just what had happened at the cabin, and also gave him a truthful account of his own and his brother's labor in making the claim, which had been jumped regardless of their rights.

"An' now, youngster, I'm goin' ter tie ye up, an' bring yer ole dad ter terms, an' the more ye cut up the wuss it'll be for ye."

The boy evidently believed his story and saw both the point and the justice of the case, for he sullenly submitted, gritting out between his teeth that "Dad 'n' Bob 'll get ev'n with ye fur this."

Jake tied his prisoner securely, unhitched his oxen and turned them loose, with the yokes on, to graze, and then, getting some quilts out of the wagon, made a bed under it, picked up the captive and laid him upon it. He then ate a cold bite of bread and meat, and taking his rifle went slowly back to the cabin.

When he arrived there he again seated himself upon a stump and gave his mind to thought. He had gained one advantage, at least, he could exchange prisoners and get his brother free, which had been his object in so roughly treating the boy, but could he do anything more?

He determined to try. Accordingly he got up and softly behind the covered wagon where he had before—the dog seemed to have exhausted its animosity or else it had followed the wagon and gone rabbit-hunting.

Jake now shouted loudly at the cabin

"Ho, Burrel! Burrel, I say!"

There was a movement inside, a light shone through a crack and an angry voice—the old man's again —replied: "Wall, what ye yawpin' 'bout now?"

Jake briefly related the story of the boy's capture, only being interrupted every few seconds by ejaculations of wrath and chagrin from his auditors, or at least from two of them. Jared was listening also, and Jake heard him give a shout and a hearty laugh of triumph at the conclusion.

For a moment there was confusion inside the cabin, and a gabble of excited discussion, then the door opened cautiously, and Jake heard somebody—evidently a woman—crying piteously.

"Oh, they'll kill 'im! they'll kill my babby!" she moaned.

"Shet up!" said one of the men, roughly.

"Say, mister!" he called, poking his head out of a crack in the doorway.

"Now, look hyer!" called Jake, sharply, "none o' that! Keep inside ef ye want to keep a whole skin."

The head was hastily withdrawn.

"Now, lookee hyer!" repeated Jake, "I'm a-goin' ter hold this hyer cabin in a state o' seige till ye come ter my terms. My terms is these:

"Yer turn my brother loose; give 'im ev'ry gun ye've got an' let 'im bring 'em out hyer to me. Then yer pick up yer duds, 'n' bring 'em out 'n' pack 'em in this wagon 'n' take yerselves off 'n this claim, n' when ye've done that I'll turn yer boy loose,

'n' when ye've gone 'n' took a claim 't ye've got a
right ter squat on, 'n' git settled onto it, yer c'n send
one o' yer neighbors after them guns. Now yer c'n
jes' do that er I'll hol' ye in thar till the crack o'doom,
'n' yer boy 't's tied up out thar in the woods c'n stay
thar till the b'ars eat 'im up, er the wolves, 'n' they's
plenty o' both round hyer. I've got plenty ter eat in
my pockets 'n' good shelter commandin' the winders
'n' door."

At the close of this speech there was another wail
inside the cabin. The woman, rough as she was, loved
her boy and was terribly frightened, and the men
seemed subdued and impressed with the gravity of the
situation. After a long parley the men, moved by the
entreaties of the woman and greatly to Jake's surprise,
did accept them and sent Jared out with the guns.

They brought out their household goods and the men
sullenly packed them in the wagon while Jake and
Jared with the guns stood guard at a safe distance.
They got up their oxen and hitched them to the wagon,
and then the woman, who had silently helped bring out
their bedding, clothing and cooking utensils, broke down
again, and begged that the boy might be "turned
loose 'n' fetched."

This was more than Jake could stand, and though he
knew the lad was safe and fairly comfortable, he had
tied him so that he felt certain he could not get loose.
He, therefore, left Jared with two guns to guard the
claim-jumpers and went and got the boy. The whole
party then drove off without a word.

It was nearly two weeks before a neighbor with
whom they had become acquainted, and who sided with
them upon learning all the facts in the case, came ov.¯

ınd got the guns, and brought the information that the Burrels had settled about twelve miles down the river. He had previously told them that he and some other neighbors, who had elected the elder Burrel a constable, nad not been acquainted with the family long, having only fallen in with them while "moving."

After getting acquainted with all the new-comers of their neighborhood the two boys found good friends and good neighbors among them.

II.

THE MYSTERY OF THE _Y N_ BRAND.

Six or eight years ago horse and cattle thieves were exceedingly troublesome to the stockmen of Montana and northern Wyoming. During a year's stay in those regions I heard many accounts of daring and successful robberies, of narrow escapes on the part of these raiders, and of various curious expedients employed by them to accomplish their object, which was, of course, to drive off stock which did not belong to them.

One of the most bold and yet cunning attempts at cattle-stealing, perhaps, ever made, occurred about that time on the South Cheyenne range near the Wyoming and Dakota lines. I do not know that the story was ever told outside the region in which it happened: but, whether or no, it seems worth telling now.

It was just at the close of the Indian troubles about the "Hills," when cattle men had newly discovered the many advantages of the range of country lying immediately south and west of the Black Hills. It would, in fact, have been impossible to have carried out so daring a scheme on an older and more closely guarded range.

One of the first ranches to occupy a portion of this excellent grass region was built at Dead Cedar Forks on West Dry Wood, and was owned by the Cheyenne Cattle Company. It started with two thousand head of stock, and its brand duly recorded in the nearest stock journals was _J V_, the initials of an old ranch man

18

and chief stockholder, Joe Villemont. The letters were simply formed, about eight inches in height and eight inches apart, and were stamped upon the broad sides, always on the right of the company's cattle, and in smaller letters upon the left hips of its horses.

"Old Joe," as Villemont's men called him, had always been averse to the cruelty of the big, complicated brands which disfigure the cattle upon so many ranges, and which must cause so much suffering in the stamping, and afterward until the wound heals. Accordingly he had always used the simplest and smallest brand that would identify his stock.

At about the time the J V ranch, as it was called, was established, several other cattle-owners came into the region, bringing large droves of cattle, and built ranches on Horse Head and Hat Creeks, and at the head of White River, and the Running Water, and the "L Z's," "Circle Bars" ⊖ "K—23's," "Goose Eggs," "OOO" and others, took their places with the "J V's" upon the range.

The circuit of a "round-up" was soon determined upon, and the cow-boys of each ranch soon made themselves familiar with the various brands upon their riding circuit.

It was at the third general round-up, in June of the second year, that the boys working to the northwest discovered a new brand upon that part of the range, and searching their record-book of Nebraska, Wyoming and Dakota brands could find no marking to correspond. The new brand was "bar Y N" thus, *Y N* stamped upon the right broad side, and supplemented by a new moon upon the right hip.

It was a camp on Lightning creek, a number of the

"Circle Bars" and "J V" men, who first found stock carrying the "bar Y N" brand, as they named it. They found several steers and eighteen or twenty cows bearing it, in the first bunch they rounded up and corralled at the Lightning Creek branding pens. The markings seemed rather fresh, and the calves which were running with the cows were not yet branded.

There was no little speculation in the camp that evening, after the stock-book had been inspected by the foreman, as to where these cattle belonged. It was supposed that they must be strays from some recently established ranch farther north—one probably that had just run in a lot of fresh-branded stock and had not yet advertised its brand.

As the camp moved north and made a new branding pen on Old Woman Creek the bar Y N stock became more numerous until it was calculated there must be a hundred and fifty or more of them; and the out-riding cowboys began to keep their eyes open for signs of a ranch.

The mystery seemed to be solved one evening by the appearance in camp just at supper time of a horseman who reined up with a hearty "How do?" and alighted. He was a slim, dark-looking fellow, dressed in a well-worn suit of corduroy, and wearing the regulation slouch hat and high top boots.

"Well," said he, as the foreman of the camp came forward, "Well, I suppose you've discovered a new brand on your range down here,—the 'bar YN,' eh?"

The foreman said they had, and then asked if he represented that stock, to which the stranger replied that he was superintendent of the ranch to which it belonged, a ranch which had been newly established on the Little Missouri range, that they had shipped out a lot of Minnesota cattle in March, and driven them down from the Northern Pacific, having hay enough on hand to keep them from running down until grass should start up fresh in April.

They had expected to hold them without trouble, but there came a three days' blizzard, which the J V and Circle Bar men had experienced also, from the north, caught a lot of them out, and ran them off to the south. There were about seven hundred of these new cattle gone from their ranch, he said, and they had found them scattered all the way from Belle Fourche to Hat Creek.

He then drew a Montana stock journal from his breast pocket and pointed out his brand advertised as the property of the "Minnesota & Montana Cattle Company," and went on to say that he had brought down three of his men to begin at the southernmost point at which their stock was to be found, and work back toward home, gathering the cattle as they went.

"We'll take what calves you leave us," he said, laughingly, "for you will be through with your branding before we fairly get to work!"

He remarked that his camp, temporary, of course, was on a creek about twenty miles east, and that he had merely stumbled upon the round-up by chance while looking for his own brand.

His story, perfectly plausible and established by an advertisement in an accredited stock journal, made him heartily welcome at the cow-camp, where he was immediately invited to take supper, and, as it rained that evening, he shared the foreman's bed, under the cover of a big supply wagon.

It was about a week after this that the round-up broke camp, and in the meantime two other cow-men were met in search of bar Y N stock. Rather rough-looking fellows they were—hardly up to the standard of "number one punchers" the men thought them. Two of the J V boys, "Griff" Mosher and Tom Dodd, with an extra pony and a week's supplies, were left to look up several ponies which had strayed from the camp at Indian Creek, while the others moved to another part of the range.

Griff and Tom "rustled" around lively for a few days, picked up all of the ponies but two, five had strayed, and giving those up for lost had started from Lightning Creek to go to the J V ranch on Dry Wood. They were riding down into the deep valley of a small run in search of water and a camp for the first evening, when they came upon a large bunch of cattle grazing upon the bottom and side hill.

Upon approaching they discovered the brand bar Y N upon the nearest ones, and struck by the size of the drove, rode through them to discover, if possible, whether they all had that mark. It seemed so; at least, they could see no other markings except the new moon looking remarkably fresh upon the right hip of each creature inspected.

"Hum," said Griff, as they rode forward, "them fellows hev rounded up a big lot of strays right here, haint they now? Say, Tom, don't it 'pear sort o' strange that they haint a spotted critter in the whole bunch?"

Tom cast his eyes over the lot with some astonishment.

"That's so," he admitted; "not a one."

"And say," said Griff, pulling up with sudden energy, "if that big yellow steer there with the wide horns haint the one we hed such a tussle with a-rebrandin' him over at Old Woman last fall, I'll eat my hat."

Tom emphatically coincided with him.

"Yes, an' what's more," fairly shouted Griff, "I can see a dozen cows I'd swear to as J V's this minute! Here, cut loose the horses an' let's down that red heifer thar with a fresh brand on 'er, an' hev a look at it!"

It was the work of three or four minutes for these practiced "ropers" to catch the heifer, throw her, and examine her brand. It also took but a hasty scrutiny to discover that an old marking of J V had been changed to Y N by adding fresh "lean tos" to the original letters, with a bar and the new moon to make the deception more complete.

Griff and Tom wasted no time, but set their wits at work, to plan a capture of the daring rascals, or, at least, to take steps at once to prevent them from running off the stock, as—from the gathering of so large a bunch—it was evident they intended doing soon.

Luckily, as they believed, the fellows had not discovered their presence in the valley, and were probably camped at no great distance above or below. As there were known to be four of them at least, the boys felt that it would be too risky to attempt to cope with them alone, and they determined to ride to the ranch at Dead Cedar Forks, and rally a crowd if any men could be found there.

They mounted, passed through a narrow draw to the creek and up another to the high ground beyond, and then rode hard all night, changing ponies frequently, and only stopping twice for water, and a half-hour's rest at noon or a little before they reached the J V ranch.

There was no one there except Lame Johnnie, the cook, and he had not seen a man, he said, for five days; didn't know where any of the boys were or when they'd be in.

Johnnie himself could not ride on account of his wretched legs; and while they were off hunting up a crowd the thieves might drive the cattle through to Montana and sell them.

Not an hour was wasted; the two bold fellows determined to make an attempt to recapture the stock unassisted. Arming themselves with Winchesters from the ranch in addition to their six-shooters, and selecting four of the best ponies from the corral, they rode swiftly back over the route they had traveled in the morning.

They gave themselves three hours' sleep that night, and the next morning halted at the creek where they had found the bunch of stock with the stolen brand upon them.

As they had feared, the cattle were gone; there was not a creature except a few head of L Z and Circle Bar stock to be seen in the region. But after two hours' search to the northward of where they had struck the stream, they came upon a well-defined and fresh trail of a lot of cattle going north, and knew they were upon the right track. The cattle had been started the day before, as near as the boys could judge, or the day after they had seen them.

They followed the trail at a racking gait until it became too dark to trace it without difficulty, then picketed their tired ponies, ate a cold lunch, and gave themselves up to a night of refreshing and much needed sleep.

All the next day they rode hard upon the trail, but did not come up with the thieves, who, they concluded, were pushing the stock at a terrible rate, probably fearing that they were pursued, as, indeed, for aught Griff and Tom knew, they themselves might have been within plain sight of some or all of the thieves, while making the discovery of the fradulent brand.

It was easy to keep hidden among these breaks and gulches.

It was not until late in the afternoon of the third day's chase that they sighted the drove just descending into a narrow and cañon-like valley of a tributary of the Belle Fourche.

Believing the thieves would stick to this narrow valley in order to keep well hidden, the boys circled, rode rapidly around them, and descended into the valley in their front, as they could tell by the cloud of dust that rose continually above the herd. They reached the level of the stream at the mouth of a gulch about sundown.

Knowing that the cattle thieves would be on the alert, the two cowboys had formed no plan save that of immediate attack upon them from the nearest point of vantage and the most unexpected to the attacked that could be gained.

The spot they had happened upon was well adapted to an ambush. They picketed their ponies some rods from the mouth of the gulch and out of sight, and then the determined fellows, with their Winchesters and revolvers, and abundance of ammunition, placed them-

selves behind a small bank and awaited the approach
of the robbers as they urged the stock along the cañon.

The cloud of dust rolled down, and the leaders of
the herd came in sight climbing out of a gulch a few
rods distant.   Yells and the cracking of stock whips
could now be heard above the trampling and lowing of
the cattle.

It was growing dusk, and the thick dust which rose
from the dry, grassless soil of the cañon made it
impossible to see more than a few rods with certainty.
But soon at the tail of the herd two horsemen appeared,
then another, then a fourth.   They were riding not far
apart, the nearest about fifty yards away, and rather
dimly outlined in the dust and growing darkness.

Griff and Tom laid down their Winchesters, and
with self-cocking revolvers opened fire upon the
miscreants.

The first shots had no other effect than to cause the
thieves to leap from their saddles and get behind their
ponies.   That they did not immediately ride out of
range was no doubt owing to the fear that they had
been surrounded, and that these shots were merely
to drive them upon the muzzles of other guns upon the
other side or in the rear.   .

They were not altogether cowards, either, for they
returned fire at once, and for a few moments the cañon
witnessed one of those fierce shooting affrays which
sometimes occur between the outraged citizen and the
desperado of the plains and mountains.

"Crack! crack! crack!" the thieves fired across their
horses' backs at the heads and shoulders which Griff
and Tom offered as marks, while the incensed and
excited cowboys emptied their revolvers, and then

caught up their Winchesters and "pumped" forty-five's in rapid succession.

These last weapons settled the affair speedily, their length and steadiness gave a better and truer aim than could be got with revolvers.

First a pony went down, then one of the thieves got a bullet in his leg and led his horse away while he limped at his side. The man whose horse was shot took to his heels and ran away. One of the others exposed himself while mounting, and rode away hanging across his horse's wethers. The other sprang upon his pony, and galloped off up the cañon.

In three minutes from the time the firing began the thieves were whipped, "cleaned out" in Western parlance, and gone, and the two plucky cowboys had come off without a scratch.

They dared not attempt to follow up their advantage, however, but rode immediately after the stock, which they succeeded in getting out of the cañon, and twenty miles on the route toward home before morning.

After that they took it leisurely, only keeping a sharp lookout, and taking turns in guarding the stock closely at night. They saw no more of the thieves who had, no doubt, had enough of cattle stealing for once.

The Cheyenne Cattle Company rewarded this bold exploit as it deserved, by raising the wages of Griff and Tom each from forty-five to sixty dollars per month.

III.

It would be hard to find in the Rocky Mountains a rougher stage road than that which runs between the mining hamlets of Thunder Gulch and Squaw Forks. Indeed, if a worse road could be found, there are few persons who would care for a seat in the coach of the most careful driver.

This road is twelve or thirteen miles long. A few years ago a lady who ventured to ride over it called it "The Twelve-Mile Horror," and by this name the road is known to miners and travelers of the region. That the name is deserved the writer can testify, for he knows it to be truly a rambling thread over dizzy precipices and among black, gaping cañons.

There are places along the verge of cliffs and around the jutting points of yawning gulches where the coach seems literally suspended in mid-air, and the rider, glancing out over the wheels into the sheer, gaping space below, hastily pulls down the "flaps," closes his eyes, and leans dizzily back in his seat, not daring to look a second time.

For five years Gideon Fletcher, or "Gid," as he is commonly called, has driven the stage once each day, Sundays excepted, from Squaw Forks to Thunder Gulch and back. Of course, he has occasionally missed a trip, when slides or heavy falls of snow along the line have prevented him from running. Yet during all his fifteen hundred "round trips" he has never met with an accident serious enough to cause the loss of life or limb to his passengers.

So trusty and sure-handed a driver is he that the "contractors of the line" will have no other, and they pay him double wages to keep him upon this particular stretch of their route. Only once has a coach been demolished or a horse killed under his management; but on that occasion he met with a double accident, under circumstances so stirring and heroic as to be well worthy of narration.

It was some two years after Gideon had begun driving the coach upon this road that one day, as he came out from eating his dinner at "The Rough-and-Tumble House" of Thunder Gulch, a pale-faced young woman appeared at the rude gate, and beckoned to him.

"Are you the stage-driver that drives the stage to Squaw Forks this afternoon?" she asked, as he came up.

"I reckon I'm the chap yer lookin' fer, mum," said Gideon. "Want ter go down? Start in half a hour."

The woman glanced about nervously, as though fearful of being overheard, and then she said, hurriedly and in a low voice:

"I'm from Corson's Camp. I'm Corson's wife; but he—they all—abuse me dreadfully, and the baby too. Look here," and she threw an old bonnet she wore back from her forehead, and showed a great fresh scar across one temple.

"I got that last night. They do it when they're drunk, and they're drunk most of the time. Night before last one of 'em threatened to throw my baby into a hot spring. He said he'd 'kill the little imp, he would,' and oh, I can't, I don't dare to stay there any longer! I'm the only woman up at the camp, and

"I'm from Corson's Camp. I'm Corson's wife." —Page 29.

to-day the men are all up at Big Horn Spring pros-
pectin' for a new place, and so I've come to you to see
if you won't take me away from this dreadful place.

" I've no money with me, an' no friends nearer than
Denver. My folks live there, and I would have wrote
to 'em to come and take me away if I dared ; but I
knew if Corson got wind of it before they got here he'd
kill me and the baby, too ; for though he's my husband
he's the most horrid and wicked man I ever saw, except
the gang he keeps around him. Oh, *will* you let me
go with you ? "

" Wal, now, I sh'd smile ! " answered Fletcher, in his
hearty way. " You jest go 'n' git yer baby 'n' yer
fixin's, 'n' we'll git out o' these diggin's in a jiffy."

" Oh, I daresn't come here to start," she replied ;
" but in an hour I'll be down at the mouth of the 'Gap'
below. If I should come here, Corson would find out
soon as he comes back that I'd started off with you,
and they'd like enough catch us before we'd got down
to the Forks.

" Some of 'em may be back any minute ; like enough
they're there now ; but I'm going to sneak away with
baby somehow, if they are. There don't seem to be
anybody hangin' round here now. All off but the
women folks, I s'pose, and it looks like I'd have a good
chance to get off without anybody's knowin' how or
where I went," and with this she turned and sped
away.

" I'll wait for ye, sure," Gideon assured her as she
started.

He hung about the stable of the Rough-and-Tumble
longer than usual that noon, pretending to one of the
women that came out presently that he had to "fix"

something about his harness before he started on the return trip.

"Everybody's gone off crazy 'bout the new *placer* up at Big Horn," they had told him at the table, "'n lef' nobody but ther women folks 't the Gulch."

In about an hour from the time he had finished dinner, Gideon and his coach were in waiting at the mouth of Melcher's Gap. It was about half an hour later when the woman, with her child in arms, came hurrying breathlessly down to him. She looked behind her frequently, and he saw as she approached that her face was white with fear and suspense.

The baby, a wretched little year-old object, dressed, like its mother, in mere rags, turned its poor and piti-ful little face upon the driver with a wan smile that, as he said, "fetched" him "clear to the boots."

"Oh, you *must* drive fast," cried the poor woman, as she clambered into the coach without waiting for the proffered help, "for they've come back, as I was afraid ! Corson and two of the men, and they're going to break camp and move up to Big Horn this afternoon. They daresn't trust me there alone, for I *am some* good to 'em in cookin' and keepin' camp. I knew this was the last chance to git free, so I took the baby and started down to the spring for a pail of water, and when I got out of sight I just run for here, and you must go, go, for they'll sure be after us !"

"I'll *go* fast enough," answered Gideon cheerily, "an' don't you be afraid they'll ketch us neither on them leetle mountain ponies."

But though he spoke with such assurance and deter-mination, he did not feel at all sure of the outcome of a race if the men at Corson's camp should soon discover the woman's flight and follow. He felt that he had taken an extremely hazardous exploit, considering the dangerous route he had to drive over and the characters of the men, who, he had not a doubt, would be upon his trail within the next half hour.

The spring at Corson's Camp he knew was in a ravine at the head of Melcher's Gap, and as this cañon was the only outlet in that direction, Corson could not long remain ignorant of his wife's line of flight after he had discovered, as he soon must, that she was truly gone.

But the woman and her baby, in such evident and distressing need of rescue, had "fetched him," and the brave driver, looking to his revolvers to see that the chambers were all loaded, drew in the lines and urged forward his horses at as great a rate of speed as the nature of the road would warrant.

For a half-hour or more the coach rattled forward at a dangerous pace, for these first few miles were the roughest part of the road. Up and down it went through deep gorges, scaling precipitous "hog backs," and swaying far above the verge of cavernous cañons. From the point of every turn that commanded a view of the trail behind, Gid cast anxious glances backward, to note if anyone were yet in pursuit.

At the "half-mile stone," which was supposed to mark a spot midway between Thunder Gulch and Squaw Forks, was a height from which a good portion of the road for two miles back could be seen, and here it was that the driver discovered, indeed, that Corson and his men were following them. A single glance sufficed to reveal them—three horsemen—riding at a breakneck gallop over the crest of a long hog-back some mile and a half in the rear of the coach.

"A flight for life," thought Gideon, and he cracked his long whip above the ears of the already fretted stage-team. The horses were not unwilling to go faster, however, on the contrary they seemed nervous and frightened at such unusual driving, and sprang forward at a pace which the driver soon found it necessary to check by vigorous pulling at their reins.

"Are they coming? Did you see them?" screamed the woman, frightened at the swaying and rocking of the stage as they rounded a curve.

"Oh, *we're* all right!" the driver shouted back, evading a direct answer. "The road ain't bad, hyar! An' I'm a-tryin' ter make up fer whar *'tis.*"

The coach tore along, pitching crazily down into deep gullies, and swaying wildly above the crests of abrupt cliffs or the sides of gulf-like ravines.

It was quite a number of minutes before Gideon caught sight of the pursuing horsemen again, but when he did, as they came around the point of a mountain spur, they had gained perceptibly upon the coach, and the question of being overtaken had narrowed to one merely of time. And now the driver began to canvass the chances of making a successful defense when he should be finally overtaken.

There was a point nearly two miles ahead, where, if he could only reach it, the road ran along the foot of a narrow ledge and above a precipitous gulch, and where he thought he might halt the coach behind a sheltering point of rocks, and "stand off" their pursuers with his revolvers. He was now determined at every hazard to keep the woman and her child out of the clutches of her pursuers.

With this goal and end in view, then, he drove with a recklessness, which in any less urgent case would have been mad, indeed. More than once the poor woman screamed with fright, as the hack lunged forward or careened over, and ran several yards on two wheels.

But Fletcher kept a steady and strong rein on his animals, and threw his weight to one side or the other as the coach rocked and threatened to overturn.

Several minutes passed in this mad flight, when, glancing back at a smooth turn, the driver caught another view of Corson and his men; they were now pressing hard upon him. There was but a few minutes more to spare in racing, but Gideon had reached a point where, if no accident should occur, he felt certain of gaining the narrow pass.

His horses were sweating profusely from fright and exertion, but still seemed full of energy.

On, on, they flew. It was wonderful that the coach kept right side up, while the poor frightened woman inside clung frantically to her seat with one arm, and to her babe with the other.

Another half-mile was passed safely, and Gideon felt a thrill of triumph as he struck the mountain spur, upon the other side of which he felt sure of making a successful stand against their pursuers. Both at the Gulch and the Forks, he was known as a "crack shot" with his revolvers, and those three fellows, he thought, with no little judgment, wouldn't care "to run up agin 'em," when once he had gained the shelter of the jutting rocks on the other side.

But just as he reached the point of the spur, and when too late, he remembered a dangerous curve in front, where, going at their present rate of speed, the hack must inevitably be thrown off the ledge by its own momentum. It was a short turn upon a steep bench with a ledge above and a chasm below.

He threw all his weight in a backward pull upon the lines, but the team, now thoroughly frightened and wildly excited by their furious run, refused to obey the reins, and plunged recklessly ahead.

They were now within a few rods of the fatal turn, and Gideon, foreseeing instant catastrophe, dropped the lines, sprang over the back of his seat, and catching both woman and child in his arms, jumped out with them upon the upper side of the road.

They were scarcely out of the hack when the vehicle "sloughed" off the road, overturned, and, as it did so, wrenched the team off the narrow "dug-way."

The poor animals scrambled resistingly for an instant, then one lost its footing and fell; the other plunged over it, and coach and all went crashing into the bottom of the gulch below. Gideon had time to note this, as he says, even while trembling with his precious freight from the bank of the spur, against which he had leaped, into the road-bed.

Luckily the bank at that point was of earth instead of rocks—the ledge was but a few steps further on—and the three, though shocked and jarred, were unharmed by their violent exit from the hack.

Gideon, however, did not stop an instant to note whether the woman or her child were injured, but gathering the baby on one arm and grasping its mother's arm with his free hand, ran forward, carrying the one and fairly dragging the other.

Just a few steps beyond the ledge were several big boulders on the lower side of the road. To gain the shelter of those before Corson and his men came in sight was now Gid's object.

Before the boulders were reached, he could hear the clatter of hoofs around the curve. The men were in close pursuit and riding hard, but by dint of great exertion_ Gideon reached the rocks with his charges a minute or two before the pursuers rounded the point.

"Set close behind hyar," he commanded the woman, "and hyar, take your babby 'n' keep es quiet 'n' es cool es ye ken."

Then he drew a revolver from one of the holsters at his hips, and dropping upon his knees at a spot where he could peer through between two of the boulders, cocked the weapon, and leveled it upon the road preparatory to halting the fellows with a shot as soon as they came in sight.

He had not a second to wait before the leader appeared at a point just beyond where the stage and team had gone off the bench and over the cliff.

It was Corson himself, but he had "slowed up," and before Gideon could make up his mind to fire, he suddenly drew rein, and gave utterance as he did so to a loud and excited oath.

He had discovered what had happened to the stage by means—as was afterwards proved—of a sheep-skin seat cushion, which had been flung out of the hack as it overturned, and had lodged on top of the ledge.

The other two men came up almost instantly and halted, and then the three dismounted and talked

excitedly together—though Gideon could not distinguish what they said—and one of them went forward
and peered long and intently over the ledge.

But either he dared not go near enough to the verge
of the precipice to see plainly to the base, or he could
not clearly make out the wreck on account of the
chaparral thicket below, for, after gazing a minute, he_
shook his head decidedly, as though convinced that
passengers and all had gone over, and then all three
quickly remounted, wheeled their ponies about upon
the "dug-way," and disappeared as rapidly as they had
come.

"Unyhugh!" grunted Gideon, with great satisfaction,
"ye think ye've ran us over thar 'n' smashed the hull
outfit, don't ye, 'n' ye've skipped mighty sudden for
fear 't' sumun 'd come along 'n' diskiver yer deviltry,
haint ye?"

Then he told Mrs. Corson to get up, and taking the
child from her arms—the scared little thing had slept
as quiet as a young partridge in hiding—helped her to
rise and led her out upon the road.

The woman had seemed like one dazed while lying
there in hiding, but now that she understood that the
man she so feared had really gone she plucked up
courage, and declared that she could easily walk the
remainder of the way to Squaw Forks—there being no
habitations at that time between the two points.

They reached the little town after a wearisome tramp
over the rough road.

Their arrival and the story of their adventure and
escape created great excitement among the miners, who
gathered at one of the stores that evening, and raised
two hundred dollars to give to the woman, besides pay-

ing her stage fare in advance to the nearest railway station where she could take a train for Denver.

The coach and the team were discovered the next day, a shapeless wreck, having taken a clear plunge of nearly one hundred feet. Only the mail was rescued.

Corson and his gang "pulled up stakes" and left the region immediately, and it was well for them that they did, for as the story of the woman's sufferings became known, the irate miners would surely have lynched them if they had not taken themselves away.

IV.

A daily newspaper widely read in the West devotes a page of each Saturday's edition, seven columns or so, to collections of ghostly doings, as related by local narrators in various parts of its own and surrounding States. These tales and brief accounts are entirely devoted to modern and, if many of them are to be believed, "well-authenticated" ghosts, surprising as this may seem to the reader who has not the advantage of an acquaintance with the "spook" columns of the journal in question.

There are stories, indeed, of haunted houses in southwestern towns where even the electric light has failed to "lay" their nightly and mysterious visitants. This local revival in ghostly matters and beliefs gives good proof of the strength and persistence of inherited tendencies.

In the backwoods annals of forty or fifty years since we expect to find strong traces of superstition, tales of weird and supernatural happenings. It was the writer's good fortune lately to listen to one of these old-time accounts in a story of a haunted rock, the incidents of which were told him by one who took part in the adventure, and are well remembered by old inhabitants about Bogey's Bend.

Bogey's Bend of the Wisconsin river received its name from its earliest settler, a Canadian Frenchman, who had married an Irish wife in his native province, but after a time moved westward with a numerous

family and finally settled upon a fine tract of land in a
sweeping bend of the Wisconsin, the only land fit for
cultivating, in fact, of several square miles contained
within the curve, the remainder being swampy, heavily
timbered, and subject to over-flow. Hence it was a
lonesome spot, and other settlers had been content with
the fertile valleys and plateaus of the bluffs which skirt
the river valley. A spur of those bluffs projects across
the valley at the lower end of Bogey's Bend, termi-
nating in a razor-like ridge, sharply descending and
abruptly ending at the river's bank. Numerous big
rocks, jagged, and broken, crown the "hog-back" of
this ridge, and at the very extremity, protecting this
bluff, indeed, from the wear of a swift current, stands
a pinnacled rock projecting about seventy-five feet
above the ridge and nearly twice that distance from
the water's edge.

To the right of this rugged sentinel, calling the river
its front, a densely-timbered swamp stretches for
several miles, while immediately at its left the earth of
the bluff has caved off, leaving an extremely high and
steep bank plainly bearing the marks of an old land-
slide. And it was told by the old trappers of the region
and also by an aged Winnebago chief, known as an
occasional visitor throughout the surrounding settlements, that the caving off of this huge bank some
thirty years before had buried a party of adventurers
who, with a Winnebago guide, had drawn their canoes
in there and camped for the night upon the river shore
beneath the beetling bluff.

Ever since that time, so the trappers and the Indian
maintained, the spirits of these unfortunates had
hovered about the big rock—had made it their home,

in fact; and almost any night of the year they might be heard moaning and sighing in a way that made the listeners shiver. When the wind blew strongly up river on a wet night, our old trapper claimed, it was "jes beas'ly terrible ter hear thar carryin's on." And the old Winnebago said :

"Heap spirit make um noise, scare Injun a heap."

The trappers and hunters, who in this locality, as in all others throughout the Northwest, had preceded the settlers, giving a nomenclature which has generally stuck to prominent landmarks and streams, had not failed in the matter of this mysterious rock, and its name, "The Moaning Rock," still clings. The stories which they told of the supernatural noises and sights which were to be heard and seen—for some of them claimed also to have seen strange things about the rock—naturally found a credulous reception among the more ignorant of the settlers, and in fact for several years the locality of the Moaning Rock was pretty generally avoided. Even among those who "poohed" at the idea of there being any ghosts at all, and boasted of having been to the rock and that nothing of the kind was to be heard or seen, very few, if any, had ever been known to go there in the night.

Some there were, of course, practical men, busied with work and improvement upon their new farms, who very sensibly paid no attention to any tales of the sort that infested this rock, and who had no interest in visiting the isolated spot.

Peter Bogey was one of these. He laughed when his children or wife repeated with awe the accounts they had heard of the "Moaning Rock," and would say good-humoredly :

"Fools dey ees ticker es de guss'oppers."

But to his Irish wife and the young Bogeys the rock was a veritable bugbear. The boys could scarce be got to go in its direction in search of the cows when the animals strayed that way. However, as "Al" Bogey, the oldest boy, got well along in his teens and began to extend his hunting excursions further into the swamps, he grew—like his father—skeptical of the ghosts and witches in which his mother firmly believed, and at length became so bold in one of his hunts as to track a deer directly up to the foot of the ledge above the crown of which towered the redoubtable rock. He had seen it once before from a height of bluff some half a mile distant—a safe point of view—beyond which few visitors ventured.

What he saw now was a steeple-like rock, triangular in shape, with rough, jagged edges and sharp projections, and growing beside it in a sheltering fashion a huge whiteoak-tree, some of the largest limbs of which had been turned aside in their growth by its nearness. Al could not but feel that it was a bold thing to stand there surveying the rock, and felt not a little uneasy, notwithstanding his lately-aroused skepticism. He lingered for some time, and though he felt strongly the influence of the old tales he had listened to, and the weird lonesomeness of the spot, he neither saw nor heard anything of an alarming nature. Yet he knew that night was the real time to settle the matter—at night, when the wind "blew strong up river." And as he wandered towards home, having lost the trail of the deer upon the hard dry soil of the ridge, he came to the determination to find out for certain whether the story of strange noises and sights at the "Moaning

Rock" were true or not. He knew a young fellow, Jet Ferris, over on Bear Creek, whom he was sure he could get to go with him.

Jet was a great hunter, afraid of nothing, and would as gladly be out all night as all day if there were any fun or excitement to be had.

He said nothing at home of his visit to the rock or of his plan, not wishing to arouse the fears and opposition of his mother, who believed in real ghosts and wizards, and that only evil could befall those who tried to pry into their affairs.

It was September, and Al had not long to wait for a wet, drizzly day which freed him from work and also promised the right sort of a night for his adventure, the wind blowing "up river," or nearly so. As soon as his morning chores were done he took down his father's rifle and set out for the home of Jet, on Bear Creek, four miles distant. Upon reaching young Ferris's home he was told that "Jet hed went up t' the Birch Bluffs t' shoot pa'tridges," and was asked to come in, "set by the fire an' dry yer clo's."

But he declined the invitation, saying:

"Wet clothes ain't nothin'."

And, well knowing that the game Jet was hunting would be found that day upon the sheltered side of the bluffs, he set out after the hunter again, and, after a two hours' tramp, succeeded in finding him.

Jet, after his fashion, gave Al a boisterous greeting, and then readily agreed to his proposal to spend the night, or a part of it, at the Moaning Rock.

"I ben awantin' ter dew it, " said Jet, "fer a long time, but I didn't know of nobody as I thought 'd wanter go long 'th me 'n' I couldn't scrouge myself clean up ter the p'int of goin' alone; but along of you I ain't afeared."

They spent a large part of the day in hunting, returning to Jet's home with back-loads of pheasants and squirrels. Then, after an early supper, or rather, a late dinner, they started for the Moaning Rock—a trip of four miles or more along the tops of the Bear Creek Bluffs.

It was yet broad daylight when they reached the rock. They went boldly up to it, walking along the base and gazing up at the ragged sides and pinnacled tops.

"No spooks up thar es I c'n see," laughed Jet. And then, as it still lacked some time of growing dark, he proposed that they should go down into the swamp with the dog and "see 'f he can't stir out a coon er a wild cat."

To this plan Al eagerly agreed. Having a lantern with them to light their way home they set it down at the base of the big oak to await their return.

After a half hour's unsuccessful beating about in the nearer parts of the big timber swamp it began to grow dusk, and they turned back for their night's vigil. The wind, instead of "going down with the sun," had risen considerably, and was blowing stiffly among the tree-tops as they emerged upon the river bank at the foot of the big rock. There was a fine rain falling also, and they started at once to pass around the base of the rock and climb the ridge to the shelter of the big oak which branched out partially on the leeward side of its neighbor. They had not ascended one-third of the way when a strange, weird sound broke out above their heads—a long-drawn wail that wound up in almost a shriek.

Al Bogey, who is now a man considerably past middle age, says though he fought three years in the war he can remember no moment of his life of such terrible fright and suspense as the one in which he first listened to this wail from the Moaning Rock. He cowered down to the very ground, expecting instantly some awful vision to present itself. But Jet stood boldly up and listened intently while yet another mournful wail broke forth and quavered, at first low and plaintively, then increased to a shrill whistle, then died away only to be followed by others, sounding sometimes singly, sometimes a number in unison.

' "Nothin' in the worl' but the wind up 'mong them snags 'n' jags of rock," he said presently, and in a triumphant, conclusive tone that brought Al to his feet with a heart that soon began to beat naturally with the sudden conviction that Jet was right. He, too, now that his "right mind" had returned, could recognize the old familiar whistle of the wind, as it had sounded from his baby days around the chimneys and the roofs of the log houses in which he had lived.

He was breathing easy again when suddenly an entirely different and more appalling sound jarred upon his ears, and once more sent a chill creeping over him.

C-r-r-a-a-i-k-k!

It was a harsh, discordant scream, such as might have issued from the mouth of the ugliest wizard of all his mother's category.

"Mercy, Jet! he exclaimed; "what's that?"

"Huh!" grunted the stolid fellow, "a feller that

runs in the woods oughter know that sound; it's two
o' them big boughs up thar that's growed crosswise a
grittin' agin eaoh other. I've hearn 'em do that a
hundred times in the woods. Now them sounds," he
went on, "is jest the long 'n' short o' the hull o' this
here sperrit business; an' es fer seein' things, why eny
body es is too skeered ter know them sounds could see
a 'most any thing they 'magined, I sh'd jedge."

This made Al-feel rather small, but he owned his
cowardly feeling.

"I was skeered, Jet, that's a fact, 'n' if I'd ben
alone," he said, "thet rock would 'a' ben howlin' with
sperrits."

"O, wal," replied Jet, with intent to comfort, "you
haint traipsed the woods es many years es I have, else
ye'd know'd them sounds. Thar she goes agin'—"

S-o-r-r-e-a-k!

"Now let's go up," he concluded, "an git our
lantern 'n' strike fer home."

The wind whistled and screamed overhead as they
climbed, and when they reached the trunk of the old
oak a new wonder greeted them—the lantern was
gone!

Although fast growing dark it was still light enough
to have discovered the lantern had it been near the
spot where they had left it; it was a bright new one,
and its polished tin base could almost have been seen
in utter darkness. In vain they lit matches, and
finally built a fire from dry sticks gathered within
shelter of the rock; their luminary was gone, and no
trace of it could be found. The wind could not reach
the spot where it had sat, and the dog had been at
their heels coming up from the hunt; therefore some-

thing or somebody unknown to them had taken it
away.

"Wall," said Jet, scratching his puzzled head, "this
here comes the neardest to speritool perceedin's of
anything I've hearn on 'bout this rock."

It was about this time that the dog began to show
signs of excitement. Suddenly putting his nose to the
ground he ran out to the river bank along the top of
the land-slide and began barking furiously.

The boys piled more sticks on the fire and then followed the animal.

"That's whar our lantern's gone, " declared Jet.
"Don't know what's got it, but that dawg's follered it
fur's he could, sure. Thar's somethin' round here that
ain't no sperrit, fer that dawg don't foller nothin' that
don't make tracks ner leave no smell."

They cautiously approached the edge of the bank
where the animal was jumping about in noisy excitement, and peered over into a black depth which the on-
coming night had made murky and forbidding enough.

Nothing was to be seen or heard; the wind's roar
drowned even the swash of the current which ran
below.

"Thar's somethin' down thar somewhar," declared
Jet, positively.

"Shucks!" said Al. "How could anythin' be down
thar on the sides of that slide?"

Just then, as if in answer to the question, there
flashed out below a little to their left a thin stream of
light. It came from the bank and projected in a funnel-
shaped glare, like the light from a bull's eye lantern.

They were startled, and yet the streak of light shone
out into the blackness with such a natural, cheerful

gleam that there could be no doubt of a genuine flame behind it, queer as the situation seemed.

"What'd I tell ye?" exclaimed Jet, triumphantly. "Some feller down there with our lantern."

"Fishin' mebbe," suggested Al. "Must be farther down than it looks."

"No," said Jet, "it's comin' right out o 'the centre o' the bank not more'n forty feet below. Somebody's in a cave or a hole down thar, 'n' if 'tw'a'nt fer this howlin' wind I sh'd expect 'em ter hear the racket up here 'n' be pokin' ther heads out."

The dog had suddenly left them again, and a moment later they heard him barking directly below and nearly beneath them.

'Thar—see!" exclaimed Jet. "Thar's a path goes down; it's out here by the rock." And he ran to the fire, and, gathering the unburnt ends of several flaming brands, in his hands, arranged a torch.

"Now, come on," he said; "let's find the path."

"Ain't you feared?" asked Al.

"Shucks, no," replied the plucky fellow; "it's only some ol' trapper that's got a good thing long of these banks which nobody won't come near, 'n' the cute ol feller's dug a hole down thar so's ter keep hid up."

This theory re-assured Al, and, hiding their guns under a dry ledge, they passed around the rock to the edge of the bank. After a moment's careful search the path was found leading from between two boulders obliquely along the steep incline. By the light of Jet's flaming sticks they could trace the narrow roadway several yards in advance. It had plainly been cut into the bank by the aid of tools, but it proved a ticklish affair, barely sufficient for safe passage in daylight, and after descend-

ing carefully the slippery way for a dozen steps or so,
Jet halted.

"'Taint safe," he announced to Al, who was cautiously following, while he held the torch above his
head. "'Taint safe to go no furder, slippery 'n' narrer,
'n' what's more, the rain's goin' to put this light out
d'rectly."

All this time the dog had barked energetically
ahead, but as Jet finished there came the booming
reports of a gun, followed by a sharp canine yelp either
of fright or pain. It was evident almost instantly that
the animal was more frightened than hurt, for, peering
ahead under his waning light, Jet saw the dog bounding
up the path. Instinctively the torch-bearer threw himself back against the bank, and the dog sprang past,
brushing him smartly, but not pushing him off his feet.
Al was not so lucky; the brute, both frightened and
hurt, as it afterwards proved, struck him squarely upon
the legs, knocking his feet from under him.

Instantly the luckless lad was sent sliding down the
slippery incline at a rate of speed which took his
breath and left him no time for thought or action.
Luckily he started feet first, and instinct, of course,
made him clutch the earth of the bank with either
hand, thus keeping his body in the same position; at
least he supposes so, for he had sense enough to feel
that he struck the water feet first, and, after a strang-
ling splash, was surprised to find himself standing up to
his neck in the current and up to his knees in mud. It
was the season of low water, and the stronger portion
of the current turned further out by the rock above
had allowed the water to fall away from the bank and

intervening bed to fill partially with the earth washed down from above.

As soon as he got his breath Al began the struggle to free his feet, which it took some time to do, as the velocity of his "slide" had driven his legs into the sticky material with no little force. He succeeded at length, and then setting to work as best he could in such a depth of water and such darkness, got off his boots and most of his clothes and made a bundle of them. He was a good swimmer, and as the water was not very cold he struck boldly out into the current and swam down stream, using one hand and his legs, while with the other hand he clung to his clothes.

He had swum but a few minutes when he heard Jet's voice hallooing at him from the bank above. He gave an answering shout, to which Jet replied with a joyful whoop.

"Down a leetle furder here, Al," he shouted; "here's a good place ter climb the bank. And Al having rounded the bluff came in shore by the aid of Jet's light and was soon standing dripping upon the bank, while Jet, holding a dimly-burning brand, danced around him in a furor of delight.

"Hurray!" he said, "I thought ye was a goner. Mighty lucky there wasn't no stones ner stumps ter hit agin. Now git on yer clo'es, fer we must be gettin' out o' this. I brung down the guns, hopin' ye'd turn up all right, fer 'twont be safe fer us ter poke round up thar any more. They's a den o' thieves, er wuss, up thar in that bank."

After a weary, stumbling tramp over the bluffs, they succeeded in reaching Ferris's house in the valley. The family got up to listen to their story, and the dog was called in and carefully examined. Two slight buckshot wounds in the jaw and shoulder attested the truth of the boys' narrative.

By noon the next day nearly all the men and boys of Bear Creek had assembled, each armed with some sort of weapon, at the Moaning Rock.

But the inhabitants of the bank had flown; their den, a roomy excavation with a small entrance just large enough to crawl through handily, was found empty, and the hay or grass which they had used for beds had been scattered over the floor of the cavern and burned, thus leaving no scrap of anything by which their business or their number might be guessed. There were two paths, one leading to the ridge above, and the other to the water below, thus giving two avenues of escape, as they had, no doubt, a boat in hiding upon the river.

The bank proved not to be so steep as it appeared in looking from the top or bottom. The cave-dwellers, whoever they were, were evidently aware of the superstition investing the Moaning Rock, and had taken advantage of the protection it offered in seeking a base for some secret and, no doubt, illegal traffic.

The settlers at once concluded that they were counterfeiters, and probably they were right in so thinking, for the country at that time was exceedingly pestered with well-counterfeited bills of the State, or "Wild-cat" banks, as they came to be called later.

As the rain had obliterated all traces of flight, however, no attempt was made to follow this band, for it was evident from the size of the cave and the work that had been done that there must have been a number of them. That they had thought themselves discovered and were prepared for fight, even before Jet and Al had returned from the swamp, seemed evident from the taking of the lantern and their warning shot at the dog.

The cave remained a neighborhood curiosity for some years, and was inhabited for a time by wolves, but at length the wash of heavy rains wore away and destroyed all trace of both path and cavern.

The episode above related, however, broke the spell which had so long hung around the Moaning Rock, and Jet and Al got, as they deserved, no little credit for their plucky adventure.

V.

MORTIMER HALLECK'S ADVENTURE.

Among the many adventurous incidents of our
frontier life in northwest Iowa, fifteen years ago, I
recall one that befell a boy neighbor, Mortimer Halleck, in which his recklessness came very near causing
his death.

There were five of us boys, who formed a little company of tried friends and pledged comrades. We
hunted, trapped, boated, went skating and swimming
together, and, when the first frame school-house was
built, we occupied the two back seats, on the boys' side.

In our hunts after deer, wolves, badgers, and feathered game, we found an exhilaration such as I never
again expect to experience in the tamer pursuits
of life. We even felt an exultant joy in the fierce
buffeting of the winter blizzards which annually
descended upon us from the plateaus of Dakota.

During the regular season of bird migration, the
resounding *golunk, golunk,* of the wild goose, the
shrill *klil-la-la* of the swift and wary brant, the affec-
tionate *qu-a-a-rr-k, quack* of the Mallard drake and his
mate, with the strange, inimitable cry of the whooping
crane, combined to form a sylvan orchestra, the music
of which thrilled us with more pleasurable sensations
than were ever awakened by the household organ or
the town brass band of later years.

In the early spring, during the alternate slush, mud
and freeze of the first thaws, there always occurred a

short vacation from school and work, in which we gathered a harvest of fun, fur and feathers.

At this season, the low, flat valleys of the Little Sioux and the Ocheyedan rivers were covered six or eight feet deep by the annual overflow; and torrents of yellow snow-water, the melting of tremendous drifts, rushed down creeks and ravines.

As soon as these impetuous currents had gathered force enough to upheave the thick layers of ice in the river-beds and break over the banks, out came beaver, musk-rat and mink, driven from house and hole to take refuge upon the masses of ice and drift stuff which lodged in the thickets of tall willows that grew along the beds of these streams. Here they were obliged to stay until the water subsided, and here they often fell a prey to the rifle or shot-gun of the hunter.

We owned three boats in common; and as the men of the settlement were not particularly busy during the freshet season, we could easily persuade or hire them to load our skiffs on their wagons, and haul us eight or ten miles up the Sioux or Ocheyedan, for half a day's run down home, in which scarcely the stroke of an oar was necessary, after getting out into the main channel. Floating leisurely down, we were able to hunt musk-rat, geese and ducks, which were plentiful on the water or on the banks.

Beaver were scarce, but we occasionally got one. A mink or two, a couple of dozen musk-rats, and a goodly bag of feathered game were often the result of a half-day's run with a single boat.

Mortimer Halleck, who at this time lived in the fork of the rivers, and at a considerable distance from the rest of us, owned a staunch skiff, which he had

himself made, and in it went often alone upon the
rivers. It was upon one of these solitary trips that he
met with the adventure mentioned.

On a raw afternoon in March, his father had taken
Mortimer and his boat on his double horse wagon six
miles up stream. At this point there was a great bend
in the river, and, by crossing the neck, the water distance to the fork was lengthened to fifteen miles.
Mortimer was thus set afloat with his boat, with a long
afternoon's run on the river before him.

For several hours the young hunter allowed his boat
to drift down with the current, then swollen to an
unusual height. His eyes, roving on either hand, were
now and then rewarded with the sight of a small brown
bunch of fur, resting on a bit of lodged drift. Then
followed a quick puff of smoke, and the echoing report
from the shot-gun. The troubles of the furry little chap
were at an end. The kinks would straighten out
of its small humped back, and, as a deft turn of the
oars brought the boat alongside, the hunter's hand
would reach over the edge, grasp the long, slim tail,
and fling the body of the sleek little *musquash* into the
boat.

Twice during the afternoon a flock of geese had
ventured low down over the drifting boatman, and
each time one of the flock had fallen a victim. The
others had hurried away in noisy confusion. He had
hardly expected to find beaver, yet as the night drew
on without a sight of one, he felt a little disappointed.
True, he had secured a profitable lot of game: two
geese, a mink, and more than a dozen muskrats.

But he wanted to show a beaver with the rest of his
bag, and he had about given up his hopes of it when,

just as the sun was setting and while he was passing
down the mid channel between two long lines of clus-
tering willow thickets, he espied the very object of his
desires directly ahead and within easy range.

The animal was rolled up in a rusty brown ball, lying
in a snug nest amid the bushy sprouts from an elm
stub which projected three or four feet above the
water. The tree had been broken off, and leaned out
from the summer banks of the river. It had grown,
as elm stumps often do, a dense fringe of short, tangled
brush about the end of the trunk. Among these sprouts
the beaver had fashioned a nest, and was lying curled
up, asleep. when Mortimer, drifting silently down
within short range, raised his gun and shot at it.

But the beaver is a "hard-lived" animal, and, even
when shot at such close quarters, will quite frequently
flop off its perch into the water, and, clutching with
teeth and claws into roots or grass at the bottom,
remain there. In that case, the hunter's ammunition
is simply wasted.

This had happened more than once in Mortimer's
experience, and, fearing that it might happen again,
for he saw the beaver floundering heavily in its nest,
he brought the boat about in great haste, circled around
the stump, and jammed the bow into the sprouts. He
then dropped the oars, and sprang forward to secure
the game.

His haste was unfortunate; for, though he grasped
at the small limbs quickly enough to have held the
boat in place if it had not been in motion, his impetus
was so great that the unsteady skiff recoiled backward
with a force that pitched him over the prow, upon the
very top of the stub. He lurched off to one side, and

his feet and legs splashed into the water; but he escaped a complete ducking by clenching the top of the trunk with his left arm, while with his right hand he grasped *one foot of the beaver!* And then he glanced around for his boat.

It was gone, and had left him in a most perilous situation. The light skiff, impelled by the force of his

Mortimer looked after it in utter dismay.—Page 58.

fall out of it, had floated back into the current, and was already more than a dozen yards out, moving down stream.

Mortimer looked after it in utter dismay.

It was now too late to make a swim for it; he could never live in that strong, icy current long enough to reach it.

With a few cautious hitches he succeeded in gaining a ticklish seat upon the broken top of the stump, where he maintained himself by resting his feet upon two of the stoutest sprouts. Seated thus, he could feel an unsteady quivering of the trunk, a trembling, wrenching motion, that told, but too plainly, of the powerful force of the flood, and of the uncertain tenure which he possessed on even this comfortless refuge.

The lad was now thoroughly alarmed, and surveyed his surroundings with a growing fear that gained not a ray of hope from the prospect. The situation was truly a grave one.

On all sides was the hurrying flow of the grim, dark waters, which rushed swirling and eddying onward, The current swashed dismally among the slender. swaying willows, on either side ; and beyond these, he knew that there was at least three hundred yards of swimming depth before either shore could be reached.

If any one should happen to pass, he could not, from the land, see Mortimer, on account of the willows. The nearest house was three or four miles distant; and a voice could be heard but a little distance, above the swash of the flood and the rush of the cold wind.

Mortimer's parents did not expect him to return until late in the evening, and they would probably make no effort to learn of his whereabouts until after midnight. The night, too, was already growing very cold, with a raw, gusty wind that soughed drearily among the willows; his bare hands and wet feet were fast becoming chilled and numb.

All the desolation, helplessness and misery of the situation were forced upon him by that keen and merciless power of reflection which so often attacks the mind in moments of extreme peril or of sudden disaster.

He saw but too plainly that it was useless to look for rescue before morning, and, clinging there to his bleak and uncertain perch, he felt that he would assuredly chill to death in a few hours.

Looking out into the gloom of the coming dusk, with the long, black, freezing night staring him in the face, tears gathered in the poor fellow's eyes, and a lump of choking misery rose up in his throat. Yet he was a brave fellow, who had never been known to yield an inch before any danger which must be met, when the balance of probabilities was adjusted with any degree of fairness. In this case, the probabilities were all on one side, and that side was against him.

"There just aint any chance for me at all," he groaned, at length. "I'm in a much worse predicament than the beaver and muskrats; for if they do get killed, it's so sudden they don't know it, but I've got to die by inches. I've just got to sit here and freeze a little at a time, till I fall off and finish life by drowning."

A wretched enough prospect! Yet that was the fate which seemed certainly awaiting him. Wet as he was, and already shivering, with no chance for exercise, there seemed little chance of surviving the cold, dismal night.

Sitting in hopeless suffering, he peered about him again and again in the gathering darkness, in the vain hope of discovering something that could give him an atom of comfort. Then, whipping his numbed hands about his shoulders until they tingled, he attemped to remove his soaked and stiffening boots; but, owing to his shaky and uncertain seat, he was baffled in this effort also.

Then, with feet and legs growing every moment more numb, he sat, clinging with one hand to the stump, whipping the other, shouting at intervals, and waiting for—he dared not think what.

An hour passed; then another; dumb, dreary despair had settled upon his mind. Insensibly he fell into a half-frozen stupor. He was beginning to think, in a numb way, that it did not make any particular difference to him what happened now.

An hour or more dragged by thus sluggishly, then a sudden shock, accompanied by a grinding noise, threw him partly off the stump. Instinctively he clutched the sprouts with his chilled fingers, but slid down, expecting to sink in the cold waters.

But he struck something solid and white. It was a large ice-cake, which had come floating down the river and touched the elm stump. The jar of his fall roused the boy; he staggered to his feet, feeling *strange* in his head, and with queer and painful sensations about the arms and shoulders.

He tried to step, but at first it seemed as if his feet must be frozen; yet, after stamping about for a few minutes, they began to lose their feeling of lumpishness and to prickle.

He then sat down upon the ice, and, after a struggle, worked off his boots, squeezed the water from his socks, and chafed and pounded his feet until they felt alive. This done, he got up and looked around; and hope revived within him.

The ice-cake was a large and solid one, twenty feet across at least; and, owing to the falling of the river, it was floating down the centre of the channel. He was, at least, floating toward home; and there was room to stamp about and keep from freezing.

Mortimer's spirits rose with the renewed circulation of the blood. He shouted, beat his arms about his chest, he even danced, the better to warm himself up again.

It seemed to him now that he was being guided by fate. He then became confused in mind—dazed, as it were. In odd vagary, as his ice-raft floated on down the river, he peopled the darkness about him with imaginary foes, and "squared off" at them pugnaciously. His blood warming with this exercise, he began delivering in grandiloquent tones the address which he had declaimed at school, when a voice from the darkness near at hand brought him back to his situation.

"Mortimer!"

"Halloo!" he answered.

"Mortimer, is it *you*?"

"Is that you, father?" cried the young castaway, "have you got a boat?"

"Yes," replied Mr. Halleck; "but we have been alarmed. What has kept—"

"Paddle your skiff this way, father. Here, this way; I'm on a cake of ice."

"On a cake of ice!" cried Mr. Halleck. "I knew you were in some trouble. What has happened? I borrowed Neighbor Wescott's boat, and was going to cross over to see if you were at Morley's with Pete, when I heard your voice."

Mortimer was astonished to find he had already drifted so far.

"How much longer could you have stood it?" Mr. Halleck asked, in tones that trembled a little.

"Not another half-hour," Mortimer declared, and probably he was right.

Next day he succeeded in finding his boat, safely lodged among some willows; but the beaver was missing, having probably been jarred off the nest on the stub by the ice-cake striking against it.

The river had lowered considerably, and Mortimer, while searching for his boat, saw numerous ice-rafts moving down the channel; yet he could not repress a conviction that something more than mere good fortune had directed the ice-cake to touch at his bleak and comfortless perch in the nick of time to save his life.

VI.

THE MYSTERY OF THE VALLEY.

Among the earliest settlers on the Wisconsin river was Robert Wheaton—now one of the wealthiest farmers of the State—who, with his pretty young wife, Jennie, came up into the Winnecon Valley to make a home about the year 1850. There was this difference between the Wheatons and many others of the pioneers here: Robert and Jennie settled there tó stay, while too many of the "old Winneconers," yielding to temporary discouragements, drifted away with the ever-moving tide of Westward migration.

Robert, like all "old settlers," greatly delighted to tell of the hardships of those early times, when he and Jennie came to live in the new log-house in one of the Winnecon "pockets," or side valleys between the bluffs.

One midsummer evening, just at twilight, Robert sat milking his cow in the little yard back of his shed, when someone near the fence surprised him with,—

"Good-e'en, Meester W'eäton! Ha' ye seän th' broout baäst yit?"

Robert knew the voice, and looking up, saw "Big Jim" Hodgson, as he was known, leaning his elbow upon the fence. Hodgson was an Englishman, with a large family, and in person an enormous man of six and a half feet in height, who spoke the North of England dialect, in a voice as rough and guttural as the rumbling of a cart-wheel. The Winnecon people among whom he had settled had nick-named him "Big Jim."

He was a brave, good-natured man, but somewhat inclined to be superstitious.

"Hullo, Hodgson!" Robert exclaimed. "What brute are you talking about? I haven't seen any one."

Big Jim explained. There was a strong flavor of hobgoblin belief in his gruff, deep tones, as he related how a strange creature had been seen in the valley roads and along the cow-paths during the past week. One of the Carter girls had seen it up on the "bluff path," between Cat Rock and the Twin Oaks. It was a large, gray, shaggy creature, which, issuing from the brush, had followed the girl as she drove home the cows. She was naturally much terrified, yet she dared not run, and the "broout baäst" had followed her silently, until she had gone past the Twin Oaks, down to the upper end of Carter's rye-patch.

There it had left her and walked off into the woods, and she had rushed home with the cows, and gone to bed in a high fever.

Continuing his account, Big Jim related how, on Sunday evening, the *thing* had followed the Mulrony boys down through the gap road.

"They were on horse-back," he said, "a-coomen' doon on a spaärkin' veesit to Carter's; and the brout baäst 'ad coom oop a-hint their 'orses, 'n' nigh scahed th' seensus oot o' um."

Nor was that all, for last evening, just at dusk, his own little girl, May, had seen it cross the turnip-patch up in the "notch" on the side of the bluff above the house. It went across the patch from one point of timber to the other like a streak of gray light, seeming not to touch the ground with its feet, and "hit warn't nowt loike onythink at all she 'ad e'er seän."

"W'aät do Muster W'eäton think o' that, now?"

The question had in its tones a strong touch of exultation, for hadn't Robert Wheaton always "toorned up 's noäse at onythink at all as was onnaäteral?"

Robert laughed, not so much at the information, as at Hodgson's tones. He soon grew sober again, however.

"We must look after that animal, I think, Jim," he said. "I'm inclined to believe, from what you say of the beast and its actions, that we've got a panther sneaking about our neighborhood."

"Mought beä," returned Jim, a little miffed; "but I'se un as b'leäves traäps'll no hoäld un, an' bullut's'll no hoort un," and he walked off toward his home swinging a heavy club as he went.

"Evidence in his hand against the belief in his head," chuckled Robert, who went in with his pail of milk, and told Jennie about the "broout baäst."

"Some stray panther, I expect," he said, in conclusion, "or a big timber-wolf, that's prowling about after pigs and chickens."

A week from the following Sabbath there was "preaching" at the new log school-house. Rob and Jennie attended, and after the service their ears were filled with excited questions, and with remarkable statements about the "broot baste," as the strange creature had already come to be called, this name being an American perversion of Big Jim's North English tongue.

Every one wanted to know whether Robert had yet seen the "thing." Not a few affirmed that they had seen it—always after dark—and it had each time followed silently a little way, and then, as they drew near houses or openings, it had slunk away into the woods. For a fortnight it had followed some one nearly every night.   Even the itinerant preacher grew interested.

" Must be a dangerous creature of some kind, Robert," he said, addressing Wheaton ; " a wild animal, of course, and you had better trap it."

Nothing, however, could convince Big Jim that the creature was not an uncanny brute ; and old Granny Bates, who was born before the Revolution, declared her belief that it was "some creatur' bewitched."

Robert promised to try his hand at trapping it, and went home.   In less than a week he had seven large double-spring traps, baited and carefully set at different points in the bluffs where the strange object had been seen.

He had to neglect his work somewhat in order to make the round of these traps ; and as they were not disturbed during the whole of this time, the affair proved most annoying to him. At last he grew sceptical about the matter, and took his traps home, declaring that he " wouldn't trap for shadows any longer."

'Somebody," he said to Jennie, "has started a ridiculous story about the creature, and now everybody that sees a dog come out into the road after dark imagines, it's the ' broot baste.' I've found a few fresh wolf-tracks, but there's no sign of any strange animal, that I can see."

But tidings of the " broot baste " did not cease. Scarcely a week passed that some one in the valley or among the bluffs did not have a fresh story to relate of the oddly-behaving creature.   It was often seen close to houses, at night-fall, but generally made its appearance to women and children.

As the creature never offered to molest any one, and spared the pigs and chickens, people ceased to fear it and only wondered what it could be.

But Robert remained sceptical as to its existence; and the matter continued to be a mystery.

Late that fall, after the first snow, which came early, there began to be heard strange yelps and cries nearly every night among the hills. These were most "unearthly noises," the people said who heard them. Robert only laughed at these reports. "Wolves always howl during the first cold snap," he said.

But one night Jennie and he were awakened by what was, in very truth, a most frightful yelping, which came from the bluff, just above their stable. They listened awhile; and Robert was compelled to admit that he "never had heard such an outcry as that from any living creature before."

The cries seemed to be half-way between the quick yelps of a frightened dog and the prolonged howl of a timber-wolf, only more wild, weird and mournful than either of those sounds.

Robert took his gun and went out; but the howling stopped immediately, and it was so dark that he could see nothing.

The next night the creature came and howled in the same place, and earlier in the evening, but it became quiet the moment Robert stepped outside the house. Wheaton's curiosity was fairly aroused.

He tried to find its tracks the next morning; but the snow had now nearly all melted and the ground was frozen again. He said nothing to his neighbors, but determined to outwit and kill the beast, in some way. But though he again set his traps and baited them invitingly with fresh meat, night after night passed and the howling increased, yet the traps remained empty.

Then he tried hiding out in the brush, lying in wait with his gun, but the animal did not appear, and that stratagem failed.

But one night, early in December, the mystery was explained in the most unexpected manner. "Young John," a Winnebago trapper, solved it for them.

Young John, as he was called by the white settlers, was an Indian who, for some offense, was under the ban of his tribe, and who subsisted by trapping and hunting along the Wisconsin.

He could speak broken English, and he evinced a liking for Robert Wheaton, who had taught him many useful things. Hence he often came to Robert's place and slept on the house-floor at night. Generally he ate supper with Robert and Jennie, but he always left before the latter awoke in the morning.

One evening, about three weeks after they had been so disturbed by the howlings of the "broot baste," Young John came to the house, and, as usual, took supper with them, having brought his blanket, prepared to sleep on the floor.

After supper, when Robert had finished his "chores," he sat by the fire with Young John, as they had been in the habit of doing, telling stories, when on a sudden the "broot baste" set up a series of its wild, mournful cries, in the same place on the bluff above the stable.

They had not heard it there for several nights; and

Robert had not yet mentioned the creature's doings to Young John.

On hearing the sounds, the Indian started and listened for a moment most intently, while Robert and Jennie exchanged meaning glances. But Young John's next move surprised them; for after listening for a moment or two, the Indian gave a most expressive guttural grunt of mixed astonishment and satisfaction, then abruptly strode to the door, threw it open, and placing two fingers between his lips, blew a shrill, ear-piercing whistle.

The howlings stopped.

He repeated the whistle, then stalked out into the darkness.   Robert and Jennie followed him to the door, and peered out curiously.

It was light enough for them to see the Indian, as he stopped near the corner of the stable; and then they saw a strange, shadowy creature come bounding down the hill and throw itself on the ground, with pitiful whines, at Young John's feet.

He stooped over and seemed to be petting it, and talking to it in the Winnebago tongue, for a few seconds.   Then he came back to the house; and the creature followed whining and leaping at his heels, until he had nearly reached the door, when it slunk quickly away out of sight again.

Robert and his wife were quite prepared for Young John's announcement, as he came up to the door.

" Me dog," he said. " Me lose um las' spling clossin' liver. Him heap 'fraid white man's."

He made no further comment, and his hearers said nothing.   They remembered perfectly well the shy, large, gaunt, grizzled wolf-dog which had always been with him, and had always refused to come near the house, on his previous visits.

Jennie at once offered the Indian some victuals, to feed the animal, but Young John said : " No, him eat plenty labbit."

The Wheatons had a quiet laugh over the solution of the strange affair. Next morning the Indian and his dog had disappeared.

The " broot baste " and its antics were from that time forth things of the past; and the neighbors enjoyed the explanation as much as did Robert and Jennie.

VII.

The most desperate and lawless men to be found in the West—I speak from twenty years' experience on the plains—are the gamblers, confidence men and robbers who follow the "end of track" when a railway is pushing through new and unsettled territory.

At every side-track a new town springs into existence, so suddenly as to suggest the Western expression "dropped there by a cyclone." At each of these new communities the first-comers are usually men of the kind I have mentioned.

Along the road-bed, wherever a siding is to be laid, a dozen or more big tents, respectively labeled "Saloon," "Dance House," sometimes very appropriately, "Satan's Hole" or the "Devil's Den," are always found set up in advance of the arrival of the track-layers.

A certain harvest awaits the owners of these groggeries, as the "railroader," of a certain class, takes his "time" from his foreman at frequent intervals, in order that he may cash his "time check" at the nearest saloon and gambling-place.

He quickly squanders the proceeds of his check in drink and play, or is robbed of them, lies about in a stupid condition for a day or two, and then goes to work again, penniless.

Such a person accepts all the evils of this mode of life with a philosophy that would be commendable if shown under adversity of a different sort. A shirt, pantaloons, shoes, and a slouch hat usually comprise the whole of his possessions, and so long as he can get the means to satisfy a periodic appetite for drunken excitement, he seems to be contented with his lot.

This description of a large class of railroad laborers, it should be distinctly noted, does not apply to the many sober, steady fellows who save the large wages they get, and often settle and become prosperous citizens in the country they have helped to open to civilization.

It is upon the earnings of floating, dissolute wage-workers of the track and grade that the gambler, whisky seller and assassin thrive, and, to secure their plunder, they follow the progress of a new railway like vultures in search of prey.

The day-laborer upon these pioneer roads is not the only victim of the robber and sharper. It is unsafe for any man who visits one of their mushroom towns to let the fact be known that he has a considerable sum of money in his possession.

Yet men who know the nature of the dangers about them sometimes neglect to take proper precaution to insure the safety of money in their charge, and thus the writer allowed himself to be caught, two years ago, in a "snap" that came near ending his career, and that taught him a lesson in caution which he hopes will never again be needed, at least by him.

I was acting as paymaster and chief commissary clerk for a firm of grade contractors upon the North-western road, which was then pushing through northern Nebraska into the adjacent territory of Wyoming.

We were doing some heavy grading and rock work,

and with a large force were pushing the work day and
night in order to get out of the way of the track,
which had then advanced to a point within a day's ride
of us.

We had let pay-day slip by without paying the men,
and hoped to satisfy them by the issue of time-checks
until the track should overtake us, and our money
could come to us with little risk on the construction
train. But, three or four days after "paying-off" time,
some of the men began to grow suspicious and to
grumble, and threatened to quit work until their checks
were cashed. They were afraid we might somehow
slip up on them and they wouldn't get their money.

As we were in desperate need of every available
hand, it was necessary that the men should be satisfied.
So it was determined that I should go to Chadron, our
supply base and banking point, and bring up enough
money to pay the men their last month's wages, which
amounted to about four thousand dollars.

I decided to go alone. I set out that night on
horseback, and I reached the "end of track" at Crawford siding the next morning in time to leave my horse
at a neighboring ranch corral and get aboard a supply
train which had just unloaded and was now going
back.

At Chadron the supply store of the main contractor,
a huge, roughly built shed, stood at a side track about
forty rods from the main street of the town. Here I
was accustomed to order supplies and get drafts for
money from the book-keeper from time to time.

That morning, after finishing my business with the
supply department, I went to the book-keeper to pro-
a draft. A crowd of railroad laborers were wait-

ing before his window to get their time-checks cashed, or secure passes to go up or down the road. I noticed that two of these men were better dressed than the others, but thought nothing of the circumstance.

I awaited my turn at the window, and handed the book-keeper a slip of paper on which was written, " Four thousand three hundred and forty-seven dollars and fifty cents, *Pay Roll*—Rodney and Curtis." He made me a draft for the amount named, folded it carelessly, thrust it through the window, and took the receipt which I had just written, and then turned to the next man.

As I left the store I passed the two men whom I had noticed at the window, and it struck me, upon a more attentive view, that they were rather sharpers than workingmen, although I had seen them cash two time-checks and get passes for some point up the road. The construction train did not leave until three o'clock that afternoon, and I lounged upon the shady stoop of the Chadron House watching the passers-by and chatting with the landlord, who was an old acquaintance of mine when I lived in the East. I had a pleasant dinner with him, and after the meal was finished, I walked across the square to Lake & Haley's bank, at the corner of the two principal streets of the town, where I cashed the draft.

The bills which I received I stuffed into various side pockets of my clothes, and stowed a sack of silver change into a small leather "grip" which I carried in my hand.

I heard a locomotive whistle and, turning, walked quickly out of the bank. As I reached the sidewalk I was startled to see the two men who had before attracted my notice step rather hastily away from the sidewalk in front of the bank windows and walk across the street.

I was satisfied that they had watched me as I cashed my draft. My suspicions were thoroughly aroused by this circumstance, and when, an hour later, I stepped into the caboose of the construction train, and discovered the men lounging upon two cracker barrels smoking their pipes, it did not need their evident avoidance of the direct stare I gave them, the moment I entered, to convince me that they were after me.

I had heartily berated myself for not having exercised greater caution while at Chadron. I should have waited until I could see the book-keeper alone before I obtained my check, and should have had my cash made up by the clerk at the bank, and brought to my room at the hotel, as might easily have been done. But it is easy enough, after you have done a foolish thing, to think how much better you might have managed it.

While I sat upon one of the hand benches in the caboose, with my "grip" lying beneath the seat, I considered how I should dodge the two fellows at Crawford. There was no danger that I should be robbed on the train, as there were at least twenty passengers on board. Presently one of the men sauntered up to my seat, sat down by me, and began to talk.

"See?" said he; "you'r with Rodney an' Curtis, aint yeh, one o' their foremen?"

I answered carelessly that I was in their employ.

"Paul 'n' I's goin' up the road lookin' fur a rock job. We're strikers. Could ye hire us, d'ye think?"

"Certainly," said I; "we need more badly, especially

good strikers. Will give you two dollars a day, and you can work a part of the night shift, if you like."

Then, as unconcernedly as I could, I went on to tell him about our work, and directed him how to find our headquarters. I told him I should leave Crawford after breakfast the next morning on horseback, and that he and his partner could undoubtedly find a freight wagon there on which to take passage for our camp.

After some further conversation with the man—a young-looking, wiry, dark-faced fellow—he went over to talk to his "pard," and no doubt they congratulated themselves on his success in throwing me off my guard.

On my arrival at Crawford I went to the company's tent, where food and other supplies brought on the construction trains were stored until they could be shipped forward by wagon to points where our forces were at work. There I explained the situation to the two clerks in charge of the tent, and said that I wished to spend the night with them.

I was armed with a good "six-shooter," and the clerks had each a light Winchester rifle. They said we could guard the money without trouble that night, and it was arranged that I should start for the grading camp at three o'clock the next morning. By leaving at so early an hour I believed that I could baffle pursuit by any robbers who might have conspired to follow me.

My pony—a tough Oregon half-breed—was picketed that evening behind the supply tent, and the clerks and I took turns in sitting on guard at the opening of the tent. I saw nothing of the two "strikers" after we left the train, and no suspicious person approached the tent that night. I shifted the silver from my "grip" into a pair of saddle-bags, and, armed with my revolver and a borrowed Winchester rifle and a belt of cartridges, mounted my pony at three o'clock the next morning to complete my journey.

Day was just breaking when I came to the fork of the trail at Fort Robinson, two miles out from Crawford siding. Both routes led to the grading camp,—one trail lay through White River cañon and the other led to my destination by way of Driftwood. One of these routes I must take, and as the men who were "shadowing" me believed that I would proceed by way of Driftwood I chose the White River cañon route, a rough, new trail that for seventeen miles led through a tumbled, rocky gorge or cañon in the bottom of which rippled merrily the little streamlet that is the beginning of the White River.

I urged my pony forward at a good pace until, after sunrise, I passed a camp of freighters who were preparing their breakfast, and later met several wagons on the move, which relieved the loneliness of my ride and caused me to feel more secure. As the morning was hot and oppressive I now proceeded more slowly.

About half an hour after meeting the freighters I halted at one of the numerous creek crossings, and dismounted to drink and to eat a part of the lunch of crackers and dried beef which I had brought from the commissary tent. As I had no cup I stretched myself out upon the rocks at the edge of the current, and buried my nose in the cool water of the spring-fed stream.

As I lay drinking, with my head just above the water, a distant sound of horses' hoofs struck on my ear. I ceased to drink, listened intently, and soon heard distinctly the noise of horsemen coming rapidly up the cañon.

I sprang to my feet in alarm. My first impulse was to mount my pony and apply the spurs, but as his gait, a racking gallop, was a very slow one, I came to the sudden conclusion to dodge into the brush and let the horsemen, whoever they were, go by. There were a few box alder-trees and several clusters of plum-bush close under the rocks on the right. I grasped the bronco's rein and led him in behind the thickets of thorn and tied him.

I had little time to think or act before the horsemen came up at a gallop; I peered through the leaves as they rattled on, and discovered that there were six riders and that the two strikers were in the lead. They passed my hiding-place without an apparent suspicion that I was concealed there, and, though still much alarmed, I was congratulating myself that I had outwitted them when, just as they rode into the water, my pony lifted up his head and uttered a shrill, inquiring whinny.

The party instantly halted. Every rider turned his face eagerly in my direction, and a half dozen rifles and revolvers were jerked into readiness for action. My pony whinnied again before I could get a grip upon his muzzle, and I felt that unless some unexpectedly fortunate circumstance intervened I should lose the money and probably my life. The horsemen were determined, villainous-looking men, and as I glanced about I saw they had a great advantage over me. The scattered patches of pine scrub on the steep bare sides of the gorge offered me but little shelter for a retreat, and the

"I thrust the Winchester through the tops of a plum bush and fired."—Page 81.

bushes behind which I stood were but a slight protection
against heavy bullets. At the second whinny of my
horse the men dismounted and stood behind their
animals.

"He's in there, sure," I heard one of them say.
"Spread out, boys, an' let's surround them bushes."

Without waiting to hear any more I thrust the Winchester through the tops of a plum bush and fired at
their nearest horse, aiming at its body back of the
shoulder. The animal went down with a groan, and
the man behind it sprang back with a fierce oath.

My only hope now was in swift action and certain
aim. A quick motion of the lever re-loaded and cocked
my Winchester, and almost before the horse had fallen
to the ground I had aimed and fired at the fellow as he
turned to run for cover.

He fell, but got up and ran again. Shifting my aim,
I opened a rapid fire upon the other horses and men.
The robbers returned a few hasty and ineffectual shots,
and then scattered in flight. When I had fired the
seventeen shots, which emptied my repeating rifle, three
horses lay on the borders of the cañon at various dis-
tances away, and one man with a broken leg was
dragging himself toward the shelter of the creek bank.
His companions had fled down the cañon, two on foot
and the others on horseback. Three or four of
their shots had struck in the brush about me, but none
had hit me.

The sudden, fierce determination which had seized
upon me, and the swift, effective firing which followed,
were as much a surprise to myself as they could have
been to the "road agents," who no doubt believed there
was more than one shooter behind the bushes that

sheltered me. I dared not stop to look after the wounded man, who undoubtedly would have fired at me if I had approached him. Mounting my pony and keeping as much as possible under cover of bushes, I rode my animal at his best speed up the cañon.

About five miles from the scene of the shooting I came upon a grader's camp, and sent some of the men to look after the wounded robber and to secure the saddles of the fallen horses.

I afterwards learned that they got the saddles but could find nothing of the man.

H. H. CUMMACY.

VIII.

There were rough times occasionally on the street of Jimtown when big Olaf Helgerson and his friends came in from the Upper Ussawau Lake and made themselves drunk with alcohol and water—not that the water stirred their blood or fired their brains. The Norse settlers of James county generally were of that sober and industrious sort who have borne such a large share in breaking up the great prairies of the North-west and subduing this big wilderness. But among this people, as among all others, there is more or less "bad blood," only in this case it showed itself boldly and badly in the carousings of Olaf and Gulik Helgerson and their neighbors, the Larsens and Joraegs.

One blustering day in December some dozen years ago they came, a half-dozen of them, to town, and began drinking and soon grew riotous. Up and down the single street of Jimtown they caroused from one saloon to another, pouring down fiery alcohol until their faces flamed and their brains reeled, and they swaggered along the sidewalk kicking and cuffing at each other and threatening everyone else who had the hardihood to meet them.

The town people kept indoors, and no one thought of making an arrest. The town depended for its main support upon the Norse trade, and so a Norse frolic was not to be interfered with.

That afternoon, though, matters "came to a head," and the men came out of their stores and shops and overawed the rough Norwegians, drunk as they were. It happened in this wise: Kneut Halvorsen, a Norse lad living at the Lower Ussawau Lake, came in that afternoon to get mail and some medicine for his mother, who was ailing with rheumatism.

The post-office was kept at "Iliff's" drug store, and as Kneut stepped in there were a number of loafers seated about the big box-stove listening to one of "Old Iliff's" many stories. The old man paused in his narrations and spoke to Kneut.

"Kneut," said he, "Helgerson and his crowd, I s'pose you know, are in town t'day, but mebby ye didn't know that they're drunk as loons and knockin' everybody off the walks? Better git yer mail 'n' go right home."

"Faal," said Kneut, "I ton't alfays pe koin to run afay fon Olaf Helgerson. I kot me yust so koot a ride to keep een te town uss he haf.

"Wall," replied the old man, "I was only givin' ye fair warnin';" and he resumed his story. But his hearers' interest flagged, in view of Kneut's combative spirit, and while Tom Iliff, Jr., was "putting up" a prescription for Mrs. Halvorsen's rheumatism they watched the young Norwegian curiously.

Presently Kneut turned from his purchases and left the store.

"There'll be a fight, sure," said one of the loungers; and he went to one of the front windows and scratched the frost from a pane that he might look out upon the street.

The quarrel of Helgerson with the Halvorsens had long since become common stock in Jimtown's affairs of local interest, and dated back to the first Norse settlement of James county, when Kneut and Gus Halvorsen were lads. It came about by the death of widow Halvorsen's brother, Eric Brakstead, who owed Olaf Helgerson for a yoke of oxen. Eric's claim joined that of his sister, and they lived together-and helped each other in improving their new land. Kneut and Gus were old enough to drive teams, and the widow had two yoke of oxen of her own, their interests being kept separate, although they worked often together. In the spring Eric had bought a yoke of steers of Olaf Helgerson, giving a note due in six months, when he expected his wheat harvest would enable him to pay it.

Bad luck followed. In June one of the steers was struck by lightning, grasshoppers came and devoured the growing wheat, and that same autumn poor Eric was taken with typhoid fever and died, leaving his claim to be immediately jumped by the first land-seeker. Helgerson went to the widow with Eric's note and demanded payment when it came due. She informed her neighbor that her poor brother had died owing her money, and that it would be impossible for her to pay his other debts; but she told him there was the other ox left, which, of course, she should expect him to take.

Eric went away in a great rage and immediately brought suit against her. The jury, of course, returned him his ox, but gave her the verdict. From that time on Olaf Helgerson, a wild, rough, passionate fellow, spared no pains to vent his hatred in all ways that he dared against the widow and her boys.

He often threatened Kneut and Gus with terrible threshings, but up till this December day he had never touched either of them. The boys often met their belligerent neighbor upon the road, at the Lutheran church between the lakes, or at other Norse gatherings. However, they had for several years carefully avoided going to town when they knew that Olaf would be there, and as the road from Upper Ussawau to Jimtown ran directly past their door they generally knew when he went or returned. Indeed, they were very likely to know when he came home, for he was nearly always "in liquor" and would shout and curse at them or at the house as he rode by.

But Kneut had grown large and strong as a man, and he had heard Olaf's threats so often that they had become tame; in fact, he had never been afraid of Helgerson, but, knowing the latter's habit of drunken brawling when in town, in keeping away he had acted prudently and in accord with his mother's wishes. Then, too, Olaf, who was a natural leader, had drawn a rough crowd around him who generally shared his drunken bouts and also his quarrels.

Kneut was of a peaceable disposition, a hard-working and honest lad, who desired no quarrel with any one. But this day as he stepped out of "Iliff's" Olaf Helgerson was coming down the opposite side of the street, boisterously drunk and aggressive. He saw Kneut and instantly started across, wading in the snow, wildly swinging his arms and shouting all sorts of threats. Gulik, Olaf's brother, Ole Larsen, and Snell Joraeg followed.

At sight of them and at the word "coward," which they shouted at him, Kneut's young blood boiled. Regardless of consequences he stepped down from the sidewalk and threw off his big knit scarf, his overcoat, and sheep-skin mittens, and with clinched hands awaited them.

"Will you pay me seventy-five dollars?" shouted the drunken Olaf, as he came up; he spoke in the Norse tongue, and flourished his big fists at Kneut's face by way of emphasizing the demand.

"No," replied Kneut; and, fiercely clinching, the two whirled round and round, wrestling and jerking each other about in the snow.

Kneut was strong and sober, and, being a good wrestler, as soon as he "got his head" gave Olaf a sudden trip and flung the tipsy fellow headlong in the snow and then sprang upon him. Then, I suspect, had it not been for his brother, with Ole and Snell, all too brutally tipsy to think of fair play, Olaf Helgerson would have received a sound hammering from Kneut's tough knuckles. But these three now pounced upon Kneut, and, seizing him by the arms and legs, tore him away from Olaf and began dragging him along the street. Olaf staggered to his feet and came after them, swearing loudly at Kneut and threatening dire vengeance.

But the man at Iliff's window, and a number of others at various points on the street, had seen the scuffle, and by that magic which draws people so quickly together at exciting scenes, a crowd gathered and attacked Kneut's tormentors, wrenching them away and driving them from him. The plucky lad was bruised severely in many places, where Olaf had brutally kicked him, but the townsmen were roughly sympathetic, a number of them insisting, in spite of his declaration that he "fan't mooch hoorted," on taking him into "Iliff's" to have his hurts examined, and, if need be, dressed. Others hunted up the constable and assisted the officer to arrest the four drunken fellows and lock them in an old coal-bin, which had been fitted up as a "calaboose."

Kneut's bruises were only black and blue spots on his legs and one arm, and after Tom Iliff had rubbed them well with a patent liniment he went out, got on his horse, and set out for home.

On the road he had time to think coolly—very coolly, if the weather were to be taken into consideration—and in spite of the indignities he had received, he began to regret that he had not walked rapidly off, as he might have done, and get out of the way of Olaf.

"I had no business fighting with drunken brutes like the Helgersons and those other fellows," he thought, "and it will make mother feel badly."

But before reaching home he had something else to think of; the wind suddenly increased to a gale, the clouds thickened and grew dark, and the snow came down in stinging scuds, driving directly in his face. The storm had come on a blizzard, and his horse, a young colt, snorted wildly and shook his head in a protest against facing it. Kneut urged the animal forward, as he had several miles yet to go, and knew from experience that the storm was likely to increase in violence rapidly until midnight or later. Keeping the colt at a stiff trot, and bending forward to break the force of the blinding drift, he managed to keep the road, which, lying in the path of the wind, was in most places swept bare. He had nearly reached the outlet at the foot of Lower Ussawau, when a team with a sleigh attached came dashing up and passed him.

He knew the team at a glance. It was Olaf Helgerson's and Olaf was lying in the bottom of the sleigh, too drunk, probably, to sit up, and one line was dragging. The horses were going at a keen gallop, and, of course, without any control; they ran with their heads low, snorting loudly, and evidently keeping the road by instinct rather than sight. They were young spirited animals, which Olaf had raised and of whose speed he boasted greatly.

"They'll break his drunken neck before he gets home with them," thought Kneut, "or they'll throw him out where he'll freeze to death." This last catastrophe seemed so probable that Kneut, in alarm, forgot, all other feeling toward Olaf Helgerson, and whipped his colt into a run to overtake the sleigh.

He came up with it just at the crossing of the outlet; here, when the sleighing was bad on the road, Helgerson sometimes turned off and went home on an old "hay road" which led through the marshes on the east side of the lake, and here his team, no doubt sheering off to avoid facing the storm directly, took up the old trail which led along the east shore of Lower Ussawau. There were no houses to be met in that direction for several miles, the land being a succession of swamps separated by "hard-head" ridges; the region, several miles in extent each way, was known as Lonesome Township.

Kneut, alarmed at being turned away from the main road even for a moment, ran his colt alongside the run-aways, and tried to reach the bridle-rein of the nearest; but the colt he rode, only half-broken, was both "skittish" and unruly, and, try as he might, he could not get the animal near enough to let him grasp a rein or a line. He then made a desperate effort to get in front of the flying horses and stop them; but again the unruly colt, frantic with his lashing and the pelting of

He then made a desperate effort to get in front of the flying horses.—Page 89.

the storm, proved intractable, and would only rear and plunge in an effort to keep out of the way of the team.

Failing in this attempt Kneut reined up for a moment, half tempted to let the team go with its helpless master, trusting their instinct to get him home safely. But no, he could not do that. Olaf was lying there like a log, with his big buffalo coat on and also a robe thrown partly over him; but even if he were not freezing already another half-hour of such stupor in a biting storm, Kneut reasoned, would surely finish him.

The tipsy fellow had no doubt broken away from his jail, or given bail, and had started for home, trusting to his horses to take him through, as they had been known to do on two or three occasions. No; plainly Kneut could not desert him in this howling storm, with all that waste of country to traverse and no guide but the instinct of dumb brutes.

All this came to the brave lad much more quickly than I have written it, and no doubt in different form, but, at any rate, he urged his colt forward in the trail of the sleigh, determined to follow until a chance offered for gaining control of the team.

Several times he attempted to ride alongside, with the purpose of flinging himself out of the saddle and into the sleigh-box, but the unmanageable colt each time foiled him by plunging and floundering and falling back in the rear.

Presently, striking a long flat where the ground had been burned bare by the fall fires, and the covering of snow was light, Olaf's team quickened their pace to a stiff run, and then for some minutes there followed a race in which Kneut could barely keep in sight of the runaways. The old hay-road had disappeared entirely, and the storm was growing thicker every moment. The snow whistled across, cutting Kneut's cheek as he bent forward and filling space with a thick white dust through which he had to strain his sight to penetrate even the distance of a few rods.

It was a perilous, a despairing chase; no road left, the lake-shore out of sight, the direction no longer certain, night coming on, and the furious blizzard growing thicker and colder each moment. Even should the horses hold out, and all survive until the surrounding settlement could be reached, darkness must first overtake them, and through that blinding drift of snow no light could be seen at a hopeful distance.

All this Kneut realized and was terribly frightened; but he pressed on heroically, digging his heels into the colt's ribs and urging it on with his voice and managing to keep the sleigh and the flying team in sight. The effort kept him warm. Suddenly the ground grew rough and boggy and the colt stumbled and fell, pitching Kneut over its head and wedging him between two hummocks so tightly that it took him some seconds to extricate himself. He had clutched the bridle-rein tightly, so tightly that it had broken at the buckle, and as he struggled finally to his feet he still held the long end in his hand while the colt snorted and floundered about him among the bogs and snow.

Kneut hastily rebuckled the rein and mounted. He could no longer see the sleigh, but there was still the trail, though fast filling up, where the plunging team had wallowed through the snow amid the bogs. He followed for a few rods and came within sight of an object which proved to be the sleigh without the horses; the beam of the front "bob" had struck solidly against a frozen hummock and the runner had broken, leaving the team free of burden.

Kneut hastily tumbled off his horse, tied its halter to a ring in the end rod of the sleigh-box, and hurried around to Olaf, who lay motionless in a kind of heap where he had been thrown by the jolt into the front end of the box.

A moment's examination proved that Helgerson was alive and not yet badly chilled, for his face was flushed and he was actually snoring in a drunken stupor of sleep. Kneut shook him roughly, and even pounded him in an effort to arouse, but could only get him to fling his arms about and mumble drunkenly while the snow pelted down in his face.

Kneut, finding it impossible to get him awake, ceased trying, and looked about in desperation to see what, if any thing, might be done to save him from freezing to death—as he must soon, exposed in this helpless condition.

The Norse lad did not stop to think of his own perilous situation. A glance about him discovered the fact that the sleigh had lodged at the edge of a slough and that a dense growth of tall rushes was in sight a few yards distant. They had been too green to burn when the early fall fire had swept across them, and it was in such rush brake, he remembered, that, years before, the deer used to take refuge from the winter's cold and storms.

His plan was formed at once, and, going to his colt he deliberately stripped it of saddle and bridle and turned it loose. "Save yourself if you can, Jan," said he, and the animal plunged out of sight while he was speaking.

Kneut then turned his attention to Olaf. He wrapped the buffalo-robe and blanket which lay in the bottom of the sleigh-box about the stupid man, rolling him in them; then, seizing him about the waist, lifted his limp body out of the sleigh. Then, with a mighty effort, he tugged his big enemy forward, dragging Olaf's long legs among the bogs, through the snow and in among the rushes. He pushed on, puffing and even sweating with exertion, until he had reached a point within the brake where the thicket became so dense that he could no longer get on and carry his burden. Then he dropped Olaf, and with his hands broke down the rushes in front, making a path some rods further. Here he could scarcely feel the wind, and, thankful enough to have found such fortunate shelter, went back and dragged the stupid Helgerson to it. Then, clearing away a little spot and piling the rushes at one edge for fire-wood, he opened Helgerson's big coat and searched the pockets of his inside garments, and luckily, with a pipe and a package of tobacco, in one of them was a box of matches. Then, rolling Olaf up in his robe and blanket again, he got down over the pile of rushes and managed to light them.

And now began a strange and wearisome night vigil.

Darkness was already coming on, and Kneut began industriously breaking rushes for fuel. He broke them upon the windward side and threw them in heaps upon the fire. An armful of them would not burn three minutes, but that made no difference; the fire must be kept going, and undauntedly he worked on for hours and hours.

He had laid Olaf as close to the blaze as he dared,

and occas onally he turned his huge bundle over that the heat might get a chance at both sides.

Once and a while he pounded Helgerson vigorously and then listened to his breathing, but he could only spare a moment in each effort to awake the sleeper, as the fire had to be kept going at all hazards.

The circle of open space in front of the blaze grew wider as Kneut broke the rushes and threw them on. They were so thick, though, that an armful could be gathered without stepping out of his tracks. Steadily he worked, while the storm whistled and howled about his head, and the swaying rushes alternated with the driving snow in dealing him stinging cuts upon the face.

It was nearly morning when Olaf, after a pounding, came to himself, and, after rubbing his eyes and mumbling in a growling voice for a bit, sat up before the fire. Curiously and half-dazedly he watched Kneut coming and going at the fire.

Presently Kneut threw on an extra large armful and stopped in front of Olaf.

"Halloo, Olaf Helgerson!" he shouted. "Do you know where you are?"

Olaf gazed at him earnestly for a minute.

"You are Kneut Halvorsen," he said. "How came we here?"

And then, while feeding the flame lightly with a fresh bundle of rushes, Kneut told his story.

When he had finished Olaf staggered to his feet and threw his arms about Kneut.

"Kneut, Kneut?" he burst out, hugging the lad close to him, "I've got my pay! I've got my pay!" And the big rough fellow, in his wonder and gratitude, wept like a child, while Kneut supported his unsteady limbs. He had sobered suddenly and thoroughly, and after Kneut had helped to walk him about a bit gained the use of his limbs, and for the balance of the night helped Kneut to keep the fire going.

While walking about Olaf told how he remembered rushing against the door of the "calaboose," breaking it down and running for his sleigh, but he could remember nothing further.

Morning came soon, and though it was still storming hard, the air was not so filled with snow as it had been, and they managed, by rightly calculating the direction of the wind, to gain the lake shore, and from that point it was an easy matter to find the way around to Kneut's home, just above Elk Grove Point. Widow Halvorsen's surprise was as great as her anxiety had been; and, when her son and her late enemy had recounted their story while warming themselves at the fire, her thankfulness was greatly increased to know that the night's adventure had made them friends as well as brought them safe out of the storm.

By almost a miracle of instinct or luck Olaf's horses reached his house in safety and found their way into his cattle-shed, where they spent the night among the cows; but Kneut's colt perished in the blizzard, and was found afterwards some five miles east of the lakes. It had, no doubt, run until exhausted, and then lain down to freeze.

Olaf replaced Kneut's loss with another horse, insisting that even then he was, and always would be, Kneut's debtor, and since that night his neighbors declare that he has been a good neighbor and a decent man.

IX.

At nine o'clock one September even ig in 1876 I took
the coach which left Custer City—o₊ Custer Village,
for the town consisted of twenty or thirty log struc-
tures—to go to Sidney, Nebraska. A coach, I suppose
it should be called, though on t'.e plains this vehicle,
which has the driver's seat on che same level as the
passengers' seats, is called a "ₐack."

I had gone to the "Hills" to engage in mining, but
after four months of prospe ,ting had decided to open a
general supply-store at tl ₊ new town of Deadwood,
and was on my way to Cₘaha to purchase goods for
the venture.

A tin lamp, fastened iₐ one corner of the "hack,"
discovered to me two passengers within as I entered
and took my seat. One was an old gentleman, apparently weak and ill, for, although it was not a cold
night, he was muffled in a coarse, heavy ulster overcoat. Moreover, so much of his face as I could see
between a gray beard which almost covered it and the
rim of a slouch hat was pale and thin, and the eyes
looked sunken and unnatural. At least, so it struck me
at a cursory glance.

The other passenger was a young fellow of twenty-
two or twenty-three years, I judged, decidedly dandi-
fied in his dress for that region. He wore a stiff hat
and a stand-up collar encircled by a neat tie, and had
on a dark suit, evidently custom-made, which was an
unusual "get-up" for that region, and one which at

once aroused my suspicion, for the only persons I had
seen about the mining towns dressed in anything like
that fashion were gamblers, a class of men I had made
it a point to avoid.

Just before setting out the driver came to the side
of the vehicle, thrust in a light Winchester carbine,
and placed it between my knees.

"I see you didn't have no gun," said he, "an' I keep
a couple of extra ones fer sech."

That was all. No further explanation was necessary
in those days.

I took charge of the weapon, although I was as little
expert in its use as I was in handling the Smith &
Wesson in my hip-pocket, which, indeed, I had never
yet discharged.

I knew enough of life in the mines to know that the
"bad man with a gun" is usually the man who gets
into difficulty rather than the peaceful and unarmed
citizen; but a stage-ride from Custer to Sidney at that
time was a trip not altogether likely to be without
its adventures, and for once I regretted my unfamiliar-
ity with "shooting irons."

It occurred to me that if we were "jumped by road
agents," as the phrase went, the freebooters of the
route would have little to fear from the occupants of
the hack, whether they got much money or not.

There were usually valuables of some sort in the iron
box under the driver's seat.

The young man who sat opposite me nau a carbine
across his lap, but I fancied he knew even less of its
use than I did. As we started he sat, without noticing
me, twirling a slight mustache and humming a tune.

" A fresh gamester, if one at all," I said to myself upon a second look at him.

The old man had no arms in sight. The driver no doubt regarded him as out of the fight at any event.

As we rolled on up into Buffalo Gap I had a few words of conversation with my companions. I learned that the elder was an Iowa farmer who had come out to see what he could do in the new mines, but he had been ill with mountain fever,and afterward attacked by rheumatism, so that he had been forced to abandon his projects and return to the East. He spoke freely, and in the careless English of Western men.

The young fellow said he was from New York. " Neh Yawk," he pronounced it. He was, he said, a student of mining engineering, but he did not mention what his business had been in that region; but that was not strange, for we could not talk much. A jolting stage bowling over a rough country at eight miles an hour does not give the best opportunity for conversation.

I soon became sleepy, and leaning back in my corner, took such momentary cat-naps as the nature of the road permitted. At eleven o'clock we made a brief halt at a temporary stage station, where the driver's four-in-hand team was exchanged for fresh horses.

I peeped out, and got a glimpse of the teams, of two men with a lantern, of a low structure of sod or adobe faintly outlined, and of the black side of a pine-covered mountain beyond. The night was quite dark, with floating clouds and no moon. It became somewhat lighter as we passed out of the gap a little later, as I noted through a crack in the swaying " flap " opposite.

The road was now smoother, and I settled back in

my corner, as my companions had done, to get a little
solid sleep if possible. I dozed off for a time, but was
awakened by the groaning of the old man beside me.
He seemed to be in great pain, and writhed about nervously. I asked him what was the trouble. He
replied that the rheumatism in his legs was nearly killing him.

"I wisht the driver'd let me aout when we git t' th'
nex' crick. He'll water likely, 'n' I've jest got t' stretch
my legs er die. Ye see I'm troubled with cramp rheumatism, an' th' ain't no room in hyer t' get the cramp
out o' my legs."

I told him I would speak to the driver when we
halted, a few minutes later, at the bank of a stream—
White River, I believe. I thrust my head out at the
side, and asked that the old gentleman might be let out
for a moment to stretch his legs.

"All right!" said the driver, as he clambered down
from his own seat. "I'm goin' ter oncheck 'n' let the
hosses take a pull at th' drink."

I then helped the old man to dismount, steadying him
by the arm as he got down. He seemed to have a good
deal of difficulty in alighting, and groaned in a most
lugubrious fashion. The flap swung to after him, as I
had unbuttoned it all around to let him out. The young
man opposite me lay curled up on his seat, but I could
see that his eyes were wide open, and that he was eying
me with a sharp, keen glance. My eyes probably
responded when they fell upon his, for he straightened
up in an alert fashion, and leaned toward me.

"Say," he whispered, "do you think that old chap's
all right? Strikes me that groaning of his was put on.
What dy'e think?"

The question startled me no less than the young fellow's manner, and I was about to make some reply when a gun or pistol shot rang in our ears, followed by a yell either of pain or surprise, and a lurch of the hack threw me forward against my companion's knees.

Either the shot or the yell had startled our team, and we went down the bank and into the stream with a lunge. I heard shots—one, two, three—as we splashed through the water. Then more yells, loud and fierce.

My notion of what had happened or was happening was confused for a moment, and then I saw my comrade—for the light still burned—crawling through to the driver's seat as we went careening up the opposite bank.

A second later he had gathered the lines, which were tied in front, and while he held them with one hand he grasped a front rib of the hack with the other. Then he leaned out and glanced back.

Luckily the horses, which were going at a gallop—they were animals which needed no urging—kept to the road, and the cool-headed young fellow was not pitched out.

" There's a lot of 'em," he shouted in at me a moment later. " I can just see four or five getting onto their horses. They've killed the driver, I guess, and after us now! "

With that he gathered up the long-lashed whip, which lay in the boot, and dropping upon his knees began yelling and laying the whip upon the team.

In a moment we were going at a fearful pace, and despite the excitement and fright of the moment I noticed that our four horses came to hand and ran with a steady, even gait which did credit to the young man's driving.

"Get ready for 'em now!" he screamed back at me; "they'll be down on us in a minute. Open the back flap 'n' pour it into 'em with your guns, and when they're empty get mine under the seat!"

He was my captain as well as driver, and I obeyed instinctively, for I certainly had formed no plan of defense or action on my own account.

I managed to unbutton and roll up the leather behind, and peering out, on my knees before the back seat, I saw that we were indeed followed. It was light enough to distinguish objects dimly at a hundred yards, and there were at least five horsemen in our rear, tearing along at the top of their animals' speed. Knowing that they were within rifle-shot I opened fire on them over the seat. I worked the lever of my gun as rapidly as I could, but made awkward business of it. Presently I got a shell stuck, and began trying to get it out. In the meantime our pursuers were gaining with every second.

They were within fifty yards before I could get out my shell and I was too excited to think of using another gun. Suddenly the light in the hack went out, and a hand upon my shoulder jerked me backward. Then a voice yelled in my ear:

"Let me get at them! Load the guns for me, 'n' let the team go. We might's well smash as be riddled by bullets. Here, here's two boxes of cartridges!"

I dropped back to the other seat and gave place to him. He threw his carbines over the back of the hind seat and began firing.

Crack! crack! crack! It seemed to me that a

steady stream of fire poured out of the back of the stage, and before I had filled the magazine of my gun, his was empty. He snatched mine, however, and thrust his own back at me.

Loading was awkward business at first, as I had to feel for the feeder, but I managed soon to thrust them into my gun as fast as he could work the lever of his own. The men, whoever and whatever they were, rode up to within twenty-five or thirty yards, and, spreading out, opened fire on us.

" Keep close down in the bottom ! " shouted my comrade, as he kept on with his firing.

The " road agents " did not come nearer, evidently fearing too great exposure to the stream of shots from the hack, and my courage rose to something near the level of my companion's. I caught glimpses, as I glanced up now and then, of a plunging horse-man with shadowy, outstretched arm, from which flashed blaze after blaze of light.

All at once we began descending into a gulley, and the hack bounced from side to side so violently that it was impossible for us to do anything but cling to the sides of the box.

" It's all right ! " rang my companion's voice in my ear, shortly after we had begun the descent ; " they've quit. They can't ride along the side of the gulch, and daren't follow straight behind. There's a stage ranch below, too. I remember the road."

Sure enough, the men had dropped back, and the shots ceased. My cool, brave comrade now clambered over me, and in some way got into the front seat of the jumping coach. A moment later I noticed that we were slowing up and running more steadily. Five

minutes more we halted, what was left of us, safe and
round in front of a stage station.

Our story was soon told, our horses exchanged and
a fresh driver, doubly armed, put with us.   Such little
accidents did not stop stages in those parts.

There was no danger, they told us, from that same
gang.   The three men who were left promised to go
immediately and look after our other driver.

It was only the darkness and the motion of the
vehicle and horses that had saved us from being hit.

We found several bullet marks about the coach next
morning; one of them, well aimed, had gone through
the back seat at an angle and into the front, and must
have passed directly between us.   My respect for my
young companion was greatly raised by the events of
that night, and was further increased by an after
acquaintance which discovered his real modesty and
worth.

On my return to the " Hills," I learned that our
driver had been picked up at the crossing of the creek,
badly wounded, and also that the brave fellow had
yelled to the team to go the very second he was hit.
He had been carried to Sidney.   As to the rheumatic
old man, he was, of course, a rascal in league with the
band who had attacked us.

X.

CARLEN AND HIS COMET.

Several years ago, if one had been traveling through Lake Township, in a county of eastern Dakota, and had inquired who was its best known and most reputable citizen, the answer in almost every case would have been Emmet Carlen, and almost any settler could have pointed out on the level prairie, from his own door, the house and buildings of the young Norwegian upon the crest of "Tip-Top Knoll," at the head of Rush Lake.

Emmet began life in Lake Township as many other Norsemen in many other regions of our New West have done, with no possessions save a change of clothing ; but, at the end of a few years, he had, by his thrift and industry, secured and improved a new farm, and placed himself on the sure road to comfort and plenty.

At the time of which I write, however, it was not so much his thrift that made him a marked man, but a certain daring, cool-headedness which he had always displayed when courage and intrepidity were demanded

Once, at his own great peril, he had carried food and extra clothing to a school-teacher and a half-dozen small children who were confined in a little school-house, nearly a mile from any habitation, by one of the fiercest blizzards ever known in that region. This happened during the first year of his stay there, and while he was working for his board and attending school with the little ones whose lives he saved.

Strangely enough, he was again to figure as the rescuer of two of these same children from another

sweeping storm, one even more terrible than the dreaded
blizzard, a storm of fire, as it swept over the tall, dry
grass of the unbroken prairie.

To this exploit, however, there was another party,
Emmet's big steer, "Comet," without whose aid, indeed,
the children must have perished.

This animal was quite as noteworthy as his master.
"Comet" was a huge, long-legged, long-horned steer.
For two years Emmet had only his help in plowing
and cultivating the "Tip-Top" homestead, except that
the breaking of sod was done by hired "breakers."

The young Norseman hitched his steer to a heavy
cart, and drove him to market at the small but ambitious town of Boomerang, eight miles distant. In winter, when snow fell and the roads were good, a light
sled took the place of the cart.

Before the sled Comet soon gained a local reputation
for speed upon the road. His gait was a steady, long-
stepping trot, like that of an elk, and nearly as swift.
At any rate, it was soon an admitted fact that there
were no horses in the neighborhood that could pass
Comet in a trotting-match. This was abundantly
proved by many races along the road to town and
back, where the drivers of the teams or single horses
had tried and failed to "go by" the fleet steer.

Comet had taken his name from a former owner, and
it was given him because of his wonderful speed and a
habit of flying his long tail as a horizontal streamer
while "cutting" away from the herd and the herder's
pony. The owner was willing to sell the animal cheap,
because he was unruly and hard to break. Emmet
heard of the chance to buy, and bethought him of the
plan, often adopted in Norway, of driving oxen singly.

But he had no ready money. Although he had strong objections to running into debt, he did so now, and obtained Comet by giving his note for twenty dollars. Then, having fashioned a yoke and harness of the Norse pattern, he set to work with characteristic patience and kindness to bring the big, headstrong animal "under the yoke."

His success, though won after a hard struggle, was complete, and, in a few weeks Comet, hitched to a vehicle made from two wheels of an old wagon, with Emmet seated upon the axle, was driven to Boomerang. There the young fellow bought a few boards at the lumber yard, nailed together a rough box, secured it by bolts and braces to the axle which had served him for a seat, and rode home in triumph.

That autumn Emmet bought a small ten-inch stirring plough, and turned over ten acres of sod. The steer pulled the implement with ease after a short training.

The next year another ten acres was broken upon the homestead, and Comet was still sufficient for all Emmet's purposes. It was in October of this year that the event which is the subject of this narrative occurred.

Emmet was ploughing. The day was one of those common to that season in new prairie regions, smoky, with a strong northwest wind smelling of burned grass, a fine dust of cinders sifting down, and sun shining through smoke and dust with a dull red glare. But as Emmet had sometime before burned a broad "fire break ' around his shanty, grain and haystacks, he noted these evidences of raging fires without uneasiness. They came at some time every autumn.

It was about the middle of the afternoon that little

Jake and Lib Walker came into his field, bringing some grain bags which Emmet had lent their father to use during his threshing the week before.

Walker lived at the foot of Rush Lake, about a mile from the school house, where the young Norwegians had taken lessons in English, and these little fellows, Jake and Lib, had been his schoolmates when the "big blizzard" came, cutting them off suddenly from home and imperilling their lives.

"Hal-lo, Yakie; hal-lo, Libbie! You a koot fays from home, aint it?" was Emmet's greeting as the lads came up, each staggering under a back-load of sacks.

"We've been a good deal further'n this more'n once," said Jake, "and we've got to go clear round the lake 'n' drive the cows home yit to-night. They're away over yonder," pointing across the lake, "where the wild rice grows 'long the edge, and pa's gone to town."

"Sit you ride town on t'em packs t'ere," said Emmet, "unt rest yo' lecks, unt I feel let Comet rest, too. I did tink meppe as I coot feenish tot bloughin' py night-time put I ton't know off I ken to ut."

And then, seated on the plough-beam, he talked pleasantly with the boys for a few minutes, then telling them that he would carry the sacks to the house when he turned out, bade them "look out unt not ket lost een t'em tall krasses,"—tall grass—as they trudged sturdily away toward the upper end of the lake.

The lads had been gone from the field about half an hour when Emmet noted with alarm that the smoke which had pervaded the air all day had thickened, until now the sun was almost clouded over, showing only a dull red disk. The smell of burning grass had grown more pungent.

His fears were aroused wholly on account of the two boys who had gone to the other side of the lake. The field in which he was at work lay upon the south side of the hill upon which his shanty stood, shutting off the view to north and west, from whence the wind was blowing.

He unhitched Comet at once, and drove him at a trot to the top of the hill.

No sooner had he reached the crest than he saw cause enough for alarm. Not two miles away to the northwest dense volumes of smoke were rising and rolling forward over a broad stretch of prairie. A big prairie fire was sweeping down at a tremendous rate of speed, the "head fire" lining out directly toward the head of the lake.

What could he do to save those two boys? was the young Norwegian's first thought. They must be even at that moment, he thought, well round the head of the lake, wading through the tall grass of the flat. There was no bank to the lake upon that side; wild rice and tall rushes grew far out into the water, and this swamp growth would burn to its very edge. He could not race with the fire on foot, and he doubted if even a horse would be able to outstrip it, but he instantly resolved to make the trial with Comet.

He had frequently ridden the big fellow, who had become as docile and obedient as a dog, to and from the field, hawing and geeing him about at will. Now, if possible, he would ride the fleet-footed steed to some purpose. To throw off the yoke and harness, tie a rope around the animal's body to cling to, and another to either horn to serve as reins, was the work of a minute; then, whip in hand, Emmet mounted and was off.

Comet, feeling a few stinging blows of the whip, broke away at his swiftest trot. Although his gait had more than once defied the best trotters of the settlement, the big steer could hold it with ease for a length of time that seemed incredible. In fact, as had been proved when Comet ran wild among the settlement herds, the animal was as nearly tireless as flesh and blood could be.

But it was a rough ride, and Emmet was obliged to cling tightly with one hand to the girth-rope, while managing reins and whip with the other.

The whip, however, was not needed, and the rider had only to yell "Hi! Hi!" to keep the steer flying at his best gait. With head up and tail streaming, Comet rounded the point of the lake, some half-mile from the knoll cabin, just as the "head fire" reached the upper end of the flat which lay to west and north of the lake.

That "head fire" was now not a mile distant, and was coming directly down the flat which followed the southeast trend of the lake.

The smoke had grown so thick that Emmet could only see a few hundred feet ahead, but he kept well within sight of the lake shore, knowing that the boys could not have gone far down as yet, and that they were not likely to wander far from the lake's edge, for fear of getting lost. Their cattle, too, would be found along shore, feeding upon the rice-heads.

"Hi! Hi! Hi!"

Away they tore through the high grass, across ditches, over rough, boggy spots, the rider getting a terrible pounding, the steer possessed of but one instinct, it seemed—to respond to those sharp yells with the utmost possible strides of his long, fleet legs.

The fire meanwhile was gaining every moment, in spite of his tremendous exertion. Emmet could see that the smoke closed in thicker, and feel that the air was growing hot and oppressive.

But suddenly two little dark objects appeared a few yards ahead, bobbing above the waving grass.

Emmet gave a shout of delight; it was the black heads of Jake and Lib, nodding as they ran. Their hats were off, and they were running as fast as the wilderness of grass would let them.

In an instant Comet was alongside, and, with a few sharp whoas and a hard pull at the reins, Emmet managed to stop him but a few yards in front of the boys.

They ran to him with eager shouts, their fright turned to joy at the sight of him. But without waiting to answer them he leaned forward, caught Lib by the arm, and swung him up in front, then helped Jake to scramble on behind.

"Hank tight to me, Yake," he said; then, throwing an arm around Lib and grasping the rope, he dug his heels into Comet's ribs, and with a shrill "Hi! Hi!" set the steer off again at a swinging pace.

The crackle and roar of the fire could plainly be heard as they started, and Comet, either objecting to his additional burden or uneasy at the smell and the roar of the fire, began snorting and throwing his head on either side ominously.

Emmet feared that the steer would become unmanageable, and as a last resort, determined to run him into the lake and make a swim for it. Somewhere not far below, he knew there was an arm of the lake about one hundred yards wide, extending out a considerable distance into the flat, and this arm, or bayou, he had hoped to reach.

He knew that Comet would not hesitate an instant to plunge into it and swim,—the steer had been known

"Hank tight to me, Yake."—Page 111.

to swim clear across the lake itself,—and once upon the other side, he could soon make his little party safe.

Suddenly the smoke lifted, and he ventured a glance backward. The sight was appalling! The smoke, driven upward by the rush of heated air, was flying above their heads, leaving the jumping flames in plain view.

The head fire was not a quarter-mile distant, Emmet judged, and was bearing down on them with terrible speed, the flames shooting higher than he had ever seen them rise before.

Little Jake and Lib clung to him without a word, while Comet threw his head about and snorted more violently than before.

But suddenly there was a strip of water before them; the arm of the lake had been reached. A moment more, and they were into it with a splash, and Comet was swimming with his heavy burden and carrying it more easily than he had been able to bear it upon land; but his body sank until the water came up to Jake's waist, and nothing but the nose and horns of the steer could be seen.

But swimming was much slower work than running had been, and by the time the opposite shore was reached the fire was already roaring at the other edge.

Emmet leaped off into the edge of the water, and pulled Jake and Lib with him.

"Here!" he shouted, giving them the ropes. "Hank tite to 'im; ton't let 'im loose off you can hold to 'im. You yust so safe as to home now."

They obeyed manfully, and Emmet, drawing a match-box from his vest pocket, dropped upon his knees at the nearest dry place, and, lighting a match, held his hat over it until the flame had touched the blades of grass which he bent toward it; then he stepped back into the water and took charge of the steer again.

The flames on the other side had now reached the

water's edge, and bunches of burning grass were blown toward them.

For an instant the heat was intense, almost scorching. Great tongues of angry flame lapped over among the waters and reached out toward them. Then, with a final cracking *whish!* they died out, leaving a black, smoking surface beyond.

The fire swept on around the bayou, but meanwhile Emmet's small blaze sprang up and stretched away, gathering force and speed as it swept a wider space.

Comet took things quietly after his swim, which had cooled his skin, and his dripping coat of hair served to protect him from the violent heat which reigned for a moment.

" Fäll," said Emmet, when the coast was clear, " Fäll, little poys, ve kin ko to you' house now."

Walker's house was only a mile distant, but they reached it long after the fire had passed, and found that Mrs. Walker had been nearly wild about her boys until she saw them coming.

" I might have known you'd save 'em," she said to Emmet, while grateful tears ran down her face, as she listened to the story of their escape. Their cattle had taken fright and come home about an hour before.

XI.

CAUGHT IN A BLIZZARD.

The tremendous hurricane of snow and wind which swept over our great, level Northwest in January, 1888, was accompanied by incidents tragic, thrilling and heroic, that will no doubt become a part of the history of the vast region over which the storm swept.

In northwestern Iowa the blizzard descended with a suddenness and fury which made the early settlers shudder as they thought of the barren, unprotected prairies of fifteen or twenty years before. "If 'twasn't for our maple and cottonwood groves and big fields of cornstalks," said they, "wouldn't we ketch it?"

Happily, we had these protections, and suffered neither loss of life nor great inconvenience, though we complained more or less because our daily mails were cut off and our freights delayed even for a short period. But really our most important grievance when we are visited by these occasional fierce storms in winter is the stoppage of hay hauling, pressing and shipping, which is our chief industry at that season.

It was in connection with hay hauling in one of our marshy, unsettled townships that there occurred an incident of extreme peril, of fortitude and intelligent exercise of the faculties amid great danger, which, at the time it came to light, was almost lost sight of in our interest in the widespread calamities which fell upon our unprepared neighbors on the more newly settled prairies of the North and West.

The little railway station of Dupont, in one of the
thinly settled districts, was built entirely in the interests of the hay-pressing business, for which the unin-
habited flats of Lowland and Gull Lake townships
furnish thousands of tons of grass.

The land in these townships is mostly owned by
Eastern speculators, who obtained it cheaply under the
first Entry Laws and the Swamp Land Act. Although
much of it is excellent farm land, these owners have
held the price so high as to keep off the actual settlers
entirely. This they have been able to do by renting
the lands for pasturage and haymaking, and getting
enough out of the rent to pay the taxes, and even in
some cases a fair interest on the first investment, which
was extremely small.

Over this tract, a dozen miles in extent, as far back
from the railway as hay can be hauled with profit, are
scattered every summer the camps of the haymakers,
and the low ricks or "stacks" grow and accumulate
until they dot the prairie so thickly as to become for
the time the distinguishing feature of the landscape.

There are at the station large hay barns, containing
steam presses, to which, from September until April,
the hay is hauled, stowed and baled, ready for shipment.

Among those who were hauling hay at the time of
the great storm were Dick Jordan and his small
brother Orr—named after an Iowa statesman—a little
fellow, too young to attend school regularly, who went
along on pleasant days to tramp down the hay in the
frame of the big rack.

It had been pleasant enough for Orr to go on every
trip that week up to the night of the blizzard, and the

day was so warm and fine that Dick's sisters, Jeanie and Carrie, younger than himself but older than Orr, obtained the permission of their teacher to go home at recess, in order that they might go with their brothers for a ride to the hay-field. Their mother had promised that they should go upon the first warm day after sleighing came.

They arrived at the house just as Dick and Orr drove up for a lunch, before going after their last load for the day, and, as it would be dark before they could get back, the girls, too, got each a slice of bread and cold meat to munch on the road.

Dick spread two heavy horse-blankets, which were always carried in winter to throw over his horses when standing, upon one of the bottom boards of the rack, and seated Jeanie and Carrie upon them. Then, little dreaming what was before them, the brothers and sisters drove swiftly out upon a new sleigh road, which led them for several miles over a prairie almost as level as a barn floor.

The haystacks were reached, and while the boys worked at their loading, the little girls raced about, tumbled in the hay, or rolled snowballs as they pleased.

The load of hay was taken from the bottom of a stack around which the snow had drifted, thawed and frozen until much of the outside hay had to be cut loose with an axe or freed with a shovel, both of which implements Dick carried for that purpose. It took much longer than usual to load upon this occasion, and evening was already drawing on when finally the little girls were helped upon the load and the team was turned toward home.

It had been mild and thawing all day, so mild,

indeed, that Dick had feared that this would be their last trip with a sleigh until snow should come again; but as he climbed upon the load to start for home, he noticed that a heavy gray bank had formed across the western sky, and that it seemed to be growing thick overhead. The air had suddenly become rather chilly.

He told his brother and sisters that it would snow before they got home, and that they had better "cuddle down" in the hay and throw the horse-blankets over their laps. He drove forward for a few minutes, urging the horses to a half-trot, and uneasily glancing toward the dense gray bank, which rapidly overcast the west and north, and threw a gloom and cold in advance, as it approached.

The darkness came on rapidly, and soon the roar of a high wind broke upon Dick's ears.

"It's a blizzard!" he thought, with alarm, for he had been bred upon the Northwest Prairies, and knew the danger of being caught out upon that mowed flat, so far from any houses, for the nearest dwelling was that of a farmer across Gull Lake, two miles and a half to the southeast.

He had not much time to think or to exercise his fears before the great storm was upon them.

It was nothing less than a hurricane from the beginning, and at the first fierce gust the big unwieldly rack careened with its load so that the little girls screamed with fright, and the horses stopped and stood turning their heads away from the pelting sleet which drove down at the first burst of the storm.

The air was filled instantly with the driving ice.

Dick shouted at the animals and slapped at them with the lines, but they could not be induced to turn their heads against the storm. They stood as if paralyzed by the fierce blast of wind and sleet. Another and more furious sweep of the hurricane came almost immediately, and this time the rack was lifted completely off the sled and overturned with hay and riders.

Fortunately, there was a considerable drift of snow beside the road, and neither Dick nor the younger children were hurt by the fall. They had all, with a common impulse, jumped from the top of the load as it careened over, and so fell, or rather tumbled, outside the sweep of the rack.

As they scrambled to their feet the stiff wind was so filled with hay and snow that they could scarcely distinguish each other. The rack turned bottom side up, and, as it was built in the shape of a "figure four" quail trap, held most of the hay securely beneath its frame.

Dick still held to one of the lines, and the horses stood shivering with fear and cold, for the temperature had suddenly dropped far below the freezing point.

"Get behind the rack out of the wind!" he screamed to the younger ones, who were clinging to each other in the endeavor to stand up before the raging wind. They obeyed him, and, hugging close against the framework, found themselves protected from the cutting blast, but snow and sleet whirled over the top and about the ends in blinding scurries.

Dick knew instinctively that to attempt to get those children on the bare sled and to drive them to a place of safety only meant certain death to them all. In the first place, it would require all their strength to cling on. Moreover, they could not endure a half-hour even of such exposure to the storm. With darkness coming on and the air filled with driving snow, there was the barest possibility of his being able to find a house—it could only be found by running against it or into a yard—even if he should be able to drive and keep the children alive all night.

His plans were quickly made, and a man twice his age could not have made them with greater good sense, or have shown a braver spirit in their execution.

He stripped the harness from his horses and turned them loose. Then, without waiting even to see which direction the animals took, he ran to his brothers and sisters.

Although it had been so warm when they started from home, their mother had insisted that Jeanie and Carrie should dress warmly, and take cloaks and comforters with them. These they had put on before the storm came, and Dick, after digging in the hay for a few minutes between the boards of the rack, discovered the horse-blankets upon which the children had fortunately been sitting when the load overturned.

While digging for them he had prepared a "nest," as he termed it, for the three small ones, and he now ordered them to get in there while he tucked the blankets around them. Frightened and hushed by the terrific storm, they obeyed without a murmur, and the brave young fellow told them that they must "cuddle close together and never peep outside" till they heard him call them.

He said that he would go and bring them something to eat as soon as he could get back from Mr. Waldeman's across Gull Lake, and then after the blizzard was over they would all go home.

He knew the snow would drift over them in a very

few minutes, and believed that if they kept quiet their breath would warm the "nest" and no doubt keep them alive for many hours. But he knew also that such blizzards have been known to last with unabated fury for two or three days, and that there was little likelihood of their being able to outlast such a storm. Therefore, his only hope was to reach help if possible, and get it to them the moment it should be possible to breast the blizzard.

Gull Lake lay over a mile distant, directly to the southeast. It was one mile and a half across it, and on the other side lay Waldeman's ranch, a large group of buildings, dwelling, barns and shedding for stock, enclosed by a large yard which stretched along the lake shore for forty rods or more.

Dick hoped that he might be able to reach this ranch and to find it.

Buttoning his overcoat tightly about him and pulling a "Norwegian cap" which he wore tightly down over his ears, he set out, going directly with the storm, which came from the northwest.

He started at a stiff run. The wind nearly lifted him off his feet at every step, and cut the backs of his legs and the sides of his cheeks icily.

He soon found it impossible to tell whether he was going directly with the wind or not, as it blew in changeful gusts and whirled violently about him. But there was a mile of lake shore in front, and he reached it at length and found himself upon the ice.

It had now grown dark, and amidst the pitchy blackness of night and the thick drift of snow he could no longer make use of his eyes. In fact, he was obliged to shut them and allow himself to be carried over the ice by the wind. A part of the time he was able to keep his feet, but often he was thrown forward and actually blown over the rough ice for rods. The skirt of his overcoat occasionally blew over his head, and the bitter wind pierced every part of his body.

It was a rough and terrible experience getting across the lake, and he was glad he had not attempted to take his brother and sisters with him.

When he at length reached the southern bank, he was so chilled and exhausted that he could scarcely keep his feet at all. The bank was high at the point where he reached it, and he knew it could not be opposite the ranch fence, as the high bank was west of that. So he turned, and alternately walked and crawled eastward, guided in that direction by the wind.

For a long time he forced his way along the edge of the ice, which was swept bare, guided by the sense of feeling and the direction of the wind, but at length he stumbled against something and joyfully discovered it to be a fence.

As it afterward proved, it was an extension of the cattle-yard, a corner of which was built down into the edge of the lake to afford water for the stock, and had he missed it by even a few feet he would undoubtedly have perished.

The discovery of it gave him new life at once and aroused all his faculties. He climbed over the fence so as to get inside the yard, and then, by feeling, followed it until he came to a connection with the cattle-sheds.

Once in the shelter of these, he whipped his numbed arms and stamped his chilled feet until circulation was partly restored, then felt his way along to the barn, and at length managed to reach the ranch dwelling, guided by the glimmer of a light which he could see through the storm.

He was welcomed and warmed and fed, and promised that by every possible effort that could be made the men should help him to rescue his brother and sisters when daylight came.

Dick found that he had escaped with only a slight frosting of his face and fingers, but his anguish on account of the little ones he had left buried in the hay was intense. He did not sleep at all, but walked the floor of the ranch kitchen, where he was allowed to keep a roaring fire all night. Every few moments he would go to the windows, scratch the frost, and endeavor to peer out into the storm.

He could gather no encouragement until daylight, when he discovered that the snow was no longer falling, and that the sky would soon be clear.

He roused the ranch hands at once, as two of them had agreed to go with him.

In a short time the men were up. Some hot coffee was drunk, a jug of it was filled from the pot, and a sharp-shod team was harnessed. The horses were blindfolded, their heads wrapped in blankets to protect them from the blinding drift which was still driving hard from the northwest.

This team was hitched to a double sleigh filled with robes and wraps. Then, muffling themselves in the bottom of the box, the party set out across the lake in the very teeth of the wind.

The horses were old and steady, and, after some snorting and tossing of the heads, as a protest against the novelty of complete "blinds," took a steady hard trot over the corrugated ice.

On reaching the farther shore of the lake and ascending to the prairie, Dick, with his head completely muffled to the eyes, took a standing position and, bracing himself, directed the movements of the driver. The short distance of a mile and the steady direction of the wind enabled him to hit the hay-road at a point so close to the overturned rack that he caught sight of the top of it as they were passing some rods distant.

A moment later they had halted and tied the team, and Dick had pointed out the spot where his companions were to dig. Then, utterly overcome, he threw himself upon the drift and buried his face in his arms. His grief and suspense at that moment were almost beyond endurance. He had no idea that the children could have survived such a fearful night. But five minutes of silent digging occupied his companions, and at the end of that time both of them gave a triumphant shout.

They had uncovered the nest and a cloud of steam rose up from the blankets. Dick was on his feet instantly. A moment later the three young Jordans were dragged forth, alive, but stupid with cold and a drowsiness which would not have left them alive many hours longer. Yet they had escaped any serious frost-bite, and a dexterous rubbing, shaking and jouncing restored their circulation and their senses. They were bundled into the sleigh amid robes and comforters, and, despite the severity of the weather and the drifting snow, were taken immediately toward home, where their welcome must be imagined

One of Dick's horses perished in the storm, but the other turned up alive and well the next day at a farmer's stables twelve miles south of Gull Lake.

XII.

A FORTUNATE CYCLONE.

"Ben down to 'Squire Brennan's, Mose?"

The speaker was a sturdy farmer, who stood mopping the moisture from his brow just outside the lane fence which divided his snug farm from that of his nearest neighbor.

Moses Bently drew the reins tightly across the neck of his dripping horse, and with a sharp "Whoa!" flung himself out of the saddle.

"Yes," said he; "I've ben thar;" and pulling a huge bandanna from his pocket, he took off his hat and followed the example of his neighbor across the fence.

"Jones," exclaimed he, with vehemence, "but ain't this a scorcher? Never seed sech hot weather in the last of August. Cuttin' up corn, air ye? Bless me, man! you'll drop fust ye know, an' hev to be laid in the shade."

"Not's long's I can keep up a sweat," replied Jones, coming forward from the corn shocks and leaning upon the fence. "But say, Mose, what's that rumpus 'bout over in your neighborhood? What's the row 'tween Blake an' Miller, anyhow? I hear they've ben down to Brennan's lawin' it to-day."

"Yaas," returned Moses, "they've ben thar lawin' it, an' they're likely to keep on lawin' to the end o' ther days. But mercy, Jones! I can't stand in this hot sun tellin' ye 'bout it."

"Come under the shadder o' this plum-tree here,"

walking toward a large branching plum which stood, loaded with fruit, just inside the fence. "Here's a good place to set down an' cool yerself off," he added, as Mose finished tying his animal and climbed over the fence.

"Yaas," said Moses, again, as he seated himself beside Jones at the foot of the tree, lifted his broad-brimmed straw hat and drew one hickory shirt sleeve across his beady forehead. "Yaas, they'll law it now s' long's they live, an' in the end all they'll have'll go to pay up costs. I left their lawyers argyin' 'fore Squire Brennan, an' a picked jury that didn't know nothin' 'bout the case, nor nothin' 'bout anything else if I'm any judge; jest like most o' the men that gets on juries, though; lot o' loafers, reg'lar nuisances, that's just got pride 'nough t' keep 'em out o' the poorhouse.

"Squire Brennan did his best, jest as he al'ays does, to get 'em to settle; but bless ye! 'twa'n't any use. They're madder 'n hornets, both of 'em. I went down as a witness, but what I knew didn't amount to nothin' 'n' I jest got disgusted with their wranglin', an' when they was done with me I come away an,"—

"But what's it all about?" broke in Jones. "Air they fightin' 'bout that new survey?"

"Waal, yaas, that's at the bottom of it, but they wouldn't had no trouble 'bout that, I guess, if 't hadn't been for them harvest-apple trees on Blake's line, that he set out when he first moved onto the place. There's only five or six of em, and they don't bear a great sight of apples, either; but they're good, what there is of 'em, an' dead ripe now. You see, Blake sot 'em out right on his south line, or jest as near as he could, an' not have 'em grow so's to spread acrost. Wall, the

Gov'ment surveyors was jest as drunk when they run the lines over Section Twelve as they was when they laid out the rest o' this township, an' so this new survey sets them apple-trees jest inside Miller's north line.

"There ain't any question, of course," continued Moses, "not the least sprinklin' o' doubt that Miller's got a legal right to them apple-trees, ef the last survey is c'rect, an' he's mean enough—which it seems he is—to claim 'em. But it seems that Blake hadn't no idea that Miller would lay any claim to the apples, or that he re'ly intended to have the line-fence sot over, bein' as 'twas only a matter of two feet or so, an' 'specially so long's there was a chance to dispute the last lay-out an' set up the old Gov'ment one agin.

"The new survey, ye know, was made last June, an' the change o' lines 'tween Blake an' Miller was so leetle that Blake never thought o' speakin' of it, only jest in a jokin' way. Ye see, the west line o' Section Twelve was changed much as three rods; but as the odds was all in favor of both of 'em, an' had to come out o' the public road, which hadn't ben used but four years, they both felt toler'ble good over it.

"But as I was sayin', Blake hadn't no idea that Miller'd make trouble about the middle line, as there was a good solid fence that they'd both built atween 'em; but when his apples got ripe, he went down one day an' begun pickin' some off'm the earliest tree. An' while he was a-pickin' of 'em, here comes one o' Miller's boys, with a bag slung over his arm, an' climbs over the fence.

" '' Mornin', Joe!' says Blake, unsuspectin' as could be. 'Got through harvestin'?'

"'Yes,' says Joe. 'Thought we'd better git some o' these apples, now they're gittin' ripe. Pop says they belong to him now, but you can have half of 'em this year, bein' as you put out the trees; or he'll pay ye for your trouble in settin' 'em out.'

"'He will, hay?' snaps Blake, settin' down his pail an' starin' at young Joe sarcastical like. 'Your dad's a mighty generous fellow, aint he, now? He'll *give* me half the apples! Give 'em to me, will he? Waal, I guess he will, for I sh'll take 'em, the whole of 'em, not only this year, but ev'ry year, and don't ye forget that now, sonny!'

"At that, Joe, he kinder bridled up a leetle. 'I guess my father's got a right in the lan',' says he. 'An' he told me to pick some o' these apples, an' I'm goin' to take some of 'em home now,' and eyin' Blake kind o' cautious-like, he reached up for a big yaller one that hung a-tempting his jaws just above his head.

"'Don't you touch that!' yells Blake, starting for him in a way that made the boy dodge from under the tree an' scramble for dear life over the fence.

"Waal, of course Miller was madder 'n a hornet, an' so, with his new survey back of him, he goes down to Squire Brennan's and sues Blake for trespass, an' sence that time each one of 'em's had one o' *their* boys watchin' them apples, day an' night, to see 't other'n didn't steal 'em. They mount guard out there like a couple o' roosters, one on one side the fence an' the other on t'other. One of 'em's afraid to touch the apples, an' the other dasn't."

"What'll be the outcome, think?" asked Jones, as Moses paused in his narrative, and again made use of the huge bandanna.

"The outcome? Bless you, man, there won't be no outcome to it. Squire Brennan can't decide the case, an' if he did, 'twouldn't amount to nothin', an' no decidin' ever will so long's there's a higher court to carry the thing through, an' then they'll take a fresh start an' go through agin. This is a case, ye see, for trespass, but how're they goin' to make trespass out of it till they can prove who the land belongs to?"

"I see," said Jones; "goin' to be a nice wrangle, ain't it?"

"I s'h'd say so," muttered Moses. "But, Jones," he added, getting upon his feet, "I must be goin'. Do you see that black cloud off in the southwest? Shouldn't wonder if we'd git another reg'lar old twister when that comes up, an it's a-comin', too."

"Thought I heard it thunderin' an' kind o' rumblin somewhar a bit ago," said Jones, rising. "I'm 'fraid you're right, Mose, and I don't know but it *is* a good plan for a feller to be gettin' around close't to his suller."

"Yaas," returned Moses. "My wife and the young ones have jest about half-lived in my dug-out this summer. Every time they see a cloud, they skedaddle for 'the house of refuge,' as Sarah calls it."

"Beats all how many o' them tornadoes goes ragin' over this country lately," said Jones; "'pears like a man aint safe nowheres," and bidding each other good-day. the two men separated.

"TWISTER," as a word in Western parlance, has attained an entirely new signification within the last two years, especially throughout the now famous storm belt extending from central Kansas in a northwesterly direction beyond the southern boundary of Minnesota.

The prevalence of those terrible storms known as tornadoes, cyclones, and throughout this region as "twisters," has become so alarming of late that in some of the counties of Iowa the citizens take refuge in their cellars during the summer season at the appearance of every dark and threatening cloud.

In this region a large proportion of the farmers and many of the townspeople dig out-of-door cellars, or "under-ground houses," in which to shelter themselves from the violence of these atmospheric disturbances.

On nearing one of their dwellings, one notices, but a few yards to one side, a heaped-up mound of earth, with an opening in one end disclosing the frame-work and top of a heavy door, the bottom of which is reached by a flight of steps cut into the earth in front. The whole is constructed much after the pattern of the summer milk-house of more Eastern farmers, and indeed, most of the dug-outs are used for that purpose also.

The genuine tornado, or "twister,"—the one which tears up everything in its track,—is generally preceded by a short time of hot, "muggy" weather, and at such times, when the feather-edged, dark-centred nimbus floats lazily a mile or two above the farmer's head, small spiral-shaped projections are often seen suddenly darting downward from their centres, curling, twisting, steadily shooting ahead, sometimes almost reaching the earth. Then, with a peculiar, writhing motion, these snake-like columns of vapor break up into little sections, or separate puffs, and disappear as quickly as they were formed.

Sometimes a dozen or more may be seen at a single glance. On such days it is necessary to be on the lookout, and if the cloud above one of those dark columns grows suddenly black and emits flashes of lightning, followed by the rumble of thunder, the "dug-out" is the only safe retreat.

About three o'clock on the particular afternoon and near the locality of which we write, the thermometer at various places indicated 98° Fahrenheit in the shade, and away towards the horizon in the south and west could be seen piled-up masses of silver-tinted thunder-clouds, their lowering bases sinking almost out of sight behind the distant woods and fields.

"My! what whoppin' old thunder-heads!" thought Billings Blake, as he sat sweltering beneath the shade of one of the disputed apple-trees; "guess Clem Miller'll get sick of his bargain sittin' over there on the south side of the fence. He dasn't come over here, though," he soliloquized, "'cause he knows I c'n lick 'im the best day he ever saw, an' he knows I will, too, if he comes."

Clem did have a pretty hard place, to be sure; for, to tell the truth, he was afraid of young °Blake, and so, as there were no trees on his side, he was obliged to content himself with the small shelter afforded by the green corn-stalks which grew beside the fence.

"I wish pa'd never made any row 'bout these miserable old apple-trees," he grumbled, as he held his broad-brimmed hat high over his head in order to shelter himself from the scorching rays which would find their way down through the corn leaves; "I don't want to be melted into taller a-watching them old apples that'll rot in two days after they're picked. I don't like the looks of them clouds," he added, a moment later.

"Haloo, Clem!"

Could he believe his ears? Yes, it was surely young Billings Blake calling him.

"Want's me to come over there, and then lick me," growled Clem.

"I say, Clem," bawled young Blake again. "Clem, jest get up an' look over the hill yender. I believe there's a twister a-comin'."

Clem got up and looked.

"'Tis sure enough, Bill," he answered. "Do ye reckon it will come this way sure?"

"Dun no," said Billings. "I say, Clem, come over here an' let's watch the thing!"

It is curious how a common danger transforms the bitterest enemies into the best of friends. Clem got over the fence without the slightest hesitation, and in a moment the two boys, who just before would not have deigned to speak to each other, stood together, gazing in common fear and wonder upon a scene that once witnessed is never forgotten.

Away to the southwest, several of those silvery-edged, harmless-looking clouds had grown together, and were rapidly approaching. Their sun-tinted columns had suddenly changed color, and, black and angry, they were tumbling together in ugly broken masses, while forks of jagged lightning darted across their lowering sides, and the distant growl of thunder could be distinctly heard.

The wind sprang up, and began to stir the leaves of the apple-trees, and to rustle the broad blades of corn, while black masses of vapor swept hurriedly across the sky, obscuring the sun, and hurling themselves into the very midst of the huge pile, thus constantly swelling its already enormous proportions.

"Mercy!" said Clem, catching at his hat as a fresh gust of wind swept past. "Mercy! Bill, the wind's a-blowin' from ev'ry direction, an' jest look at them clouds; they're a-comin' from every way, an' goin' every where. Don't ye think we'd better git for shelter?"

"Where sh'll we go, Clem, to better ourselves?" asked his companion. "Ye can't tell where she'll strike the hardest, and fer one, I'd rather be in the open field than in the woods when there's a hurricane comin'. But jest look at 'er."

Even as he spoke, the roar of the approaching hurricane drowned his voice, and a round black column, darting down from the center of the hurrying mass, struck the timber across the hill with a roar and a crash that was fairly deafening.

"Run, Clem! Git for the field!" yelled Bill; and the frightened boys scurried away toward the north, and the fifty yards' run which they were then able to make probably saved their lives.

On came the twisting, writhing storm, tearing the earth, trees, grain and fences in its track, and filling the air with a hideous din. Swiftly as the boys ran, they were not fleet-footed enough to escape the effect of the fearful side wind which accompanied the whirling cloud.

Clem felt his legs suddenly wrenched from under him, and in a trice found himself turning the most astonishing summersaults he had ever dreamed of. His hat and shirt were literally torn away from him, and a moment later, scratched, bruised, and lacerated by the corn stubs over which he had been tumbled, he found himself lying on his back in a deep, dead furrow, with six inches of muddy water slushing around him.

Bill had fared but little better, as, spattered with mud and bleeding from half-a-dozen bruises, he picked himself up from between two corn rows, where he had been carried bodily.

"We are in a bad fix, sure," said Bill. "But jest look down yonder in the track of 'er, will ye? There's a strip forty rods wide where there aint a thing standin', an' the ground's all ploughed ready for winter wheat. Yes, an'—an'—an'—can I believe my eyes—*the apple trees are gone!*"

"If they haint!" answered Clem. "Hurrah, Bill! your dad an' mine'll quit their quarrellin' now, won't they, an' we'll all be friends an hunt ducks together like we used to?"

HUNTING STORIES

BY

FRANK W. CALKINS

CHICAGO.
M. A. DONOHUE & CO.
407-429 DEARBORN ST.

CONTENTS.

HUNTING STORIES.

I.

TRAPPED BY "TRAVELING MOUNTAIN."

It was when we—my brother Judson, Jack Imly
and I—were staying one spring at my father's cattle
ranch in Nevada that the curious and perilous adventure I am about to tell happened to us.

It all came of Jack's getting acquainted with
Washoe Pete, a half-breed cow-boy employed on the
ranch, and "worming" out of him curious information
about the country where his tribe of Indians lived and
hunted.

Jack "pumped" every new acquaintance. Moreover, he was an inveterate curiosity hunter, and was
then collecting "specimens" to present to the museum
of the university at Sacramento, where we had been
students. His special pursuit was fossils and small
animals, birds and insects. He was a good taxider-
mist, and while at the ranch he secured and mounted a
number of rare specimens of *batrachians*, and also of a
queer little piping bird that was new to us.

From Washoe Pete he obtained a piece of intelligence that excited him greatly. Pete told him of a
traveling mountain of sand that shifted about in the
great basin country near the Humboldt Mountains.
This mountain was, he said, steadily but slowly moving
across the basin plains, driven eastward by the prevailing winds.

It had moved a considerable distance within the memory of the old men of his tribe, and had stopped for nothing. It had crossed hills, cañons and sage plains with equal ease and speed. It sang a low, mournful song, that could be heard night and day, and it had a great conical hole, like the crater of a volcano, Jack explained, in its top. Whoever passed over the rim into the basin, or crater, was immediately engulfed by the sands, and sank out of sight, to be seen no more.

Several Washoe Indians had, according to Pete, paid the penalty of their lives for daring the experiment of attempting to cross the mountain-top.

Furthermore, he said, on the east side was a cañon-stream fed by the Humboldts that flowed down to the sand mountain, and was "drunk up" at its base — as other Nevada streams are by the sands of the Great Basin. In the rocky walls of the stream were great fissures and caves, where, according to the Indian folk-lore, dwelt the spirits that sang in the mountain.

This was Jack's version of Pete's story translated from the half-breed's cowboy-Indian dialect. Of course, when this Indian superstition was added to the story, we were disposed to make a considerable discount on the rest of Pete's account of this wonderful mountain; but there seemed to be enough in it to arouse curiosity, and it certainly impelled us to investigate it.

As the mountain was said to be but little more than one hundred miles from the ranch, we finally concluded to go down and explore this curious phenomenon, and had no difficulty in persuading the ranch superintendent, for neither father nor any other members of the family ever *lived* there, to let us make the trip. He allowed us to select three ridden ponies, a pair of burros for pack purposes, and to take Washoe Pete, with his riding pony, for a guide.

We completed our preparations on the morning of the 5th of May, and set out in the gayest spirits imaginable. We had the burros well "packed" with blankets, flour, bacon, coffee, canned fruit and cooking utensils.

We found it hot and disagreeable work riding over the dry sand and alkali plains, and through the belts of sage and grease-wood; but Pete proved a trustworthy guide, and at night we always camped near a plentiful supply of water, brackish and unpalatable, however, until boiled, when it made very good coffee.

We had guns and ammunition, but there was no game in the country save jack-rabbits and sage hens, and these were not fit to eat at that time of the year.

The Humboldts were in sight most of the time, looming up in the east, and the snow, which had not melted off their crests and out of their gulches, lay in white patches and streaks about their tops.

About noon on the fifth day we were jogging along over a hot, shimmering alkali flat, when Pete, who was riding ahead, halted, and pointed away in the distance to a great yellowish, gray mound that showed indistinct through the haze.

"That *him!*" said he. "He tlavel (travel) that way," with a sweep of his hand off to the left. "My peop (people) live 'way yonda now," and he pointed again, this time to the right of the mound.

We watched, with curiosity, "Traveling Mountain," as we had named it already. On one side of the moun-

tain the country was a barren plain, broken only by
heaps of sand and by gullies, out of which these mounds
seemed to have been scooped.

We neared the base of the sand mountain at about
four o'clock, and found before us a great oblong hill
that was, as near as could be judged from our point of
view, some four or five hundred feet high, and perhaps
three miles in length—not much of a mountain, but an
oblong, irregular sand bluff, with curious serrated
ridges running from the top down nearly to the base,
where they seemed to blend together.

There was no air stirring at this time, and, of course,
no sand moving, but I remember a distinct feeling, that
we boys all spoke of, that the big mound looked all
ready to move ; that it had an air about it of seeming
to be merely resting.

However, we did not stop long that evening to view
the mountain ; it was hot, dry, and hard traveling, and
as our ponies' and burros' small, hard hoofs sank deep
into the sand, Pete said we must keep them going, in
order to get around and reach the " cave cañon," where
we should find water and a cool camping spot, and
where, also, there was feed for the animals.

We found the country quite different when we had
got around on the opposite side, the side facing the
Humboldts ; it was rough and broken by cañons, in
several of which, as we scrambled down and through
them, we saw pools of brackish water.

At first we were compelled to make a considerable
detour away from the sand mountain, but at dusk we
came back near to it again, above the mouth of a rocky
cañon, through which ran the stream that Pete had

mentioned, where the singing spirits were supposed to
dwell.

Below us in the gray dusk we could see the big
mound stretching diagonally across the cañon, and
Pete told us the water was backed up below, and
soaked into the sands of the mountain by degrees.

The soil of the cañon was a hard-baked, red clay.
Clumps of grease-wood grew here and there and
in patches a short, thin, wiry grass, that was
already nearly burned dry by the summer heat, though
it offered the best of feed to our close-cropping ponies
and burros.

We found the water the best we had met on the trip,
and had a pleasant camp that night, as the weather in
this region is always cool between sunset and sunrise.

The next morning we were up at daylight, and ready
to begin explorations. We joked Pete about the
spirits, and asked where the caves were in which they
lived, and also why they had not "turned up" during
the night; but the half-breed had suddenly grown
reticent, and refused to answer our badinage. In fact,
he began to act very queerly.

After repicketing the ponies and burros upon new
ground, while we boys were preparing breakfast, Pete
wandered up through the gap at the mouth of which
we were camped, and stood for some time upon a high,
rocky point overlooking the country to the northeast.

When he came down, he announced that he had
seen a smoke "'way off"—he pointed toward the
Humboldts—and that he thought a hunting-party of
his "peops" were up there killing young bush-rabbits.
We had before learned that they are extremely fond of

these tender creatures, and make forays upon them every spring.

After this, while we were eating breakfast, we noticed that Pete frequently glanced uneasily at the big yellow-gray mound that stretched obliquely across the gap some half a mile below.

"That mounting," he said at length, with seeming indifference, "that mounting he come 'way up this away since two yea' now. He got mad at speyets, an' have bayed (buried) um in um cave. You neveh hea' um sing no mo' now."

Then he arose, and coolly announced that he should ride off to see the party of his "hunt folks," while we stayed at the mountain. He would be back the next morning, he said, and then we should go home.

Nothing we could say would induce him to remain, and he rode away and left us, provoked and disappointed enough.

It seemed, after all, that there was nothing to see but a big pile of sand, that was blown about by the winds, as we had seen other smaller heaps blown about on sand-flats in California.

Pete, we surmised, must have ascribed the marked change in the position of the sand mountain, since he had seen it last, to some occult cause, and, possessed of his superstitious notion, had, Indian-like, made haste to get out of the neighborhood.

We suddenly lost interest in the "big sand heap," declared the trip a flat failure, and were thoroughly disgusted. If we had not been angry at Pete, we should have packed the burros, mounted our ponies, and set out after him in the hope of meeting with an adventure of some sort.

As it was, we stayed, and met with one which seems incredible to relate, yet which came about from as natural a cause as any phenomenon connected with the traveling mountain.

It happened thus :

We had gone down the stream, bent upon exploration, and had easily discovered the process by which the great mound was encroaching upon and filling up the cañon. The wind, prevailing from the west, had blown the sand across its top and along its sides above the level of the cañon's walls, and piled them in ridges and heaps, which, like snow accumulating upon a steep mountain-side, had caved off, slid, and settled into the abyss below.

We could see several fresh "breaks," where huge piles of sand—probably from the settling of the mass below them—had recently given away, and had precipitated their bulk in a long shooting slide down the side of the mound to the very foot of its base in the cañon.

The mound loomed up above us like a huge embankment, and reminded us of the big "dump" of a gigantic piece of grading.

We tried to climb, but found the sides too steep and the sand too soft and yielding, and, in fact, we never got to the top of the traveling mountain. We searched for caves along the cañon walls, but found only some big cracks and fissures in the gray sandstone at their bases.

The atmosphere was still; there had been no wind since we had arrived the night before, and, as the sun mounted, the air of the cañon grew hot and stifling. We bathed our heads and limbs in the water that lay backed up in the channel soaking into the sands, but the liquid was **hot and oozy,** and had a depressing effect.

The sun had got round so that there was no shade from the rocky walls, and we were thinking of going back to camp and making a shade by spreading our blankets over grease-wood bushes, when Jack proposed that we should crawl into a fissure in the rocks that we had discovered, where a sand-slide had poured over the cliff and shot obliquely across the opening.

We had laughingly wondered if there were any "spirits" living in that "big crack," and now Jack thought we might crawl in there and cool off at the risk of disturbing them. We went over and looked in.

It was a fissure wide enough to creep into and sit down in, and extended back some eight or ten feet before narrowing away, as it did, again to the solid wall. We got on our hands and knees and went in, getting back into a wider space behind the sand-slide where the sun had not been able to beat in that morning, and we found the place tolerably cool and comfortable.

As the roof of the fissure slanted downward, the sand, of course, could only fill in to the natural angle or slant of its fall, and so there was plenty of room for us in a sitting or lying posture.

But, to hasten the story, we had been sitting there but a few minutes when Judson, who was a good marksman, proposed that we should try our rifles upon the sand-rocks of the opposite cañon wall, which we could see by looking obliquely past the line of the "dump", as we termed the great mass which had slid down there.

" I'll bet," said Judson, "that I can make the sand fly most awful close to that crack in the big gray rock that stands out on that point yonder ; " and, bringing his knees up in front of him, and "resting" his Winchester across them, he took careful aim and fired.

Sometimes even yet I fancy that explosion rings in my ears. It sounded as though a hundred cannons had all been fired off at once.

Before the echo of it ceased, we were startled by a swift, rustling, whistling sound, and like a flash a heavy rush of sand shot down across the opening in front of our eyes, falling with a heavy *whoosh* and shut the fissure in until we were left in almost total darkness.

For some seconds we sat in silence, utterly stunned by the calamity which had befallen us. During that moment I think we were all staring fixedly at the slim line of light left at the farther end of the fissure, then Jack broke the silence in a scared voice.

" We're buried alive ! " he exclaimed. " We can never get out through that crack yonder in the world."

" It was the gun," said Judson. " How horrible ! "

As for me, I was too much frightened to find my voice yet. But Jack, who was the smallest, and, I think, the coolest and quickest-witted, immediately got on his hands and knees and crept forward to explore the chances of getting out.

As he wriggled up into the narrow space that was left between us and the only remaining crack of light, Judson and I were enveloped in the densest of darkness.

" Well, how is it ? " asked Judson at length, and I held my breath for the answer.

" Slim chance," he answered. His voice, though

sounding hollow and weird, seemed strangely cool. "Cracks 'bout six inches wide where the sand cuts across. I can reach out nearly to it with my hand from where I lay, and back about four feet here there's space enough to crawl through by tight squeezing. Only show's to dig out, and I don't believe it can be done from the inside, for the sand'll run in fast as we can dig. If one of us was only *outside!*"

"Try digging," said Judson.

Jack went at it. He dug for some time, while we sat in perfect silence, fearfully awaiting the result.

"It's no use," he announced, despairingly, after working desperately for what seemed an age; "there's such a tremendous bulk above outside that it pours in faster than I can dig. If we try to dig out we shall only fill this hole all up and be worse off than we are now."

We groaned in dismay. The situation was truly horrible. We were literally buried alive. I shall never forget the terrible emotions of that time, when escape seemed impossible.

Jack, after lying some time longer peering out at the crevice, said: "I've thought of a way to get us out, fellows, when Pete comes."

My heart bounded at the mention of the half-breed's name; I had not thought of him.

"It'll take some time," continued Jack, calmly, "but it can be done, if only there don't come another slide, and Pete has sense and wit enough to come and look us up. I don't think there can be such slides every day, and Pete'll surely come down here in the morning when he finds we're not in camp."

We now began to hope that there was a chance of

rescue, but we knew that it would be a terrible trial of patience and endurance to be cooped up in that dark hole, no one could say how many hours, without food or water.

Jack crawled back to where we were and told his plan. It was to watch for Pete in the morning, hail him through the crack when he came within sight, explain the situation, have him bring biscuits, water and a lariat, and while we were satisfying our hunger he could begin digging at the sand near the crevice.

He would need to remove a great deal of sand, but Jack thought the opening might be made large enough to admit of our being drawn out one at a time by the lariat, though he admitted it would be "tight wriggling and an awful sight of work." At any rate, we should not starve, and if only another slide did not occur, he felt sure "the thing could be done."

But then, if Pete should be frightened and not come within reach of our voices, or if another slide *should* take place.

Ah, that terrible if!

The chance of escape from that living tomb seemed frightfully small, even when calculating it in our coolest moments. For the present there was nothing to do but to wait. Such a waiting! The agony of that suspense cannot be described.

At first, after pulling in sand enough to make a comfortable bed to lie on, we only suffered from the natural terror and suspense of the situation, but, as the hours wore on, the pangs of hunger, and more especially of thirst, became little less than torture.

The day passed slowly, and my memory of the night that followed is confused. I spent it tossing about in a burning fever, induced by fright, anxiety and extreme thirst. The other boys fared little better.

At daylight, however, we had life enough to discover that our chance of escape had not been diminished by the falling of more sand, and Jack, gaining hope and courage, crawled forward to be on the lookout for Pete.

We tried to talk, but our tongues were parched, and a burning sensation of the throat and stomach proved too depressing for effort in that direction.

The hours dragged on, and still Pete did not come.

How we raged at the cowardly half-breed!

We waited until near noon, and then, in a fury of despair and terror, I declared to Jack and Judson that we "*must dig*," that I would "dig into the sandpile and die there, *smother*, rather than burn up in this horrible hole."

At that we began digging. Jack, at the narrowest part of the opening where it was thought we could crawl through, pawed the sand out and threw it behind him to Judson, who passed it on to me, and I threw it still farther back into the fissure.

We had worked an hour, perhaps, and I for one had started the sweat and felt better, when Jack suddenly exclaimed:

"*Thank goodness, there's Pete!*"

The open crack, though small, still commanded, from where we lay, quite an extensive view of the cañon, and, peering over Jack's shoulder, Judson and I saw Pete slowly and cautiously moving down along the channel of the stream, peering this way and that as he came.

He had discovered that something was amiss, and

was evidently both frightened and filled with some
superstitious notion. When the half-breed had come
up within a few yards, Jack put his hands to his
mouth so as to throw the sound outside and spoke to
him.

Pete was startled and looked frightened enough, but
as Jack, in a husky voice, proceeded to explain our
situation, he glanced up at the mountain and down at
the crevice with quick intelligence. Without waiting
for Jack to finish or give any instructions, he flung up
one hand with a gesture of comprehension, and saying,
"Wait; I come back quick?" bounded away toward
the camp.

He was back in a few minutes, and with him came
three Indians, all on their ponies. Pete had brought
coffee and biscuits, which he passed in to us, the liquid
in a tin cup, and the biscuits by tossing them through,
while his fellows stood about giving vent to grunts of
amazement.

In five minutes we were new beings, filled with hope,
courage and strength.

"We git you out," said Pete, and they all went at it
and dug with might and main.

As they dug, the sand slid down from a great space
above, and it took them hours to remove enough to
enable them to get at us, and then only by a piece of
ingenuity of Pete's devising.

They *burrowed* in by using three big Mexican saddles
to make a tunnel. These saddles they placed hollow
side to the crevice, shoving one ahead of the other
until an arched tunnel was formed through which each
one of the prisoners was drawn out by lariat.

We came through somewhat bruised and jammed, but *thankful*.

The wind was blowing when we got outside, and the sand was falling over the bluff, sifting down with a rustling murmur which indicated to Pete and his brother Indians that the mountain spirits were free again.

"We git you out," said Pete.—Page 17

If they really were, and felt as light-hearted as we three boys did, they were spirits truly to be envied.

We set out for home the next morning, having had quite enough experience with Traveling Mountain. The Indians rode all the way back with us, for the sake, as we believed, of the food which we were glad to furnish in consideration of their services to us.

THE HORN-HUNTER'S ADVENTURE.

Trophy heads of Buffalo, elk and other animals have been favorite tavern signs ever since the days of our Saxon ancestors, but the "craze" for polished buffalo and Texas steer horns is of much more recent date. Indeed, it has been but lately discovered by relic-venders that the horns of the American bison are susceptible of a very beautiful ebony-like polish, which renders them highly ornamental. Since this fact has become known, however, the demand for them has increased, until the present traffic in them has grown to be both extensive and lucrative.

The new stations and towns along the line of the Northern Pacific and of the Canadian Pacific railways are the present headquarters of the trade, since these new railroads penetrate the old haunts of the bison.

Here the bone-picker, horn-gatherer and relic-hunter have, for two years past, been reaping an abundant and profitable harvest. Bones for fertilizing purposes, at from twelve to sixteen dollars per ton, buffalo horns at fifty cents a pair, and occasionally a set of elk-antlers, worth from five to fifteen dollars, according to their size and beauty, furnish a virgin harvest for the few who have the hardihood to scour the great solitary plains and lonely mountain ranges of this wild region.

Some months ago the writer chanced to fall in with two young men, then on their return from the Yellowstone country, who related, in the way of conversation, several interesting instances from their experience in horn and "specimen" hunting along the Rose-bud and its tributaries.

They were then, and are now, students at a Western college, and having their own expenses to pay, had gone out on the plains last summer, during the vacation season, to see what could be done in the way of making money. They set off prepared for the work, and had made a market in advance with a friend in Chicago, who kept a general curiosity shop, for all the buffalo horns which they might be able to gather and polish.

They took with them a stout wall tent and a couple of breech-loading rifles, and after arriving at Rosebud purchased two strong pack-ponies, some cooking utensils and provisions. Thus equipped, they moved out to a distance of twenty miles or more, to a region which had been famous for buffalo-hunting during the previous winter, pitched their tent, and began operations.

As the horns have to be polished perfectly in order to command the highest price, one of the boys was obliged to stay at the tent and work constantly with knife, glass, and paper and emory. The other, meantime, scoured the plains on horseback, with pack-sack, rifle and horn-hammer (a light hammer for knocking the horn loose from the skull), and came in at night invariably loaded down with big "tossers."

The ground there in many places was literally strewn with buffalo skeletons.

As was quite natural in such a region, some exciting incidents befell them, several, in fact, with a genuine flavor of adventure. One of them, whose name is Hollingsworth ("Rufe," his companion called him), gave the following account of an adventure with two mountain lions, or rather with a family of those dangerous beasts. It happened during the first part of August, shortly after they had moved their camp up a small branch of the Rosebud, to the mouth of a timbered, rocky cañon, known among hunters as Starving Crow Gulch.

Rufe was riding down the gulch late one evening, after an unusually long trip after horns. He was leading the other pony behind him, packed with two large sacks, astride of which, and tied on, rested a magnificent pair of elk antlers. As he jogged on, he was congratulating himself on the prospective receipts of their next shipment from Rosebud, when, with a low growl, some big creature sprang from a thicket of underbrush near at hand, and drew itself up directly in front of his pony!

Surprised and greatly frightened, the animal which he rode sprang snorting backward, pitching Rufe forward upon the pommel. At the same instant the other pony, whose stout lariat was securely fastened to a ring in the rear of a saddle-tree, dashed wildly ahead. The shock proved too much for the girth, which was an old and long-used one; it snapped, and Rufe was thrown heels over head to the ground. Worse still, one foot hung in the stirrup, and for several rods he was dragged, sprawling, over the rough ground, after a terribly rough-and-tumble fashion; then the stirrup lost its grip, and he lay for some seconds so stunned and bruised as hardly to recollect what had happened.

But at length he pulled himself together—as an

Englishman would say—and staggered to his feet.   As
he did so, he heard the distant clatter of his ponies'
hoofs as they fled one up and the other down the gulch.
First he rubbed his bruised arms and legs vigorously,
and concluding that he had no bones broken, bethought
himself to look about and pick up his gun, which he
knew must have been thrown from its open holster on
the saddle.   The full moon was shining brightly in the
east, but the steep, black sides of the gulch, the shadows
of the rocks, trees and undergrowth, rendered his
search an uncertain one.   He was, as he frankly
acknowledged, afraid to go back where the wild creature
had sprung out and frightened his animals, for he
strongly suspected the nature of the beast; and he
had heard stories of the mountain lion which made him
feel rather weak-kneed at the prospect of meeting one
in such a place.

He continued back through the bushes, however,
until he reached the small opening where he had been
thrown from his pony.   But as he stepped out into the
clear space, a shrill scream came from the bushes close
by—a horrible, unearthly cry, utterly beyond description—that literally raised his hair, and sent a prickly
chill over his whole body.   This scream was followed
by a whining, snuffling sound, as of a young puppy
badly frightened.

Rufe drew back from the bushes into the middle of
the opening, where the light was strongest, and looked
nervously about him.   He could see nothing; but he
dared not run, fearing that such a display of alarm
would invite an attack from the "lion."   Again the
creature sent forth from the brush a terrific scream;
and this time an answering cry came from the opposite

side, so close at hand that Rufe turned in terror, expecting to see this second lion ready to leap upon him.

A moment later a long-bodied animal stalked out from the shade of a clump of willows, showing itself in the open ground, scarcely thirty feet distant from where Rufe stood! Its attitude was threatening, its eyes glowed, it snarled savagely, and its long tail swept from side to side!

For a moment the horn-hunter was too much frightened to stir from the spot; yet he retained sense enough to fully comprehend the situation. He was facing a full-grown male lion, which had undoubtedly come at the call of its mate, to help in protecting their young! In a word, he had stumbled on a nest of mountain lions, in the night, and had nothing but a small hunting-knife with which to defend himself.

For an instant he gave himself up as lost, then seeing that the beast did not spring, he recovered his nerve a little, and began thinking of escape.

There stood the powerful brute, its outline quite distinct in the moonlight.

Rufe now determined to try the effect of a movement; for he could endure the strain of such suspense no longer. Accordingly, he stepped slowly backward; but as he did so the creature's furious lashings and snarlings grew louder, seconded by deep growls from its mate.

Determined, if possible, however, to reach and climb one of the nearest cottonwoods, Rufe took another backward step. As he moved his foot, the spur on his heel clinked faintly against something, with a metallic sound; and divining instantly what it was, he looked

down and saw the barrel of his rifle lying directly
between his feet. He had been standing almost over it,
while looking in vain on all sides!

At sight of it, his heart gave a joyful throb; he
stooped quickly, picked it up; and as he straightened
up to look out for the enemy again, he saw the male
lion walking slowly across the moonlit space, not ten
paces in front of him!

It was circling around him preparatory to an attack.
It walked with a sidling motion, lashing out its tail,
its big head turned towards him.

Slowly and carefully, as one whose life depended on
his skill in shooting, Rufe drew the gun to his face,
and taking aim as perfect as the light admitted of,
fired!—and instantly threw another cartridge forward
for a second shot. But the animal had dropped in its
tracks, as though struck by lightning; and without a
sound, save a little gurgle in its throat, it gave two or
three kicks, and lay as lifeless as a log!

It was a powerful animal, even though lying dead,
and seen by moonlight. Its body, including the head,
was more than five feet in length, and its tail some four
feet more.

Rufe had no more fear of lions that night. He spent
some minutes examining the animal, satisfying his
curiosity generally with regard to its species. Then
he started for home, but met Mayhew, his partner,
riding out the pack-pony—which had run directly to
camp—to see what had become of him. Together
they went back, built a fire for light, and skinned the
lion before returning.

Next morning the other pony came in; and during

the forenoon they found the elk antlers undamaged, and secured also a part of the buffalo horns, which had been scattered along the pack-pony's route, as it ran away.

III.

A FRIGHTENED HERD.

During the autumn of '82 and the winter following a number of the writer's friends (among them "Mell" Green) spent several months in buffalo-hunting, upon a branch of the Powder River, in Montana Territory.

They had gone to that region with the idea of forming a "cattle company;" but after some prospecting, the plan was given up, and then the young men—there were six in the party, all sportsmen by instinct and some practice—speedily took the buffalo fever. For there were here, even at that late date, considerable "bands" of these animals along the branches of the Big Horn and Powder Rivers; and the killing of them for their skins had not yet ceased to be an exciting and a profitable business.

Much is said about protecting elk, deer and buffalo in the West. No one doubts, I suppose, that these noble game animals should be protected by law strictly enforced, or that the slaughter of them for their hides merely is infamous. But so long as foreign sportsmen are permitted to come here and shoot to their hearts' content, it is hardly to be expected that the American settler will refrain from so doing. For why should he spare the game—for English and French sportsmen to shoot? So, at least, he reasons, though it is not the broad view of the case.

My friends were well equipped with the best of modern sporting rifles; and after purchasing riding ponies, pack animals, provisions, blankets, and the necessary articles of camp equipage, it only remained to select a hunting-ground and build a "shack." They finally pitched upon the Chalk Buttes region as their range. There are a chain of white-capped mounds skirting a small branch of the Powder River. There are a considerable number of these buttes—high, conspicuous bluffs, capped each with ledges of chalk-rock and having their steep sides covered with stunted pines, loose boulders and hill grass.

The valley of the stream, and all the rough country lying around the buttes was then carpeted thickly with the short, curly, nutritious buffalo grass. Many small "bunches" of buffalo and deer, and immense bands of antelope, fed over this range, which was also grazing--ground for their ponies and mules. So the boys "preëmpted" this locality early in the season.

They built their *shack* of logs cut from the tall, slim cottonwoods which grew along the creek. It was a commodious affair, sixteen by twenty-six, with a stone fire-place, two small windows and a roof of poles covered with turf. The situation was picturesque. For they were on high ground, overlooking the creek valley on the west side, but at the very base of a high butte on the other, almost *in* the base, in fact, space having been dug back into the abrupt bank for a part of the foundation. The steep, conical bluff, with its *chevaux de frise* of charred, stubby pines and its battlements of chalk-rock, towered above the low cabin like a sheltering fortress.

At this comfortable "headquarters" the party lived for several months, fetching their water up hill and bringing their wood down from the side of the butte.

Hereabouts they hunted, going off for many miles on all sides of the shack, starting early in the morning and often coming in very late at night. Sometimes they were lucky, and came toiling back to the shack from all directions loaded with pelts and with exciting after-supper stories to tell; and sometimes, though rarely, they all came in empty-handed.

By midwinter a score or more of three-cornered curing racks, made of light poles set in crotches, had been erected and were plentifully hung with buffalo skins. These robe-draped racks added not a little to the picturesqueness of their surroundings; and the incidents of their daily life here were rough, venturesome, and often wildly exciting. I am indebted to my friend "Mell" for the following account of an adventure which occurred at the shack one morning:

"We had just eaten breakfast," said he, "and were bringing up our horses to saddle and get ready for the day's hunt, when Tom Wrisley, who was just ahead of me with his pony, stopped short, and sang out: 'Look at old Jack, Mell!'

"Jack was a large pack-mule that we had bought at Miles. He possessed all the characteristics of the mule in general, and had besides several striking qualities peculiar to himself. He was blessed with the keenest eyesight and the finest sense of hearing of any creature I have ever seen, and he was a *pointer* too. Yes, a genuine pointer, and as good a one as any bird-dog you ever hunted over.

"There couldn't an animal come within sight or hearing, no, or a bird, but he was sure to clap his eyes upon it and to make a straight 'point' at it. Then he would stand stock-still, ears and nose aimed in the same

direction and on parallel lines; and he would stand so
until his curiosity was satisfied, and he had concluded
whether to run or keep his ground. And when he had
once concluded, he stood or ran without regard to consequences.

"When Tom called my attention to him, I looked,
and there stood the old fellow gazing up the side of the
butte, his nostrils wide open, his big ears making a
straight point for the chalk-ledges, and his hair all
bristled up on end. I had never seen him look that
way but once before, and that was when he had sighted
a cinnamon bear. He usually wore an air of mild
curiosity at the sight of strange objects; a kind of
gentle surprise seemed to beam out all over him.

"'Something uncommon up there,' said Tom; 'cinnamon, I reckon.' And we both stared hard up at the
top of the ledge.

"We didn't see anything at first; but in a few
seconds we both started in the same breath and
exclaimed—

"'*Buffalo!*'

"And indeed it was queer we hadn't seen them at
the first glance; for they stood on the extreme edge of
a narrow 'bench' at the foot of the chalk-ledge, their
dark bodies outlined plain against the white crag, and
not more than seven hundred feet above us. They
seemed to be looking down at us, over the tops of the
stumpy pines, with as much interest as we were regard-
ing them.

"'Twenty-seven of 'em!' muttered Tom. 'We must
have them!'

"By this time the other boys had sighted them, and
were scudding to the shack for their guns.

"In a minute or less time we had the ponies tied, and the six of us were outside, guns in hand, watching the herd from behind the curing racks and the corners of the cabin.

"The game didn't seem in any hurry to move, but just stood and looked down with a lazy curiosity that was rather tantalizing. Jack was still staring up at them, but his hair had slicked down, and the old air of mild and ruminating wonder had taken the place of his first ferocious stare.

"Tom and I stood by the corner of the shack. 'I'm going to fire,' said he.

"'All right,' said I; 'try that big bull near the centre.'

"Tom had a heavy 40-90 Sharp. He laid the barrel across the end of a projecting log, sighted up at the bull and fired. All the rest of us followed suit, and five more bullets went whizzing up the butte. The balls did execution; four of the unwieldy creatures, hard hit and unable to turn, fell, or leaped off their path; and these knocked off several others, half the whole herd, in fact. They came plunging and tumbling down the steep side of the butte like an avalanche.

"I wish I could describe that scene just as it looked! I have heard a great many stories how buffaloes climb the buttes and post sentinels, and how they will sometimes charge down a bluff; but I never saw nor heard anything like that. At every lunge those great brutes made clouds of loose dirt and dry dust flew up in front of them, while close at their heels rattled a volley of small stones and not a few good-sized boulders.

"We could see it all plainly through the burnt and scattering pines; and we opened a rapid fusillade on them. Yet they never swerved—they couldn't—but just bore down on us like a young cyclone. As they neared the foot of the butte, we all scuttled in behind the shack, and then kept firing up over the top of it.

They came plunging and tumbling down.—Page 30.

"Old Jack and the ponies had snapped their tie-ropes and galloped wildly away. The buffaloes, most of them, scattered out somewhat; but there were three or four of them pointing straight down for the shack. A lucky shot brought down one of them and ended him off to one side, so that he missed the shanty and

rolled past our corner; two more of them sheered off
at this, but the last one, a bullet-proof old bull, came
lunging straight down for the roof of the shack. Several shots hit him; but on he came, like a locomotive,
and with a mighty bound landed squarely in the middle of the roof. A cannon-ball could not have struck
it much harder. He went plump through, and—
mercy! how the turf and broken poles flew away to
make room for him! Almost at the same instant, several great boulders came bounding down; and one of
them, striking the top of our stone chimney, sent a
shower of rocks flying away in front of it. Still other
big stones came thundering down; the uproar was
something tremendous.

"Of course we were awfully excited and a little
scared; and though we didn't run we did some lively
dodging, firing away cartridges with desperate energy.

"The buffaloes didn't go past us all in one herd, so
we had quite a chance at them while they were smash-
ing through the curing racks and rolling over on all
sides; and we secured seven of them.

"About the time the rest had got well past, the old
bull in the shack, after knocking things endwise generally inside, came 'bousing' out of the open door.
Tom brought him down with a ball through the neck.

"Then we looked about us and took a survey of
things. It was a crazy-looking camp. It looked as if
an Iowa 'twister' had just passed over. The shack was
badly damaged inside as well as out, and the curing
racks knocked all to pieces, while skins and carcasses,
boulders, dry logs, sticks and stones lay scattered all
about us. It took the six of us all that day to find our
ponies and repair damages.

" That was the first time that we had seen buffalo so
high up on the buttes ; but afterwards, when the snow
got deep in the valleys, we found them up on the very
summits of some of the highest peaks there, where the
wind had swept the ground bare of snow and uncovered
the dry hill-grass."

IV.

There were just six of us, camped in the big woods on Cache Lake. Col. W——, the "Fat Man of Texas," whose feats of muscular strength have made him famous throughout the Southwest, was the most important figure in our expedition—important as chief, as a shot, and lastly on account of his tremendous strength and colossal proportions.

Mac was a celebrated individual also. Mac was a conjurer and "sleight-of-hand" performer. One of his first exploits, after we were fairly settled in camp, was to frighten nearly to death a Comanche chief and two of his braves.

These Indians had ridden down from their village to pay their respects and beg a little "tobac," when Mac was prompted to try his arts on them. His audience was at first considerably astonished at the feats exhibited; then a little frightened and overawed, and finally so terribly scared that they took to their heels, or rather their horses, in indiscriminate flight.

They had held out courageously until Mac appeared to swallow a huge bowie-knife, and immediately to draw it out of the pit of his stomach. That finished the scene, and we saw no more Indians during our stay. The rest of us were individuals of far less brilliant attainments, who had in various ways gained permission to accompany the illustrious colonel on this his annual hunt in the woods of the "Nation."

The cook, or "camp rustler," was a fifteen-year-old *protégé* of Mac's, who was enamored of the conjurer's art, and who went by the somewhat indefinite title of "Son." Jimmie H——, a telegraph operator at one of the frontier posts; "Jack," a seventeen-year-old freighter and the son of a freighter on the Ft. S—— route, with myself, made up the party.

"We'd oughter av'rige from ten ter fifteen turkeys apiece every day we're out," the colonel had declared before we started.

Here let me remark that we did *not* average ten or fifteen apiece each day out, and that, despite the colonel's stories of former exploits, we don't believe any one else ever did, not in those woods, at least.

About nine o'clock on the first morning, the writer shouldered his eleven-pound, ten-gauge Baker, and sallied forth into the "deep and trackless" woods. He carried a hearty lunch in the pockets of his hunting-coat, expecting to be gone all day, and to return at night laden with at least six large gobblers; the other nine were to hang upon the limbs at some conspicuous point near the edge of the creek-bank, and to be brought in the next morning upon a horse.

As this was my first experience in turkey-hunting, being a fair shot, I of course expected to make an "average" bag during the day.

As the others all went up the creek, where our leader said turkeys were most abundant, I determined to go down the stream, and have the whole field in that direction to myself. It was a beautiful sunshiny morning in December, and little streaks of mellow light straggled in through the tangled growth of vines and branches overhead, strewing golden patches over the dark gray clothing of the massive trunks between which I stole with soft and easy tread.

Not a breath of air was stirring, and in picking my way among the great bodies of the white oak, elm and cottonwood, every twig unluckily stepped upon snapped with a sharp, spiteful report that could have been heard at a hundred yards' distance.

The stillness and this cracking of brush were unfavorable, yet I concluded that where turkeys were so thick and so tame that ten or fifteen was merely the average bag of a day's hunt, the breaking of a few small sticks could be no great obstacle in the way of success.

But as time wore on in the same ghost-like stillness, broken only by the sound of my own foot-falls, with not even a sight of game to enliven the monotony of the tramp, I began to feel somewhat discouraged, and rather inclined to believe that the "Fat Man's" turkey stories were humbugs, or much too large for the expected amount of truth entering into them.

For six long hours I wandered wearily through those woods, wading creeks, scrambling over meshes of tangled vines, wallowing in sweet-brier thickets that tore my clothing and scratched my body in a hundred places, and was not rewarded with a solitary glimpse of the game which had been the object of all this tramping.

I made my way campward, firm in the conviction that Col. W——was a nuisance.

The first object which met my eyes upon reaching the camp was the huge hulk of this same Fat Man, deposited upon my new blankets, which were spread upon the ground near the fire.

He was reclining upon one elbow, with a great flabby hand under his fat face.

He didn't look a bit tired, but as comfortable, sleek and well-fed as ever. I came at once to the disgusted conclusion that he hadn't been forty rods away from the "wicky up" during that whole day.

"Kill any turkeys?" I asked, with a sarcasm born of disgust.

He shook his head gravely, without raising his eyelids. "Too still for huntin'," he muttered, sleepily.

I attempted no further conversation with him.

Mac came straggling in shortly, and dropped upon a log near the fire.

He said nothing, but looked as though he might have swallowed another bowie-knife, and for once have failed in extricating the weapon from his stomach.

At any rate, I had not the heart to break in upon his meditations, and the colonel still gazed contentedly at the end of his nose.

But we were destined for a surprise soon. At sundown Jack and Son came in lugging seven great brownish-black birds, which, upon close inspection, proved to be turkeys. Jack had killed three with his Winchester rifle, and Son had slain the others with an old single-barreled shot-gun.

We were all elated. The turkeys had been discovered at last. Even the colonel roused up, and deigned to examine the birds. They were not as large, he said, as those he had been in the habit of finding, but still they would do to fry.

"Son," said Mac, as we sat down to supper, "Son I'm proud of you. You shall go with me to-morrow, and stay with me all day, too."

I edged around near the young freighter.

"Jack," I whispered, "let's you and I keep together to-morrow."

"All right!" he replied.

At daylight the next morning we two started off together, leaving the others busy in preparing to follow.

"Now," said Jack, after we had crossed the creek and were out of hearing; "now, then, you just pull yer freights right on my trail fer about an hour, an' I'll take you to where there's turkeys, an' lots of 'em, though they're purty wild. The fellers from the Fort have hunted 'em all the fall. There ain't no use in lookin' fer turkeys through no such big woods as these here, 'cause ther ain't nothin' here fer 'em tu eat. You've got ter git out 'mongst the hackberries an' pecans."

At length we struck the mouth of a sandy creek, and Jack led me out of the woods and on to the prairie, where the walking was excellent.

"'Bout two miles up this creek," remarked he, as we hurried forward, "jest about two miles on, we'll take into the woods agin; but ye won't find no sech woods es there is down round camp an' you'll see turkeys in 'em too."

A half-hour later he announced himself ready to enter the nearest grove.

The timber was, as he had said, small; little more, in fact, than a dense thicket of hackberry poles and young pecans, but there was no underbrush, and the ground was bare of all growth but the trees.

Here's where we'll find 'em," declared my companion, sinking his voice to a whisper, and halting to give instructions.

"Now," said he, "I don't b'lieve we'd best keep together in here. We'll git more shots a heap to go separate. You keep 'long in the out edge, an' I'll take down next the creek, an' then we'll drive 'em all out ahead of us inter the nex' grove. Ye see, this here ground's all covered in hackberry seed, an' this is jest the time o' mornin' they're scattered all out feedin'."

"All right, Jack; just as you say," I returned. "Shall we meet at the upper end of this grove?"

He nodded, and turning away, stole silently as an Indian down towards the creek.

Following his example as nearly as possible in my movements, I stole forward on tiptoe among the slender tree-trunks, keeping a sharp look-out on every side for any appearance of game.

I had not gone a hundred yards when my ears were assailed by a chorus of *Quit! Quit! Quit!* and the ground on every hand seemed suddenly alive with big black birds scooting away from me on all sides.

I had tiptoed into the midst of a whole drove of feeding turkeys, and had alarmed them before seeing them.

My gun was quickly at my face, and catching sight at a vanishing gobbler over its polished tubes, I fired and secured him.

I turned to shoot again, looking in all directions, but the distant pattering of foot-steps growing rapidly fainter each moment was all that rewarded my attention. Not a thing was to be seen save bare poles, dry branches, and the leaf-strewn earth.

Well satisfied, however, with my first shot at the wild turkey, I chucked a loaded shell into the empty barrel, took up my bird—a splendid glossy fellow, with

a pendant brush four inches in length—and made my
way stealthily forward as before.

A sharp report from Jack's Winchester now admon-
ished me that he too had found game.

Five minutes or more passed in silently stealing
through the hackberry grove, when I suddenly came
upon an open clear of trees of any description. It was
a large field of dry reeds such as seldom grow so far
from the edges of streams and ponds.

My drove of turkeys had mostly fled in this direction; perhaps there were some of them hiding in this
same reed-patch. If so—but I had no time to speculate upon the problem before my attention was arrested
by a sudden rustling among the dry stalks just ahead.
Whuh! whuh! whuh! a great black and bronze bird
rose not twenty feet away, and as he flopped off in a
direct line, presented a mark which no hunter who had
not lost his head entirely could have missed.

My Baker ordered a sudden halt to the flying bird.
Another rose almost instantly at the report and dropped
but a few yards to the right of the first. Greatly
excited, I hastily reloaded and hurried forward to
secure the game. The first bird was dead, but the
other, undoubtedly winged, had taken to its long legs
and was nowhere to be found.

I left the patch carrying five—three males and two
hens. Jack met me at the appointed place. He carried
three great birds.

My confidence in the Fat Man and his stirring tales
was now somewhat revived, and it began to seem as
though with hard and persistent hunting one might
average ten per day for a few days at least.

At about noon Jack and I built a fire, and we dined

off the broiled hearts and gizzards of turkeys, eaten with the baking-powder biscuits brought in our pockets —a dinner which under the circumstances we relished greatly.

That afternoon our chase proved almost a failure; we hunted until sundown, only securing one bird, a lucky wing-shot from the Baker, made at a remarkable distance. Just before sundown we ensconced ourselves in the bed of a dry, sandy run near the edge of a large grove, and but a few yards from a fresh turkey-roost, which Jack had discovered during the day.

Turkeys usually roost near the edge of the prairie or on the bank of a stream, and when they go to roost at night, walk out upon the open ground, take a hard run, then rising gradually on the wing, sail easily into the top of the desired tree.

If you can find the roosting-place and hide near by, or succeed in crawling under them after dark, you are pretty certain to make a bag of two or three, or if they be thick upon the tree, even a larger number may be secured. We had lain upon the sand under the overhanging bushes but a short time when we heard a rush of wings near by, and the next instant four great dark birds sailed over our heads and out into the woods beyond.

Jack looked at me in disgusr. "Knew there wasn't but four or five of 'em roosting here," he said, "but I didn't reckon they'd be so mighty sharp. Ye see, they've been chased all day, an' they've got mighty cunnin'. 'Taint no use to hunt 'em now, only when they're feedin' in the mornin'."

We both rose and peered through the tree-tops. There was but one to be seen, seated upon the topmost bough of a tall tree some three hundred yards away. Though its form was plainly outlined against the yellow twilight of the western sky, the bird did not look larger than a small chicken from where we stood.

"No use tryin' to git under 'em through all them sweet-briers and thick brush; he's too skeery."

"Jack," said I, "you can show me a long shot now."

"All right, boss," he answered, in a pleased voice. "It's gettin' powerful dim here in the woods, but I can see my sights plain against that sky, an' you jest watch that old feller a minute, please."

Instead I watched Jack's steady motion, as he raised the Winchester to his face. He certainly could not hit so small a mark at such a distance, even in broad daylight.

For several seconds the young hunter stood motionless as a monument, his lithe figure growing uncertain amid the shadows that seemed momentarily growing higher among the tree-trunks; then his face was lit up for a brief instant by a bright blaze of light from the muzzle of his rifle, and the woods rang with its sharp, spiteful report.

Instantly lifting my gaze to the distant tree-top, in utter astonishment I saw the turkey roll off its high perch, and plunge down into the darkness.

Fairly satisfied with our bag of ten turkeys, we left eight of them hanging at the noon camp, and after a hard, adventurous tramp, reached the Cache camp late in the evening.

The boys were all in, and all but the colonel had met with fair success. The Fat Man had remained at camp to guard the horses and camp equipage.

He did not kill a single bird while we were out. Five days later we drove into the town of G—— with half a wagon-load of turkeys, and as we were tired and hungry, unloaded, stowed them away in the colonel's shooting-gallery, and repaired to our various places of resort for supper and rest.

The next morning upon gathering at the gallery to divide the spoils, we found a new proprietor in charge. The turkeys had been sold to parties in town, and the famous Fat Man had gone, no one knew when or in what direction. Numerous creditors mourned his loss.

It was near the holiday season, and the birds sold well. I could but think how differently we provide for the table on the Red River than do our friends in the East. Here nature furnishes the stores for which others toil in different manner. Generous, indeed, in the far West are the gifts of the autumn and the early winter days.

V.

THE BIRD-CATCHER'S ADVENTURE.

The catching, taming and training of young mocking-birds is a favorite pastime with numbers of young people living in the vicinity of New Orleans and other cities of the South and Southwest. It often proves a quite profitable pursuit, too; for the bird-fanciers, who buy for Northern or foreign markets, pay from five to eight dollars for a trained singer, and the young birds, when first caught, will bring fifty cents a pair.

As may be imagined, however, there are far more "catchers" than "trainers," since there are three somewhat rare qualifications necessary to the trainer's success in rearing a mocking-bird singer.

First of these necessities may be mentioned a natural sympathy with, and recognition of, the modes and peculiarities of the bird; that is to say, the trainer must be a bit of a naturalist by instinct, with a touch of the imaginative in his study of the bird's habits. Second, it is quite necessary that he should possess some musical accomplishment or play some piping instrument, and do this fairly.

The third condition to success is that of favorable surroundings. That locality where may be heard the greatest variety of out-door musical sounds is certainly the most favorable to the rearing of a good singer. As is well known, however, there are many *unmusical* sounds which will suggest a strain or a snatch of unwonted song to the ear of this delightful bird; the

44

whine of a dog or the mewing of a cat are often quite exactly imitated.

Johnny Trumbull, a Northern-born lad who lives in the famous "Cross Timbers," of Central Texas, is a bird-catcher, who, with favorable location, combines the personal qualifications above hinted at. His home is surrounded by hills, rocks, and the beautiful post-oak and live-oak of this peculiarly attractive region; a region too, which in birds, animals, reptiles and an innumerable variety of insects, is a very paradise, indeed, for one who is blessed with the tastes of a naturalist.

He catches and rears but few birds, however, and never sends a bird to market until it has become an accomplished singer. It is his special business to rear extra good singers, and he leaves the wholesale trade to those who have no higher artistic ambition. His birds are never sent out with less than a year's tutelage, and should one of them prove rather dull, or lacking in quality of voice, he opens the cage-door and sets it free.

Twice each year Mr. Trumbull makes a business trip to the city of New Orleans, and the train that carries him conveys also a half-dozen or more of Johnny's bird-cages, each containing one or two rare singers. He has made some remarkable sales for the lad, one bird bringing the fine sum of twenty-five dollars, and the total quite frequently reaching one hundred. As the gentleman stays in the city two or three weeks each time, the fancier to whom he takes the birds has ample opportunity to test their powers and to price them accordingly.

The mocking-bird, like the quail, is a quite domestic

little creature, and often builds its nest in the immediate vicinity of human habitations. The Cross Timbers
seem to be the natural summer home of these birds.
All day long the woods and hills are "tintinnabulat-
ing"—if I may use such a word—with their trilling
melodies; and I have never seen them so numerous
elsewhere.

They are caged and carefully fed for a few weeks,
when, in response to the singing of other birds and the
variety of musical sounds with which the young trainer
regales them, they begin to ruffle their feathers, cock
their little heads on one side, swell their youthful
throats and imitate.

When one of them "gets a going in good style,"
Johnny carries its cage out into the door-yard, seats
himself beside it, and assails the little fellow with a
volley of warbling notes and quivering trills. If it be
quick and apt, with a good range of voice, it will respond
at once, catching here and there a cord and nearly
bursting its small throat with its " *Quillopy—willopy—
quirk—a—wirk—sweet— tweets !* "

If the bird be at all lively and emulative, Johnny
will soon work the little chap into a perfect frenzy of
mad *musicalness*, in which it loses all desire to imitate
and launches out with wild improvisations of its own.
Then the lad studies its moods, and whistles or plays
accordingly. When the bird feels gay and festive, he
whistles his liveliest tunes ; when, as is often the case,
its song grows pensive and sad in tone, he plays low,
sweet strains upon the harmonica. Then, also, the
cage often hangs in the sunshine, in the out-door air all
day long, and other out-door songsters are brought
into requisition as trainers.

But Johnny has other pets besides his mocking-birds; a tame antelope, an opossum, a pair of jack-rabbits, and of the feathered tribe an eagle, a raven, a "scissor-tail" (paradise bird), and several varieties of the beautiful Southern red-bird. And my story is of an adventure which befell him while on a bird-hunting trip last summer; it occurred, in fact, at the time he secured the eagle now numbered among his pets.

This eaglet Johnny captured from a nest in the top of a tall oak, back of Quarry Peak, a long, ledge-crowned ridge, distant a mile and a half from his home. On his return from the trip to the eyrie, he had determined to cross the crest of the ridge and descend the crags, instead of making a circuit of it, as he had done in going to the nest. The ledge does not average more than forty feet in height, but in most places on that side it was so steep that ascent was impossible, and at any point quite arduous. There were two places, however, which Johnny had discovered in his rambles and hunting excursions, where the ragged, jutting rocks afforded a sort of stairway which might be descended by a hunter with steady nerves and flexible muscles. At both these places there were points where the descent must be made by dropping from the edge of one rock to the top of another six or eight feet below.

Having the eagle as an incumbrance, Johnny this time selected what he considered the safer "stairway," and strapping the bird-to his back, began carefully getting down. He had got about half-way to the bottom of this niche in the ledge, and had just dropped from an overhanging "step" of the stairway to the broad, flat surface of the one next below it, when a laintive, half-human cry reached his ears, ...ng to come from the base of the crag beneath.

A cold chill crept all over the boy's flesh and set all his nerves a-tingle with fearful sensations. He had heard that cry before.

A great branching oak with limbs shadowing the jagged rocks and almost touching them, had grown up from below. He peeped cautiously down through its foliage, not daring to make the slightest noise and almost fearing to breathe.

He could see nothing.

But soon again that wailing, womanish cry came quivering up from below. Johnny clenched his hands and set his teeth hard to keep from giving way to his terror.

It was the prolonged, moaning caterwaul of a panther. Johnny had never heard one in the daytime before; but now he remembered a large, long crevice in the rocks near the foot of the big oak; he knew instinctively that there must be a den of these dangerous beasts beneath him, and that he had just heard the plaintive scream of a young one calling to its dam.

Immediately the cry was repeated. Johnny listened intently. It began in a soft minor key, sliding gently upward to a thrilling, heart-moving climax, then dying gradually away in a woefully pathetic and wistful cadence. Yes, it *was* a young one, there was not volume enough of sound to have come from the lungs of a full-grown panther. But where was the old mother-beast?

Should he go up or down? He had no weapons with him save his jack-knife and a small pocket revolver, a mere toy; and with panthers he concluded that the

knife was equally to be relied upon with the pistol.
He cast his eyes wistfully at the rugged, disheartening
rocks above, and then bent forward and took another
anxious look among the limbs and brush below.

While bending over thus, the shadow of some flying
thing seemed suddenly to pass over him; there was an
ominous rattle of loosened stones above and a rustling
shock among the upper branches of the tree. Then on
the instant, another shrill scream,which now seemed to
come up triumphantly from the foot of the ledge, was
answered by a snarling cry from the oak-top.

Johnny knew just what had happened, and crouched
quite faint and limp with fright, upon the shelf of
rock. For a few moments he dared not look upward,
then another horrible snarl and a ripping of bark
among the high limbs drew his eyes irresistibly upward. At the sight which met his gaze, he shrank and
cowered still closer beneath the overhanging rock from
which he had dropped but a moment before.

The old panther was there, the mother of the young,
at the base of the ledge. Swaying to and fro, she
clung to a branch and glared fiercely upon him, her
white fangs gleaming as the lip quivered in rage above
them. Through the shaking foliage the lad could see
her lithe, tawny body stretched back in a crouching
attitude along the bending branch, as if about to leap
down upon him, while the snarling cries grew louder.

Johnny tried to think, to plan briefly, some way of
escape or defense. If he leaped down, the danger of
an attack would be increased he feared. If he
attempted to climb back up the rocks, he must approach
nearer to the angry beast, already at such frightfully
close quarters.

The bird-catcher's dilemma was a terrible one.

For several moments the beast kept her menacing attitude. At length, puzzled, perhaps, or awed by the death-like stillness and steady eyes of the lad, the animal ceased her threatening manœuvres abruptly and turned round upon the branch as if to descend or go back up the cliff. But just then the wailing cry of the young one rose again, when as if mistrusting treachery on Johnny's part towards her cub, the old panther suddenly whirled about, and at a single bound landed on the shelving rock beside his body.

With an involuntary yell of horror, the boy kicked out both feet spasmodically, and with such violence that his boot-heels, striking plump against the beast, pitched her off the narrow edge of the rock. But even as she fell over, the agile brute, *quirling* about, struck her claws into his legs and drew him after her.

As he slid off, Johnny threw a desperate clutch at a branch of the oak a little below, and grasping it with both hands, stayed his fall—though a part of each leg of his pantaloons disappeared down the crag in the panther's claws.

In an ecstasy of terror, he drew himself on the bending limb and got to the trunk of the tree, expecting every instant that the fierce creature would be upon him.

But having found her kit, the old beast was, perhaps, reassured and content; and our young naturalist, climbing hurriedly upward, swung off upon the rocks higher up and escaped to the top of the crag. As he made off, the eaglet shook its rumpled feathers and gaped dolefully; the breath had been nearly jammed out of it by the weight of its captor's body as he lay on the shelf of rock, with the panther watching him.

The week following, one of their neighbors, to whom Johnny had recounted his adventure, succeeded in trapping the old panther at the foot of the oak and capturing the young one by throwing a horse blanket over it. The little creature was offered to Johnny as a pet, but he declined to undertake its education, his interest centering in birds rather than in the *felidæ*.

VI.

To the lover of rod and gun who needs a change of air and a few months of out-door recreation, few places can be more interesting than the region of the Upper Red River.

There is a strip of country about one hundred miles in breadth along this stream and its branches, including the middle and western frontiers of northern Texas, and also the south and southwest of the Indian Territory, which, if not a veritable "hunter's paradise," is at least plentifully stocked with a large variety of game. Deer, antelope, turkey, wild goose, duck, crane and prairie chicken abound there, while smaller varieties of game, the "Jack," or "mule ear," the common rabbit and the quail are almost overabundant.

In the deep woods that skirt the " Nation branches" of the Red may be found the bear, panther, wild cat, wild hog and opossum. In winter the waters and sand-bars of the Red River are a famous resort for wild geese, and the fields belonging to the scattering farms along the south bank are often seen swarming with crane, geese and brant. There is plenty of hunting in the region for at least six months in the year, and of the most exciting sort, too.

But there is fish as well as other game, for Red River and all its deeper branches are well stocked with great "cats," buffalo-fish, red-horse and sucker.

The writer's notions of fishing as a business had

been pretty much confined to sea-coasts and lake-shores, until he became acquainted with several persons on the banks of these streams who make a living, and a good one, by catching the great lazy cats and buffaloes that loll about the bottoms of the Red and its tributaries.

Of course, there is nothing in the operations of these individual fishermen that is worthy the name of commerce, and their work is lacking in the exciting romance of the rolling wave and the smacking breeze of the sea, but these lone fishers sometimes meet with exciting adventures nevertheless. Trot-line fishing may, as a usual thing, prove tame business; but when you are required to detach from the main line a forty-pound cat, and bring him safely to land, or pull him into your boat, you are quite likely to have a lively time of it, and to conclude when the task is ended— if indeed the attempt is not a complete failure—that you have had excitement enough for one day.

Forty pounds sounds pretty large, but there are fish of even twice that size in these very streams, and it is with the catching of one of these giant cats that my story has to deal.

Aleck and Sam Mosby are two stout lads, who live with their widowed mother upon a small farm on the south bank of Red River. Their father died in New Orleans, some years ago, of yellow fever, and since that time the boys have been the main stay of the widow and their two young sisters. They have but little land under cultivation, and in fact the soil bakes so hard in the heat of the summer sun that not much can be raised, except in the garden, where they keep the earth constantly loosened with their heavy hoes.

But the sterility of the land gives these enterprising youths very little uneasiness, so long as the streams are stocked with fish, and the annual season of bird-migration brings thousands of geese and brant flocking into the river and among the fields above and below.

Twenty miles away is the frontier railroad-town of H——, a lively place, and the home of a score of "cattle men," worth half a million or more. Fish and game find a ready market here, at good prices, for what is not consumed at home can be easily shipped to the large towns east and north, or on the Gulf coast.

Thus Aleck and Sam are able with fish net, trot-line and gun to support their small family in comfort; and with the aid of the garden, the cows and butter, they even manage to lay by a small sum each year.

"It seems like a shiftless kind of life," says the widow, "this hunting and fishing; but the boys work real faithful in the garden at whatever they're a doing; and they buy a good many books to study in the long evenings. So I believe they're going to come out all right in the end."

Scarcely a week goes by during the months in which game can be preserved, that either Sam or Aleck does not go to town driving a span of mules hitched to the spring wagon, laden with twenty or thirty dollars' worth of fish and birds. Surely there's not much "shiftlessness" about such a thrifty business as that.

Their fishing operations are mostly confined to a large, deep pond, formed at the mouth of a fine creek, —one of the largest of the "Nation branches"—which empties into Red River, nearly opposite their dwelling. This pond, or rather deep hole, is some half a mile in length, and has been formed by the peculiar shifting process with which the longer stream manages so often to change the channel of its water course.

The red sands of the bottom have been banked up at the mouth of the creek until, in this case, a permanent dam has been formed, and the original channel is completely blocked. The water finds an outlet at the lower end of the bar, however, running over in a shallow, swift current, that is not easily ascended in a row-boat.

The boys "pole" their skiff through this channel, and then find themselves floating easily upon the deep, narrow sheet above, which nearly fills the bank of the creek for some distance back into the woods.

This hole of water, in many places twenty feet deep, is the home of the largest cat and buffalo known to the channels of the Upper Red and its branches. But the fish are scarcely more at home than the fishers, for Sam and, Aleck go the rounds of their trot-lines and take the big fellows in in a way that would do credit to the ingenuity of more experienced fishermen than they.

Their trot-lines consist of large ropes stretched across the channel, an end tied to a tree on either bank and knotted once in six feet for the whole length. Each of these knots holds a small iron ring, from which depends, fastened with a common harness-snap, a stout line and hook, the latter baited with fresh meat and reaching nearly to the bottom of the channel. The big cat and buffalo feed low down in the water, and must be baited in their favorite haunts if caught at all.

The boys' method of landing these big fish is ingenious. In the stern of their boat is a stout, free roller, wound with a heavy reel-line. A ring in the end of

this line allows them to take off the short line, upon
which the fish is hooked, and take him in tow. If
the fish be an extra large one, the ring of the reel-line
can be placed within the snap before it is unhooked
from the rope, and then the stout denizen of the
waters is allowed to amuse himself on the reel until
tired, when he is drawn to the top and landed by the
aid of a boat-hook.

One foggy morning last October, they repaired as
usual to the trot-lines, of which they then had three,
thrown across the "Hole in the Cache," as they have
named the long pond; and upon nearing the first
stringer, discovered that something unusual had
occurred. The rope, which had been drawn quite
taut several feet above the water, was pulled downward at a point near the middle until several yards of
its length were completely submerged.

"Must be a whale or an alligator on that line!"
cried Aleck. "Just look, Sam! It's done pulled
clean under water, an' stretched harder'n a barbed
wire, an' 'taint much bigger, neither."

Sam was as much astonished as his brother.

"There ain't no alligators here, Aleck," he answered,
gazing at the line with wide-open eyes. "But I don't
know but you're right about the whale."

Aleck was in the bow of the boat, while Sam had
been seated in the stern, paddling, until this event had
caused him to rise and stare wonderingly through the
light fog.

"Well, don't let's stand gaping here any longer,"
exclaimed Aleck, at length. "Do you paddle her forward easy, Sam, till I can reach down in the water an'
find that rope. We'll soon know what's got a-hold of

that hook. Good thing them lines are linen and stout enough to hold a horse, or else that one'd break, sure. I reckon, though, that the rope'd snap afore one o' them lines."

By the time he had ceased speaking, the prow of the skiff was directly over the centre of the submerged rope, and in a trice Aleck was down on his knees, with an arm thrust into the water.

"Mebbe," said he, "an old wet log's rolled down with the under-current and caught the hook, for you see it's sort a bent down-stream. No, it ain't!" he exclaimed, excitedly; "there's a "—but before he could finish, the rope upon which he was tugging flew out of his hand and straightened up with a "swish," catching the rim of his hat as it went, and throwing that article clean over the boat's stern and into the water beyond.

The next instant there was a deep swirl in the water just ahead of the prow, then a heavy splash, another little eddying whirlpool, and then a quick strain at the rope which wrenched it down to the water's edge again.

"Back water! back water!" shouted Aleck, seizing one of the oars which had been shipped and paddling furiously at the bow. "Back water, Sam. Fetch the stern 'round an' get the reel ring into the snap quicker'n lightnin'! Another sech a jerk'll break that rope."

The boat was brought about with a sudden energy that nearly pitched Aleck over the prow.

"I've got the reel-ring snapped," cried Sam a moment later, "but how'll I get the other ring out? The old fellow's quiet just now, but he's pulling like a steam-engine, an' if I try to pull him in an' unhook his line, I'm afraid he'll cut up again an' break it."

"I don't know how we'll fix it," returned Aleck, anxiously; " but we *must* have that old fellow; why, Sam, he's as big as you or me, but—there—now's your time! Quick! he's slackened up for another rush."

Sam had the snap free from the trot-line ring before his brother ceased speaking. And none too soon, either, for the great fish made another quick run and shot away up-stream at a surprising rate of speed. The roller fairly whistled as the line reeled off, but Aleck soon had the oars working, and a lively chase began.

"We ought to keep up with a cat-fish!" cried Sam, as he saw that in spite of his brother's exertions the line was still fast paying out. " You ain't a goin' to do it though, Aleck, 'less you work livelier'n this. The reel-line never'll hold that old monster—'tain't stout enough, an' it's mighty nigh paid out now."

Aleck did his best, but, not a minute later, the roller stopped and the line snapped.

"There, we've lost him!" shouted Sam, in disgust, as he saw the broken end of the line rapidly retreating up stream.

"Grab the paddle! jump over behind here an' help!" yelled Aleck. " He won't go out of the hole, an' we'll pick up the line again at the other end."

"Aleck was right; the fish slackened his speed soon, and Sam gathered in the end of the still floating line.

" You take the oars, Sam, and let me handle him this time, please," said Aleck, coaxingly.

Sam reluctantly exchanged places. He wasn't so stout as Aleck, and he *did* want to secure that fish.

Aleck slowly hauled in the slack, and then with great

caution *felt* the mouth of his victim. But the fellow was gamey, and didn't propose to stand any trifling. He turned his course and ran swiftly down stream, coming almost directly towards the boat.

"Now, then," said Aleck, exultingly, "now, then, we'll have him an' no mistake. Jest wait till he gets past, Sam, an' then show what you're made of for half a minute, an' then that old cat can do the rest of our rowing."

In a few seconds the line had doubled and the farther string was gently rippling past, not ten feet distant from the boat's side.

"All ready," said Aleck, and away went the boat. The young fisherman now began rapidly hauling in the line. He would not trust the roller again.

The line was soon drawn taut, and bracing himself in the bow, Aleck carefully tested the powers of the runaway. The boat forged ahead, and the line showed no signs of yielding. Aleck gave the command to quit rowing, and a moment afterwards the boat was gliding along close in shore, with no other motive power than that given by the gigantic cat which had thus been made to take them in tow.

"We'll soon tire him out now, Sam," said Aleck, in triumph; "and how's this for a free ride?"

"But you've got the line wound round your hand an' wrist, Aleck," said Sam. "Remember there's big snags just under water along here, an' if we should strike one, you'd be in a nice fix."

"Oh, I can hold any cat there is in here," answered the other, confidently. "All I'm afraid of is that he'll break the line, an' then he'll go over the riffle into the river, as they do sometimes when they're hard-pushed.

You know we've lost two old whoppers that way, an' I believe this one's goin' to try it. See, we ain't fifty yards from the end of the bar an' he's goin' yet; there won't be no "——

Aleck concluded not to finish that sentence. A sudden conviction seemed to have seized upon his mind that he ought to take an immediate cold-water bath.

At any rate, he took a meteoric header over the bow of the boat. A sudden plunge, a glimmer of heels at the agitated surface of the water, and the astonished eyes of Sam sought in vain for any trace of his brother.

Sam, himself, had received a considerable shock from the striking of the boat against a sudden stub projecting from the bank. He thought nothing of this, however, but really began to feel alarmed about Aleck.

Could it be that the big fish had drawn his brother under and swallowed him?

It seemed an age as he stood staring blankly at the water, before he saw the rise of a dozen bubbles, which preceded the popping up of Aleck's head, some dozen yards below.

"Got 'im yet!" spluttered the diver, blowing the water from mouth and nose as he still floundered along in the wake of the fish. But by this time he managed to keep his head above the surface, using his free arm in lusty strokes to keep from being drawn under again.

"Goin' down Red River," he shouted back at Sam. "Git to Shreveport to-night; pick up your oars an' come on, or you'll be left!"

The demoralized boatman siezed the oars and began

a pursuit. He sat with his face to the bow, however, so as to watch the swimmer in front.

Aleck was now fast nearing shallow water, and an instant later Sam saw the great gray back of the cat away out on the "ripple."

Suddenly Aleck gathered himself up and stood waist-deep in the water. Rapidly hauling in the line, with a hard pull on the mouth of the tired fish, he rushed ahead shouting triumphantly.

And now the big cat had made a fatal mistake. The water was too shallow for his great body ; he was tired, and the hard pulling of his pursuer held him at a stand-still. He grew sulky, gave up the fight, and rolled over and over.

An instant later Sam saw his brother seated in triumph on the half-submerged body of the floundering monster.

"Got him safe now!" cried Aleck, as Sam brought the boat alongside. "He's a whopper—as big as a good big hog!"

He wasn't quite as large as that, but after they had flopped him over the edge of the boat and taken him home, he was found to weigh eighty-nine pounds and four ounces.

VII.

I have often met old hunters who have heard of battles between the grizzly bear and the immense, tawny panther of the Rocky Mountains; but I have only once known a man who had seen such a combat.

Sergeant Roseman of the —th United States Cavalry, whom I met in Wyoming while on a hunting expedition in '86, told me of a fierce fight between "Old Eph" and two mountain lions which he had "umpired"—as he put it—near Caspar Mountain several years before.

At that time he was stationed at Fort Fetterman. A party of citizens had come out from St. Paul, Minn., to hunt the big game, then so plentiful in eastern Wyoming, and the sergeant, one of the best hunters in his regiment, was allowed to go with them, taking a small detachment of soldiers to look after the camp, and take care of the game. The party had been hunting elk among the foot-hills of the Caspar range, and near the great ragged mountain which is their chief feature, when the adventure befell him.

"I killed an elk," said he, "early one morning, and as I often did in a region where there were grizzly or silver-tip bears, I left it where it fell, for bear bait. There is nothing the big bears of this region are more fond of than a freshly killed elk or a black-tail. I had already, at one time and another, shot seven bears by baiting in this way, and watching by the bodies of the dead elks.

" Perched comfortably in the branches of an ever-
green, or lying upon the top of some high rock within
a few rods of your bait, it isn't such a desperate adventure, the killing of a grizzly. A good gun, using heavy
ammunition, decent markmanship, and a steady nerve
are all that is required. If you are fresh at the business though, you probably won't fret a great deal if
the bear fails to come.

" This time I had killed an elk in just such a spot
and with just such surroundings as I would have
selected could I have had full choice. I shot it in the
act of drinking at a small basin of water in the bed of
the cañon, which cut back into the foot of old Caspar
Mountain. The side of the mountain on either hand
was rutted with deep gorges leading into the cañon.
Quaking asp thickets clustered around the heads of
these ravines, while the bottoms, wherever vegetation
could take hold, were grown to willows, currant and
bullberry bushes. It was just the place for bears, and
their sign was as plentiful as I had ever seen it anywhere.

" The spot was only a mile from our camp, and when
I came in from my hunt—for we hunted singly or in
twos and threes as the notion took us—I found three
of the St. Paul men taking a late dinner. I told them
of my success, and invited them to go with me, and lie
in wait for bears that evening. They declined, declaring that they hadn't lost any bears, and, therefore,
didn't feel called upon to hunt for 'em. I was welcome,
they said, to gather all the stray grizzlies in the region,
and put my particular brand on 'em.

" So about three o'clock I went up to my bait alone.
I found it undisturbed, and perched myself in the

crevice of a ledge of rock, some thirty yards distant, which position I reached by making a ladder of dry poles that lay among some drift of a recent 'washout.' My hiding-place was perfectly safe from the attack of a bear, should I be lucky enough to lure one within shot, as it was fully fifteen feet from the base of the ledge, at a perpendicular height.

"I found the crack, in which I could stretch myself at full length, such a comfortable place that I concluded to watch all night, provided no bear came to my bait sooner. I had not long to wait, however, before I was treated to the most thorough and thrilling surprise of all my hunting experience.

"I had lain, perhaps, an hour, and the sun had just sunk behind the mountains back of me, so that their shadows had crawled over the tops of the lower ones in front, when I heard the sound of soft foot-falls just on the other side of a fringe of bullberry bushes, which skirted the stream above the spring where my elk lay. I pricked my ears and looked sharply for game, which from the muffled sound I took to be two or three bears running down the cañon.

"I had no time to speculate on the nature of the animals before there bounded in sight two big tawny mountain-lions! They were racing down the cañon, jumping sidewise and running against each other in a way that was, no doubt, intended to be playful, and I was just about to stop one of them with a shot from my rifle, when in the same breath each of them caught a scent of the elk's carcass, and came to a sudden halt.

"They stood for a moment with heads erect, ears pricked forward, and tails switching eagerly, their yellow eyes gleaming and scintillating, the white spots on their **breasts** offering a splendid target if I had cared to shoot at once. They were fine, sleek animals with glossy coats, far more imposing in looks, and much larger than the panther of the East and South, and I was anxious to bag both of them, which I thought I might make sure of doing if they attacked my bait, as I might easily bore them both with a single shot from my Winchester express if they got in range.

"They hesitated but an instant, a few seconds rather, then leaped the channel of the stream with cat-like jumps and approached the elk which they cautiously sniffed with pointed noses. I rejoiced at the prospect of securing two such magnificent cats.

"One of them, the larger and a male, came up to the bait first, snuffed it over, licked the fresh blood about the neck, then with a sudden proprietary air he mounted the carcass with his forefeet, gave a satisfied purr, that sounded like the muffled drumming of a partridge's wings, and switched his tail about with a snapping motion at the end, just as a cat with a fresh-caught mouse in her paws might have done.

"The female took her turn at licking the bloody neck, and snarled her cat-pleasure at the prospect of a gratuitous feast. They did not seem to be in the least hungry, for they made no move toward devouring, but after snuffing and examining the game for a bit, they sat about scratching leaves and dirt over it, with the evident intention of preserving or hiding it for future use.

"Thinking my time had now come, I shifted my position carefully, and brought my gun to bear upon them, waiting only for an opportunity to make one bullet to kill or cripple them both, as I feared that the unhurt one would get out of sight before I could get a fair shot at it.

"Suddenly, the big one threw himself upon the elk with a harsh snarl, his hair raising on end, his ears laid back, and his tail switching viciously as he lay at full length, his head turned away from me, evidently watching some object down the cañon. The female, too, advanced nearly beside him, her hair sticking out like bristles, and her angry snarling was deeper and more threatening than his.

"At first I could see nothing of the intruder against which this fierce threatening was launched, but I more than suspected its nature, and my excitement rose. Either another lion or a bear was approaching, I felt certain, and so it proved; it was a grizzly, and one of the largest I had ever seen!

"He reared himself suddenly out of the bed of the little stream, only a few yards from the lions and the elk. He had been traveling up the bed of the creek, —as bears often do in a shallow stream,—and attracted by the snarls of the lions who had heard him coming had emerged to see what the fuss was about.

"To my delight he took in the situation at a glance, and without a minute's hesitation he shambled toward the belligerent cats, mingling his hoarse growls with their savage snarlings.

"I had heard that the mountain lion would not run from a grizzly, but did not believe it, and despite the fearful threatening of the two before me, I expected to see them give way as the monstrous bear came up. Imagine my astonishment when, as the grizzly charged within leaping distance, both of the panthers sprang upon him instantly.

"I could not properly describe the scene which followed; both brutes pounced upon the grizzly tooth and nail, and closed with him in such a fury of savage outcries as made my hair rise, and my whole body prickle with intense excitement.

"The grizzly reared as the two animals struck him; as he came up in a sitting position upon his haunches he shook the female lion from his shoulder. But the male lion held him by the throat, his tawny body lay along the bear's belly, and his hind legs were working with lightning-like speed and strength.

"The bear opened his mouth wide, and roared as he turned his head sidewise and downwards, and strove to catch his antagonist's neck with his teeth. He failed in his attempt, but at the same moment he caught the lion's body just below the shoulders in a clutch of his terrible claws, which seemed literally to flatten the animal between them.

"The lion relaxed his hold of the bear's neck, threw back his head, and sought to writhe loose from the bear. It would have gone hard with him, had not the female lion by a desperate spring fastened herself so strongly upon the back of the bear's neck that he was forced to drop the male and turn to her.

"Over and over they rolled about the elk carcass. They clawed, bit and tore at each other with deep, muffled snarls and growls. Sometimes the bear was on top of a lion, and again both lions were on top of him.

"The grizzly would gather one of them suddenly in his huge forearms, bear it down upon the ground in the effort to crush and bite the life out of it, then feeling the teeth of the other which would invariably seize upon the back of his neck, the infuriated monster would loose his hold, and whirl upon that one.

"Soon, in one of these whirls, he caught the smaller lion, and gave her such a terrible bite before the male's attack—which was from behind as usual—could induce him to release her, that she lost 'sand' completely, and slunk limping away, evidently badly hurt.

"The male lion immediately took the defensive, dodged about the grizzly, and leaped easily out of reach of his furious charges. I saw that Bruin had the best of the fight and was likely to maintain his advantage; and as I was far more anxious to secure the tremendous beast than I was to get the lions, I opened fire upon him with my Winchester, and gave him a ball behind the shoulder as he turned broadside in one of his rushes at the lion. Luckily the first shot killed him.

"The lion, more frightened at the report of the gun than he had been at the bear, bounded across the creek, and though I fired two shots at him before he got out of sight I missed him. The male got off scot-free, as I do not think the bear had given him more than a few scratches, but I followed the female, and overtook her in a crippled condition some half a mile up the cañon ; a single bullet killed her."

VIII.

IN THE CACHE CREEK WOODS.

We had been watching an opportunity to talk with father for a week, but, to tell the truth, he had not been in a very good humor. The crops were light, pork bade fair to be low too, and we knew he had interest-money to make out on the first day of December, a fact that troubled him a good deal, for it was October already. However, he looked rather more cheerful this morning; so my brother, Ad, mustered up courage, and said:

"If you will let Lew and me go after 'cons' this fall, we will engage to pay you fifteen dollars a month for our time, and board ourselves."

Father looked at him a moment, and then sharply at me. He evidently did not favor it.

"Who will do the fall's work?" he exclaimed. "Who will look to the hogs?"

Ad did not like to say: "It will be necessary for you to do that yourself," so he simply said: "It seems to me that ninety dollars would help a good deal on the bills that are coming due."

Father rose and went to the door; then, as mother had breakfast about ready, he sat down at the table. "Well, you may as well eat your breakfast, boys," he said.

We ate in silence. Just as we were getting up from the table, father said: "If you feel quite sure that you can save thirty dollars a month, as I need the money, I think I will try to spare you."

That was enough. Weren't we glad, though!

Perhaps the reader is wondering what we meant by going "after 'cons.'" Did you ever eat a pecan nut? Here in northern Texas, and in the Indian Territory, along the upper course of Red River, boys earn pocket money by gathering and selling pecans. It is quite a business, in fact. We make camping-out trips of a month or six weeks' duration. The nuts are ripe by the first of October, and the gathering season lasts till the first of the following January. The pecan nut tree is a variety of hickory, as many know.

At this season of the year our climate is almost perfect. There is an occasional "norther," of course; but a day or two of cold north wind may well be served up as a spice for the long dessert of genial sunshine with which the winter solstice favors us.

Our summers, however, cannot be so highly recommended; for though the thermometer stands at 968 in the shade nearly all day, one-half of the inhabitants are commonly shivering every other day with the cold. Chills and fever! These are the blots on our summer climate.

Pecan trees are very numerous on the banks of all the wooded streams of Texas and the Indian Territory, but it is among the groves along Red River that the nuts are most abundant. There, too, the "camp of the picker" will be most often seen.

Let me say here that gathering pecans, as a business, involves *work*: and the industrious picker goes from his camp in the morning provided with a "strap sack" and a long, slender pole. The sack, made of stiff ducking, with leather-covered bottom, will hold a peck or more of nuts, and is carried by a broad strap thrown over the shoulder. The pole is a light, strong sapling, as long as the picker can conveniently carry or handle. This is a very necessary part of his outfit. Without it he could accomplish little, for the pecan tree is tall and slender, with slim branches that offer little aid to climbers; while the nuts themselves are incased in hard, oblong shucks, and yield very slowly to the forces of nature, but very quickly to the smart raps of the gatherer's pole.

An active picker will gather from two to three bushels a day. When gathered, the nuts are worth, on an average, two dollars and a quarter per bushel at the nearest " store," or frontier town.

Thus the sons of farmers living along Red River frequently make good wages during the pecan months, and get some sport into the bargain. Not that there is much sport in the picking of the nuts, but the deep woods into which the picker must penetrate are still well stocked with game. Deer, turkeys, wild cats and panthers are to be met in these wild places. The wild turkeys are especially abundant, and the nut-gatherers carry guns, of course.

Another kind of game is met in some places, too frequently met, let me say, and this is the wild hog. These vicious brutes, like those in the swamps of Mississippi, the descendants of the domestic animals—are indeed a "thorn in the flesh " to the pecan-picker. Not only do they devour bushels of the windfalls, but they often make a raid, in the absence of the picker, into his camp and plunder his larder.

Nor is this all. The old boars are fierce and vicious, and many of them seem determined to drive all trespassers from the woods through which they roam. The pecan-picker is very willing to avoid encounters with them, and never shoots one unless forced to do so to escape injury, for many of them bear the brand of an owner.

But occasionally a pitched battle takes place between some savage old "tusker" and an exasperated picker, which usually ends in the death of the brute. It is a dangerous encounter, however, even when well armed, for the brush and sweet-briers are usually more than waist-high, and a boar's motions are very rapid and uncertain.

This introduction was necessary before beginning my story, in order that I may be understood.

Our home is on the south side of Red River; and having made up an outfit, something as above indicated, and procured a six weeks' stock of bacon, lard and corn meal, we set off on the morning of the 4th of October with old "Buck"—one of our horses—harnessed into a farm wagon, containing tent, blankets, etc.

Fording the river, we went ten or fifteen miles up Cache creek, to a tract of timber which we had previously "prospected." It was a good place for nuts, and one not likely to be visited by other pickers.

Our method of disposing of the nuts, which otherwise would accumulate on our hands, or cause much waste of time in hauling across the river, was a very convenient one. We were within half a day's drive of one of the numerous freight roads into the Territory; and the "freighters," returning without load, from a trip to one of the northern posts or agencies, willingly gave us two dollars per bushel for all the nuts we chose to bring them; for they were sure to sell them at an advance of from twenty-five to fifty cents per bushel.

There is no trouble in catching a "freighter" at the creek crossings, on almost any morning or evening.

Our camping-place was near a little tributary of the Cache, called the Deep Red, in the midst of the pecan and hackberry woods. For the first two weeks, we did not see a man except the passing freighters. By the afternoon of the fourteenth day, we had gathered over fifty bushels of nuts, for which we had received from the freighters over one hundred dollars; more than enough for our "freedom money" till January. There seemed no limit to the quantity of pecans on the trees. Turkeys were plenty, and, as yet, we had not heard a hog nor seen a trace of one.

That afternoon Ad took old Buck and the wagon, to go up the creek a few miles after a load of "windfall" nuts, which we had scraped together on the ground under the trees, the afternoon before, leaving me to pick, as usual, nearer the camp. We had seen deer signs on the creek, and he took our breech-loading carbine (a Winchester) along with him. There remained to me only the light shot-gun.

"Bring back a deer," I called to him, as he drove out through the timber; "and I will have a turkey all ready when you get here."

"I'll do it," he said. "Have your turkey ready, for I shall be hungry."

For three or four hours I was busy, rapping limbs with my pole and gathering the nuts that fell; and in fact came near forgetting the turkey altogether, in the castles I was building for expending the three hundred dollars which I hoped to clear that fall, and by which I could make a grand tour to New York and Boston. The late afternoon sun-rays falling in between the hickory trunks at last reminded me of my duties as cook, and hastily taking my fourth sack-load of nuts to camp, I loaded the shot-gun and started for my turkey.

From previous experience, I knew that the creek-bank was the place to look for them, at this time of day; and, indeed, I had scarcely reached it when a plaintive "Yeap, yeap, yeap, yop, yop, yop!" came to my ear, from a few rods below. The bird had evidently strayed away from its mates, and was complaining loudly of its separation. I had to make my way very cautiously through a thick growth of young hackberries, but at length reached the desired position, and peering through the bushes from the top of the bank, was rewarded by the sight of a fine young gobbler trotting back and forth upon a sand-bar, on the opposite side of the creek. The turkey seemed bewildered and unable to decide which direction to take; but in a moment I raised my gun and the stricken turkey lay dead on the sand.

With the report of the gun, however, quite another sort of game turned up. Close at hand, in the thicket, I heard a surprised Whoogh! whoogh! then a crash in the brush followed by the angry chop! chop! chop! of a boar's jaws.

Knowing how rapid these ugly brutes sometimes are in their rushes, I lost no time in jumping down to the partly dry bed of the creek, and wading quickly through the water, caught up my turkey, with the intention of leaving such a dangerous neighborhood, without loss of time. But the thicket was very dense on the other bank, and I was obliged to follow up the bed of the creek, for a few rods, to get out of it. I went on tip-toe, and it seemed to me I hardly stirred a pebble, yet I had not gone more than twenty yards, when with another gruff whoogh, and a clash of his long tusks, a great, gaunt, spotted boar plunged out from amongst the sweet-briers, and throwing the froth from his mouth high into the air as he "clacked," came at me like a shot.

My gun was empty. I knew that I stood no chance with such a creature by clubbing the breech To run was all that I could do, and run I did, down the bed of the creek, at my very best pace.

But let no one think that he can outrun a wild boar; I had not taken ten jumps, when a loud whoogh at my very heels told me that the brute was upon me and would the next moment rip me up.

I did what 'most any one, overtaken, will do—leaped aside as far and as lithely as I could.

The boar went by me with a rush, plowing through the sand and making the pebbles fly, as if a hundred-pound shot had struck beside me!

I did not wait to even look at him, but tacked about, as if on a pivot, and ran up stream, with all my might and main! But the boar pursued almost as quickly as I, and I had not run a hundred feet before he was at my heels again!

Again I leaped for life, to one side; and again the boar plowed by! The next instant I was running for dear life's sake down stream again! Four times I ran back and forth in this manner, and every time the boar came so close that he threw the froth from his mouth all over my back! It seemed as if he came closer to me each time. I felt my strength, or at least my breath, failing me. The thought that I must be ripped and killed by that savage animal was an awful

one; and catch me I knew he would in less than
another minute. But just as I tacked the fourth time,

my eye fell on a hackberry sapling that leaned out
from the thicket on the bank, over the creek bed. The
trunk was, perhaps, four feet up from my head. As I
ran under it, I summoned all my energy, jumped and

caught it with my hands. It bent under the weight, but I drew my legs up, and clapped my feet round it, just in time to escape a spiteful upward slash of the boar's tushes! He just missed my body. Another foot and he would have struck me!

I wiggled round to the top side of the sapling, into a more secure position, and was now perhaps six feet above the boar's head.

There I lay and panted; while beneath, the old tusker stood and looked up at me, whetting his tusks, his wicked little red eyes fairly sparkling with fury, and the long bristles standing up all along his fore shoulders and back.

Finding that he could not reach me, the boar began rooting and tearing out the bank at the roots of the sapling. *Rip, rip* went his old tusks through the turf and fibres. I felt the sapling jar, and soon began to fear that he might tear enough of the roots and the earth away so that it would fall over into the creek bed.

Every few moments the malignant brute would stop and eye me for an instant, then fall to ripping at the roots again. I really think that the creature had some plan of getting me down.

Already it was past sunset, and twilight would soon come on. Ad ought to be back by this time, I thought, and in hopes of his assistance, I now began to shout for help. For a time the forest echoes were my only responses, but I kept shouting at intervals of half a minute, or less; and at length got an answering *hullo!* from away up the creek.

"Help!" I shouted. "Help, help!"

Ad was at this time about half a mile from camp,

coming home with a wagon-load of pecans. When he heard me call "help!" he unhitched old "Buck" from the wagon, jumped on his back and came down at a gallop. In a minute or two, I heard him dashing in through the sweet-briers at a great pace.

"Hold on!" I shouted. "Get your gun ready. I am treed by a savage old boar. You must look out for him. He's full of fight."

"I'll settle him!" cried Ad cheerily.

But the boar no sooner heard his voice than he gave one of his *whooghs!* rushed up the bank and out through the brush, toward the sound.

I could just see Ad over the briers.

"Look sharp!" I called out. "He's coming for you!"

"Let him come!" Ad exclaimed; I heard the carbine hammer click; then *crack* went a shot! Old "Buck's" head reared up in sight, at the same instant. The boar had charged blindly at the horse. In the fracas, Ad was thrown violently into the briers.

Fearing the worst, I jumped down from the sapling, and ran through the brush on the trail of the boar. But before I got through, another shot cracked, and Ad cried out : "All right! I've settled him this time!"

When I got through the thicket, he was standing in triumph, over the still heaving body of the boar.

"Missed him the first time," said he, "then the horse jumped before I could catch the reins an' threw me. Old 'Buck' ran off in no time; and then the boar turned on me, as I lay sprawled out here. I continued to work the lever and shove the muzzle down, as he came towards me. See, the bullet went in at his mouth, an' came out at the back of his head."

I got the turkey and the shot-gun; and we went back

to camp—where the first living objects we saw were fifteen or twenty sows—the old tusker's family, probably, champing up our supplies, and ripping our tent and blankets to pieces. In fact, they had pretty nearly ruined our domestic arrangements, and it was four or five days before we got fresh provisions, and were in trim to resume pecan-picking.

Yet, despite our misadventure, we made a very handsome sum of money—for boys—that year.

IX.

Numerous accounts of adventures with Old Ephraim, as the grizzly is called in his native mountains, have come to me through an extensive frontier acquaintance. Usually these accounts bear a strong resemblance to each other in the details of incident.

A bear is seen; shots are fired, and sometimes the animal is killed by a lucky first shot; but generally — either owing to its almost bullet-proof toughness, or the hunter's excitement — Bruin is not hit, or is only wounded. If wounded, the grizzly invariably attacks his assailant, and the hunter must trust to his legs, or to his horse, if he has one, or to the effectiveness of his repeating rifle at quick sight and short range.

Old Ephraim comes with a tremendous rush when hit not mortally. Many hairbreadth escapes occur, and stirring fights take place between him and his human foe. However, an account both amusing and stirring is told by a mining engineer of Montana, in which the grizzly plays a — for him — rather novel *rôle* of camp thief and house burglar.

"Ed" Crandall, chief engineer for a Montana mining company, tells the story, and I will give it, as nearly as I can, as he related it to me.

We had been talking about grizzly-hunting.

"My first sight of Old Ephraim," said he, "in fact, my first experience with him, was just after I came out here, fresh from the Polytechnic Institute.. It was in

September, 1877. I landed off the stage at Virginia City on the 3d of August, and on the 5th I had the luck to meet an old friend on the street. His name was Adam Fuhr, and he was a school-mate at the district school where I learned my A B C up in the mountains of western Pennsylvania.

"Adam was delighted to see me, and he had a scheme to unfold immediately, in which he proposed I should become a partner with himself and another, who, he said, were going to prospect a quartz lead in the mountains west of Bannock City.

"They had struck a lode near the head of Horse Plain creek, where there had been a placer excitement some years before.

"The placer digging had played out soon, but Ormsby, Adam's partner, who was there while it lasted, had become impressed by the quartz croppings he had seen among the rocks above the valley, and, though he left with the rest, he had intended to go back at some time and prospect. He had fallen in with Adam, and the spring before I came they had gone up, stayed nearly all summer, and found a lead that they thought worth going into.

"As I had come out to obtain employment as a mining engineer, I of course fell in with the plan, as, perhaps, offering something better than wages. When I met them, Adam and Ormsby were getting together an outfit for their work—provisions, drills, picks and blasting-powder.

"As Ormsby was willing to take me in, I paid my share of the expense of outfitting, and we hired a fellow with ponies and burros to take us up.

"We got up there about the middle of August, and

took up our abode in one of the five log buildings of
what had once been known, in fact was still known, as
'Dead Mule's Diggin's' a name given it by the disgusted miners when the 'pay dirt' ceased to 'pan out.'

"We found ourselves quartered very comfortably.
The building was a one-story log structure, about
eighteen by twenty-four, with a board roof, two single
windows, high up, and a heavy plank or puncheon
door. It had no floor, but there were two stout sleeping bunks, a rough table, a number of stools, and a
good fire-place. Somebody, evidently, had lived there
who cared for the conveniences of civilization.

" After we had got comfortably settled and sent our
'packer' home with his animals, we went to work with
drill, pick and powder upon the quartz lead which
Ormsby had discovered. I had come prepared to assay,
and, as we advanced on the lead, I found the out-look
daily more favorable, but suddenly, after two or three
weeks of hard work, the lode gave out entirely. It was
a 'blind lead'; one of those fragments of a vein broken
off, and shoved to the surface in some ancient upheaval.

"We concluded, as we were prepared for a several
months' stay, to put in the time prospecting and hunting. We had a good time; for prospectors, you know,
are never discouraged; they are always expecting to
'strike it rich' soon, and I found it took a 'tenderfoot'
but a very short time to attain a solid state of exuberant
expectancy.

"There was an abundance of game up there; the
black-tail, or 'mule-deer,' were especially numerous,
and there were grizzlies and mountain lions to be met
occasionally, besides smaller game—grouse, mountain
quail and rabbit; but we had been there several weeks

before we saw *ursus horribilis,* and when we did meet
him, it was at most uncomfortably close quarters, and
in a trying situation.

"It was a strange experience—one, probably, that
never occurred to hunters before.

"We came home one night, toward the last of September, from a prospecting trip, and found that the
carcass of a black-tail that was hung up on the outside of
our cabin wall had been pulled down and dragged away.
The boys, Adam and Ormsby, thought it was the work
of a mountain lion, but they were not certain, for the
ground was so hard and dry that the beast, whatever
it was, had left no tracks. Only the faint, slightly
blood-marked trail of the carcass was to be seen.

"But when we went into the cabin they changed
their minds about its being a lion, for the brute had
been in there and had done plenty of mischief.

"The door must have come open after we left, for
the latch, a big wooden one on the inside, was defective;
sometimes it caught, and sometimes it didn't, and the
region was so solitary and so seldom visited by strangers
that we had not thought it worth while to make the
fastening more secure.

"But a trespasser had been there at last, though
not a human one. The table, upon which had stood
the most of our cooking utensils and the remains of
our breakfast, was knocked over. We never cleaned
the dishes from one meal until we were ready to get
the next. The greasy platters had been licked, and all
the scraps eaten. A wooden pail of sugar and an
opened can of lard had been devoured.

"Not satisfied with these depredations, the creature
had pulled the blankets off the bunks, torn some of

them, and scattered them all about the room. A sack of coffee also, in the 'provision corner,' was ripped open, and the contents were strewn about.

"Adam and Ormsby at once concluded this to be the work of a bear, and, as there was no other kind about, of a grizzly, although they had never heard of a grizzly entering a human habitation before. They thought, too, that the creature would return, and we immediately made up our minds to lie in wait with our rifles—one at a time—until it should come back, when we believed, from the cover of the cabin, it could be killed without danger.

"It would come back about the same hour the next day, Ormsby thought, and we all agreed that the creature must have had enough to eat to protect us from its return that night. Accordingly we hung up our guns—there were old hooks of deer's horns along the walls—cooked and ate our suppers, and after a time crawled into our bunks and fell fast asleep.

"The bunks were both on the same side of the room; I slept on the one next to the door, while Adam and Ormsby occupied one in a corner near the fireplace. It was a fairly warm night, and, as usual, in order that we might have a good supply of out-door air, we covered ourselves well with blankets, and left the door slightly ajar.

"Some time after midnight I was awakened from a disturbed sleep by a sniffling and a rasping sound that seemed to come from the center of the room. I seemed to have heard something before, a creaking and scratching sound was my impression of it, and, now thoroughly aroused, I raised myself upon my elbow and looked.

"The door was half-open, a flood of moonlight was pouring in from a full moon, and the sight that met my eyes was, to say the least, startling.

"The grizzly was there, a monstrous great creature standing on its hind legs in front of the table and holding in its forearms a six-quart wooden pail freshly filled with sugar, and licking out the contents with sniffs of evident satisfaction.

"It was that temptation, the bear's uncontrollable liking for sweet, that had brought it back so soon.

"I was not only startled at the discovery, I was thoroughly frightened, and before I could collect my senses or make a move, I heard a sharp, frightened whisper from my partners' bunk.

"'Great Scott? Look there.'

"It was Adam, awakened by the licking sounds, and the grizzly, which had stood with its back to me noticed either his whisper or his movement, and suddenly letting the pail fall, gave a growl, dropped down upon all fours, and began backing toward the door. Ormsby awoke and started up, but Adam seized him and held him down.

"'It's the bear,' he whispered. 'He's in here, but he's backin' out. Keep still?'

"Just then, however, the grizzly, unable to steer its unwieldy bulk backward through so small a space, struck the door, and, as a matter of course, caused it to shut. It swung noisily and latched.

"We had trapped a grizzly, but we were in the trap with him. The big brute turned round as the door brought him up and sniffed at the planks with a hoarse whine of anxiety.

"Under the bunks, everybody,' said Adam; 'we're

penned in with him.'   And, with an excited scramble, we plunged out and under cover of our beds like frogs jumping from bogs down into the mud. I rolled over the foot of mine so as to go under as far away from the bear as possible.

"Our movements excited the bear and frightened him evidently, for he now began plunging wildly about and giving vent to hoarse, frightened grunts.

"He knocked over the table again and sent things flying in every direction. I crawled back snug against the wall under my bunk and lay there in a condition of fright that I should have hard work to describe.

"We were truly in a pretty predicament, shut in there with that big raging brute, not a weapon to hand —for our guns were hung up on the *opposite* wall—and the bunks, our only protection, liable to be smashed down at any moment by his powerful paws.

"The grizzly, however, was as much alarmed as we were. He tore about the room like a mad bull, bellowing and puffing as he tried his strength, buffeting the door and walls with blows that made them shiver.

"The windows, I should have said before, were nothing but square holes in the walls, and had been closed by nailing boards over them. As they were high, and admitted no light, the room was totally dark.

"We could only judge of the grizzly's whereabouts by its movements, and these brought him frightfully close at times. Once he sprang with his full weight on top of my bunk, and I could hear it creak and strain beneath him as he reared up and pawed desperately at the logs above.

"It was a fearful moment for me; but at length, old Ursus lunged off to the floor again, and then a lucky thing happened. The bear must have caught a gleam of out-door light between the boards nailed across the opposite window, as he turned on the bunk, for he charged straight across there and reared up against the wall, and the next instant we heard a ripping sound of breaking nails and the clatter of the boards as they fell to the ground inside.

"'He's opened a window!'" I shouted, with the recklessness of great relief.

"He was certainly trying, and we could hear him puffing and tugging as he struggled to pull his huge body up into the opening.

"'Ed!' called Adam, 'if you dare get out and open the door we can get rid of him now.' It required a good deal of determination to make the attempt, but I was close to the door and I crawled out, flung it open, and scrambled back to cover, in the briefest possible space of time. That let in the light again, and we could see Bruin with his forepaws and head out of the window trying to strain his big body after them.

"Then Adam did a daring thing. He got out from under his bunk, sprang across to the wall, caught down his 40-90 Sharp, that hung there, loaded as usual, for emergency, and, stepping close to the struggling brute, shoved the muzzle almost against its side, fired, and leaped back to shelter again.

"I think he wasn't out from under his bunk more than fifteen seconds.

"The shot too was a well-calculated one. The grizzly answered the roar of the gun with a fierce grunt, struggled and scratched for a moment to get through the window-hole, and then fell back with a

great flop and lay on its back pawing the air and
gasping for breath.

"We peered out from under the sheltering bunks
fearfully, watching the great, heaving body until at
last it rolled over on its side and lay limp and motionless.

"Then we got out and lighted a lantern and examined it. It was a magnificent brute, a male, and
weighed nearly eight hundred pounds.

"'Ad,' said Ormsby, after looking the great beast
over, and seeing from the position of the wound that
the ounce and a quarter ball must have gone through
its heart, 'Ad, that was the coolest, grittiest thing I
ever saw done.'

"I had always known that Adam was plucky, and
his action that night completely won my admiration.
I joined Ormsby in hearty praise of it.

"Altogether it was a strange encounter, both fearful and funny—funny *after it was over*—and I think it
was only explainable from the fact that those buildings
had stood there within the grizzly's haunts solitary and
unoccupied so long that the animal had lost all fear of
them. As the one we lived in was the only one with a
door left hanging, it is quite probable that this bear,
and perhaps others, had been inside them all before.

X.

CAUGHT.

One summer evening, several years since, the writer, with a party of young men who were traveling by wagon from Cheyenne to Fort Laramie in Wyoming, camped near the "trail" on the bank of a pretty and swift little stream called the Chugwater. Some hundred yards away and opposite their camp were "Chugwater Ranch" buildings.

These buildings were neat-looking adobe houses—there were two of them—surrounded by a high, strong picket-fence. Outside the adobe enclosure were several sheds and corrals ranged along the slope of a hill. In one of the latter were several calves trotting about and bleating anxiously—the only signs of life about the houses.

After we had picketed our animals, and while we were cooking our supper, it was suggested that one of us should cross over and see if he could buy a bucket of milk at the ranch. It seemed probable that there must be a woman there.

The result of this suggestion was that I was asked to go over and make the trial. Taking a tin pail, I jumped across the brook, walked up to the gate and rattled it. There was no response. I undid the fastening—a hook and chain—and rapped at the front door of the first adobe. Again there was no response. Thinking there might be some one in the next building, I walked around and tapped on its door also.

While I was waiting, I was startled by the appearance of a big black-antlered elk that came with a stately strut around the corner of the adobe, and stopping within a pace or two, stared at me with its great brown eyes.

He was a magnificent animal. At first I felt somewhat alarmed, lest this apparent guardian of the premises might conclude to toss me over the picket-fence on the points of his big horns. But the mild expression of his great eyes reassured me, and after looking at me a few seconds, he stepped forward and laid his velvety nose against my shoulder.

As I stood for some minutes stroking the big elk's tawny red neck, I heard a long-drawn "*How* ŏ-ŏ-ŏ-ŏ up!" and looking out through the space between the pickets, saw several cow-boys racing a "bunch" of cattle down the hill toward the corrals. I at once went outside, and one of the boys, seeing me standing by the gate, came down at a gallop, and drew rein with a hearty "*How*, stranger! Want some milk?"

"How do you do!" I replied. "Yes, I would like to get some."

"Come right up to the cow-corral," said he, turning his horse about, "and Ed'll strip you some. He's the only stripper 'bout the ranch, but he can pull milk to beat the oldest man."

I followed him to the corral. "Here Ed," he said, as a boyish-looking fellow, wearing a buckskin shirt and a wide-brimmed slouch hat, rode up and nodded to me, "take the stranger's bucket and pull it full of milk for him as lively as ye can. Wants it for supper, I reckon."

Ed hitched his pony to the corral, and took my pail. The other man dismounted, and we sat down, crossed our legs, and proceeded to "swap talk." In the course of a brief conversation, I learned that he had been for some time " boss" of the ranch, and also that he was a bright, intelligent fellow.

Presently I pointed to the pet elk, and asked how they had succeeded in taming it so thoroughly. "Oh, elks tame easy enough, if they are caught young," he said. "I had a pretty hard time of it, though, when we got Dudad, as we call him. You'd like to hear about it, perhaps ? Well, I reckon you'll have time before Ed gets through with his milking.

"When I first came here, five years ago, tnere were a great many elk in the country, but hunters have driven a great many of them off since. They used to come down in spring from the Black Hills to the north and west of here, and stay all summer and fall along the Chug, and out east on the plains. They scattered out in summer to breed their calves, and then in the fall came together in good-sized herds, and I tell you there were some old settlers among the bucks; big as good-sized steers, and ugly as grizzlies when they were wounded or cornered.

"But the king among them was ' Old Highflyer.' I heard the boys telling about him almost as soon as I got here—a tremendous old buck, that overtopped all the others by five or six inches.

"Every boy on the range had seen him and knew him. They knew him by his size and by his motions. The first time I saw him, *I* knew him too; there couldn't be but one such elk in the country at a time. What horns he had!

"The first time I saw him was during the June round-up, about a month after I came here. I was down on the Chug, about five miles below here, gatherin' steers, and was pushing a bunch along up through a gap in the hills, when all at once I saw the big elk going at a lightning trot over a point of hill straight before me.

"He was as tall and big as a large five-year-old Texas steer; and his branching horns were longer and wider than the biggest elk I've ever seen. He got out of sight before I had time to use my carbine.

"Well, I saw him once or twice more that summer, and then not again till about the first of October, down at the Eagle's Nest, four miles from here. That was when I caught Dudad. It was the queerest thing, the way that calf was caught, jammed in between two rocks where he'd tried to jump through, just in play, I expect.

"I'd gone down the Chug to see if I could bring in some maverick steers that had cut loose from a Government herd, that a day or two before had been driven north for the forts. It was just above a cañon gap that we call the Eagle's Nest. I was poking around down in there, looking for the steers, when I found Old Highflyer instead.

"He was standing on the side-hill across the Chug, right in front of two big boulders that stuck up close to the edge of a quakin' asp thicket. There was a cow-elk with him. She was trotting back and forth around him, acting kind of anxious and queer, while he stood tossing his horns up and down, scrapin' the rocks now and then with a sharp scratching noise, and stampin' his feet savage and nervous like.

"They didn't notice me, they were so busy with their performance. I knew there was something that seriously disturbed them, but I couldn't make out what it was. My carbine was at the ranch, but I had a Colt six-shooter with me, and at close range I could handle it as well as a rifle. There was a little clump of quakin' asps to the left, and between me and the elk, and I thought if I could just get behind that, I should be within safe shooting distance.

"So, slipping off my pony, I led him back and tied him out of sight, and then began to work my way up the hill behind those bushes. It was slow work, for the hill was steep and covered with loose stones, but I managed to worm along without making much noise.

"Well, I got up behind the bushes at last, and out one side where they were low, and peeped out through the tops. I was as careful as possible, but before I caught sight of the elk I heard a snort, and the next minute I saw them both standing, heads and ears up, facing my bushes. They had heard, or scented me, and I saw I must be quick to get a shot.

"They were about a hundred feet away—close enough range—and I took a quick aim and pulled the trigger. But I wasn't quite quick enough, for both elk whirled to run, and I missed my big buck.

"The two scurried away up the hill and were out of sight behind the quakin' asps in no time, though I fired a couple of shots after them, jest for luck. Then I went over to the rocks to see if I could find out what had been going on there.

"I rather reckoned I'd find a calf, either badly wounded by a mountain lion, or hurt in some way, but when I got round where I could see in between the boulders, I reckon I was about as surprised as if I'd been suddenly jumped at by a band of Sioux.

"There was the calf, sure enough, and in the queerest fix. He'd probably been playin' round the rocks and all of a sudden took it into his head to jump through between them, and was *stuck* there fast as a bear-trap could have held him. You see, the rocks came close together, in a kind of cone-like shape, and the crack between them widened away from the point where he was caught, and there he hung, the crack not being wide enough to let him through into the space beyond. All he could do was to kick and blat. As soon as I stood above the crack he saw me and broke out in good earnest, bawling like a crazy thing, while his feet flew like the spokes of a buggy-wheel.

"I stood there a moment, and could not help laughing at his predicament. All at once I heard a savage wheeze and a clatter of hoofs, and looking back, saw Old Highflyer coming for me like a steam-engine.

"He wasn't a hundred feet away, and was coming with his ears laid back and his hair sticking up on end. But short glimpse as I had of him, I noticed that his head was bloody, showing that he had been wounded.

"In a second I drew my Colt. Getting a quick aim, I fired, and then made a spring for the crack in the rocks.

"But I wasn't quick enough. The old fellow reached me before I had time to get into the crevice, and with one sweep of his big branching horns, struck me on the left hand here—you can see the scar yet. I had it behind me, I expect—so; and he threw me into a heap on the ground.

"Only my hand was hurt, and I scrambled to my feet as the big critter went ploughin' down the hill— for he couldn't stop at once, he was going so swiftly.

Then I scrambled in between the rocks just as he turned to come back.

"The crevice was slightly higher than my head, and I was in a hole, as it were, between the heels of the calf and the southern end of the crevice. My revolver was gone—knocked out of my hand.

"But I tell you, stranger, for a few minutes I found that crack in between the boulders the most uncomfortable place I was ever in. The old buck came rushing up, and glared at me with his big flashing eyes, while the blood dropped out of his nose and mouth from a wound in his upper jaw.

"Then at my side were the calf's heels, from which I had not room enough to get away—the little wretch raining upon me thick and fast, kick after kick—thump-a-thump! thump! Yes, and it hurt, too. I thought he'd drive me wild!

"I tried to catch the little brute's legs with my right hand, but I might jest as well have tried to seize the buck's antlers and to *hold him*. But something had to be done, and that soon, for I felt that I should soon be used up unless I could get away from that calf's heels. Lucky for me, I had a butcher-knife, such as most of the boys carry, in a sheath at my belt.

"I got that out, and as the old buck threw down his head, making a sideling rake along the crevice with one horn, I struck him in the face, and the point of the knife took hold of the corner of his eye.

"It was a lucky stroke. He staggered back a few steps, holding his head high up in the air; then he kind of settled back and shook his head, gave a wild squeal and shot away as fast as his legs could take him.

"I got out of that place in a hurry, and found

myself rather used up. I was smarting and aching
from the hurt on my hand and from I don't know how
many bruises on my back and legs. The fact is, I
didn't get entirely over the battering I had had for
weeks. I was glad even to get out alive.

"I found my revolver and managed to get to my
pony and ride back to the ranch, where I found one of
the boys and sent him up after the calf, which you've
seen down at the 'dobes, for that calf was Dudad.

"We've never seen Old Highflyer since, and whether
he got a wound from which he died, or whether he was
frightened off the range we never knew."

Long before the ranchman had finished his story,
"Ed" had set the bucket of milk at my feet. The
"boys" positively refused pay for the milk, and after
thanking them, I carried my treasure back to camp,
where I was found fault with for "gassing" so long
with the cow-men.

XI.

A FIGHT WITH WOLVES.

In the winter of 1860–1 a family of Trebolts was living in a frontier settlement west of the Des Moines River.

Jesse and Peter Trebolt were stout, healthy fellows who helped their father during spring and summer, in breaking up land and cultivating the new claim of half a section upon which they had lived for two years. In the autumn and winter, however, when they were not attending school at the log school-house three miles away, they were engaged in trapping and hunting the musk-rat, mink and beaver.

Like thousands of the first settlers of Iowa and Minnesota, the Trebolts found their annual *fur harvest* the most profitable of the year. Musk-rats were the most plentiful of the fur-bearing animals, and during the early autumn the boys took them in small steel traps, which they set in "run ways" and at the foot of "mud slides" along the edges of sloughs and the banks of a creek which ran through the Trebolt homestead.

But after the ice froze so as to bear their weight upon the surface of the sloughs and little lakes in which the region abounded, they killed the *musquash* with their "rat spears," sometimes spearing it through the thin ice as, frightened out of one "house," it swam toward another.

When the ice became too thick, as it did upon the second or third cold snap, to spear through, they cut open the tops of the rat houses—conical heaps built of rushes, flags and muck, and projecting several feet above the surface of the water—exposing the hollow nest of the little animal. Over this the fur-hunter stood guard with unlifted spear until the musk-rat, recovered from its fright at his thumping and cutting, popped inside with eyes blinking and fur dripping, when it was pinned with a quick thrust of the pointed rod.

The rat-spear was made of a sharpened rod of iron or steel, without barb eighteen or twenty inches long, and fastened by a ferrule to a light ash or hickory pole from five to six or seven feet in length.

Upon their rat-spearing excursions Jesse and Peter carried two of these weapons, made of strong, steel rods and ash poles, and a heavy hatchet for cutting open the houses.

It was upon an extended trip of this kind that the adventure which follows befell them.

Late in November of that year, the two lads had received a brief letter from an old Quaker uncle who had left the settlement in which they lived the year before, and moved with his wife and a maiden sister to a new Quaker colony west of the Raccoon River thirty-five miles distant. It ran thus:

"To My Dear Nephews Jesse and Peter:

"Greeting: I have to say to you that I and your Aunt Sarah and my Sister Alzina would be much pleased to see you at Christmas time, if it be the will of God and your father that you should make such a journey from home.

"Knowing that your time is well occupied, and with much profit in the taking of the skins of wild animals, I have to say further that the ponds and wet places around about my land do greatly abound in musk-rat, and that I have staked out certain of them, warning off them which trap about here.

"Now if you will come with your spears, I think you may hunt these animals two or three weeks with much profit.   I will be content with one-third the peltry taken for my share.

"Affectionately and with brotherly love,

"Your uncle,

"ABRAM JESSE GREEN."

As both muskrat and beaver were already getting somewhat scarce along the Des Moines, Jesse and Peter were glad to adopt the plan of their shrewd old uncle.

Then came a severe blizzard which lasted, blowing and snowing with more or less violence, nearly the whole of Christmas week, and it was not until the morning of the thirtieth of December that they finally set out.

They traveled with snow-shoes made of hickory "shakes" turned up at the front, and with straps nearly in the centre, which held the foot at the instep and toe.   They carried their rat-spears, a hatchet, and a lunch of bread and meat.

The weather had turned much warmer, and during the middle of the day it thawed so that the snow yielded under their shoes, and so retarded their progress that night came on before they had reached the Raccoon River, twenty-eight miles from home. The country at that time was very thinly settled, and it so happened that there were no houses in sight during the latter half of their route until the " Quaker Colony " was reached.

They would gladly have stopped at some settler's cabin for the night, but fearing they might be compelled to go down the river nearly as far as they would have to travel to reach their uncle's, they guided their course by the "Big Dipper," and plodded on.

They had nearly crossed the narrow valley of the river—it was little more than a large ravine at this point—and were pushing along the crest of a huge drift which had blown out from the top and point of a hill between two gullies, when Peter, who was ahead, noticed a number of dark objects moving along the side hill, near the head of the drift a hundred yards or more in advance of him. He thought at first that a drove of deer was coming up out of the valley to feed upon the bare knolls where occasional patches of grass were exposed.

He turned and spoke to Jesse.

"Look yonder, Jess, 'f we'd jest brought the shotgun we might'a'got a ven'son!"

"Them's no deer," said Jesse, who had stopped just behind his brother. "They're wolves, Pete, an' a lot of 'em too; one, two, three, four, five, six, seven, eight, nine of 'em, an' big buffalo wolves, too."

While he was counting, the animals, which were going at a trot, had filed up to the hill-top, and stopped so that their bodies were plainly outlined against the sky.

"They've stopped to have a look at us, but I guess they won't dast tackle us," said Peter. "That's the most of them big wolves I ever saw in one drove, but come on, Jess, less scat 'em off, an' be gettin' to'rd the col'ny."

But the big brutes were not to be *scatted* so readily as Peter had fancied. They squatted upon their haunches, and waited immovably while the boys approached.

, " Scat ; git out o' the road you brutes," yelled Peter, as he came up within twenty paces or so of where they were sitting.

Several of them moved cautiously a little to one side, and squatted themselves again, but three of them sat there as though cut out of rock.

Both Peter and Jesse, as they afterward admitted, began to feel nervous and afraid, and they halted facing the wolves. The big animals, now plainly distinguishable, looked fearfully gaunt and hungry and their small eyes sparkled viciously in the starlight.

"Let's take down the side hill, an' leave 'em alone, Peter," said Jesse. "They're dangerous brutes, them big fellows. You know how they chased old Larry McGinigan up at West Bend three years ago."

"Yes," returned Peter, "but there was more'n thirty of 'em. I don't b'lieve 't nine wolves 'd dast to tackle two men."

Still he took his brother's advice, and leading the way turned to the left and started down the side of the hill. Jesse moved along close behind, and each kept an anxious eye over his shoulder to see what effect this move would have on the wolves.

They had advanced a few yards to a point nearly opposite the squatting animals, and were just about to pass out of sight when the pack, setting up a fierce yelp and shrilly *Ow—ow—ru—ru—ru*ing—this is Jesse's attempt at mimicry—came leaping down toward them.

"They're goin' to pitch into us!" shouted Jesse, in alarm, and with a sudden backward movement he attempted to get out of his snow-shoes; but the straps, wet when it had thawed, had frozen to his boots, and the heels of his shoes catching in the crust tripped him. He fell down the hill sliding and rolling for several yards over the slippery crust of the side hill drift.

The wolves had slackened their speed as Jesse shouted, and the foremost were sliding and scratching in an effort to halt as he fell, and whether they would really have attacked him had it not been for this accident cannot be known. Probably not, but seeming to realize his plight, the three foremost animals sprang forward again, and passing Peter, who struck at them with his rat-spear, they jumped savagely at Jesse, snapping and snarling.

Jesse had lodged in the hollow of a drift, and as the brutes came at him he began shouting and trying to get up, but the snow-shoe on his right boot still stuck. He had let go his spear, and as he raised himself to a sitting posture one of the wolves in its mad rush caught one of his coat-sleeves in its teeth, and jerked him over upon his face. All three of the animals passed him, but gathered themselves again and came at him savagely.

But Peter, who had got out of his shoe-straps, now rushed at them, made a hard thrust with his spear at one of them, and luckily struck it in the flank with a force that jammed it down upon the snow. Throwing all his weight upon the handle he succeeded in pinning the howling brute, and forced its wriggling body through the crust.

The outcries of the struggling animal seemed to madden the other two and they turned from Jesse, and sprang upon it, snapping and tearing it recklessly.

Jesse, who had turned over and snatched the hatchet from his belt, now managed to scramble to his feet. He rushed at the maddened brutes, struck one of them upon the head, crashed its skull and killed it instantly.

Encouraged by this he attacked the other, and would no doubt have killed it, too, had not the beast jumped back as he struck. It ran off down the hill yelping.

Peter was still holding down the one he had speared, but a few raps from Jesse's hatchet quieted the squirming beast, and the two panting boys looked about them. Several of the pack were squatted on the bank above them yelping, and licking their chops, and the others were moving about below. These, though they were evidently ravenous with hunger, did not seem to have the hardihood to come nearer.

"Are ye hurt, Jess?" Peter asked, when they had discovered the attitude of the remaining animals

Jesse replied that he was not injured, but that he was awfully scared, and that one coat-sleeve was nearly torn off him.

"Well," said Peter, "I guess if we go off 'n' leave these dead ones the rest'll eat 'em up 'n' be satisfied for to-night, but let's skin 'em first."

Jesse agreed, so they got out their knives, laid their spears and the hatchet close at hand, and set at work The seven remaining wolves were interested spectators of the task; they gathered around at a few rods distance, sniffing, yelping occasionally, and anxiously shifting about.

When the boys had finished skinning the dead animals, each fastened a pelt at his belt, got on their snowshoes, and shouting and brandishing their spears at the nearest wolves to "warn 'em not to follow," set out again in the direction of the Quaker colony.

They had not gone a hundred yards when they heard the pack behind them yelping, snarling and fighting over the carcasses of the dead wolves.

They reached Abram Green's cabin, having awakened one of his neighbors to inquire for it, a little after midnight. The old gentleman and his wife got up to give them welcome and while "Aunt Sarah" made a cup of coffee and got them a "a bit to eat" they related their adventure.

The old gentleman and his wife were much concerned at the narrative, and the old man then told them of the trouble he and his neighbors had been at to keep their chickens, pigs and young animals out of the hungry maws of these same brutes. There was a drove, he said, infesting the neighborhood of somewhere from ten to fifteen of these animals, and the nine which had attacked them must have belonged to it. Their boldness had been extraordinary, but as there was not a gun in the whole colony, he thought this fact and the late severe weather had probably lent courage to the bolder ones, and driven them to the point of attacking the two young men.

During the three weeks of successful rat-spearing which followed, Peter and Jesse saw numbers of these wolves, and at length several of them became so bold as to follow them about from pond to pond in broad day, eating the carcasses of the musk-rats which were thrown upon the ice near the small hummocks where they had been speared.

XII.

Jean Darblaye, who is now a Montana ranchman, is a modest man, and seldom recounts any adventures in which he bore a prominent part; but he was lately persuaded to tell the story of one of his experiences, which deserves wider currency than it has yet had.

Jean was the son of French-Canadian parents, but was born at a frontier post in northern Minnesota. At seven years of age he was sent to St. Louis to school, and for eight years attended the Academy of St. Philippe, but returned every spring by boat to spend the summer with his father at the post.

His time while at home was occupied in athletic sports and, as he grew older, in hunting. His comrades were Indian boys, young Sioux, who taught him to shoot with bow and arrow, to ride their stocky and often stubborn little ponies, and to play at lacrosse. He used also to paint his face and join them in their mimic war-dances, in which he could yell as loudly as any of his companions.

When Jean was fifteen years of age, his father moved westward and established a trading post on the Upper Missouri, near the Belted Buttes. Here he bought furs in connection with the Northwest Fur Company.

Jean left school, and for the next four years assisted his father in buying and trading "Indian goods" for furs, and in caring for the great bales in the store-room, which had to be "camphored" and "tobaccoed" to protect them from dampness and moths. When he was nineteen years old his father died of a wound received from a drunken Mandan. Mr. Darblaye's business affairs were not in a prosperous condition at this time, and when his accounts with the fur company were settled, there were but a few hundred dollars remaining for Jean.

Left to shift for himself, the young frontiersman set to work at once with an enterprise characteristic of his race. Feeling that he had not the means nor the experience to enable him successfully to compete with the agents of the Northwest Fur Company, he went to St. Louis, and there made arrangements for the sale of buffalo hides, tongues and "hump steak." He engaged a boat to make regular spring and fall trips to the Belted Buttes region for the loads of hides and meat which he proposed to furnish to the St. Louis market.

Having purchased some improved guns and other articles needful for his undertaking, he went back to the Great Bend of the Missouri, hired three half-breeds and their squaws as assistants, and turned buffalo hunter.

The young hunter's first season was a prosperous one. He kept two yoke of oxen, a wagon and a driver busy for six weeks in hauling hides and meat to the storehouse to be cured and stored.

Jean sent two boat loads down the river the first autumn, two the next spring, and cleared about three hundred dollars off each cargo. This amount he regarded as a fair return for his labor and investment, as risks were scarcely counted in that region.

The months of September and October and of May and June were the periods in which the great herds

migrated between their summer pastures on the high
prairies of the British possessions and their winter feeding-grounds along the Niobrara and the Platte. At
these times the country about Jean's headquarters
swarmed with buffalo.

Almost daily throughout these months great herds
of buffalo crossed the river above and below the young
trader's block-house, and his most profitable method of
hunting was to shoot them from a boat as they swam
above his post. The dead bodies were floated down to
within a few rods of the post stockade, and hauled out
upon the bank, where they were skinned, and the
tongues and hump steaks cut from them. In this manner buffaloes were killed and brought down from
points twenty and even thirty miles distant.

During the season when the buffaloes were migrat-
ing, half-breed scouts employed by Jean scoured the
hills and the rolling prairies above the post, watching
for any herds which might be pointing toward the
river, or feeding in situations whence they could be
stampeded toward its waters.

While the scouts were out, Jean and his hunters
were accustomed to remain at some favorable point on
the river, with canoes and ponies at hand. If there
was time after a scout came in to give warning, they paddled to a point just above where the herd was expected
to cross, and waited.

But if greater haste were necessary, they mounted
their ponies and rode at a flying gallop for the point of
crossing, and taking their position on the bank, shot
the big animals as they lunged into the water or swam
past.

During the second autumn of Jean's buffalo-hunting,

there came down from the north the largest herd that
he ever saw, except the mighty one that afterwards
came into the vicinity of Fort Rice, and is known in a
legend among the soldiers, scouts and hunters as the
"Eight-Mile Square Herd."

About the twentieth of September one of his hunters
rode to Jean's station with the information that a herd,
"as wide as the eye could see," was moving slowly up
from the Buttes in a direction that would bring them to
the river at a point twenty miles above the station.

A young fellow of eighteen years, the son of a boat
captain who lived in Vicksburg, was staying with Jean
at the time, having come up the river for a hunt. He
had been out several times after buffalo, but had not
succeeded in killing one. When the news of the big
herd came in, he was wild with excitement.

"I can get one this time!" shouted he, after Jean
had interpreted the Indian's report. "Where there's
no end to 'em, there's a mighty sure chance."

"Well, Louis," said Jean—the lad's name was Louis
Longstreet—"you shall have a try, only don't get so
nervous, or you won't be able to handle your gun."

Five minutes later the two young hunters were in the
saddle. Jean had sent his scout back with instructions
to stampede the big herd as soon as he and the other
two scouts who were waiting out among the hills could
get in behind it.

Jean and Louis then started, keeping to the hills
which skirt the valley at a distance of from one to
three miles from the river. This route was taken that
they might keep a lookout for the herd, and avoid also
the danger of being caught by the front of the stam-

pede and forced into the river, which might occur if
they kept too near the bank.

It is not often that the accidents we fear happen to
us, but in this instance Jean's very precaution served to
get himself and his companion entrapped at a point
where escape from contact with the wide front of the
immense herd was impossible.

Jean and Louis had set out about the middle of the
forenoon, and Jean calculated that, if nothing unusual
should disturb the buffaloes, the Indians would get
them started shortly after mid-day, and thus the foremost buffalo should reach the river at about three
o'clock.

There were two canoes hidden among some willows
at the mouth of a small creek about twenty miles
above the post, and Jean expected, after finding the
buffaloes, to reach the canoes in time to paddle down
to some bar or island from which they could advan-
tageously shoot the swimming animals. He dared not
trust so inexperienced a hunter as Louis in a boat
among swimming buffaloes.

For about two hours they proceeded on their way.
Jean all the time watched for some sign of the big
herd. About noon several small bands of buffaloes
were sighted upon some elevations directly south of a
high point upon which the riders had halted to take
observations. These, the young trader concluded,
were outposts of the main herd, which he had no doubt
were quietly feeding upon the short, dry grass of the
depressed prairie which lay between his point of view
and the Belted Buttes, the conical tops of which could
be seen in the distance.

Just in front of the horsemen were some hills, higher

than the one they had mounted. In order to avoid climbing these, Jean, who thought that he had sufficiently located the game, determined to travel in the river valley for the rest of the distance. He pointed out to Louis a willow-grown island in the river opposite to where they had halted.

"We'll ride up the valley about five miles to where the canoes lie," said he, "and then paddle down to that island, where we'll land and wait for 'em. It'll take us an hour and a half, and by that time the big herd will be moving this way with a noise like thunder."

They descended into the valley and urged their ponies on at a sharp gallop. Just in front of them the river curved and flowed for several miles to the east.

They had turned this bend and had pushed on for two miles or more, the valley narrowing constantly as they proceeded, when, just ahead of them, there burst over the high ground, amid a cloud of dust, a great rolling mass of dark objects, which covered the sloping hill-sides almost instantly.

The riders came to a sudden halt.

"The big herd!" said Jean, hurriedly. "We'll have to scatter, Louis—too bad—but down stream's the only safe route for us, and we must hurry, too—some mistake—confound those rascals!" meaning the Indian hunters.

They could now hear the heavy rumble of hoofs which, coming in the distance, had been lost in the clatter of their horses' rapid gallop. Louis thought it did, indeed, sound like the mutter of distant thunder.

They wheeled their ponies and struck the spurs into their flanks. To their right stretched the range of hills which had hidden the coming herd, and to their left, a mile distant, ran the river, sweeping round nearly in front of them, a few minutes' ride ahead.

"Ride hard!" shouted Jean.

They were close to the foot-hills, and the herd was bearing down on them with a roar that increased like the sudden rising of the wind.

They spurred their ponies vigorously, and were getting a good rate of speed out of the short-legged little fellows, when out from a big ravine, not three hundred yards ahead, there shot a great solid tongue of buffaloes, and over the hill to the right swept a dense black mass, filling in the gap between those behind and those ahead.

Jean and Louis were trapped! hemmed in on all sides but one, and on that side was the river.

Instinctively both riders veered off and made for the head of the stampede, which was now rapidly rolling on in front of them. The buffaloes had evidently received a wild alarm from some source in the rear, for the huge, irregular *crescent*, literally a living, moving wall, bore down on the young hunters at a fearful speed.

Less than a minute of riding toward the head of the column before him convinced Jean of the impossibility of overreaching and passing it. There was only one thing left to do—make to the river and swim for it; and, motioning Louis to follow, he headed his pony straight for the river bank.

Jean glanced back over his shoulder; the central

mass of the big stampede was about three hundred yards behind them, nor could the small ponies, already winded with twenty miles of hard riding, increase the distance. Foremost in the stampede were the biggest, swiftest, bulls, their sides almost touching as, with heads down, they bowled their huge, lumbering bodies forward, reckless of anything ahead in their fright at what was behind them. In the rear of the bulls was a confused, heaving mass, lost, at no great distance, in a rising cloud of dust that seemed endless.

Louis was badly frightened, but kept his wits and followed every move of Jean's. They rode directly for the river and reached its bank together; but here both ponies so quickly and stubbornly halted that Louis, though a good rider, was pitched clean over his animal's head and alighted upon his shoulder on the edge of the bank. He clutched at the top of the bank with his right hand—his left arm was bruised and numbed from the shock—clung for a brief instant, then slid down some ten or twelve feet into the current.

Jean made one more effort to force his animal over the brink, but failed; then, too much alarmed for Louis to wait longer, he sprang from the saddle, threw away his gun and jumped after his comrade.

Louis was thrashing the water with one arm in a desperate effort to swim away from the bank, but his wounded arm and the weight of his clothes and heavy boots impeded him, the thick muddy water dragged him down, and the poor fellow would have sunk even before the buffaloes were upon him had not Jean come to the rescue.

Jean's ideas of what followed during the next few

seconds are confused; but he remembers that he got hold of Louis, and helped to buoy him up while they kicked and struggled hard against the current; that they managed to get a few yards from the shore.

Then buffaloes seemed to *rain* down over the bank, ploughing its steep sides and sousing into the water with heavy splashes, making the current boil around them.

The next instant the desperate hunters were in the midst of a puffing, snorting mass of big, hairy swimmers, a sea of humps, horns and noses. As a big bull came grunting alongside of the two young men, Jean, who knew that the buffalo is inoffensive in the water, made a grab with his free hand and caught the old fellow by the long hair on his hump. "Now, Louis, get hold here!" he shouted, and Louis, who was recovering the use of his arm, got hold with both hands.

"Now we're all right," said Jean, "only keep well behind so he won't turn." The bull snorted wildly at the sound of the shouts, and swam frantically in the effort to get free from his unwelcome freight.

Jean, still keeping fast hold of the great brute's mane, drifted backward as far as he could and then flopped himself over the creature's sunken hindquarters, so that it now towed one person on each side. Once the bull turned his head as if about to face about, but Jean promptly let go with his right hand and struck him a blow on the eye.

"Don't let him turn your way Louis," said Jean. "Let's keep him as straight ahead as he can go. Kick hard and help all you can; we must get across before the rest of 'em if possible."

Louis readily comprehended the situation. The cool

HUNTING STORIES.

115

water helped him to regain the use of his arm, in which, fortunately, no bone was broken, and he worked vigorously to relieve the bull of a part of the burden of drawing him on behind.

The old fellow proved to be a strong swimmer, and exerting himself to the utmost to get rid of his hangers-on, he reached shallow water several rods in advance of the nearest others of the herd. Here the boys let go the bull, which lunged himself out upon a projecting sand-bar and thence up the bank beyond.

Jean and Louis followed the bull to the shore, and ran to some scattered cottonwoods which grew along the bank. Each got behind a tree, and there stood wringing his clothes and slapping his arms to warm himself, while for fifteen or twenty minutes the dripping herd lumbered past them, the swelling sea of humps stretching for half a mile on either side.

An hour later Jean's hunters, who had ridden up on the other side, discovered Jean and Louis, who were pacing the bank as they awaited their comrades' arrival. One of the hunters went for a canoe and came across after them. Then they learned that a party of Aniskaras from above had stampeded the herd and had hung upon its outskirts until they had killed as many buffaloes as they wanted.

Since he left his saddle to plunge to the rescue of his comrade, Jean has never seen nor heard of either of the ponies which he and Louis rode on the day of the stampede. They were undoubtedly forced into the river, and either were drowned or swam to the other bank and ran on with the herd. He is inclined to think that they crossed safely and were picked up by some straggling band of the Assinneboines or Crees, who hunted upon that side of the river.

One of the half-breeds, after much diving, recovered Louis's gun from the mud of the river, and it was found to be uninjured. But Jean's gun, which he also recovered, was bent, broken and useless.

XIII.

IN NICK OF TIME.

Round our camp-fire again at the West Fork after a grand day of wild-goose hunting, Capt. Buck regaled us with the following story of his boyhood, and old times here on the Red River.

"Ah, those were pleasant days!" said he. "You can hardly appreciate the agreeable life we used to lead on the Mississippi in the old days before the war. You see, my old gentleman owned a large plantation and many negroes on the river above Baton Rouge. We spent our summers there and our winters at New Orleans. There was a large family of us children— ten in all—and we were educated at home. Our tutor was generally some graduate from Yale or Harvard, who kept us at our studies for five hours each day for eight months in the year.

"We always had a vacation, however, from Christmas until the first of February; and then my older brother, Chester, and I—we were the eldest of the six boys—were allowed to do our hunting for the year, and did the most of it, too, along the banks and bayous of the Red River here. My whole boyhood was associated with this muddy, red current, that glistens so brightly out there in the moonlight.

"Every winter we used to take a trip as far up as Shreveport, then a little place of not as much consequence as now. Father owned land and raised cotton and horses on both sides of the Mississippi, and kept a small steam wherry for transporting stock and hands back and forth.

"This wherry was usually in the charge of an old negro named 'Gub,' one of father's best hands in his younger days, and in the winter time, when there wasn't much use for the boat, Gub was allowed to accompany us on our up-river hunting trips.

"There was a comfortable cabin on the *Corbeau*, as we called the boat. The wherry was a broad, light paddle-wheel, a sort of scow, barge and steamer combined; and as she drew but little water, we had no trouble in guiding her among the snags and over the bars, or out upon the wide bayous and lagoons of the tamarack swamps below Shreveport.

"We took our first trip in '53, when I was a lad of fourteen and Chet but two years older, and we kept up those excursions every winter until the war.

"It was in '56, though, that we had our most memorable hunt. Chet and I had finished our regular studies, and Willett, our tutor, a young fellow from Harvard, now a noted college professor, was to leave us and make room for a governess, as the girls all came between us and the younger boys. We liked the fellow thoroughly, and determined that he should make one trip with us before he went North.

"He consented, for he liked sport and was a fair shot; so after the holidays we left New Orleans for the plantation, and found old Gub and the *Corbeau* ready for our use and provisioned for eight weeks.

"For guns we had three fine rifles, an extra double-barrel fowling-piece and two big English duck guns, with spears and fishing tackle. Besides these, we carried several dogs, the best of the plantation pack, for the bear and deer of the woods and hills above Alexandria.

"It was to one of these dogs, a half Cuban, half foxhound, that I owed my life on that trip. Yes, old *Brian* was, I think, the keenest hunter I've ever known, though I've seen finer bred house-dogs that were as intelligent as he.

"Point Roseau, or Roseau Point, as we called it, was always our first stopping-place after leaving home. It is a three-cornered peninsula, formed by the banks of the Red on one side, and one of the Bayoux Des Roseaux (Reed Bayou) on the other.

"These bayoux were broad strips of green water, grown up with reeds, rushes and cane about the edges, and full of mud bars, old logs, snags and alligators. The Point, a low piece of land two or three miles in extent, was a wild swamp of tamarack and red elm, dark and tangled with vines and undergrowth.

"It's not a very inviting country, as you may suppose, but we were obliged to 'wood-up' somewhere, and there were large quantities of dry elm along the bank here ; and dry red elm is the best kind of fuel.

"And then, too, those bayoux were usually alive with geese and ducks. The reed patches and the long flat mud bars, grown over with moss and wire grass, made fine feeding-grounds for these birds; and we carried a light boat for use in this kind of hunting. If more stirring adventure was wanted, there were the bear and . panther and tiger-cat of the swamp, fierce enough to satisfy any man's thirst for excitement.

"Well, we had reached this point on our trip about three o'clock in the afternoon, and had tied up to the same tree that we always hitched to, on the Point just at the mouth of the bayou.

" Willett was anxious to get a shot at the wild geese that we could hear squalling up at the first neck of the bayou; and Chet and I drew cuts to see which of us should go out first with him. The lot fell to Chet, and they went away, while Gub and I were left to keep company with the dogs and to cut up the dry elms upon the bank.

" We worked away cheerfully enough, cracking jokes and telling stories—Gub's black pate was crammed with both—until sundown, when the old negro dropped his end of the saw with a significant gesture that meant ''nough o' dat.'

" 'Marse Pink, yo' jes' tu'n up yo' nose dis way. Yeh?' spreading out his palm toward the northwest and rolling up the whites of his eyes. 'Yo' smell sumpin', yeh? Yo' don' yah now; ye' an' got no smell no how, yo' ain't. I kin smell 'possum shoah,' rolling his eyes again. ''Possum not mo'n two mile up yivvuh 'mong de high banks 'n' de yoke trees; shoah be thar, marse!'"

" 'All right, Gub,' said I, willing to humor the old fellow with a bit of his favorite sport. 'Go after 'em, old man, and I'll get supper.'

" 'Thankee, mars!' returned the grinning old black, with a profound scrape and bow. ' Bring a fatun 'n' tress 'im foh dinnah de morreh;' and in no time he was on board, had down the remaining duck gun, and had gone among the dogs for his favorite hunter, Bug, a genuine 'possum dog, if ever there was one.

" But while unleashing that cur, the old black made

a discovery, and came to meet me at the bow with both hands up.

"'Marse, dem dawgs Brian un Nig, dey is bofe done gone. Dey is boke de lease shoah.'

"Sure enough, they had jumped over the railing at the bows, and sneaked off without our seeing them.

"'That comes of tying them with ropes, Gub,' said I. 'But never mind; they've only gone after Chet and Willett, and will be back with 'em. Spoil some of their sport, though, quite likely.'

"'Dat so,' replied Gub; 'yo' don' heah 'em no mo' now;' and with that Gub jumped ashore and left me.

"It was a pleasant, warm evening; I watched the twilight fade and the moon grow bright. The big gloomy swamp grew blacker and gloomier; the green, dead water of the bayou changed to a slaty gray; and the snags and logs just outside the line of reeds looked like the ghosts of snags and logs in the shadows of the tall trees.

"I sat there and sat there, I don't know how long, only that I had begun to feel surprised that the boys did not come in, and that I heard nothing of them.

"Suddenly there broke on the wind that was blowing gently from the west, a long, deep howl, like the blowing of an immense brass horn.

"I knew *that* voice. It was Brian's, and by it I judged that the dog was not a half mile away. It meant game, and big game, too; for Brian would never lay himself out like that for anything smaller than a bear or a 'painter.'

"I listened a minute, excited, I assure you, and then Brian broke out with his fog-horn bay again, and Nig rung in with a chorus. I waited only long enough to locate the sound over my side of the bayou, then I rushed into the cabin, snatched down a rifle and bullet-pouch, and bounded off the boat upon the point.

"I had no doubt that the dogs had treed a bear, and of course I was eager to outdo the boys, who might be nearer the hounds than I was. I knew they could not be *very* near, for Brian would only have exercised his lungs in that powerful style to bring somebody from a distance.

"Well, away I went, crashing through brush, briars and brake like a mad fellow, till in about a quarter of a mile I came to an arm of the bayou that stretched out as far as I could see into the thick woods.

"It wasn't very wide, and the water only stood in little pools; but I knew better than to venture upon the slimy surface of that black, oozy mud. It was as much as life was worth, and more dangerous than the deepest, snaggiest part of the main branch.

"So I turned and pushed my way up the bank in the hope of finding a crossing, or the end. All this time the loud baying of the hounds was stimulating my ears. Scrambling on, I presently came to an old dry elm, leaning out over the mud, its top resting on several stout limbs, driven, in its fall, into the bank, on the other side. It was a safe and easy crossing, but I had lost my wits and my breath in my excited running, and I rushed out upon it without a bit of caution, trusting to the sureness of my legs.

"About midway, the rotten bark cleaved off under my feet, and I went over and down like a plummet into the mud and slime. So quickly did I fall, that I did not touch the log with my hands, yet I alighted on my feet! alighted on them and went up to my thighs in a thick mud pudding at the very first plunge.

"Scared! I reckon I was. I tried to jerk my legs out, but I couldn't move them. There I stuck tight.

"I held my breath a minute and kept quiet. Yes, *I was sinking!* I could feel the downward movement, slow, but sure.

"Then I screamed for help. As scared a lot of yells, I reckon, as ever came from a human throat. When their echoes died away I listened. The dogs had stopped howling; there was no other answer.

"The bank opposite was hardly twenty feet away, so near had I come to crossing, but there was nothing within reach that I could lay hold of. I held to the rifle, and laid that along the top of the mud and bore some of my weight on it with my hands; but notwithstanding this, I was slowly sinking. I screamed again, at the top of my lungs.

"I tell you, gentlemen, it's a horrible feeling, that slow settling down into a frightful bog that's sure to be your grave. if help is not secured. I wish I could tell you half the thoughts and sensations I had while settling into the bottomless depths of that slimy mire. But I couldn't do it; I won't try.

"I screeched again, like a madman, and then I suddenly heard a crackling in the brake and the tramp of some animal that proved, almost as quick as I heard it, to be Brian.

"The big hound broke from the cane-brake close at hand, and came bouncing upon the low bank in front of me, where he halted with an anxious whine, and a pricking up of his ears, as much as to say:

"'Well, you're in a fine mess, aren't ye?'"

"Can't you bring me that long limb, there?"—Page 125.

"'Brian, old fellow,' said I, 'I'm gone up, sure.' I should have said 'gone down,' but that was no time to make a choice of words. 'Can't you bring me that long limb, there on the bank, old boy?' I asked, pointing to a broken branch of elm that lay by him.

"Now, I believe I asked that just to make believe he was human and could understand, and that I was going to get help; but the hound looked at the stick, then at me again curiously, and whined pitifully.

"I repeated the words and then pointing several times and—will you believe it? Whether you do or not, it is true—that dog stepped back, grabbed that pole near the middle, balanced it an instant, then made one mighty leap off the bank toward me. Yes; and before he had sunk too deep for his strength, he made another plunge and reached me with the branch:

"It was a pole, big as my arm in the middle, and several feet in length. There were some smaller limbs branching out of it; and only a powerful hound, like Brian, could have lifted and jumped with it.

"As you may reckon, I seized that stick in a hurry, got it crosswise in front of me, laid the gun crosswise of that, and then leaned over, bearing all the weight I could upon them. That eased up the settling business, for a time, and I kept myself buoyed up by the gradual sinking of the limb, which, owing to its surface and branches, went down slowly.

"As for Brian, he had wheeled about and splashed out of the mud at a fine rate, spattering me all over with the batter that flew from his feet. Then that noble old brute got up on the bank and set up such a *ki-yi-ing* as I never heard before, or since. I tried to make him understand that I wanted another stick; but

he either thought he had done enough in that line, or
didn't propose to trust his legs in the mire again; for
he only howled the louder.

"After a while Nig came and joined in with his
howls; and altogether, with my halloos, we must have
made the woods hideous.

" Bless those dogs! they knew I was in a predicament,
as well as human beings could have known. Brian
had started at the first frightened yell which he heard
from me; and at last Nig had left the—we never knew
what 'twas—and came too.

"I was still in a dangerous condition, settling a little
in spite of the pole, and was beginning to despair of
ever getting more help. As much as an hour had
passed, when a cracking of cane begun to be heard and
I knew that somebody was coming. The dogs stopped
yelping and whined; then old Gub came in sight in
the moonlight on the opposite bank. Nothing but
calamity could have brought him in from a 'possum-
hunt before midnight.

"'Wha' wha's de mattuh, 'n' wha' is yo', mass'r?'
he called out.

"'Here,' said I, 'in the mud. Cross over on that
tree and help me out. I'm sinking and half-froze in the
cold slime. Careful, now, or you'll be in too?'

"'Lawd ob musseh, Marse Pink! how'd yo' go 'n'
git in *dah?* Yo' poah chile, peah's like yo' defful mis-
fawtnit!'

"But without waiting for a reply the old negro
stepped out on the log and hurried across. To make a
long story short, the old fellow was mighty handy at
whatever he undertook, fell at work like a beaver and
soon had a bridge of dry logs and sticks built over the

muddy hole and a staging of wood laid all about me. Then by digging and wrenching, twisting and working we accomplished the feat of unearthing my legs and bringing me safe to dry land.

"I went back to the *corbeau* with old Gub, almost prostrated from the reaction from my fright, and in a sorry enough plight. But a change of clothes, a wash, a good fire and hot coffee soon set me to rights again.

"As for Willett and Chet, they had got lost in the bayou and didn't find their way in till after midnight.

"That dog Brian was surely the most knowing hunter I ever saw. Dogs of that breed usually are fit for trailing and do not know much else; but you could teach Brian anything. He was only two years and a half old when that thing happened. We kept him for eight years after that, and I could tell of a hundred instances where he proved himself just as intelligent as when he saved me from a muddy grave; for I certainly should have gone down but for him."

XIV.

CHASED.

Duck-hunting is not usually considered a dangerous sport, provided one is careful and knows how to handle a gun ; but at least one duck-hunt of my boyhood came near causing my death.

My parents, with several other families, were at that time living upon the extreme frontier of western Iowa, in a little settlement not yet laid down on the maps.

The country for miles around us, with the exception of small groves of timber which skirted the nearest stream, was an open prairie, covered with thick, coarse grass, which even on the very highest and dryest ridges would reach to a man's knee.

Until the region became thickly settled, prairie fires raged with each recurring autumn; and when there were high winds the flames sometimes reached across the country with the speed of an antelope.

The only protection we had from these fires was the cultivated fields that surrounded the houses; and even about these a wide strip had to be freshly ploughed each fall before the grass dried, for the fire-fiend, when once started, with a dry wind to urge it on, would run accross the stubble and the ripe corn-fields with scarcely retarded velocity.

Wild game, of many varieties, was then very abundant thereabouts; and during the second autumn after our arrival, geese and ducks were so plentiful that nearly every man and every boy large enough to carry a gun spent his whole time during the month of October

in hunting these birds, for their feathers were needed
for beds and pillows, and could always be sold for
cash when there were any to spare.

The nearest railroad station was eighty miles away,
but when our geese feathers were delivered there they
could be sold for one dollar a pound. Furthermore,
the breasts of these birds, sliced clean from the bones
and dried, furnished excellent meat for months to
come, and they also could be sold for a good price at
the station.

There were three boys in the settlement—Mort Halleck, Pierre Lanfrey, the son of a French Canadian
whose place joined my father's, and I.

One bright morning about the last of October, we
set out together for a trip up the river. It was a calm
day, and not a very good time to shoot wild geese and
ducks had they been less plentiful than they were that
season.

Early in the day we had noticed that the horizon
away up the river to the northwest had a hazy, smoky
appearance.

"I'll bet there's a big old fire over on the Sioux,"
said Mort, as we trudged along.

"'Twon't hurt us any," said Pierre; "'cause there's
hardly any wind blowing, and what little there is
comes from the south."

So we felt no uneasiness, except that we feared the
fire might later on sweep over our region when the
wind changed, and thus put an end to our hunting.
For where the prairie is burned black and the wild rice
and seeds are consumed about the edges of the sloughs
and streams, water-fowl soon take leave for better
feeding grounds.

We had good luck during that forenoon, shooting three wild geese and thirteen large mallard ducks. And after eating our dinner in a small grove, we decided to hang up our game on the branches of a scrub-oak, and push on two or three miles further, to a large slough which we knew to be frequented by water-fowl of all kinds. Even if we should shoot more than we could carry home, the weather was cool, and the game would keep, and we could bring a horse the next day to carry them home, as we had often done before.

Pierre made a scare-crow of his coat, which had become a burden to him, as he wore it over a hunting-jacket, and placed it in the branches of the tree, to frighten away eagles and hawks.

We soon traversed the distance to the slough, and found it, as we had hoped, alive with geese and ducks. Quite a breeze had sprung up from the south, and the birds were constantly flying in at one end and out at the other.

Mort and I stationed ourselves in the tall grass at the south end and Pierre went round to the northern quarter. We were soon blazing away as fast as we could load, taking the birds on the wing as they passed over our heads.

The foolish birds circled about, loath to leave the rich rice-patches which lay along the edges of the slough. Some, indeed, would take fright and bear off for other haunts, but others were constantly coming towards us, and our guns soon became heated from rapid firing.

Toward night the wind suddenly veered round to the northwest and blew a gale—not an infrequent occurrence in this country, after a calm autumn or spring morning. We had forgotten all about the fire, —about everything, in fact, but our all-absorbing sport.

Mort and myself had gathered around us a stack of game, more than we had ever bagged before at one time. Pierre's gun had also been busy; and we were loading up for our farewell shots, just after sunset, when Mort suddenly sprang to his feet.

"Look up yonder, Frank! Goodness, we must get out of this!" he exclaimed.

A glance to the northward disclosed the cause of his alarm. A great cloud of smoke stretched across the horizon and seemed rolling down upon us like a thunder gust. At the same time a dull but ominous roar was audible; and we noticed that cinders, borne by the strong wind, were flitting by. Pierre had taken alarm also, and now came bounding through the grass toward us.

How suddenly it had all come on! The air overhead was even now clouded with smoke; and it began rapidly to grow dark. For a moment we stood, hardly knowing which way to turn.

"Fling yer game inter the water," shouted Pierre, as he neared us. "The fire won't burn it there. We've got to make for the river lively."

Mort and I at once began pitching geese and ducks into the water.

"Don't you s'pose we can run into the slough and stand it?" I queried.

"No!" said Pierre. "We've got to get behind the river-bank. Don't ye see the fire will leap across through them reeds and rushes? We'd be roasted. The smoke'd smother us! Jerk off yer boots an' fling 'em inter the water, and hurry!" he cried.

He was barefooted himself, and we quickly followed his advice. Pierre had been brought up on the frontier prairies, and we always found it safe to follow his lead.

"It's a mile to the river," said he, "an' the fire ain't more'n two miles away. Ready now! Skedaddle! But hang to yer guns if you can."

So accustomed were we to the weight of our musket-guns, that we ran almost equally well with them in our hands. Away we sped. But the smoke was driv-ing over us and filled our heaving lungs at each quick breath with a smarting, suffocating sensation. To the west and far up overhead a wild, angry glare was mounting—alternately glowing and darkening in the twilight.

The roar grew louder.

"Hurry! Hurry! *ou noo song perdu!*" gasped Pierre. "The fire's on both sides the river." —

Hurry we did. But the awful roar in our rear grew in volume each instant. An occasional shift of the wind wheeling aside the clouds of smoke disclosed a long, unbroken line of red "leapers" rushing on with the speed of wild buffaloes.

It was indeed a race for life. Every moment it grew hotter. The tall, dry grass that fed the flames served but to tangle and trip our feet.

"Run! Leg it!" shrieked Pierre. "We haven't a second to spare."

The dense smoke hid everything, but we knew we were nearing the stream, from the small patches of wil-low which we began to pass through. The crackle of the fire was now getting terribly loud. The heat became almost too intense to bear. Sweat ran down our limbs, while our faces felt scorched. There seemed to be not a breath of air.

"Oh, I'm smothering," gasped Mort.

"No, yer haint!" yelled Pierre. "Keep after me, boys, or we'll"—— He never finished that sentence, for at that instant all three of us went headlong over the river-bank—twenty or thirty feet—down to the water's edge. Mort indeed fell into the water, gun and all, and we hauled him out, sputtering.

"Dis way," cried Pierre. "Don't stop here." And we hurried along the edge of the steep bank down to where the bluff was higher and more abrupt, and almost jutted out into the water into which we waded waist deep.

"*Bong!*" ejaculated our leader. "Now off with your hats and souse 'em in the water, then clap 'em over your faces and keep under the bank."

We had barely time to do it, when, with a tremendous crackling and roaring and a hissing, seething noise, accompanied by a sensation of choking and of fierce, smarting heat about our heads and shoulders, the fiery hurricane swept over the bank above us.

For a few moments the air seemed full of flame—long tongues shooting out and playing over the river as if to reach to the farther bank. Then, as when a bubble bursts, it all went out at once.

A cool draft of air rushed in. The blaze had passed. Nothing but smoke was left behind, with here and there a bit of burning twig.

"'Twas a hard scratch for us!" exclaimed Pierre, who in moments of excitement was apt to mingle Canadian French and backwoods English in about equal measure. "*Sapriste!* But I think we *perdu* sure one spell."

It was such a narrow escape as comes to few in the whole course of a lifetime.

After an hour or so we were able to cross the burnt prairie, and during the evening made our way home, where we found there had been no little anxiety concerning us, the flames having been plainly seen sweeping along to the northwest of the settlement.

Next day we recovered a part of our geese and ducks from out of the slough; but Pierre's coat and the birds we had hung up in the oak had been burned to cinders.

XV.

A resemblance between two persons so strong as to give rise to a prolonged case of mistaken identity is rarely met with outside the pages of fiction. Of his own personal knowledge the writer can speak of one instance where, for a short time, such a resemblance seemed to baffle the inquisitive eyes of old acquaintances.

It happened not long ago to a friend of mine, a civil engineer in the employment of a great railway company, to be most awkwardly mistaken for a fugitive from the primitive justice of a mountain district in Arkansas. His adventure was exciting and full of danger, and seems worth relating.

Conrad Hurling, though a young man, is one of the most efficient engineers in the employ of the M. R. & P. Railway Company. He belongs to the "Locating Corps," and his work is in "preliminary" and "locating surveys." Last winter he was sent alone upon an important mission which required a journey through the State of Arkansas, a journey not by rail in a Pullman sleeper, but on horseback over three hundred miles of mountainous and swampy country, much of it little better than a wilderness.

The Missouri, Rio Grande & Pacific directors, jealous of a competing line which was building an extension pointing in that direction, determined to forestall it in occupying Arkansas territory, and Hurling was sent out to look over the ground in advance of a preliminary survey. In fact, he was to make a sort of "preliminary " by the aid of his eyes, his powers of gathering information from inhabitants, a sectional map of the State, and certain charts which he carried upon which to trace the route and all prominent landmarks and water-courses.

It was about the first of December that he set out from the mountain village of Ozo, where he had pur-chased a horse and saddle for the journey. He had attired himself in a rough corduroy suit, a broad-brimmed white hat, a pair of high-topped hunting boots. He carried a revolver in a pocket of his saddle-bags, which also contained his maps and papers, with room for a noon lunch.

The first day's travel led him into a wild and pic-turesque region of the Ozarks, a rough country of rocky peaks and ridges of deep ravines and yawning gulches, the home of not a few suspicious moonshiners, and, if report were trustworthy, of some other charac-ters still more unpleasant to meet.

However, the young engineer was well on his guard, he knew the characteristics of the inhabitants generally, and was usually possessed of the lucky faculty of mak-ing himself "at home with everybody;" in other words, of winning the stranger's confidence.

The weather was fine, and for several days the traveler found his leisurely journey pleasant and full of interest. The few inhabitants with whom he met and conversed on the road, or at occasional cabins where he put up for the night or stopped for a meal, seemed well disposed, and generally gave him such informa-tion as they had about the route he proposed to take.

Some of the more intelligent of them were very hospitable upon learning his errand, and evinced much enthusiasm at the prospect of a "shore 'nough railroad" and "cyars" running past their very doors.

"I knowed I'd see a engine a-humpin' up this valley some o' these yere days," said one shrewd old farmer, "an that is jus' the reason why I tuck 'n' sot myself en my fam'ly down on this yere piece o' lan' w'at I got pa'chelly fenced, en ben a livin' on hit ever sence the wah. Hit air boun' ter be a valleyble piece o' prop'ty, hit air.

Conrad passed an enjoyable evening at the old man's cabin, where a large family of overgrown youths of both sexes sat with them about the fire-place conversing, after the first shyness had worn off, in their uncouth, roundabout dialect.

For several days he pursued the route marked out for him through the valleys of deep water-courses, through mountain passes and over plateaus, or "bench lands," and without adventure of an unpleasant sort. Occasionally he met with surly or suspicious mountaineers, who eyed him askant, and spoke to him guardedly or not at all.

But on the sixth morning, at a creek "crossing," he met upon the bank of the stream a lank, leather-faced man, in coon-skin cap and leather leggins, bearing a long rifle upon his shoulder, with a half-dozen or more squirrels strung upon the barrel, and the lean hunter stood, as he rode up, gaping at him in undisguised amazement.

Somewhat surprised at the hunter's stare, in which there seemed such extraordinary interest, Hurling drew rein and saluted the gazer.

"How d'ye do?" said he, pleasantly.

"Tol'ble," answered the hunter, with an unpleasant

grin. " How air you-uns ? " and Conrad noted a look
of cunning upon the leathery face.

" Well," said the engineer, " I'm getting on all right,
but I'll be much obliged to you if you'll put me on the
right trail on the other side of the creek there. I see
the road forks, and I want to go through Horrigan's
Gap."

The hunter's grin became enormous as Con finished.

" Waal, Dave," said he, drawlingly, " I al'ays
knowed ye were right peart in yer makin's-up, but ye
cain't projeck ole Jake outen the youst uv 'is eyes. I
reckon ye done knowed which road air the best fer ye
ter take afore ye comed nigh hyar."

" So you take me for somebody who's been here
before, eh ? " said Hurling- " Well, my good man,
you're off in the matter of eyesight for once in your
life. I've never been here before, and am very certain
I never saw *your* face."

The old man grunted half-angrily : " Don't ye be
lettin' on ter be a plumb fool, Dave ! Ye nachelly
cain't 'possum noways with me. I done knowed ye
comin' away up the rise yander."

This was rather exasperating, but the stranger bore
it with outward patience, at least, and again denying
his identity with that of " Dave," whoever the individual might be, he dismounted, opened his saddle-bags,
took out his maps and explained the purpose of ,his
errand through the country.

The old man looked and listened, still incredulous.

" Ye don't talk exactly like Dave, en ye hev riz a
baard," was the only admission the engineer could get
out of him. He refused, in fact, to talk, evidently
believing that " Dave " was trying to play a trick on

him, and after pointing out—rather reluctantly—the road to Horrigan's Gap, the old hunter started off, shaking his head.

Hurling was not a little disturbed by this incident,

The old man looked and listened, still incredulous.—Page 138.

for he did not know what unpleasant consequences might arise if other mountaineers, acquainted with the mysterious " Dave," should also mistake him for this person, who, he doubted not from the old hunter's manner, had left the region in bad odor with some of

its inhabitants. How well founded this surmise and his
fears were, he discovered soon enough.

The road to Horrigan's Gap led along the bank of a
deep run, with here and there a dark pool of water
lying in a depression of the bed. At some distance
from the ford, while taking observations along the
road, he met two mountaineers on horseback, and
almost held his breath as they rode down toward him ;
but though they gave him curious and not very friendly
looks, and responded rather surlily to his salutation, they
evidently did not recognize in him a likeness to any
one they had known, and this fact gave him no little
relief as they rode past. He began now to fancy that
perhaps the old hunter might not be quite right in his
mind.

A little farther on, however, this illusion was dis-
pelled. At a turn of the road a boy had ridden one
horse and led another to water at one of the pools at
the bottom of the run. Conrad rode to the edge of the
bank, and called to the lad, who was leaning lazily over
his horse's wether while the animal drank.

The young fellow looked up with interest and surprise at being thus accosted unawares ; he looked, then
stared, as the hunter had, in open-mouthed amazement,
then shouted, " *Dave Kennedy !* " and giving his horse's
halter a jerk and letting go the other, turned his riding
animal about and fled at a gallop, digging his heels into
its ribs and flopping his elbows in the wildest excitement.

Here was more mystery, and keen cause, also, for
alarm.

His likeness to " Dave " could no longer be doubted,
and as to the reputation of this individual, he con-

cluded it must be that of a desperate character of some sort. The old hunter had been surprised and suspicious, and the boy was evidently frightened half out of his wits. The engineer rode on with many misgivings, and yet he was not prepared for what followed.

He had ridden rather more than a mile from the spot where the boy had been encountered, and was going slowly for the purpose of careful observation, when he heard a distant but fierce and rattling clatter of horses' hoofs.

They were behind him, horsemen, who had evidently just struck the road.

Hurling's fears of trouble were instantly confirmed; he felt an immediate conviction that the riders whose horses' feet clattered louder with each passing second were after him, and that the boy at the pool had given the alarm. He halted, got off his horse, took his revolver from the saddle-bags and stuck it in his coat-pocket, then waited, calmly as he could, their coming, determined to have the matter of his identity established if possible; at any rate, to put on a bold face and stand his ground.

He had reached very nearly the head of the run, and before him stretched a wide, gently inclining valley which he knew from previous description to be Horrigan's Gap. There were high mountains on either hand and much timber on their sides. The valley was bare of woods and some of it cultivated; he could distinguish several cabins and small fields from where he stood, and grouped against the clear blue horizon at the highest elevation of the gap, several miles distant, were some buildings which no doubt made up the village of Horrigan.

Nearer and nearer rattled the riders and soon they burst into view around a point several hundred yards below.

There were five of them, and upon coming within sight of him they reined up and came to a halt; they sat gazing at him for a moment, and then seemed to be holding a consultation.

Hurling waited uneasily. Were they afraid of him, he wondered, and had they started out with the intention to capture or to kill him? Surely, he thought, they would give him a chance to prove himself—if only they would come within speaking distance.

But while he was thus questioning within himself one of the men dismounted, and Conrad saw that he had a gun in his hands.

The fellow stepped out a few paces to one side, and deliberately took aim at him. At this alarming demonstration the engineer sprang behind his horse; as he did so the mountaineer's gun cracked; the ball struck the road, falling several rods short of the horse, at which it was probably fired; it glanced upward and went *yeun-yeuning*, above the man's head.

He waited no longer, but sprang upon his horse and sank his spurs in its flanks, determined to lead them a race to the village, where he hoped to find shelter, or at least protection, until he could satisfy the people as to his identity.

That the party after him was in dead earnest was plain enough, and that an attempt to parley with them would only bring the peril nearer he felt assured—

therefore he plied spur and whip, using an end of the long halter-strap as a quirt.

Hearing no more shots fired, he looked back to see what his pursuers were doing. They were after him fast enough, riding in single file at the top of their animals, speed, with a trail of flying dust in their wake.

The poor fellow felt that his case was indeed desperate; his unlucky likeness to "Dave Kennedy" was likely to bring him to peril in front, as it had upon the road behind.

His horse, fortunately, was a fine roadster, and had both speed and wind, and after a mile or so Conrad noted with delight that he was drawing gradually away even from the foremost of his pursuers, and that this one was several hundred yards in advance of the rest.

If only they were all mounted on such old farmhorses as he had seen at the pool, he thought it would be an easy matter to get away from them.

He neared a small cabin by the road and several ragged children scuttled in at the door in a great fright as he shot by. A little farther on, a small cornfield lay beside the road, and three men, who, with a single horse and cart, had started shucking among the first rows, turned and gazed at him as he flew past.

He wondered if they wouldn't get into the cart and take after him. They did not; but farther on another cabin stood on a slight elevation near the road, and as he neared it Hurling saw a man at one corner shading his eyes and evidently watching both pursued and pursuers.

As he came clattering up nearly abreast of the cabin the man gave an excited jump, slapped his leg with one hand, and then, dodging around the corner, darted in at the cabin-door.

The fleeing man went by like the wind, but looked back, expecting to see the fellow come out with a gun. He was not disappointed; out the man came and fired two shots in quick succession after him. A double-barreled shot-gun was evidently the weapon used, for the rider, was already out of range and saw several shots strike along the road behind him, each of which knocked up a little spurt of dust as it bit.

Truly Dave's enemies were numerous!

The engineer rode directly along the rode toward the village which he was now rapidly nearing. His horse had done well, still kept its wind and steadily gained on those behind.

Luckily there was no one at home, or at least in sight, at the two or three cabins which he had still to pass before entering the village, and he rode unannounced up to the very door of a log store which also had a sign "Post-Office" printed upon a board and nailed to one of the logs.

Hastily hitching his horse to a post he entered the door, a plan of action having occurred to him while riding for his life.

A group of half a dozen men had already gathered, seated upon and leaning against the counters of the country store.

"Gentlemen," burst out Hurling, "some men are after me on horses and with guns determined to take my life because they fancy I look like Dave somebody—"

"*Kennedy*, true's you live!" put in one of them; "that's what ye does, mighty like him."

"That's so," said several others, who got down off the counters in the stir which followed to get a good look at the stranger.

"Well," said Conrad, hurriedly, "whoever Dave Kennedy may be and whatever he has done I am not he, and if there is any one in the store who can get me a razor, a piece of soap and some water I can very quickly prove what I say."

"Mebby ye ken, but I'd swar 't ye war Dave," said the first speaker of the crowd. "It's no more'n fa'r, though, thet ye should heve a squar' deal. Boys, is they ary razor round hyar 't the feller ken use?"

"I've got one," said a young, smooth-faced fellow who was evidently clerk in the store. "Come back this way, stranger."

Hurling stepped to the back end of the store, was given a razor, a gourd with brush, water and soap and shown a broken mirror which hung beside a small back window.

A curious silence reigned in the room while he hastily made preparations to remove a luxuriant growth of beard.

Soon a clatter of hoofs announced the approach of the horsemen in pursuit.

"Hyar they come," said one of the men; "it's them Kirby boys jes' es I 'lowed 'twar. I'll go out, boys, 'n' tell 'em how hit air. O' course they air nachelly boun' ter give the man a show."

And he went out followed by two or three more. While Con was industriously scraping away he heard them in earnest conversation with the fellows who had just ridden up. Presently they all came tramping into the store.

Then for several minutes there was an ominous silence.

Conrad finished shaving, wiped his face on an old towel which hung on the wall and then "faced the enemy."

There were a dozen slouching fellows in the room now, and nearly all armed with rifle or revolver.

They stared hard at his face, which had, indeed, undergone a striking change. Pale and hollow-cheeked he awaited their decision.

"Sho!" exclaimed one of the nearest, " he don't look ary bit more like Dave Kennedy nor I do. Hit didn't seem ter me like Dave 'd git oudashus 'nough ter come projeckin roun' hyar agin."

" 'Tain't Dave," was the flat admission of all of them, and the men who had followed him so hotly looked crestfallen enough.

" Well, gentlemen, if you've no further business with me I'll ride on," said Hurling. " Much obliged for the use of your razor, young man," and nodding to the clerk he walked out while the crowd rather shame-facedly made way for him.

"I didn't care to inquire who Dave was or what he had done," said my friend. "I had had quite enough of those fellows and I wanted them to know it."

He received generous hospitality from most of the people whom he met on the long journey which fol-lowed, and though he had many other adventures, he was never in so much peril as on this occasion, when, as he puts it, he " was saved by losing his beard."

                    THE END.

CONFESSIONS OF A CON-MAN

By Curt Jeffreys.

This is the humorous and dramatic adventures of a professional sharper, who made his living by his wits. The deceptions he practiced upon the guileless and upon the well-informed in the country and cities of the United States, forms a sparkling story of how the American people like to be fooled. Incidentally the reader can also learn the "ways that are dark and the tricks that are vain," as practiced to obtain money in the world of confidence games and graft. The reader gets his money's worth many times over in humor, entertainment and instruction.

Price Prepaid, Paper, 25 cents

M. A. DONOHUE & CO., 407—429 Dearborn Street. CHICAGO.

The Philosophy

Of

Johnnie

the

Gent

By

Frank Hutchison

Author of

"The Barkeep Stories," "Told by the Wise Guy," etc.

A Series of Up-to-date Humorous
"Slang" Stories

Illustrated by the Author

Any one desiring entertainment by the freaks of the foolish can get it here on every page.

Price, prepaid, paper 25 cents.

M. A. DONOHUE & CO., 407—429 Dearborn Street, CHICAGO.